Torquere Press Novels

911 by Chris Owen • *Achilles' Other Heel* by Tulsa Brown
An Agreement Among Gentlemen by Chris Owen • *As It Should Be* by Sean Michael
Bareback by Chris Owen • *Big Enough for Five* by Willa Okati
Broken Road by Sean Michael • *Broken Sword* by Emily Veinglory
Bus Stories and Other Tales by Sean Michael • *Caged* by Sean Michael
Catching a Second Wind by Sean Michael
The Center of Earth and Sky by Sean Michael • *Clear Cut* by Alexa Snow
Cowboy Up edited by Rob Knight • *Date Night* by Kathleen Dale
Demon Princess by Kathleen Dale
Deviations: Submission by Chris Owen and Jodi Payne
Don't Ask, Don't Tell by Sean Michael • *Dreams & Daymares* by Willa Okati
Dust and Violets by Mike Shade • *Farr Anderson Lane* by Kathleen Dale
Fine as Frog Hair by Sean Michael • *Fireline* by Tory Temple
The Floating World by Wheeler Scott
Freighter Flights by Drew Zachary • *Fresh Starts* edited by Rob Knight
Gemini by Chris Owen • *A Gentleman of Substance* by Julia Talbot
Gods and Monsters by Sean Michael
The Happy Campers by Gale Chester Whittington • *Historical Obsession* by Julia Talbot
Honor Bound by Wheeler Scott • *In the Rough* by Laura Baumbach
In the Strangest Places by Willa Okati
Jazz and Sapphire by J. Falcon and Kim Burke
Jumping Into Things by Julia Talbot • *Keep You* by Cindy Rosenthal
Landing with Both Feet by Julia Talbot • *Lassoed* by BA Tortuga
Latigo by BA Tortuga • *Lightning in a Bottle* by Mike Shade
The Long Road Home by BA Tortuga
Manners and Means by Julia Talbot • *Masque* by Julia Talbot
Men in Uniform edited by M. Rode • *Monsters* edited by Rob Knight
Mysterious Ways by Julia Talbot • *Myths* edited by Rob Knight
Naughty edited by M. Rode • *Need* by Sean Michael
Night's Kiss by Catherine Lundoff
No Place Like Home by BA Tortuga • *Old Town New* by BA Tortuga
Oil and Water by BA Tortuga • *On Fire* by Drew Zachary
One Degree of Separation by Fiona Glass
Out of the Closet by Sean Michael
The Peacock and the Firebird by Julia Talbot • *Perfect* by Julia Talbot
Personal Best: Going for the Gold by Sean Michael • *Play Ball* edited by CB Potts
Playing with Fire by Sean Michael • *Post Obsession* by Julia Talbot
A Private Hunger by Sean Michael •*Racing the Moon* by BA Tortuga
Rain and Whiskey by BA Tortuga • *Roses in December* by Fiona Glass
Scarlet and the White Wolf: Book I by Kirby Crow
Second Sight by Sean Michael • *Shifting and Shifting Too* edited by Rob Knight
Sleeping Beauty, Indeed edited by JoSelle Vanderhooft
Sound and Fury by BA Tortuga • *Soul Mates: Bound by Blood* by Jourdan Lane
The Sound of Your Voice by David Sullivan
The Stallion and the Rabbit by Mike Shade • *Stress Relief* by BA Tortuga *Switched* by Sean
Michael • *Tempering* by Sean Michael
Three Day Passes by Sean Michael • *Timeless Hunger* by BA Tortuga
Touching Evil by Rob Knight • *Tripwire* by Sean Michael
Trouble by Mike Shade • *Wheel of Fortune* by Julia Talbot
Where Flows the Water by Sean Michael • *Winning Hand* by Sean Michael

Fireline

Fireline
TOP SHELF
An imprint of Torquere Press Publishers
PO Box 2545
Round Rock, TX 78680
Heat Copyright © 2005 by Tory Temple
Flashover Copyright © 2006 by Tory Temple
Cover illustration by SA Clements
Published with permission
ISBN: 1-933389-99-0
www.torquerepress.com
First Torquere Press Printing: August 2006
Printed in the USA

Fireline

Three hundred and forty three firefighters were killed in the events of September 11, 2001. They all reported to work that day, ready to do nothing more than their jobs. They died doing exactly that.

For the 343.

Heat From Tory Temple

Fireline

Chapter One

June

"You going to grad, Chance?"

Chancellor Shanahan turned from wiping down the shining silver bumper of Engine One-Eleven to see his engineer, Alex Jenkins. Alex had his shirt off and a sheen of sweat covering his chest, a testament to his afternoon run on the treadmill.

Chance spared a discreet glance for the bead of perspiration making its slow way down Alex's abdomen before looking back at the rig for any smudges. "Nah," he shrugged. Fire Department Academy graduation wasn't his thing. "Buncha rookies, don't know any of 'em."

"You could find out who scored highest," Alex offered, and Chancellor laughed.

"You just wanna know who's coming here."

"Don't you?" Alex asked, unconcerned.

"Don't care. He just better be a good medic." Chance finished swiping at imaginary smears with the rag and sat back against the front of the engine. "Sick of those damn overtime assholes not giving a shit about working here. Ever since Cahill went downtown, they haven't put the same guy twice in his spot. Makes it fucking hard to work with a partner when I have no idea who that partner's gonna be from day to day, you know?"

Alex nodded in sympathy. "Yeah, I got that. At least they're all lateral hires, so whoever it is has experience."

Chance grunted in response. "Who's cooking dinner?"

"Double," Alex gestured, referring to the crew that rode on Engine Eleven. They differentiated the engines by either "Double" for Engine Eleven or "Triple" for Engine One-Eleven. The fire truck was just "the truck".

Chance knew most civilians had no idea that fire engines and fire trucks were two different animals, but the fact that he and every other fireman knew it was one of the reasons Chancellor loved his job. Being a firefighter was like being a member of an exclusive club that had its own language and rules, and Chance had adored every second of his eight years with Oceanside Fire.

He had been hired full-time at twenty-eight, after three years as a reserve firefighter and interviewing like crazy with every department in the state. And some out of state, too, traveling to Nevada and Arizona and getting as far as being put on their A list for hiring, but never actually securing a job. It was too competitive, this field, and being a white male in a sea of minorities and women, well … it had taken a while.

A white *gay* male, he amended, although there were few in the department who knew it. It was much like the army, the fire service was, with their don't ask, don't tell policy. It grated on him sometimes, but he loved his job more than screaming from the rooftops that he liked to fuck guys, so don't ask, don't tell was okay with him. For now, at least.

The ones who knew had been all right with it. His battalion chief. Matt Perkins, the captain on his engine. And Erik Cahill, his old paramedic partner, who was now working for department headquarters as a fire investigator. Chance had held his proverbial breath when he told them all at separate times. The chief, Ross Stevens, had arched a brow and said, "Any particular reason you're telling me this, son?"

"It could come up in the future," was all Chance had said, and the chief nodded.

"Hopefully not."

And that had been it.

Matt and Erik had both looked warily at him until Chance assured them he wasn't after their hot bods. He was only telling them because they had to work closely together, and he hated questions about his personal life. Erik had shrugged. "Whatever, man. You do what you do, yeah? No skin off my nose."

Chance had grinned at him. "It's cool?"

"It's cool."

Matt took longer to size Chance up, scrutinizing him until Chance shifted uncomfortably under his gaze. "This ever gonna be a problem on my shift?"

"No, sir."

"Off my shift?"

Chance didn't know what to say to that. "Um, I'll try not to let it be… I guess." His personal life had never clashed with his professional life before, so he didn't see how it would be a problem for his captain if they weren't even at work.

Matt nodded. "You're a good fireman, that's all I give a shit about." And he had walked away to check the day's call printouts on the computer. Chance breathed a sigh of relief, and that was that.

He figured more of the guys at the station knew, and probably a lot of the ones who weren't even on his shift. "Tell a fireman, tell a friend" was the unspoken department motto. Firemen gossiped worse than a bunch of women at a bridge party, which was one of the reasons Chance never discussed his personal life. It was also one of the reasons he rarely showed up at holiday functions and station gatherings, preferring to stay home rather than answer questions about why he didn't have a date. He'd tried bringing his best female friend, Bonnie, once or twice, but that caused even more issues with the matchmaking wives of his coworkers.

But he'd never been questioned directly, and never experienced any of the sort of weirdness that he'd assumed would occur when a bunch of straight, macho men discovered they had a queer living in their midst. It was high up on his list of reasons for making sure he was the best fireman he could be. Less for the others to discuss.

It helped that he lived where he did, Chance knew that much. California was a fairly liberal state, and beachside towns like Oceanside seemed to attract gays. He didn't live in any of the scattered gay neighborhoods, but he wasn't so far away that he didn't know where he could go on a Saturday night if he felt like some action. There was the Seagull on Beach Street and Temptations on Pacific Coast Highway, and as much as Chance really didn't like the bar scene, sometimes it was just fucking necessary if he wanted to get laid.

His own right hand got pretty damn boring, even if it did do the job.

"Chow!" came the shout out the back door, interrupting Chance's thoughts, and he threw the rag into the dirty laundry bin.

Yeah, he thought on his way in to dinner, at least he knew where his own hand had been, and it wouldn't fuck him over when he least expected it. Better that way.

Pretty damn boring, though.

***

He worked a regular fireman's schedule of twos and fours. Two days on, two days off, two days on, four days off. His next shift was two days later and he'd nearly forgotten about the rookie.

Chance caught sight of his own reflection in the mirrored window next to the door leading to the station kitchen. The sunburn he'd gotten on his neck and chest yesterday at the beach was starting to fade already, adding to the nice early tan he'd started for summer. It had been a good day for waves, and he'd surfed longer than he'd intended, stopping only when he had to battle tourists for water space. Chance noticed his hair was already lightening, another side effect of the strong California sun and ocean saltwater.

He was forty minutes early for his eight o'clock shift, and the kitchen was quiet, only the captain from last night standing at the sink. "Sutter," Chance greeted, and the man half-turned from washing his cereal dish.

"Hey, Chance. I borrowed some of you guys' milk."

"Why don't you just take our fucking blood, too," Chance joked, reaching for the door of the refrigerator marked with a blue "B". Three fridges stood side by side in the alcove, each marked with the letter of the corresponding shift. Chance was on B shift, but occasionally they all would root through another shift's refrigerator for food staples if they ran low.

Two other firefighters appeared in the large kitchen, hair tousled and blinking blearily. "Bad night?" Chance asked, and they glared at him.

"Double ran two calls and Triple ran three," Sutter offered by way of explanation, and Chance winced. Some nights were like that. It came with the job.

Contrary to popular belief, most of their calls were not for fires. Chance had fought plenty of fires in his day, but most of their responses were for medical aid to the local retirement community or traffic collisions on the freeway. The occasional ocean accident came their way, if it was something the lifeguards couldn't handle. Fighting actual fire was only about thirty percent of Chance's job. He loved it, too, and sometimes considered moving further inland where there was more chance of brush or structure fire.

But one look out the window at the Pacific Ocean, blue and sparkling, and Chance would remember why he stayed at Station Eleven. High tide was a powerful motivator.

The kitchen got noisier as more of B shift arrived, and C shift got ready to leave, shoving back chairs and thunking coffee mugs into the dishwasher. There was good-natured ribbing for C shift about their crappy night, complete with calls of "hero!" when it was discovered that one of the medics had revived an old man having a heart attack.

Chance was leaning against the fridge, contemplating putting more chocolate syrup in his coffee, when the back door opened. He noticed the lull in conversation more than the actual arrival of the newcomer.

Glancing up at the sudden quiet, he was greeted with the sight of one of the prettiest men he'd ever seen. *Oh, fuck,* was his first thought, then Chance stopped thinking at all.

The new hire strolled into the greatroom next to the kitchen and stopped beside one of the twelve recliners in front of the television. Leaning against it insolently, he sized up each and every man in the room before saying, with a slight drawl, "Tucker McBride."

Matt rose from his chair, coming forward with hand extended. Chance watched as the rookie shook it firmly, knowing he had already met Matt at his academy graduation, and the two men seemed to have an easy accord. "Welcome to the Big House," Matt said, and Tucker lifted his eyes to where the station's nickname was carved in the wood beam above his head.

The other firemen called greetings to him, and Tucker made his way to the table, shaking hands with his right while holding onto his gear bag with his left. Chance kept a surreptitious eye on Tucker while he went around the table, noting details he wished he hadn't seen.

Longish legs encased in regulation blue department pants. Strong muscles in his forearms that flexed every time he shook someone else's hand, and his skin was like nothing Chance had ever seen. Almost copper, it was tanned differently than Chance's own California glow. Smooth and burnished, it seemed to shimmer. Chance wanted to touch it, to see if it was as silky as it looked.

He wanted to do a hell of a lot more than that, his body began to tell him, and Chance shifted uncomfortably. Good thing he still had track pants on and hadn't changed into his uniform yet. His track pants were a little more roomy.

Chance continued his perusal of Tucker until the man had shaken hands with everyone in the room but him. Chance was just thinking it was fine if they never touched each other when the captain called out, "And that's Shanahan, lurking by the fridge. Don't let his glare scare you."

Tucker stopped in front of Chance, dropping his bag on the floor and meeting Chance's eyes. "You're the other paramedic," Tucker stated, extending his hand.

Chance nodded, taking in the dark eyes and even darker hair, praying to any God that would listen that Tucker did not look down and see evidence of Chance's arousal. "Chancellor," he managed to get out. "How's it going?"

"Last ten minutes've been fine," Tucker said seriously, and again Chance detected the slow drawl.

"How'd you get a name like Tucker?" Chance asked, and heard several snorts from the table. His own name had been joked about enough, but it wasn't his fault his mother was pretentious and snobby.

But Tucker smiled easily, revealing a hint of dimple in his cheek – *oh, fucking hell,* Chance thought – and shrugged. "Momma named me after our home state. Said I made her think of Kentucky bluebells."

Chance had no time to wonder why the hell Tucker's mother would think he reminded her of flowers before Matt was clapping him on the shoulder. "Show him his dorm, Chance."

Dammit. Chance nodded and willed his body back to normal, jerking a thumb over his shoulder toward the sleeping area. "Back this way."

He was aware of Tucker following him silently, taking in all areas of the station as they walked. The computer room, the classroom, the chief's office, the workout room. Chance heard him grunt appreciatively as they passed the small gym. Instantly his mind was flooded with images of Tucker sweating, Tucker lifting weights, Tucker running on the treadmill – fuck! He felt his dick begin to push against the front of his boxers again and swore under his breath.

Chance stopped abruptly at the last dorm on his left, suddenly enough for Tucker to almost run right into him. "Yours," Chance said.

"I get a phone?" Tucker brushed past him into the small room, and Chance shrunk back, unwilling to let any part of his traitorous body touch Tucker's.

"You're the probie." Chance laughed. "It's only there because you're the one who has to answer it."

"Whatever," Tucker shrugged. "Fine by me."

Chance noted the way Tucker elongated his vowels in true southern fashion and decided he liked it. "So put your shit in your locker and come have breakfast," he offered. "Then I'll show you around."

Tucker opened his gear bag and withdrew bed linens. "Lemme make up the bed. I'll be in after."

Chance couldn't help darting a glance at Tucker's light blue sheets and wondered if they smelled like him. Then he cursed himself, turned on his heel, and stalked back to the kitchen.

Chapter Two

July

Chance woke up with his hand on his cock, and the sheets tangled around his ankles. He had obviously started jerking off while he was still asleep, because now he found himself more than halfway gone to a good orgasm, and he couldn't have stopped if he wanted to.

Glossy hair and smooth, copper skin teased him when Chance closed his eyes, stroking harder and clutching the bedsheets with his other hand. He imagined Tucker's mouth on him, hot and wet and doing talented things with that tongue, whispering nasty words in his ear that were only made hotter by that soft southern accent.

Chance fumbled blindly in the bedside drawer for lube, finding it and flipping the cap with one hand. He hissed through his teeth at the first touch of slickness, stroking himself harder and lifting his hips off the mattress. Chance strained toward release, flicking his thumb over the head of his dick and using his free hand to squeeze his balls, images of Tucker just behind his eyelids. It felt so fucking good to jerk off when he thought of Tucker these days, something Chance tried to completely ignore when he wasn't hard as a rock and in bed at home. He had to work with the man, after all, and sleep two doors away.

But right now, he was close enough to coming to not really care; Chance felt his balls grow tight and he was leaking pre-come all over himself. He thrust up into his hand twice more before drawing a deep breath and shooting over his fingers, squeezing his eyes shut and picturing Tucker.

This really had to stop.

Chance lay there for a while, ignoring the stickiness and staring at his ceiling. Damn, damn, *damn*. Tucker McBride had been at Station Eleven for three weeks and Chance found himself putting distance between them, despite the necessity of working as medic partners in close proximity. Chance did what was called for when it came to administering medical aid, brushing shoulders with Tucker while they took vitals or started an intravenous line. But he was constantly on edge, wondering if today his body would give him away or if Tucker – or any of the other guys, God forbid – would notice his reaction to Tucker reaching across him or peering over Chance's shoulder at a patient.

He was a good paramedic, Chance had to admit. The other guys had taken to him easily. He was an obedient rookie, too, answering the phone at all hours and getting to work well before his shift started. Plus, he could cook. Chance's mouth watered, remembering the other night's chicken pot pie with mashed potatoes. But Chance cursed Tucker silently for being those things, plus so damn hot to boot. It had made Chance's job hell. But if Tucker noticed Chance's reticence around him when they weren't running calls, he hadn't said a word.

Glancing at the clock and realizing he was about to be late for work, Chance groped under the bed for a towel. He received only an annoyed meow when his hand closed on soft fur. "Sorry, Smoke," he murmured, grabbing the towel next to the cat. Smokey darted from under the bed and out the door of the bedroom. Chance watched his twitching tail disappear. "Yeah, run while you can," he muttered. "I'm so hard up these days I might start thinking you look good."

He managed to avoid jerking off again in the shower.

***

"Shanahan!" Robert Lopez shouted at him. "Fuck, we need you to play, you asshole!"

Chance looked up from where he was polishing the engine again. He polished the engine a lot these days. The truck bay was the quietest place – away from Tucker – that he could find. "Fuck you, I'm doing work!"

"You're not doing work," Alex yelled disdainfully. "The rig's spotless. Come on, or the rookie's gonna take your place as point guard!"

Chance looked over at Tucker. He stood shirtless, his chest heaving with the exertion of playing basketball in the late afternoon heat. Chance swallowed tightly, and Tucker grinned at him, wiping his forehead with his arm. "I'm just the probie," he shrugged. "I do what they tell me."

Alex laughed and slugged him in the shoulder, giving up on Chance and passing the ball to Robert. "Fine, screw you, Shanahan. McBride can do the job."

I bet he can, was Chance's automatic thought as he watched the muscles cord and flex in Tucker's back when he reached over his head to shoot for the basket. Chance tortured himself by watching the game for another minute before turning back to the engine, steeling himself against his own arousal. Damn it all to hell.

He listened to the game go on behind him for another fifteen minutes before it dissolved into a good-natured argument about which team had how many points. "Fuck you all, I'm thirsty anyway," Chance heard his captain say, and then their voices faded as the back door slammed. The yard was quiet, and Chance could breathe.

Which is why, Chance told himself later, he was so startled when he turned abruptly and found Tucker standing less than two feet away, his shirt in his hands. "Hey," Tucker said with a lift of his chin.

Chance noticed that their gazes were almost level, Tucker only a couple of inches shorter than Chance's own six foot two. Chance cleared his throat. "Hey." *God, you smell so fucking good,* was what he really wanted to say, but mercifully he held back. And it was true, the sharp, clean smell of sweat assaulting his senses and making his head spin.

"I wasn't takin' your place or nothin'," Tucker said, motioning toward the small basketball court. "They just needed a fourth guy."

"Huh?" Chance inwardly rolled his eyes at his own lack of finesse. "Oh, yeah. No, I know, it's all good." He swallowed a mouthful of saliva and concentrated hard on not staring at Tucker's bare pecs glistening with perspiration.

The corner of Tucker's mouth turned up, and he took a step closer. Chance was pinned in place by nothing but Tucker's gaze, and somewhere in the corner of his mind he noticed a tiny, brown freckle right above the man's left cheekbone. Chance wanted to suck on it. To his own credit, he didn't look away, just stood where he was and willed his body to behave. It didn't listen.

But then it didn't matter, because Tucker reached out a tanned arm and squeezed Chance's cock through his pants. There was no way Tucker could miss Chance's erection, heavy and full, and Chance closed his eyes for a fraction of a second.

"Thought so," Tucker murmured in the stillness of the bay, and when Chance opened his eyes, Tucker was gone.

***

He skulked around the dorm area for the rest of the day, avoiding anyone else and wishing like hell he was at the beach instead of trapped at work with the hottest fireman he'd ever seen. The one who'd felt him up like a teenager this afternoon.

Chance was hard again just thinking about it. He threw himself on his bunk with a disgusted sigh and buried his face in his pillow, willing his shift to be over so at least he could go home and jerk off. Again.

But no chance for that when he heard two dings of the alarm, so he lifted his head to listen for the announcement of which engines were to go into service.

His, naturally, and then he didn't have time to think, only react. It was what made him a good firefighter, and he knew it: the simple, easy reaction time in response to any emergency. Chance was down the hall and in the garage before most of his crew arrived, tugging on his yellow turnout gear and heavy boots. He swung into his seat behind the engineer and pointedly looked at his watch when Alex got in thirty seconds behind him, laughing and flipping him off at the same time.

Chance congratulated himself on not looking over at Tucker, who he could practically feel smirking at him.

The computer printout had said the call was a teenager with an asthma attack, and the radio confirmed it on the way there. They were at the small apartment complex in less than five minutes. The hysterical mother pointed a shaking finger toward the bedroom, and Chance raised his eyebrows at his captain to keep her out of the way. He followed Tucker into the room and both of them switched immediately into the easy patterns they'd come to know in the past weeks; Chance attaching a cardiac monitor and oxygen mask, and Tucker preparing to administer Albuterol. Chance saw him wink at the wheezing girl.

"Hello, darlin'," he said to her softly, and Chance's stomach tightened at the low tone.

She turned desperate eyes on him, and he grinned at her. "You'll be all right. 'Less my partner here screws up. You got yourself a name?"

"Candace," she managed, offering her arm to Chance so he could take her pulse.

"Well. I had me a horse named Candace at home. Called her Candy 'cause she was darn near the sweetest thing I'd ever ridden."

It was the first glimpse into Tucker's background that Chance had learned, other than where he came from, and he filed it away for future reference.

"My older brother calls me that," the girl gasped, still struggling for a deep breath.

"Does he, now?" Tucker murmured, checking her vital signs. "You live up to it?"

"No," she smiled, and Chance urged her to sit up so he could use his stethoscope on her back. Listening to her clearing lungs, he looked up and met Tucker's eyes. He motioned with his head toward the door, and Tucker picked up on the signal easily.

"Gotta go to the hospital, hon," Tucker said to her. "Those big, handsome firemen out there talking to your momma are gonna bring in a stretcher for me, all right?"

Chance almost laughed when she looked wistfully at Tucker. "You're gonna come, too?"

"Sure thing. Back of the ambulance with ya and everything."

Chance went to the door and crooked a finger at Matt, who finished up his interview with Candace's mother and motioned to Alex for the stretcher.

Outside, the two young ambulance drivers opened the back doors for the patient to be loaded. Chance realized that Matt had talked the mother into taking her own car to the hospital instead of riding in the ambulance so she'd have a way to drive back home. Once again, Chance found himself trapped in a small space with Tucker and only the teenage girl for a buffer. Great.

"I'll do radio," he said shortly, reaching for it to tell the hospital they were coming. And goddamned if Tucker didn't look up and *wink* at him over the girl's head, smirking just enough so that his fucking dimple flashed at Chance. Bastard.

Chance kept his eyes either on his patient or his watch for the rest of the trip.

***

Dinner was pizza, since it was nearly seven when they got back from the hospital, and no one wanted to cook. Chance took his slices to one of the recliners in front of the TV and wished for a cold Heineken and even colder shower. Tucker's dimples were haunting him.

He got bored of TV and watched two of the guys play cards for a while, but his mind kept straying to the noticeable lack of Tucker, and Chance kept wondering where he'd gone off to. It was irritating.

Finally, frustrated with himself and needing to blow off steam, he retreated to the workout room. He set a treadmill on high and ran for twenty minutes. It helped a little. The racked weights caught his eye, and he figured he could lift for a while. If nothing else, he could at least exhaust himself so that maybe he wouldn't dream tonight and wake up at four a.m. with a raging hard-on.

Chance was lying on the bench, staring up at the barbell and wondering if he should go ask Alex to spot him or just give up on working out altogether, when the door opened. If he had been blind and deaf he would have known it was Tucker, because wouldn't that just be his goddamned luck?

A dark head appeared in his line of vision, and Chance got an excellent view of Tucker's t-shirt pulled tight across his chest. "Want a spotter?"

No, Chance thought. "Yes."

"Gotcha. Go."

Thankfully, it took most of Chance's attention to focus on the weight, because he'd added eight more pounds than usual. His muscles were screaming, and he could feel sweat standing out on his forehead when he was finished, Tucker helping him put the weights back on the bar above him. Chance let himself lie there and breathe for a minute.

He was about to get up with a mumbled "thanks," but before Chance could even sit up, Tucker had come around to the front of the bench and straddled Chance's legs. Tucker didn't sit; merely stood above him and gazed down with a serious expression. Once again, Chance found himself frozen by only a stare.

"I do my job, yeah?"

Chance blinked, not expecting the question. "Yeah."

"Then why the shitty attitude, man?" Tucker was as straight-faced as Chance had ever seen him, and it occurred to Chance that Tucker really wanted an answer.

Because I'd like to turn you around and nail you to the wall was probably not the answer Tucker was looking for. Chance opened his mouth, and then closed it again, not willing to tell the truth and not wanting to lie. His eyes strayed to the front of Tucker's shorts, and then back up to his face.

Tucker cocked a dark brow and slowly lowered himself until he was sitting astride Chance's hips. "This why?" he whispered, giving a slow, downward nudge. Chance felt Tucker's cock through his shorts, full and solid.

He darted a panicked look at the door. "The guys," he said, his voice sounding hoarse to his own ears.

"Watching a movie. Come on, Shanahan. You don't waste your breath talking to me if we're not on a call. I wanna know why not." Tucker leaned forward, placing both hands on Chance's chest and bringing their cocks into fuller contact. "You afraid?"

"Fuck you," Chance growled, and grabbed a handful of Tucker's hair, bringing Tucker down to him for a vicious kiss.

Chance felt Tucker grinning against his mouth before Chance shoved his tongue inside, sweeping and claiming and growling. He fisted a hand in the back of Tucker's t-shirt and rocked up against him, trying like hell to release some of the pressure of the last few weeks. Tucker groaned into Chance's kiss, pushing back against him, and before Chance could get his bearings, they were humping each other like kids.

"Been starin' at your ass for weeks," Tucker was muttering. "So fuckin' cocky, the way you parade around here with your shirt off and your tan line peekin' out over your shorts. You fuckin' bastard, Chance."

"Shut up," Chance hissed, arching his neck so Tucker could bite at it. "Shut the fuck up, or they'll hear us."

Tucker shut up, but only because his mouth was busy sucking a mark into Chance's jawline. Chance strained upward, hips thrusting to meet Tucker's downward rolls, wishing desperately that they didn't have fabric between them. Then he realized it didn't matter anyway, he was about to come from a little dry humping, and wasn't *that* a nice memory of high school?

Chance tried desperately to shove Tucker away from him, trying to maintain some semblance of dignity despite the urgent need in his crotch. "No," Chance moaned against Tucker's shoulder. "Not gonna come like this, like a fucking horny teenager."

Tucker lifted his head and grinned, giving Chance the full force of both dimples. "Oh, yeah, Shanahan," he said softly, "you are." And he reached down a hand between them, palming Chance through his shorts while still managing to rub his own cock against the back of his hand.

"Yeah, I am," Chance gave up, and wrapped both hands securely around the bar over his head. He planted both feet firmly on the floor and pushed up into Tucker's hand, sucking his bottom lip between his teeth to keep from groaning out loud again. Tucker buried his face in the hollow of Chance's neck, and Chance could hear his breathing grow harsh and ragged, the two of them straining for release together.

"Knew it," Tucker was muttering between panting breaths. "Knew you were so damn hot, knew it from the first fuckin' day I walked in here, with your whole stoic attitude and your goddamned cock gettin' hard every time I looked at ya. I knew it." He lifted his head and stared at Chance. "Do it, Chance, come on. You know you wanna come right now, right here in my hand."

"Asshole," Chance whispered, and threw back his head and came with a jerk of his hips, feeling the warmth soak into his shorts.

Tucker talked him through it, murmuring in the low voice he used to calm patients and drive Chance out of his mind. "You got it, baby. Come on, feels so good, don't it? Nice and sweet and hot. Gimme a little more."

By the time he finally finished coming, Chance could still feel Tucker thrusting against him, hard as stone. "You," Chance whispered, leaning up to close his teeth around Tucker's earlobe. "Go, McBride. Lemme hear you." He pushed up hard, snaking an arm around Tucker's back to hold him in place, and rubbed against the other man. "So fucking hot."

"Christ," Tucker groaned into Chance's hair, jerking against him. "Oh, Christ." And Chance could feel the faint pulsing, even between two layers of clothes, and the resulting damp warmth.

They lay panting together on the weight bench for a minute before Tucker raised his head. His face was close enough for Chance to see the tiny birthmark on his cheek and the eyelashes that were so long they curled on the ends. Chance studied him for a moment, taking in Tucker's features greedily, using this stolen time to examine him in ways he hadn't been able to before. Something drew his attention suddenly, and he blurted out, "Blue."

Tucker raised an eyebrow in question, then understanding dawned. "Oh, yeah. My eyes."

"They look black from far away."

Tucker shrugged, endearingly bashful. "I know. They're not. Kentucky bluebells, remember?"

Chance thought back to their first meeting. "Your mom. I wondered what part of you reminded her of flowers."

Tucker laughed, and Chance could feel the low rumble in his own chest. "Yup. Momma called 'em indigo. Most people just said they were dark blue, which was good 'nuff for me."

Chance had a moment to wonder who else had been close enough to discover the secret of Tucker's eyes, but then Tucker was kissing him again, and Chance felt his cock stir. The next time Tucker looked up, Chance studied him. "So pretty," he murmured without thinking, using his thumb to brush against Tucker's thick lashes. "Your eyes, and those dimples. Pretty as a fucking girl."

And then Tucker was up, moving away from him, and Chance blinked at the loss of warmth. "Hey," Chance said, and Tucker wheeled on him.

"Fuck off," he said curtly, and Chance watched with astonishment as the door closed behind Tucker.

Chapter Three

Chance started a four-day break the next day and was glad for it.

He hadn't spoken to Tucker since the man had left him alone in the weight room, and Tucker had hightailed it out of the station when his relief showed up early the next morning. Chance didn't care.

That's what he told himself, anyway.

He spent Wednesday surfing, glad it was a weekday and there were few people on the beach. He stopped at lunch to eat a Power Bar and gulp down a Gatorade, then he returned to the water and didn't have to think about much except keeping his balance. He stopped at four, resting on the sand for a while and watching the sea lions sun themselves on the large rock next to the pier.

Chance grilled himself a steak for dinner on his back patio, lifting a hand in greeting to the young couple next door when they came out to have a drink on their porch. He sat at his kitchen table, one eye on the six o'clock news, and washed down his supper with two Heinekens.

He only woke up once during the night with a vague recollection of dreaming about indigo eyes and wicked dimples. Chance didn't remember most of it in the morning.

***

Thursday was housework, a necessary evil.

Chance did laundry in the morning, changing sheets on his bed and washing loads of work uniforms and underwear. He cleaned Smokey's litterbox, the cat sitting a safe distance away and pretending to not care by washing his paws. "You stink," Chance told him as he dumped the dirty litter in the trash. Smokey blinked green eyes at him.

He took a look around his roomy condo in the afternoon, decided the real cleaning – floors, countertops, bathroom – could wait 'til next week, and contemplated calling Bonnie to see if she wanted to go eat.

Chance was still thinking about it when the phone rang at seven. Figuring it to be her, since it was her usual day and time to call him, he answered on the second ring. "S'up, Bon?"

"Shanahan?"

Not Bonnie, *definitely* not Bonnie, and Chance was instantly alert. "Yeah."

"It's McBride."

"Hey," Chance said carefully. He didn't wonder how Tucker had gotten his number. All of the crew's phone numbers were up on the bulletin board at work. Chance did wonder why he was calling, however.

"Um. You busy?" Tucker sounded unsure of himself, the first time Chance had ever heard that tone in his voice.

"Nah. Was thinking about dinner."

"Yeah, um. You wanna go grab something with me?"

Chance glanced down at his ratty fire department t-shirt and swim trunks. The last thing he wanted to do was put on a good shirt and try to look nice for someone who had told him to fuck off two days ago. "Don't wanna change clothes, man." He knew it was a shitty thing to say, but maybe he was more irritated with Tucker than he'd thought.

Tucker laughed, a sharp, hollow sound that echoed on the line. "Right, okay. See you Sunday."

It made Chance feel even shittier. "No, hey. Don't wanna change but I still gotta eat. You feel like coming over here?" The invitation was out before he knew what he was saying, and Chance waited, sure Tucker would turn him down.

"Come over there? Yeah, I guess. You want, uh. You want me to bring food?"

"Hell, yes."

Tucker laughed again, the sound more genuine. "Got it. There's a little Italian place near me. That okay?"

Chance's stomach growled at the thought. "Sure, whatever. You got a pen to take directions?" He gave them quickly, learning that Tucker was renting a small place not far away, and hung up the phone.

He tried to pretend he wasn't looking forward to seeing Tucker.

***

Tucker dropped his fork and pushed his chair away from the table. "Oh, fuck me, I'm done," he groaned.

Chance shoveled in one more bite of pasta and let his own fork clatter to his plate. "God. Same."

Tucker looked at the heaping pile of leftover food. "We didn't make a dent."

"Save it," Chance shrugged. "I'm king of leftovers. Cook so much at work that I don't wanna do it at home."

"You can have it," Tucker offered. "Little old lady who lives behind me is always handin' food over the fence. 'Just 'til you get yourself a girl,' she says." His wry tone made Chance snort.

"Yeah, the couple next door tried to set me up with her girlfriends for the first year I lived here. They figured it out soon enough when D – uh. My old boyfriend came out on the back patio with a cup of coffee one morning. Naked." He'd almost said Derek's name, but stopped himself in time. Chance wasn't sure he wanted Derek intruding right now.

Tucker looked amused. "Yeah, that'd do it."

They grinned at each other in the silence of the kitchen. "M'gonna have a beer," Chance sighed. "You want one, or another diet Coke instead?"

"Beer," Tucker said without hesitation, getting up from the table. Chance handed him one. They clinked bottlenecks and wandered into the living room, settling themselves on Chance's overstuffed couch and propping their feet on the coffee table. Chance had time to notice that Tucker's dark blue t-shirt matched his eyes. Chance shifted and adjusted his shorts, not willing to show Tucker that just sitting close was making him hard.

Smokey jumped up to examine the visitor. "Oh, hey," Tucker said, surprised. Chance watched as Smokey rubbed his whiskers along Tucker's bare leg.

"You can shove him off. He's a pest."

"Nah, s'all right," Tucker replied, holding out a hand for the cat to sniff. "I always forget people keep cats as pets."

"Why?"

Tucker shrugged apologetically. "Didn't have no house cats on the farm. Cats lived in the barn to catch mice. We had dogs for pets."

"Yeah, I had a dog growing up. But the job doesn't lend itself to keeping one now, you know? Smoke's way more independent." Chance mulled over the fact that Tucker lived on a farm and figured that explained how he'd had a horse. Tucker nodded in agreement, and Smokey lost interest, stepping delicately over Tucker's lap to sit next to Chance. Chance stroked his head absently. "Farm, huh?" he asked.

"Yep. Tobacco. And a little corn, but mostly tobacco." He sounded bored.

"Farming wasn't for you, I take it," Chance laughed, and was rewarded with dimples.

"Nope. Was supposed to take over, o'course. I even thought I would, too, 'til Daddy died. Dropped dead right there in the fuckin' fields. Had a heart problem, we found out later, and wasn't takin' the meds the doc prescribed. Momma didn't even know he was seeing a doctor at all." He glanced over at Chance, probably gauging his reaction, Chance thought, so he kept his expression carefully neutral.

"Sorry to hear it," Chance said, and Tucker sighed.

"Thanks. Was a long time ago, though. I was fourteen."

Chance tried to picture a fourteen-year-old Tucker and could only come up with midnight-blue eyes under a mop of silky black curls. "Musta sucked for you. And your family."

The look on Tucker's face grew darker. "I'm an only kid. It was hard on Momma, which was why she – ah, fuck it, you don't wanna hear my tales of woe."

But Chance did. "Nah, come on. Tell me. Unless you don't wanna talk about it, which is cool."

Tucker laid his dark head on the back of the couch and looked over at Chance. He appeared suddenly very young, although Chance knew Tucker was only a couple of years behind him in age. Chance felt a twinge of protectiveness that he shoved back down where it belonged. "Yeah, I kinda wanna talk about it," Tucker said quietly. "It's the reason I wanted to see you, actually." His eyes darted away and back.

"Do I need a refill for this?" Chance asked, indicating his empty bottle on the table.

"We both do."

Chance retrieved four more bottles from the fridge, effectively depleting his supply, and brought them back to the living room. He lined them up on the table. "M'not gettin' off the couch again except to piss," he explained, and Tucker flashed a dimple.

"Fair enough." He reached for a bottle and took a long pull. "Okay, yeah. So Daddy died, and it sucked, and Momma sort of went a little bit haywire for a while. I tried to do what I knew how to do, but at fourteen, you don't know shit." Tucker paused, laughed without humor. "Thought I could order the hands around like Daddy did and they'd actually listen to me. Assholes just stole money, mine and Momma's, and then one night I started cryin' at the dinner table."

Tucker paused, his eyes on the wall in front of them, but Chance knew he wasn't looking at it. He was tempted to reach out, to lay a hand on Tucker's leg or shoulder or somewhere he could offer comfort, but this thing between them – whatever it was – was still too unfamiliar. Chance just nodded and fiddled with the label of his beer.

"So Momma sorta woke up, I guess, and figured she had to get someone to at least oversee the crop haulin'. The tobacco was just sittin' ripe in the fields. She called my uncle Tim, Daddy's brother." He paused there, and Chance saw a muscle jump in his jaw. "It was good at first. Tim took care of that season's crop, at least. There was food on the table, and the bank stopped lookin' to foreclose."

"I'm assuming it didn't stay that way," Chance said, more to assure Tucker he was listening than to actually have something to say.

"Nope," Tucker said flatly. "But not the way you're thinkin'. I mean, we still had dinner to eat, and the farmhands didn't quit, and Momma stopped cryin' all hours of the day. But things got … shittier. For me, anyway."

He stopped again, taking a deep breath and meeting Chance's eyes. Chance was caught beneath that gaze, no different tonight than the first time Tucker had ever looked at him. "He caught me in the barn a lot," Tucker said, and his expression was closed, shuttered. "Would come up behind me when I was cleaning stalls or somethin' and back me into the corner."

Chance's stomach rolled, knowing where this was going and not wanting to hear it. But Tucker was here, in his house, trusting him with information that he obviously didn't share easily. "Motherfucker," he whispered, wishing he could have done something to protect the boy Tucker used to be.

"Yeah," Tucker agreed, and gave him a half-smile. "He never got away with much, though. I was smaller and faster. Couple of gropes here and there, nothin' too damaging. Except…" he trailed off and took a deep breath, blowing it out between puffed cheeks.

"He would grab my face. Used to tell me how pretty I was. Pretty as a girl, he used to say, and it just made me feel so fuckin' sick, you know? Aside from the fact that I was startin' to think I preferred guys anyway, it just really fucked me all up."

Chance wanted to die, despite the rational voice in his head that told him he couldn't have known. All he could hear was himself saying those words to Tucker, brushing his thumb over Tucker's eyelashes.

Pretty as a fucking girl.

Chance opened his mouth to say something, anything, then closed it again. There was nothing to say. There was nothing to do, either, except just look miserably at Tucker and wonder how to fix it.

"Oh, hey," Tucker said gently. "No, come on. I just wanted to tell you so you would know why I freaked out the other night, not to make you all guilty or nothin'. My fault, not yours. It was so long ago, I was just surprised to hear it, is all."

It made him feel worse, not better, and Chance hung his head. "I'm so sorry," he said softly. "I'm an idiot."

"Yeah," Tucker agreed, "but not 'cause of that." The teasing tone made Chance look up. "You're an idiot, Shanahan, for tryin' to deny the inevitable." And then Tucker leaned over to kiss him, threading his fingers through Chance's hair and moving closer on the couch.

It was the last thing Chance had expected to spend the night doing, but he wasn't about to complain. The freedom of not being at work, of being in his own place with the luxury of no prying eyes or listening ears was a huge turn-on in itself.

The fact that Tucker was a co-worker was an issue he'd work out later.

Chance brought up both hands to hold Tucker's head and was rewarded with a small sigh. Tucker turned on the couch and sort of nestled into Chance, fitting the hard planes of his abdomen along Chance's. Chance felt his own cock stir and swell and he moved also, seeking some pressure.

Tucker pushed him back against the arm of the couch and straddled him, reminiscent of the position in the workout room at the station the other night. Chance drew a deep breath when their erections rubbed against each other and saw heat flare in Tucker's eyes. "How come I'm always findin' you underneath me?" Tucker asked, and Chance narrowed his gaze.

"Not always," he replied, and flipped them both until he was sitting atop the other man, grinding down suggestively.

Tucker just grinned up at him. "Knew you were a top. So fuckin' bossy all the time."

"You don't know the half of it."

"Show me, then," Tucker challenged. "Been waitin' a fuckin' month, man."

Chance had never been one to back down from a challenge. He nudged Tucker's legs apart, fitting a thigh in between and thrusting, making Tucker roll his head back on the arm of the couch and groan. "Yeah, do it."

But then a moment later Tucker was gasping and pushing against Chance's chest, tugging at Chance's hair. Chance lifted his mouth from the hickey he was making along Tucker's collarbone and looked at him. "S'matter?"

"You gotta slow down a little, else 'm gonna come in my shorts," Tucker panted, belying his own words by thrusting upwards anyway. Chance bit back a moan.

"You mean like the other night?" he reminded, and Tucker laughed.

"Yeah, I know, you owe me. And I probably should just shoot right now to take the edge off … but damn, Chance, I'd rather feel your hands on me than the inside of my clothes."

It was the best invitation Chance could have asked for. "Off," he demanded, tugging at Tucker's shirt. He drank in the ridges of muscle greedily when Tucker divested himself of the t-shirt, dipping his head to circle one copper nipple with his tongue. Chance listened to Tucker's breathing increase for a minute before saying "Off," again, this time hooking a finger in the man's waistband and dragging it downward.

Tucker managed to kick his shorts off over his straining cock and breathed a sigh of relief when he was naked, taking hold of his dick and giving himself two short, hard strokes before Chance knocked his hand away. "Quit that."

"See?" Tucker murmured, closing his eyes and arching up into Chancellor. "So fuckin' bossy."

Tucker's cock just begged to be tasted. Standing up and proud away from his body, one clear drop of pre-come glistened at the tip. Chance slid down on the couch and flicked out his tongue, tasting bittersweetness. Tucker stopped breathing. "Again," he moaned, so

Chance complied, this time opening his mouth around the head, letting his tongue dance briefly over the slit.

He could feel Tucker straining beneath him, muscles trembling as Tucker tried not to buck up into Chance's mouth. Chance relented and took more of him in. Sliding his lips down, teeth carefully covered, he used the flat of his tongue to make long strokes and put his hands under Tucker's ass, urging the man to move if he wanted to.

Given permission, Tucker arched up with a hiss and put both hands on Chance's head. "How are you so fuckin' good at that," he asked, then, "No, I don't wanna know, just go, don't stop, my God."

He kept up a litany of mumbled words while Chance sucked on him, and Chance loved it all: the small, needy sounds Tucker would make when Chance licked him, the little jerks of his hips when he tried to push deeper, the urgent fingers in Chance's hair that tugged but didn't pull. It was hot, all of it, and Chance couldn't help dropping a palm to his own crotch and rubbing himself while he got Tucker off.

It didn't take too long until Tucker was whimpering above him and twisting his hips on the cushions. Chance put the hand that wasn't on his own erection on Tucker's balls and squeezed gently, feeling them draw up at the same time Tucker gasped and arched his back. "Move," Tucker managed to say, and as soon as Chance drew his mouth away, Tucker was coming with a series of shudders and jerks, his come falling hotly over both of them.

The instant Tucker was done, Chance ripped at the velcro fly of his swim trunks and shoved them to his knees. Still curled against the warmth of Tucker's body and the stickiness of his come, Chance wrapped a hand around his own cock and stroked, squeezing his eyes shut tight. Once, twice, and then he felt another hand, pushing his out of the way and taking over where he'd left off.

Chance didn't know how he'd lasted this long when he felt Tucker jerking him, he just grabbed onto Tucker's wrist, feeling his nails bite into Tucker's skin. "Harder," he heard himself grunt, "hurry up, McBride, harder, goddammit."

"Bossy," Tucker whispered in his ear, and then Chance was coming, finally, thank God, the orgasm being wrung out of him while he gritted his teeth together and rode it.

Fireline

"Wow," Chance said a long time later. Tucker grunted in agreement but didn't move from where he was nestled into Chance's side.

***

The ocean air coming in through the window brought goosebumps to their skin. They retreated to Chance's room, Tucker raising his eyebrows appreciatively at the king-sized bed. "You like your space."

Chance shrugged. "Most things are sized too small for me. Figured I might as well sleep comfortably. When I'm at home, anyway," he amended, referring to the twin beds they slept in at work.

Tucker sat on the edge of the bed, looking unsure of himself as he glanced around the room. "S'pretty nice. How long you been here?"

"Eight years. Since I got on with Oceanside. I needed something that had space but was affordable, so I went for a condo." Chance didn't know what exactly prompted him to share more information than was asked for, but maybe Tucker's confession from earlier was part of it.

"I rented a place in Kentucky," Tucker said vaguely, but didn't offer more. It occurred to Chance that he wasn't sure what exactly had happened to Tucker between the ages of fourteen and thirty-three. It also occurred to him that he wanted to know, which was unsettling.

Tucker's gaze had fallen on the framed picture over his bed. "Cool," he said softly. "Where'd you get that?"

It was a picture titled "Ready to Go". A firefighter's turnout coat hung on a hook, and assorted other gear, like helmets, boots, and a toolbox were scattered on the floor. The thing that made the picture stand out, though, was Chance's last name printed across the bottom of the turnout coat in an exact duplicate of his real one. The yellow helmet off to the side had an "11" on it, representing the station where he worked, and the wooden beam from which the turnout coat hung had a Maltese cross painted on it. Next to the cross was a small blue caduceus, the paramedic symbol.

"Bonnie," Chance explained, then remembered Tucker hadn't met her. "Best friend from high school. Fire Academy graduation present. The only thing she didn't have the artist personalize was the toolbox."

Tucker looked at him. "Personalize it with what?"

Chance grinned sheepishly. "Usually he'll paint the name of the firefighter's spouse and kids on it. Bonnie said that he offered to fill it in later. She actually took it from me and sent the picture back to him after I finished medic school so he could paint the caduceus on, but I don't think he'll be putting anything on the toolbox."

Tucker snorted. "Guess not. Still a cool piece, though." He studied it for a while until Chance saw him yawn.

"It's late," Chance said with studied casualness. "You can, uh. Stay. If you want."

It was a stupid thing to say, since Chance didn't even know if he really wanted Tucker to stay in the first place, but the invitation was already out there, and he couldn't call it back. But Tucker saved him.

"Ain't it a little early to be spendin' the night?" he grinned, standing up and stretching.

It was at the same time a relief and a disappointment. "Just offering. Since you brought dinner and everything."

"You paid me back," Tucker winked, and Chance's cock showed interest.

They walked to the front door and suddenly the two days before their next shift loomed large and lonely. Chance wanted to see Tucker before Sunday, wanted to touch him and be with him before work necessitated formal behavior. And yet … he couldn't ask, he still didn't know what this thing with them was, or if he wanted it at all. Easing some sexual tension was one thing; enjoying each other's company was totally another.

But once again, Tucker saved him. "You work out when you're not on shift?"

Chance blinked, startled. "I run."

"Me, too. One of the paths by the beach. Wanna go with me tomorrow? I'll cook ya dinner after."

"Ooh, just like a real date," Chance laughed, but Tucker's eyes narrowed.

"I don't date. You wanna go or not? And fuck you, you're not gettin' a five-course meal or nothin'. Momma's macaroni and cheese." He folded his arms and looked mutinous, and it occurred to Chance that Tucker might have thought he was being laughed at.

Chance stepped closer, bringing up a hand to brush a thumb over the tiny mole on Tucker's cheek. "Yeah," he said softly, right before he kissed Tucker, "I wanna go."

Chapter Four

Tucker was renting a place right on the beach, Chance discovered the next afternoon. "And you don't even surf," he said disgustedly as soon as Tucker opened the door. "What a waste."

Tucker grinned at him. "I still like the water."

Chance hadn't taken two steps inside before finding himself pinned against the wall, a hard, horny Tucker rubbing up on him and kissing him breathless. "Hello to you, too," Chance managed, his own cock suddenly standing at attention as well.

"Dreamed about you all damn night," Tucker murmured against his neck, fitting a leg in between Chance's thighs and grinding into him. "Was jerking off at four this morning just so I could sleep."

The pictures *that* image brought to mind would be fuel for Chance's own fantasies for weeks to come, and he groaned inwardly. He had a feeling he was in trouble.

Chance had just managed to drag Tucker's head up for a deep, wet kiss when Tucker shoved away and shook his head. "Damn it all to hell. Sorry. Told myself I wasn't gonna do that." He ran a hand through his hair and looked sheepish. "'Til after dinner, anyway."

Chance was still letting the wall support him, his legs spread and heart pounding. "Right. After dinner. Are we running, or what?"

"We're running."

They jogged for forty minutes along the beach path before Tucker waved at him and turned to go back. Chance kept it up for another fifteen minutes or so, liking the difference from his early-morning runs. He had never realized the sun made different colors on the water when it was setting rather than when it was rising.

He made his way back a while later, toeing off his shoes before entering the house. He followed the smell of baking cheese toward the kitchen and stopped short in the doorway.

Tucker had showered. He stood at the stove, clad only in a pair of black shorts that hung low on his hips. His hair was wet but combed, and as Chance watched, the dark curls at his nape dripped miniscule droplets of water on his neck. Chance wanted to pin him against the counter and suck the drops from his skin.

Tucker held out a bottle of water without turning from the casserole on the stovetop. "Dinner's ready, but you can shower first, if you want."

Chance took the offered bottle and drank a long, cold swallow. "Starving. Is it bad manners if I eat first?"

"Nope. Sit."

He did, and Tucker put a plate of home-baked mac and cheese in front of him, along with a basket of crescent rolls and a bowl of peas. "Damn, McBride, you're gonna make someone a good wife some day." Chance's mouth watered, and he tore off a piece of roll.

Tucker laughed. "Only way I get good country grub's if I make it myself. Don't get to make it that much, really, since all Momma's recipes were for like fifteen people. Eat up, there's plenty more."

Chance had two and a half helpings before shaking his head and throwing his napkin on his plate. "God. No more. M'gonna explode."

"Amateur," Tucker said easily, reaching over and gathering both of their plates. Chance watched him walk to the sink, admiring the way his ass looked in his shorts. "You can shower," he offered over his shoulder. "There's a clean towel in there."

Chance was becoming aware of how tight and sticky his dried sweat was getting and he grimaced at himself. "Yeah. Shoulda done it before dinner."

"Peach cobbler when you get out," Tucker said over the running water in the sink, and Chance groaned.

He found the bathroom easily and closed the door only partway so the steam could escape. Chance was under the spray in seconds, relishing the hot water on his skin, turning his face into it and letting it soak his hair.

He had no idea he'd been expecting the sure hands at his waist until he felt them. Half turning, Chance met Tucker's gaze, and his stomach clenched. Tucker was staring at him, eyes an even darker blue than usual, dick hard and nudging for attention against Chance's thigh. "You want help?" Tucker murmured. "You know, with washing your back or somethin'."

Chance grinned at Tucker. "Help would be good," he said. "But not with washing."

He caught Tucker's smile right before Tucker leaned in to kiss him, fingers tightening at Chance's waistline. They moved together easily, already knowing how the other liked to be touched. Chance had to break the hungry kiss to draw a deep breath. "What is this," he asked softly, his lips moving against Tucker's neck, but the words were drowned out by the shower and his own blood in his ears. Chance guessed it didn't matter, his cock was throbbing, and Tucker was sliding against him eagerly, and there would be plenty of time to puzzle it out later.

Their panting mingled with the spray and the steam. Chance listened to Tucker's words roll over them, loving how he liked to talk during sex, letting the melodic southern drawl make Chance even harder. He started to thrust against Tucker's hip, the water creating delicious slickness as he listened.

"Need you," Tucker was murmuring, his hand dropping to Chance's erection. "Need you so bad, you made me wait for a fuckin' month, Jesus Christ, never waited that long for no one. Forget all my goddamned good manners when you're around, Shanahan. So hot."

Tucker had both of their dicks in his hand, jerking them both slowly, one hand scrabbling above Chance's head for the soap. He found it and used it to lather them up, their cocks sliding and soapy, and Chance leaned his head back against the wall. "God," he muttered into the steam, "can't wait, won't last, Tucker. Don't bother taking time, just get me off before I go out of my fucking mind."

Tucker's free hand slipped down to cup Chance's ass and Chance tensed, wondering how far he should let things progress, but when Tucker teased his entrance with one soapy finger, Chance found himself moaning and spreading his legs.

"Yeah, that's it. Knew you'd like it," Tucker whispered, pushing that finger in farther. Chance relished the slight burn, savored it, wanted more. Spreading his legs even more, he slid both hands to Tucker's ass and hauled Tucker up against him, trapping their pricks between them. Tucker's finger brushed over Chance's prostate and he bucked involuntarily.

"Do it again," he demanded, and saw Tucker's mouth form a word.

Bossy.

Again, a small brush against his prostate that made him want to slide down the wall. And then Tucker's hand was gone, making

Chance almost whimper with the emptiness of it, until he saw Tucker reach for a small bottle in the soap tray. "Soap's not so good for ya," Tucker grinned, flipping the cap on the lube and coating his fingers. He brought his hand back down immediately, sliding the same finger back inside Chance's hole, but this time it was cool and slick and Chance thought he might come just from that.

Chance started pumping his hips, and Tucker moved his finger, still pulling on their cocks, for what seemed like forever. Chance was helpless against it, holding tight to Tucker's ass while he ground against Tucker's hand on his dick and thrusting back against the finger in his ass, until Tucker withdrew again and urged Chance to turn around and face the wall.

At once, Chance was alert, though the urgency in his cock almost overpowered him. He watched warily as Tucker reached up to the soap dish again and retrieved a condom. When Tucker ripped the wrapper with his teeth and started to roll it down over himself, Chance grabbed his wrist. "Put it on me," he said firmly.

Tucker stopped, their eyes meeting, and for a minute Chance thought he was going to refuse. Then he shrugged, and his dimples were back in full force. "Told ya I knew you were a top." He handed the condom and the lube to Chance and turned, putting himself against the wall and offering his nicely muscled ass.

Chance couldn't resist the gorgeous invitation, and he slicked his shaking fingers liberally with lube. One hand on Tucker's hip, he slid in two careful fingers and watched Tucker arch his neck. "Yeah, you got it, baby," Tucker murmured, one hand going to his own cock and pulling at it lazily. "Gimme one more."

So Chance complied, feeling Tucker contract around his fingers and marveling at the tightness. Managing to get the condom on with one hand, thankful he'd had years of practice, Chance replaced his fingers with the blunt head of his cock. "Okay?" he asked, leaning over to suck at the water pooling in the hollow of Tucker's neck.

"Fuck, yes," Tucker groaned, thrusting his hips backward. "Do it."

An inch, then another, until Chance was buried to the hilt and they were both gasping and shuddering against each other. "Damn, damn, damn," Tucker was whispering, his hips making short, shallow jerks as he stroked himself.

Chance tried to stay still and let Tucker adjust, but he couldn't, not when Tucker was whimpering and thrusting back so gorgeously, his head on Chance's shoulder and his neck beautifully exposed. Chance tried a small push and was rewarded with a moan from Tucker, so he tried it again.

"Quit playin'," Tucker said, his voice harsh in the small shower.

"Not playing," Chance growled against his neck, and pulled out almost all the way before thrusting back in with a grunt.

They started a rhythm of pushing and pulling that soon had Chance gasping and clutching at Tucker's hips with urgent fingers. "Good," Tucker was moaning. "You feel so good."

It was like being in a storm of want and hunger. The shower poured down like rain, and all of Chance's sensation became focused on his cock. He drove into Tucker again and again, panting for release, and managed to slide one hand around Tucker's waist and grasp his dick. "Come on," he whispered in Tucker's ear, his hips jerking. "Come for me, McBride. You waited this long, lemme see you do it."

The words were magic. Tucker slammed both hands onto the tile above his head and cried out, his cock pulsing. Chance could see long strands of spunk hitting the shower wall in front of them, and then he couldn't see anything at all except the white-hot flashes behind his eyes as he came, too, shuddering uncontrollably against Tucker's back.

They came down slowly. Chance pulled out, one hand carefully on the condom, and cracked open the shower door to toss it into the trash. He and Tucker spent several minutes kissing and cleaning under the spray, letting the water soothe and quiet them. When the water turned cool, they shut it off and reached for towels.

Unable to stop touching each other, they made it out of the bathroom and collapsed together on Tucker's bed. Tucker looked as if he wanted to say something, so Chance asked, "What?"

"You don't let guys fuck you?" Tucker asked, and Chance blinked. Not what he had expected.

"No, I have," he said slowly, unsure of what Tucker was really asking. "Just not usually."

"Me either," Tucker said. "Not usually."

Chance didn't know what to say to that, so he settled on dropping a kiss on Tucker's bare shoulder before they slept.

***

Chance woke up an hour later to an empty bed and the sound of Tucker humming in the kitchen. He went searching.

"Hey," he said in the doorway of the kitchen. "Where's mine?"

Tucker spooned a bite of cobbler and ice cream and nodded at the table. There was another bowl of dessert sitting there, the ice cream melting. "Was about to put it in the freezer. You sleep heavy."

"When I'm not at work, yeah." Chance crossed the floor and sat at the table, eagerly pulling his dish toward him. He took a bite and sighed happily, looking over to where Tucker was perched on the counter. "Momma's recipe?"

Tucker nodded, his mouth full. Chance wanted to lick at the drip of ice cream in the corner. Tucker heaved himself off the counter and took a chair next to Chance, turning it around to straddle. "Reckon we should talk."

"Yep."

"This gonna be weird for you? You and me?"

Chance thought about it. "Is there a you and me?" Tucker raised a brow at that and Chance looked down at his bowl. "Or are we just getting off, or what?"

Tucker didn't answer for a while, and Chance fiddled with his spoon, waiting. "I don't know," Tucker finally said. "But regardless, whatthehellever's going on, you all right with it at work?"

Chance met his eyes. "We'll handle it."

Chapter Five

August

Chance discovered their way of "handling it" at work was not to discuss it, mention it, refer to it, or come within ten feet of each other while in the presence of the rest of the crew. It was okay with him, actually, since he really had no idea at all how else to deal with a situation he'd always been smart enough to avoid in the past.

Tucker was another matter. Although they had agreed that it would stay private, Tucker found it difficult to keep his hands to himself. Chance found himself being groped and nuzzled at every opportunity. He was getting used to walking around with a hard-on, but it was getting more and more difficult to hide it from the guys.

Chance woke up one night not to the sound of the alarm, but to Tucker's hand over his mouth. "Shh," Tucker whispered, his eyes gleaming.

Chance knew that look. "Are you crazy," he hissed, motioning with his hand toward the other dorms. They weren't really even in a different room; all the dorms were just separated by partitions. Sound easily drifted over the tops of the walls.

"Yup," Tucker confirmed, throwing off Chance's light blanket and stretching out on top of him. "Crazy as a loon. You got lube in here?"

Chance knew he was done for when Tucker started grinding against him, and he could feel Tucker's erection through they gym shorts they both slept in. "Oh, Christ. Bottom of my locker."

"You're so easy, Shanahan."

"Fuck you."

"Yes, please," Tucker whispered, already shucking Chance's shorts and rolling a condom down, slicking it with lube and kissing Chance with a hot, wet mouth. "And hurry the fuck up. If we get a call like last time, I'll lose my shit."

Chance grinned, remembering how he'd been giving Tucker some pretty sensational head in one of the bathroom stalls when their engine had been called into service. Chance didn't think he'd ever heard anyone swear quite like that.

Quickly, he flipped them so Tucker was lying on his back. Chance urged Tucker's legs back and rested the head of his cock at Tucker's opening, hesitating there for a minute. "Didn't prep you," he said, not willing to hurt Tucker.

"Don't matter," Tucker whispered, "the condom's all lubed. Can't wait, Chance, just go slow for a second."

Chance looked down at Tucker's cock, straining and hard against his stomach, and didn't think he'd be able to stand prepping Tucker anyway. Taking a deep breath, he nudged inside and felt Tucker open even wider. "Christ," he murmured. "You kill me."

Tucker wasn't listening. He had his prick in his hand and was stroking himself, his eyes squeezed shut and his nostrils flared. It was one of the sexiest things Chance had ever seen. His eyes were pinned to the sight of it while he thrust shallowly, trying not to groan or gasp or breathe for fear of waking up their crew. The fear of discovery was hot in itself.

Chance's orgasm snuck up on him from behind, his balls tightening and his arms shuddering as he held himself over Tucker. When he stopped shaking, he opened his eyes to find Tucker looking at him with a half-smile, one dimple peeking out. "Watch," Tucker whispered, and when he was sure he had Chance's full attention, he stroked his full length twice before shooting over both of them. Chance could feel him trembling with the effort to not cry out.

It was fucking hot, and Tucker knew it. Chance had discovered Tucker loved baiting him, pushing him to his limits and beyond, making him lose what Tucker called his 'uppitiness' and just give in to the pure pleasure they found together.

Even now, having just come, Chance felt himself stir inside the other man, his cock filling once again. Chance thought it might be a good idea to find another condom.

Until the alarm made two soft dings and twelve pagers started beeping frantically in the stillness.

"Fuck," Tucker swore, pulling off of Chance with a wince and searching frantically for a towel. Chance got up and threw one at him from across the room.

"You got lucky," he said with a grin, and Tucker scowled.

"Looks like you're the one who got lucky," Tucker pointed out, before dashing past him out the door. Chance watched Tucker make it across the hall to his own room right before Matt opened his door and strode down the hall to the bay.

"Go wake up McBride," Matt barked at Chance. "Fucker'll sleep through anything."

Chance had to bite back a grin. "Sure thing, Cap."

***

It was a structure fire in a small building right outside Chance's own neighborhood, and he could feel the hum of excitement through the crew, himself included. Firefighters liked serving the public and helping in medical emergencies, but when it came down to it, fighting fire was their passion, what they lived for.

Engine One-Eleven went screaming out of the garage, breaking the quietness of the night, followed by Truck Eleven. Chance heard Matt through his headphones. "Shanahan, help the truck drop hose as soon as we get there. I'll take McBride with me while Jenkins goes through the front, if it's not fully involved yet."

Chance and Tucker both gave a thumbs up and grinned at each other. Fire was good.

They were the only engine company that had been called out since the fire was small and looked easily containable. It burned on the second floor of a narrow, two-story building. The truck had beaten them there and was already laying hose; Chance leaped out of his seat as soon as they stopped and obeyed captain's orders by going to help. Out of the corner of his eye he saw Tucker follow Matt to the front door.

Hose got laid, and a line was formed to do search and rescue, although Chance was pretty sure there was no one inside the business at this hour. Still, you never knew. More than once a homeless person had broken into a place, seeking shelter.

Chance knew by now that Matt and Tucker had gone inside to ventilate, and he itched to be in there too. Alex motioned toward the front door, so with a couple of guys from the truck, he picked up some hose and headed that way.

They dragged it into the building and up the smoke-filled stairs, Chance's breathing sounding loud and ragged through his helmet and hood. He felt Alex behind him on the hose and suddenly the temperature spiked incredibly as they found the seat of the fire on the second floor. He was covered in sweat, and the clothes under his turnouts were sticking to him. Chance forced himself to breathe easily and conserve the air in the tanks he knew he'd need.

Alex had told him on the ground that the ceilings in the place were a concern. "Cement-based plaster," he'd said with a grimace. Matt had nodded, too. "Yeah. Everyone be careful, they could come down."

Chance glanced upward now, but there was no sign to tell him if the ceiling would hold. Watching Tucker and Matt ahead of him, he signaled over his shoulder to Alex, and they lifted the hose together. He was about to pull the lever to let the water loose when it happened.

The ceiling directly over Matt and Tucker caved in with no warning at all. It fell silently, knocking both of them to the ground, and Chance felt Alex duck reflexively behind him.

"Tucker!" Chance shouted, knowing McBride wouldn't be able to hear him. *No*, Chance screamed in his head, *no, goddammit, get the fuck up, get up right now!* And then off to his left, two more firefighters crashed through the window in a rain of glass. They had a chainsaw and axes, and it spurred Chance into action. He and Alex lifted the hose again and let the spray loose, soaking the walls and dousing the flames that licked in the doorway from the next room over. He kept his head turned toward Tucker, though, praying for him to move, to get up out of the plaster covering him. Chance saw one of the guys go to work with the axe, hacking at the fallen ceiling, trying to free both men, and he felt a surge of relief when Matt scrambled out. If Matt could get out, then Tucker could, too … except he wasn't, he was just lying there, even though the firemen surrounding him had lifted the fallen ceiling from his body.

Chance made himself remain calm, because it was either that or scream his fool head off, and he still had fire to put out. He watched as two of the guys lifted Tucker and passed him to the window where Chance knew the truck's ladder was waiting. Once Tucker was out, Chance was able to concentrate on the flames in the next room.

It was the first time in his career he had ever wanted to get the fuck out of a burning building.

It seemed an eternity until Chance knew there was no danger of the flames reigniting. Leaving the hotspot check to Alex and one of the firefighters from the truck, Chance turned and headed back down the hazy stairs. He reached fresh air at the door and tore off his helmet, searching wildly for Tucker.

He finally spotted Tucker sitting in the back of the ambulance. Heading toward him at a run, Chance was halfway across the parking lot when Tucker looked up. The relief on Tucker's face was unmistakable.

Chance reached Tucker, oblivious to anyone else who stood nearby. "Tuck," he murmured, "Tucker, oh my God, say you're all right." He leaned his forehead to Tucker's and stood that way for a moment, closing his eyes and feeling Tucker bring his arms up to encircle Chance's neck.

"I'm good," Tucker assured him, his voice hoarse. "S'all good, baby, don't worry."

Chancellor took a deep breath, smelling smoke and sweat and the unique scent that was Tucker. He swallowed hard and willed his eyes to stop stinging. "You stupid fuck. You scare me like that again and I'll wring your fucking country boy neck."

Tucker chuckled, one of his hands squeezing the back of Chance's head. "Got it."

When Chance finally raised his head to look around, he wished instantly he was back inside the burning building. Six firefighters stood at varying distances from the ambulance, and all of them had helmets in their hands. They were all staring at Tucker's arms looped around Chance's neck.

* * *

Matt at least had the decency to wait until Tucker was released from the emergency room and the sun came up before calling both Chance and Tucker into his office.

It wasn't as nice as the battalion chief's office, but Chance still felt slightly intimidated as he stood before the man he'd worked side by side with for the past eight years. Matt sat in his padded chair and regarded them both.

"Shanahan," he said carefully, "I believe a circumstance like this was already discussed. I also believe you told me it wouldn't be a problem."

"Matt – " he started, then thought better of the form of address when Matt cleared his throat. "Cap. With all due respect … I don't think it's been a problem."

Matt narrowed his eyes, and Chance could feel Tucker shifting uncomfortably next to him. "I take it this isn't new."

"No, sir."

"How long?"

"'Bout a month," Tucker piped up, despite Chance's attempts to mentally will him to keep his mouth shut.

Matt considered Tucker thoughtfully. "You've only been here two months. You're a fast mover."

Tucker grinned, and Chance groaned. "That's not a compliment," he murmured, and Tucker just grinned wider, his dimples teasing Chance. Matt looked like he was trying not to laugh.

"So … whatever you've got going on here," Matt waved his hand vaguely and looked uncomfortable, "should stop immediately, you know that, right?"

"Yes, sir," they both mumbled.

"But," and here Matt paused, studying the ballpoint pen between his fingers, "if there's nothing going on, then there's nothing to stop. I mean, if I don't see anything, then there's clearly nothing going on." He pinned both of them in place with a stare. "And if no one else comes to me, complaining about something they've seen that bothers them, then that's a sure sign that nothing's going on."

Chance figured it out. "Yes, sir." He knew Tucker was eyeing him.

Matt blew out a breath and threw his pen down on the desk. "McBride, you feeling all right?"

"Sore." Tucker rolled his shoulders as he said it, and Chance winced in sympathy. "Chest hurts from the smoke. But I'll be all right, Cap."

Matt nodded. "You did well. Go home. Call in sick tomorrow." Tucker opened his mouth to protest, but Matt pinned him with a stare. "Call in sick. That'll give you four days before your next shift, and I expect you healthy."

Tucker nodded, subdued. "See you Saturday." He left the room, and Chance turned to follow, but Matt stopped him.

"Shanahan. Wait a minute."

Chance inwardly rolled his eyes. Here it came. "S'up, Cap?"

"Sit."

Chance sat.

Matt watched him for a while, long enough to make Chance squirm in his chair like a kid. "Chancellor. You've been at Eleven for eight years."

He nodded, not sure if he should speak.

"I don't give two shits where you stick your dick, long as it doesn't interfere with work." Matt was measuring his words carefully, holding Chance's gaze. "This thing you got going with McBride. Just for fun, or what?"

Now there was a question.

"Um. Yeah, it is. Mostly," he added, not even sure if he knew the answer.

"Mostly. What's that mean?"

Chance took a deep breath and tried not to raise his voice. He was tired and grimy and wanted to sleep for a hundred years. His stomach growled for its breakfast, and he couldn't get the picture of Tucker pinned under the fallen ceiling out of his head. "It means," he said loudly, "that I have no fucking idea what it is, but as soon as I do, I'll update you."

To his surprise, Matt laughed. "That tells me what I need to know." He sobered slightly and asked, "What happens if it ends?"

Chance had thought about it. "I'll leave. Transfer out."

Matt shook his head. "He should go. Not you."

"Well ... I'm thinking about taking the captain's test in January, actually." Chance hadn't been ready to admit it yet, but he also hadn't been ready to let anyone know about the thing with Tucker. Funny how things had a way of getting out. "If I pass, I'll have to transfer to wherever there's an open captain's spot anyway."

Matt broke into a broad grin. "Good for you," he said, and Chance nearly blushed under the praise of the older man. "Department could use more decent captains."

"Thanks."

"Now you get your ass home, too. You're *not* calling in sick tomorrow."

Chance smiled ruefully and turned to go, then remembered something. "Hey, Matt. The guys ... they saw."

"Yep, they did. You think they'll give you shit?"

He considered for a minute. "Alex won't. And I think Robert knew I liked guys. But the rest, I dunno." Chance sighed, not ready for any of this. Life had been peaceful before Tucker. Celibate, but peaceful.

"I won't fight your battles for you," Matt said, "but if you need my support, you've got it. And McBride, too."

Chance gave him a half-hearted smile. "Might need it. Thanks, Matt."

Chapter Six

Chance drove straight to Tucker's and found the front door unlocked and cracked open for him. Entering the quiet house, he made his way toward the bedroom.

Tucker lay face down on the bed, his shirt off. The room smelled very faintly of smoke, and he still had streaks of dirt on his cheek. He obviously hadn't showered yet, and Chance was pondering how to get Tucker into the water without it looking like Chance just wanted to fuck, when he saw it.

The bruise spanned the entire length of Tucker's back, from shoulder to waist, and was almost perfectly cylindrical. Chance knew it was from the air tank, but that didn't stop the sickening feeling he got when he looked at it. It was still mostly red, but the edges were already turning blue and the center of it had darkening patches. He sucked in a breath between his teeth before he could stop himself.

Tucker lifted his head from the pillow, blinking sleepily. "Hey."

"Sorry," Chance murmured, moving to the bed. "Didn't mean to wake you."

"Was waiting for you," Tucker yawned, curling into Chance's side and flinching when the muscles across his back were stretched. "Need a shower."

"Me, too. Need help getting up?"

"Nah." He shrugged off Chance's help, but faltered when he tried to push himself off the bed, so Chance sighed and looped an arm around his waist.

"If you let me help you, I'll blow you in the shower."

"What are you waiting for?"

Chance sucked him off until Tucker was gasping and clutching at Chance's shoulders, his legs shaking. Afterwards, when Tucker looked as if he was going to pass out, Chance got him out of the shower, dried him off, and collapsed into bed with him.

They slept heavily.

***

Chance woke up to late afternoon sun slanting in the west window and the sound of his cell phone vibrating angrily from his pants, which were across the floor. He glanced over at Tucker, still sleeping soundly, and climbed out of bed.

Throwing on a pair of Tucker's shorts, he wandered to the living room to check his voice mail and found a message from Bonnie. He punched in her number and waited for her to pick up.

"Were you in that fire?" she demanded, in lieu of a hello.

"My day was great, thanks for asking," he prodded her, sinking into the couch.

"Sorry. But were you? It was on the news this morning." She sounded worried, not the norm for her. She was used to Chance's job by now.

"Yeah, yeah. It's fine, it was small." He looked toward the bedroom and swallowed tightly, remembering the actual danger, but didn't feel like going into it. Because that would mean explaining Tucker, and Chance still didn't know how, exactly, to explain Tucker McBride to anyone. Even Bonnie.

" … want to come over tonight?" she was asking, and Chance realized they hadn't spent any time together since Tucker had arrived. He owed her.

"Not tonight," he said, "and I work tomorrow. How about Thursday? I'll even cook," he offered, and she laughed.

"You're just feeling guilty, Chancey. Where the hell've you been for the past month? You got yourself a date?"

He snorted, hoping that was enough of a response to appease her. "Just come over around seven. Bring a DVD if you want. And booze."

"I always bring booze," she said. "Silly." And she hung up, leaving Chance grinning at the dial tone.

He wondered if he should wake Tucker up for dinner or just let the man sleep through, but one look into the bedroom told him Tucker was awake and trying gingerly to sit up.

"Hey, easy," Chance said, kneeling on the bed and helping him into a sitting position.

"I hurt," Tucker said simply, and Chance knew he wouldn't admit it unless it was really, really true.

"I know," Chance said, sitting back against the headboard with him and letting Tucker drop his head to Chance's shoulder. "You want one of the painkillers from the hospital?"

Tucker made a face. "No sense in feelin' all hung over if I ain't got the empty beer bottles to show for it. I'll take some Tylenol later."

"Okay. Anything I can do?"

"Well," Tucker sighed, "now that you mention it ..." he trailed off and dropped a hand into Chance's lap.

Chance shifted, already growing under Tucker's touch. "Maybe not. How bad do you hurt?"

"Never bad enough to not want it," Tucker leered, and Chance had to laugh. It turned into a groan when Tucker squeezed him, hefting the weight of Chance's shaft through his shorts.

"You drive me crazy," Chance whispered, turning to thread his fingers through Tucker's hair. "Outta my goddamned mind." He kissed Tucker then, hungrily, need unfurling low in his belly.

Tucker growled into his mouth. "Same here. Ain't never wanted no one so bad all the fuckin' time."

It was an admission of sorts, but Chance was already too hard to think about it for long. Tucker was still squeezing and rubbing him through his shorts, which were suddenly a hindrance, and Chance pulled at the waistband impatiently.

Tucker kneeled over him, pushing him back into the pillows and stripping Chance of his shorts. "Mm, yeah." Tucker was staring at Chance's stiff cock, his tongue coming out to wet his bottom lip. "Like it, don'tcha."

Chance just grinned up at him, knowing Tucker would start a steady stream of chatter from here on out. He loved to talk in bed, and Chance loved to listen to him. But Tucker didn't follow his usual pattern this time. He opened his mouth to say something else, but closed it again and met Chance's eyes, his fingers stroking Chance's dick lightly. "S'matter?" Chance asked, bringing up a hand to Tucker's jaw.

Tucker shrugged. "Stupid."

"C'mon. It's just us. What?"

"I was – " he stopped, licked his lips again, still stroking Chance absently. "I was scared. Last night, when I went down. I ain't never been scared like that."

"I was too."

They looked at each other in the fading light of the bedroom, and something passed between them, something Chance didn't know how to name. He only knew he wanted Tucker, wanted them to wrap around each other until the scared feeling went away and they couldn't tell where one ended and the other began.

He sat up, Tucker still straddling his lap, and kissed Tucker again. They thrust up against each other, seeking friction, until Tucker whispered, "Hold on," against his mouth. Chance watched Tucker get up and go to the top drawer of the dresser, retrieving a condom and lube. He couldn't help tracing the lines of Tucker's bruise with his eyes, noting it was already darker than this morning, but then Tucker was back on the bed with him, mouth hot on Chance's chest.

"Want you," Chance mumbled into his hair, seeking out Tucker's cock with hungry fingers. "Want to feel you inside me."

Tucker looked up, eyes glowing dark, dark blue in the last light of evening. "Yeah?"

"Yeah. Want it now."

And then Chance was on his back, his feet planted flat on the bed and his legs spread, feeling wanton and slutty and not caring because Tucker was pushing in one slick finger and brushing up against his prostate. "Oh, *God*," he groaned out loud, "do that again."

"You're damn tight," Tucker whispered. "You sure you been fucked, Shanahan?"

Chance was pretty sure, all right. It had just been a while. Since Derek. "Believe me."

Then there were two fingers working their magic, and Chance couldn't help bucking his hips up, his hand automatically going to his dick and pulling hard. "Gonna go slow," Tucker told him. "You're so tight."

"Don't care, just do it, Tucker, don't care," Chance panted, trying not to sob out loud when Tucker's fingers pushed hard on his prostate again.

Tucker withdrew his fingers and rolled on the condom with a shaking hand while Chance watched. He pushed Chance's legs back, and Chance felt Tucker nudge right at his entrance, right where he'd been dying to feel him. "Ready?" Tucker asked, and Chance just thrust his hips forward in answer.

Tucker gasped and pushed in, pausing to see if Chance was all right, but Chance just threw his head back on the pillows and tried to open his legs wider. "Don't wait," he begged, not even knowing he needed this until now.

He felt Tucker's abdomen flex and tighten against his stomach. "Quit talkin'," he murmured, "or I'll just pound you into the fuckin' bed."

"Now you're getting the idea," Chance whispered back, and started stroking himself.

Tucker groaned and pushed all the way in, both of them sighing with relief. He withdrew just a little and then buried himself to the hilt again, as if he couldn't bear to pull all the way out. Chance wanted to tell Tucker again to hurry, but he couldn't talk anymore, all he could do was jerk upwards in an attempt to get Tucker to hit his prostate.

"Oh, fuck me," Tucker swore. "I'm never gonna fuckin' make it, you're too tight, Chance, you're gonna make me shoot in about five seconds." He started thrusting in earnest, muttering to himself in the way Chance loved, losing any pretense of rhythm.

Chance stopped bucking up and just let Tucker pound into him while Chance stroked himself, his own pre-come lubing him enough for his cock to slide easily in his palm. It was almost over, he could feel it, his balls growing tighter with each thrust Tucker made. But he wasn't doing this alone. Reaching up to draw Tucker's head down, Chance tongued the edge of Tucker's ear before whispering, "Gonna come right *now*."

It was all Tucker needed. With a groan, he said, "Oh, fuck," and Chance could feel Tucker's cock jerking and pulsing in his ass. Then Tucker was pushing Chance's hand off his prick and stroking firmly, bringing Chance with him. Chance slammed one hand down on the bed and threw the other arm over his eyes, his whole body shuddering with the force of his orgasm, his come spreading over both of them.

They kissed lazily for what seemed like hours after that, stopping only to let Tucker slide out and dispose of the rubber. Then they curled around each other while the dusk slipped into dark and they whispered.

"What'd you do after your father died?" Chance asked, idly tracing the Maltese cross tattoo on Tucker's bicep.

He was quiet for a long time, and Chance wasn't sure he was going to answer, until he did. "I couldn't leave Momma and the farm, even with Uncle Tim makin' grabs at me every chance he got. Momma still wasn't doin' so good."

Chance wondered if Tucker knew his accent got thicker when he was tired or upset; he tended to drop more word endings and draw out his vowels. Chance realized he used it for indication on Tucker's mood. "So you stayed," he said, feeling the anger well up in him again.

"Had to. 'Til I was eighteen, anyway, and I was smart enough to finish high school and go to junior college. Knew by then I sure as shit wasn't no farmer."

"When did you figure out you liked guys?"

"Hell, I knew that when I was fifteen," Tucker laughed. "Right after I kissed Carol Sue Harper down by the old riverbed. She got her hand down my jeans and jerked me off, and the whole time I was picturin' her older brother Joey." He shook his head, smiling. "Eventually I got Joey to stick his hand down my jeans, too. He was a hundred times better than Carol Sue."

"Being gay in the south must've sucked," Chance said quietly. "Although I guess Kentucky's not really south."

"It's redneck country," Tucker said with a snort. "Even worse. Had my share of fights. Guess I ain't never gonna be done fightin', you know?"

"I know."

"So after high school, I took off. Never told Momma about likin' cock, it would have 'bout killed her anyway. Never told her about Tim, neither. What would have been the point? Headed up to Louisville where we had family. Had a little cash from Daddy's will, used it to get a cheap place and start Jefferson Community College." He paused, closing his eyes and sighing.

Chance nuzzled into his hair. "You need to sleep."

"I ain't the one who's gotta work tomorrow."

"Don't remind me," Chance groaned.

Tucker opened his eyes and turned his head on the pillow. "Might as well finish tellin' ya. Not much more to it."

"I'm listening."

"Wrote to Momma on and off. Told her where I was workin', that I was takin' classes. Asked if she needed money, and she always said no. I never asked about Tim, but she always told me what a great job he was doin' anyway. She was lyin', which I didn't know til I got a letter from him tellin' me she died." His voice was flat.

"Oh, man. Tuck, I'm sorry."

"I was three classes from gettin' my AA in Fire Science."

Chance nodded, he'd done the same program himself.

"Went home for her funeral to find the farm completely gone to shit. Hadn't even had a decent crop that year, Tim was just livin' off what Daddy had left Momma. She finally just died of the broken heart she'd had for six years." He lay perfectly still, staring at the ceiling, and Chance realized this was not a story that many others had heard.

"Did you stay?"

"Nope. Took off again after the funeral, even though Tim asked me to stay and help. Fucker even apologized, can you believe it? Got all drunk and fucked up and cried to me. 'Stay, Tucker,' he begged. 'It's what yer momma woulda wanted.' I told him to go fuck himself. I left the next morning, went back to Louisville, finished school, worked some shit jobs just to make money. Got on with Louisville Fire when I turned twenty-three." He sat up in bed and put his hands to his waist, twisting to release pressure in his sore muscles.

Wordlessly, Chance got out of bed and headed to the bathroom. Finding the unopened bottle of painkillers on the counter, he shook one out and filled the cup on the sink with water. He brought both back to the bed and handed them to Tucker.

Tucker made a face. "Hate that shit."

"I know. But you can sleep late tomorrow, and it'll be good for you to get some rest tonight."

"You just don't want me mauling you while you sleep," Tucker grumbled, and swallowed the pill.

"Maybe I'll maul you."

"A boy can hope."

Chance climbed back into bed and let Tucker drape himself over his chest. "So how'd you make it out to the west coast?" he asked, drawing designs on Tucker's back.

Tucker yawned, the pill already taking effect and making him drowsy. "Was with Louisville Fire for seven years. Thinkin' about making lieutenant. Didn't tell none'a my crew I was queer; didn't need that kind of shit. S'different out there. Not as easy as here."

Chance knew it wasn't exactly easy here either, but kept his mouth shut, unwilling to interrupt.

"So if I wanted to get laid, had to drive over the border to a gay club in Indiana. Wasn't gonna risk goin' anywhere in the city. Didn't go that much, just when I had an itch to scratch, but obviously it wasn't far enough away." His voice was getting softer, but not as a result of the pill. "Some of the department's guys were waitin' around outside one night, all piss-drunk. Recognized my truck on their way back from some concert."

"I can guess," Chance said, smoothing Tucker's hair away from his forehead. "Fight."

"They beat the shit outta me," Tucker said matter-of-factly. "Broke ribs, kicked my head in, the whole deal. Spent the night in the hospital and missed my shift the next day, and when I went back, didn't have a job no more, easy as that. 'You're not the kind of example the Louisville Fire Department wishes to set,' my lieutenant said. They made up some bullshit reason for firing me – something about responsibility issues 'cause I missed one fuckin' shift in seven years – and sent me packin'."

"So you came to California?"

"Not yet. Spent almost a year being drunk and ornery and basically a mess. It's damn near a miracle I didn't get picked up by the cops for all the bar fights I got in. Woulda ruined my chances forever with any other fire department. Then, when I finally sobered up, I called a friend from school who lived out here. He let me stay for a couple months, long enough for me to know I liked it, so I went back to Kentucky and packed up my shit. Been here for a year before I got brave enough to test with Oceanside."

Chance couldn't do anything but continue to run his fingers through Tucker's already tousled hair. It wasn't the story he'd been anticipating – Tucker's general attitude seemed way too good to have such a crappy past behind it.

But everyone was good at hiding one thing or another, Chance knew.

Chapter Seven

Chance dragged himself out of bed at six. Tucker didn't stir, and Chance snuck a peak under the sheet at his bruise. It was dark and angry, as was to be expected, and it would grow worse before it got better.

He made it home to shower and grab clean clothes before hopping back in his SUV. Getting to the station, he automatically scanned the parking lot for Tucker's truck before remembering he'd left Tucker in bed. Chance realized it would be his first shift since June without Tucker there, and it felt odd.

Chance didn't realize he was being ambushed until he walked into the kitchen through the back door.

All of B shift was there before him, either sitting at the table or standing around by the counter. They all turned and faced the door when Chance came in. The sinking feeling in his gut made him want to turn tail and run, but he wasn't a coward.

"You got something to say to me?" he asked, and went to the refrigerator for something to drink. He wanted a nice shot of bourbon, really, but he settled on milk. Chance didn't miss how two of the guys who rode on Double shifted away from him.

Shit.

There was silence for about ten seconds, and Chance was just going to shake his head and walk away when Alex spoke up. "You queer, Shanahan?"

He steeled himself. "Yup."

"You and McBride?"

For the first time, Chance was thankful Tucker was at home. On top of everything else, the last thing he needed was to be here getting grilled. "Yeah, Tucker, too."

Alex eyed him for a long minute. "Don't guess I really give a shit," he shrugged. "Long as you and McBride don't go fucking around at work."

Chance swallowed, thinking of all the times they'd done exactly that, but what Alex didn't know wouldn't hurt him. "Look," he said, addressing all of them. The only sound other than his voice was the slow drip of the coffeepot. "If you didn't know before today, then obviously it's not gonna make any fucking difference in how I do my job." He paused and glanced at Matt, who watched him from over the rim of his coffee cup. Not going to fight Chance's battles, he had said. Okay.

"If you got a problem with it – with me – let me know now. 'Cause I've been here for eight years. I put my head down, I do my job, and I'm sure as fuck not gonna leave because one of you has a problem with fags." He thought he saw Matt grin into his coffee.

There was only silence in the kitchen, and Chance didn't know if that was good or bad. Finally, someone spoke up.

"Shanahan?" It was Jack, from the truck.

Chance rounded on him. "What."

"My uncle's a New York City police officer."

Chance blinked. "And?"

"And he's gay." Jack shrugged. "Doesn't stop him from being a good cop. I'm gonna go get on the treadmill before we get a call." And he left the room.

A couple of the others gave tentative grins at Chance and followed Jack. They'd be okay, clearly. He looked at the remaining guys in the kitchen. "Anyone else got something to say?"

Robert got up from his chair and faced Chance in the middle of the kitchen. "Lemme ask you a question."

Chance looked him in the eye as best he could, considering Robert was an inch taller and outweighed him by twenty pounds. "Yeah."

"You really prefer McBride's scrawny ass over this fine specimen?" he leered, running his hands over his chest, and the kitchen exploded with laughter.

Chance grinned. "You're a close second."

"That's right," Robert nodded, looking pleased.

They all dispersed after that, wandering off to do morning chores. Chance took note of the two guys that gave him a wide berth and sighed. Despite them, it had gone better than he'd anticipated.

Head down, do the job. It's all he'd ask from anybody else.

***

"So you're really not going to tell me?"

"Just … busy," he said to Bonnie the next night, dodging her question again about where he'd been lately.

"Hmm," she said, waving her empty wineglass at him. "You were 'busy' with Derek, too."

Chance tipped the bottle and poured the rest of the wine into her glass. It was so tempting to tell her about Tucker, about the third degree he'd gotten at work yesterday, about how the fear had climbed into the back of his throat when Tucker had gone down in the middle of the fire.

About how Chance hadn't even known he was lonely until he wasn't any more.

But telling her would lead to the inevitable questions that women always asked. She would want to know about hearts and flowers and *feelings* and all the ridiculous shit that women got into their heads. Chance didn't want to deal with it. "There's more food," he said instead, indicating the stir-fried chicken and vegetables on the stove, but she shook her head.

"No thanks, I'm stuffed. And I'm not a moron, Chancellor Shanahan, so it's okay to just tell me you don't want to talk about it." She took a swallow of wine and raised her eyebrows at him.

He felt the usual flash of affection for her. No, she was anything but stupid. Bonnie White had a sharp wit and sharper intelligence, well disguised by her pretty face. They had dated in high school, had even slept together twice before discovering they were both really in love with Scott Logan, their school's star pitcher on the baseball team.

"You're gay?" Bonnie had said on prom night, after both of them were drunk on Bartles and Jaymes strawberry wine coolers. They were watching Scott be crowned Prom King or something equally as stupid.

"I guess," Chance had shrugged. "Do you hate me?"

"Yes," she replied dryly, "because I could have been chasing him this whole time." She nodded her head at Scott, who had a blinding smile.

"Me, too," Chance said sadly, and both of them had laughed 'til they cried.

He looked at her now. "I don't want to talk about it."

"Fair enough," she said, never one to dwell on a subject. "I brought movies."

Two hours later found them lying together on the couch, her head on his chest while he slouched down and propped his feet on the coffee table. Chance never thought anything of their physical contact with each other, it was as natural as breathing for Bonnie to snuggle up to him while they watched TV or for him to tangle a hand in her hair.

So when Bonnie looked up at him to make a catty remark about Angelina Jolie prancing across the screen, Chance didn't think twice about laughing and dropping a chaste kiss to her temple.

"Well," Tucker drawled from the doorway, "you shoulda told me you bat for both teams, Shanahan."

Chance nearly dropped Bonnie to the floor in his scramble to get off the couch, but by the time he got to his feet, Tucker was gone.

"Who was *that*?" Bonnie asked in the following silence.

"That," Chance sighed, "was what I didn't want to talk about."

***

Chance did his level best to explain why he hadn't told her about Tucker until she was rolling her eyes and waving him out the door. "Just go," she finally said, exasperated. "Trust me, he looked more mad than I am."

He had kissed her forehead and promised to buy her dinner.

Now he stood on Tucker's front steps, wondering if his knock would even be answered, when the door was jerked open. "The fuck do you want?"

Chance eyed the bottle of Jack Daniels in his hand. "You drunk?"

"Jus' about."

"You drove that way?"

"Christ, I thought my fuckin' momma died already. No. Didn't start drinkin' 'til I got back home. The fuck do you want?" he asked again, his tone belligerent.

"To come in." Chance didn't usually have to explain himself to anyone, this was new territory.

Tucker didn't answer, just turned and walked back into the house, leaving the door open. Chance took it as consent and followed.

It was dark, the only light in the house coming from the kitchen, so that's where he went. The kitchen was illuminated by the little light over the stove, throwing shadows into corners. Tucker sat stiffly on the counter with his bottle and made no move to invite Chance to sit.

Fireline

Chance lingered in the doorway "I wasn't expecting you," he ventured, trying to gauge how much whiskey Tucker had drunk.

"Clearly," Tucker laughed, and took a long swallow. "Jesus, Chance, you coulda just told me. Didn't need to make me think I was the only one you were fuckin'."

Chance didn't recall having any kind of conversation about exclusivity – not that it mattered, since there was no one else anyway – but the only thing that was important at the moment was that Tucker was apparently jealous.

Huh. Chance thought probably he shouldn't be that pleased by it, but couldn't help it.

He approached Tucker cautiously, taking the bottle from Tucker's hand and fitting himself in between Tucker's legs. "You jealous?" he asked, ducking his head to nuzzle at the soft skin below Tucker's ear.

Tucker cleared his throat and tried to shift away. "So the fuck what. Pissed off's more like it. Not gonna compete with a woman, they always win. Done that shit before." He sounded disgusted with himself.

"You don't have to compete," Chance answered, a laugh threatening to make its way out. If he'd known it would be this cute, he would have baited Tucker long before now. He wrapped both arms around Tucker's waist and hauled the man forward to bring their bodies in contact. Just like he'd thought – Tucker was hard.

"That's right, I don't," Tucker scowled, arching up in spite of himself.

Chance pulled back to look at him. Tucker's hair looked as if he'd been running an angry hand through it, his cheeks flushed with liquor. His shirt smelled like whiskey and aftershave and faintly of the fabric softener Chance knew he preferred, and it all combined to make the heady scent that Chance had grown used to over the past month.

"You idiot," Chance said softly. "If you'd stuck around, I could've introduced you to Bonnie."

"Why the shit would I wanna meet – oh. Bonnie, Bonnie? Like, your ..." he brought up a hand and nibbled at the side of his thumbnail.

"Like my."

A furrow appeared between Tucker's brows. "Damn. You pissed?"

"Do I look pissed?" Chance went back to nuzzling Tucker's neck and started grinding slowly against him, since Tucker seemed to be finished protesting.

"Either I'm really loaded, or you look like you wanna fuck."

"Both right. How's the back?"

"Hurts."

"Sorry. I'll stop." Chance made as if to pull away.

"The hell you will." Tucker grabbed Chance's head with two hands and kissed him with an open mouth and hot tongue, his legs coming up to wrap around the backs of Chance's thighs.

Chance moaned and pushed back, feeling Tucker's cock hard against his hipbone and wanting him badly. He nibbled at Tucker's lower lip and dropped a hand to Tucker's waistband, pulling ineffectually at his shorts.

They were on the floor of the kitchen almost before Chance realized it, Tucker having practically leapt off the counter at him. Shimmying out of shorts and t-shirts was getting easier and easier the more they did it. Then they were naked, cocks hard and leaking and pressed together as they rocked and kissed and panted.

Tucker's mouth tasted like whiskey and need, but then it was gone as he slithered down to wrap his tongue around Chance's aching cock. "Oh, Jesus," Chance said, not expecting the sudden warmth around his dick, and bucked up. He could feel Tucker grin against him before getting down to business, alternating between sucking and licking.

Chance arched his back on the hard floor and let him go to it, absorbing the feeling of getting well and truly blown. The man knew what he was doing, that was for damn sure, because Chance's toes were curling with every suck and Tucker was doing something with his tongue that made Chance's eyes roll back in his head. "More," Chance moaned, and knew he had about five seconds before he came.

Tucker gave him more. He swallowed him nearly to the root, making Chance moan and fist a hand in Tucker's hair. "God, please," he begged, not ashamed of it, not as long as Tucker gave it to him. Then he felt it – one of Tucker's fingers teasing at his hole, not slipping in, just circling the outside and pressing on the soft skin right behind his balls.

"Fuck," he hissed, and tried to pull away before he came, but Tucker latched onto his hips and held him in place.

Fireline

Chance shuddered and clenched his muscles, pouring gushes into Tucker's mouth. Tucker swallowed it like a pro, taking it all and licking Chance clean with easy swipes of his tongue while Chance lay limply, trying to come down.

"We ain't done," Tucker murmured to him after a minute, stretching out across Chance's body, and Chance could feel just how 'not done' they were against his stomach.

"Hmm," he said, licking at Tucker's mouth. "Surprised a drunk like you could get it up."

Tucker reached down and stuck a finger in Chance's ribs, making him yelp in surprise and try to wriggle away. "Flip over. I'll show you just how up this drunk can get it."

Chance grinned in anticipation and turned over, wriggling his ass in the air. Tucker smacked it, then turned to dig behind him in a drawer. When Chance heard the rip of a condom and the cap being flipped on a bottle of lube, he asked, "You keep that shit in the kitchen?"

"For emergencies," Tucker said, as if that explained everything, and then Chance really didn't care why Tucker kept that shit in the kitchen because there were two fingers in his ass, stretching him.

Chance lifted himself slightly on his elbows, trying to push back onto Tucker's fingers, doing his best to make Tucker hit his prostate.

"Eager, ain't ya?" Tucker was leaning over him, cock brushing against one of Chance's ass cheeks, fingers still working.

"For you." It was the truth, Chance realized, glancing down at his own cock. He was hard again already, seemingly a common occurrence whenever he and Tucker were fooling around.

The thick head of Tucker's cock pushed at Chance's hole, searching gently. "Okay?" Tucker asked, his voice hoarse.

In answer, Chance rocked backward, forcing Tucker inside. They groaned in unison. "Go," Chance ground out, needing to feel him.

Tucker went. Grasping Chance's hips, he thrust in all the way, angling himself to brush the spot where Chance wanted him most. Again he did it, and again, until both of them were moaning in unison and Chance's head was hanging so low his forehead nearly touched the floor. "Can't ever last with you," Tucker gasped. "You make me come like a goddamn kid."

"Doesn't matter," Chance panted, a bead of sweat rolling off his side and dropping onto the linoleum. "Oh, shit, this is about to be over." He could feel his balls draw up tightly and watched a drop of his pre-come land a few inches from the sweat.

Tucker started slamming into him, urgent fingers clutching at Chance's skin, muttering profanities to himself.

"You before me," Tucker gasped out, and since Chance's hand was already jerking at his dick, it was only a matter of seconds before his second orgasm was sneaking up on him.

It rolled over him with even more power than the first, and Chance cried out with the force of it. His come hit the floor with a splatter while he tried to hold himself up on trembling arms.

Ten seconds later, Tucker froze behind him and sucked in a breath. Chance felt Tucker's cock pulsing and jerking, even though his body stayed perfectly still, and then the two of them were on the floor, tangled about each other.

"See?" Tucker said, after a while. "Not so drunk."

Chance smirked at him, amused. "We'll see how your head feels in the morning."

Chapter Eight

October

Fall came but the cool weather didn't, although the ocean dropped in temperature enough for Chance to start wearing his wetsuit. More often than not, Tucker was in bed with him when the alarm would go off at five-thirty in the morning.

"Christ," he would mumble, and pull the sheet over his head. "Can think of lotsa reasons to be awake at this hour and none of 'em involve you gettin' outta bed."

"You heard the surf report last night. Good swell coming in off the Mexican coast."

"*You* heard the surf report last night. I was just sittin' in here gettin' lonely." Then he would throw the sheet off and bat those lashes.

A lot of times Chance ended up not making it to the beach.

***

They settled into a routine. Work, play, eat, fuck. Spending nights at whoever's house was closest. Chance liked it – and most of the time he thought he more than liked it, but wasn't sure what to call it. Or maybe he did know, and didn't want to admit it.

They found new, creative ways to fool around at work, though the fear of being caught was always there. If they were, Chance knew not only would one of them get transferred to another station – probably Tucker, but Chance was on the line, too – but they'd also get written reprimands in their files. Not good for being promoted to captain.

But it was awfully hard to resist when gleaming blue eyes woke him up in the middle of the night with Tucker's finger over his lips and a hand on his dick. The latest escapade could have gotten them both fired, come to think of it, and Chance shook his head.

Fucking on top of the fire engine. Jesus Christ.

It had been hot, though. The feel of the hose rough against his back while Tucker rode his cock from above, being so high off the garage floor, the anticipation of knowing they could get a call at any minute. It had made Chance come like lightning, and Tucker too. Then both of them a second time, sucking each other off.

Chance was hard now just remembering it. It seemed to be his permanent state these days, not that he minded, and he wondered briefly where Tucker was. The open books on the table mocked him. Chance was trying to use the relative quiet time between calls to study for his test in the station's small classroom, but his thoughts kept turning to sex. Specifically, sex with Tucker. Chance was just wondering if he could find Tucker for a quick grope in the bathroom when the door to the classroom opened.

"You hidin'?" Tucker's dark head poked around the door.

Chance grinned, absurdly pleased to see him. "Not from you. Just studying. Can't seem to concentrate on it, though."

"Got somethin' to show ya." Tucker came in and let the door close behind him, perching on the edge of a desk. He held a white envelope in his hand and Chance knew exactly what it was.

They had taken their fitness tests the week before. The entire department was required to be tested once a year in a complete physical exam. They were hooked up to heart monitors while they ran, their body fat was tested, and nearly four vials of blood and a sample of urine were taken from each firefighter. Last year, Chance's cholesterol had been high enough to surprise him, so he appreciated the yearly reminder.

And also the proof that he was clean, though there hadn't been worry over that in eighteen months.

So when Tucker twinkled at him and waved his envelope, Chance knew what he was going to say. "Results," Tucker announced, unnecessarily.

Dread curled in his stomach. "Yeah?" he said, clearing his throat.

"You get yours?"

"You know I did," Chance answered. They had all gotten them in their office mailboxes this morning.

"Saw it on your bunk." Tucker was practically wriggling with glee, dimples flashing. "Did you check?"

"No," Chance lied. Of course he had checked. He always checked, after what had happened.

"Come on, then!" Tucker jumped off the desk and headed toward the door, anxious as a pup.

"Tuck, I'm studying."

Fireline

Tucker stopped, his hand on the door. "You want me to bring it here?"

"No. I'll look in a little bit, after I'm done."

"Aw, come on," he wheedled. "It'll take two seconds."

"No," Chance snapped. "Damn, leave it be. I'll check later."

Tucker narrowed his eyes. "Right," he replied, and left the room.

Chance made a sound of frustration and shoved his books to the floor.

***

Tucker had avoided him for the rest of their shift, although Chance woke up around two a.m., thinking he had heard his door whisper open. Turned out to be his imagination. Tucker hadn't even looked his way at breakfast this morning.

The boy knew how to pout, that was for sure.

Chance lay on his bed now, yesterday's envelope in his hands. A check of the clock showed it to be six-thirty, ninety minutes later than usual for Tucker to show up at his house. Chance guessed he wouldn't be coming, and ignored the voice in his head that told him he wasn't exactly rushing to Tucker's place either.

He propped his head up with a pillow and took the folded sheets of paper out again, bypassing the page that detailed heart rate and body fat and turning right to his blood work. Cholesterol looked good. Less ice cream and cheese had helped with that. There was a full liver and kidney panel, both of which were functioning normally. All internal organs were doing what they were supposed to do. Iron level was good.

Chance skimmed down to the bottom. Hepatitis B: negative. Hepatitis C: negative. Human Immunodeficiency Virus: negative. Thank God.

Crumpling up the paperwork and lobbing it toward the trashcan, Chance picked up the phone.

***

Tucker appeared an hour later, still mutinous and quiet.

Chance greeted him at the door with a kiss that had enough tongue to melt his stubborn exterior and soon had Tucker panting and clutching Chance's hips. "I'm sorry," Chance murmured against his lips, "I should have just told you."

Tucker pulled back far enough for Chance to marvel once again at the length of his lashes. "Told me what? Are you dyin'?"

Chance laughed. "No. The opposite."

They sat on the couch, some distance apart. Tucker folded his arms across his chest and waited patiently, though Chance knew it went against his nature to do it. "Go," Tucker finally said with a fidget, and Chance was sure he was imagining the worst.

"So our tests came back," he started, then faltered. This had sounded much easier in his head.

Tucker watched him for a minute before sighing and moving closer on the couch. Nudging Chance's knee with his own, he said quietly, "I ain't one for judgin' people."

It was what Chance needed to hear, so he picked up again. "I was in a relationship for a while. Three years or so."

Tucker nodded, he knew that much. Chance had mentioned Derek by name, but that was all.

"So we were careful, right? Used condoms." He stopped, licked his lips. "'Cept for once or twice. Times when one or both of us was too drunk to care. But most of the time we were safe. I kept pushing him to go get tested with me so we could throw out the goddamn rubbers once and for all, but he always shrugged it off. So finally I went to the clinic myself."

Tucker was listening intently, a hand on his leg. "And? You were clean?"

Chance nodded. "I was, yeah. So I brought Derek my results that night, thinking he'd be happy, and maybe it would make him want to go get it done."

"What stupid fuck wouldn't want to?" Tucker asked.

"Turned out, he'd already been. Two months earlier."

"Why didn't he tell you?"

Chance chewed on his bottom lip for a while before looking up and meeting Tucker's eyes. "Because he was positive."

"Positive." Tucker looked momentarily confused before understanding what Chance was getting at. "Like … HIV positive?"

"Yes." Chance's voice was low, dreading Tucker's reaction.

"What the fuck!" he exploded, pushing off the couch and pacing to the center of the room. Turning, he faced Chance with his hands on his hips. "You're tellin' me he endangered you for two fuckin' months? What the *fuck*!"

"We didn't have unprotected sex during that time," Chance sighed, "but we'd had it sometime during the last year. So the fact that my test was negative was meaningless, since you know HIV can take up to six months to show on a blood test." He paused to judge Tucker's reaction, but since Tucker was staring at a point over his head, it was hard to tell. "Anyway," Chance continued, "I left him. I got a lot of shit from his friends for leaving him because of the HIV, but that wasn't it at all. It was the dishonesty, you know?"

Tucker still didn't look at him, but nodded curtly.

"I got tested twice more, six months apart. Clean both times. I passed the eighteen-month mark this year. I don't worry about it any more, but I also don't ever go without a condom. I was just … I dunno. I knew why you wanted to see my results. I figured you would want to … you know. And I'm just not ready for that, not yet. I might not ever be." He stopped, aware of talking too much, but the following silence was painful to hear.

Tucker finally dragged his gaze from the wall and looked directly at Chance. He walked forward and dropped to the floor, pushing Chance's legs apart so he could kneel in between. "Hurts that you didn't tell me," he said, and Chance nodded. "But hurts more to think of you in that situation. To think he was such a fuckin' coward that he wouldn't warn you."

To his absolute horror, Chance felt the sudden sting of tears. He didn't know if it was from Tucker's soft words or from having to relive the whole Derek situation, but he swallowed tightly in an effort to shove them away before he embarrassed himself.

Tucker, who was always more perceptive than Chance wanted him to be, put his forehead to Chance's and slid one hand around to cup the back of Chance's head. "None'a that," he murmured, his voice warm. "Asshole ain't worth it."

Chance shook his head and said hoarsely, "Not 'cause of him."

"What, then?"

"He's not worth it," Chance whispered, "but you are." And he kissed Tucker, plunging his tongue in deep and clutching at the front of Tucker's t-shirt desperately.

Tucker met him kiss for kiss, sliding his mouth up to the corner of Chance's eye and kissing away tears Chance hadn't even known were leaking out. He kept a hand on the back of Chance's head, grounding him, giving him support. "S'all right, baby," he said between kisses, and suddenly Chance couldn't get enough of him.

Chance tugged at Tucker's t-shirt impatiently, making Tucker laugh and lift it over his head. Reaching over to shove the coffee table out of their way, Chance sank to the floor with him. They knelt facing each other, hands roaming, mouths joined, Tucker alternating between giving Chance gentle kisses and then trying to swallow him whole.

Clothes were shed. Still kneeling, Chance lowered his mouth to Tucker's shoulder, nipping and sucking a small red-purple mark into his skin. Their cocks brushed, sending goosebumps up his arms and over his back. Chance lifted his gaze to see Tucker's head fall back, offering Chance a sweet expanse of skin on his neck, and he licked a long stripe up to Tucker's chin. "Want you," Tucker whispered into the quiet. "Always want you."

"How?" Chance asked, bringing a hand down to lightly trace the head of Tucker's dick.

Tucker shuddered and glanced around. "Table," he said, turning and bracing his hands on it, offering up his ass. "Like this." He dropped his head between his arms and waited quietly, though Chance could hear his breathing quicken.

Chance leaned over Tucker, taking his cock in hand and using it to tease up and down Tucker's crack until both of their breathing was coming in gasps. It would be so easy to lick his palm, coat himself, and slide into Tucker's ass with no protection, no barriers in the way. His dick twitched at the mere thought, but what he had said earlier still held true. Chance knew he wasn't ready for it, Derek had taken that freedom away from him, even if it was only temporary.

Tucker was looking over his shoulder, eyes dark with heat. "Go get it. Hurry the fuck up, I'm wantin', here."

Chance smiled his thanks and went to the bathroom, tearing apart his medicine cabinet in search of the condoms and lube. He didn't waste time rolling one on as he walked back, and when he got to the living room he froze in the doorway. Tucker had taken matters into his own hands and was stroking himself, dick hard and leaking, one hand leaning on the table. Chance was mesmerized by the sight of it, especially when Tucker's tongue darted out to wet his lower lip. "Better hurry up, Shanahan," he muttered. "Else I'm gonna finish your job."

Chance crossed the room and knelt down behind him, already using a lube-coated finger to probe at his hole. "If you come," Chance whispered in Tucker's ear, "I won't blow you for a month."

Tucker stopped abruptly, chest heaving.

"Oh, no," Chance grinned, "I want you to keep going. Just don't come. Understand?"

Tucker nodded, his breath hitching, his hand already going back to his cock and regaining its rhythm. "Don't know if I can do it," he gritted out.

"Try." And with that, Chance withdrew the finger and pushed inside.

Tucker cried out and squeezed his prick just below the tip, shaking his head. "Oh God, oh God," he mumbled to himself, "please Mary mother of Joseph don't come, don't come."

Chance would have laughed if he weren't so close to spilling as well. He pulled out, and then eased his way back in, torturing them both with slow, measured strokes. He felt rather than saw Tucker start jerking off again and gave him another warning. "You don't shoot until I say so."

Tucker's only answer was a whimper.

Chance managed to keep it up for a while longer, gritting his teeth against the waves of sensation that rolled over him with increasing strength, watching the muscles flex in Tucker's arm as he jacked himself. Chance drove in at an angle, knowing when he hit Tucker's prostate because Tucker's arm would freeze for a fraction of a second before continuing.

It was only when Tucker was practically holding back sobs of frustration that Chance gave up the power Tucker had allowed him. Feeling the telltale tightening in his balls, unable to hold off any longer, he leaned over and murmured one word in Tucker's ear.

"Go."

Tucker came instantly with a body-wrenching shudder and a stream of profanity.

Chance followed almost immediately, pulling Tucker up tight against him and gasping hard against Tucker's shoulder. His cock throbbed as he filled the condom, and Chance felt a tiny twinge of regret that they weren't skin to skin.

"Jesus," Tucker was gasping, both hands braced on the table, though his arms were trembling. "Jesus fuckin' Christ."

Chance's knees were killing him so he pulled out carefully and collapsed to the floor, hauling Tucker down with him. They kissed lazily, sleepy and sated.

Tucker nuzzled Chance's cheek, his eyelashes tickling. Chance could feel him grin. "What?" Chance yawned, wondering if he'd be able to get up and make it to bed.

Tucker nipped at his ear. "So fuckin' bossy."

Chapter Nine

October wore on and the cold weather finally made its appearance toward the end of the month. Fire season officially ended but Station Eleven was still busy with traffic accidents and medical calls, and Chance figured he'd better get his ass in gear if he was serious about the captain's test. The fucking books wouldn't open by themselves.

Tucker was his biggest supporter, leaving him alone to study at work, or sitting quietly next to him on the couch on their nights off while Chance pored over his test material. After he was done for the night, however, was another story; Tucker pouncing on him as soon as he closed his books.

Not that he minded.

Oftentimes he'd go back to his books after they'd messed around and Tucker was asleep. Chance had picked up some of the old captain's tests in the station's files, and he studied these the most, afraid of how many multiple-choice questions there were and how similar the answers all seemed.

A lot of times he thought he was insane for trying. He'd only been on the department for eight years, and most guys who tested for captain had been there for twelve or more. There were no captains in the department with less than ten years' experience. What was he thinking? These thoughts usually came on the rare nights when he was alone, Tucker either working overtime or spending the occasional night in his own bed.

But he persevered, soaking up as much information as he could.

So when he woke up one morning at work with no appetite and his head slightly aching, he attributed it to nothing more than exhaustion.

Tucker offered him a cup of coffee when Chance finally stumbled into the station's kitchen, blinking against the fluorescent lights. "I'm on an eight-hour holdover," Tucker said, frowning when Chance made a face and pushed the cup away. "Whassamatter, you gettin' too spoiled on Starbucks?"

"Nah. Just don't want it. You coming over later?"

"Yup. Kirby's got some Little League game he wants to watch his kid play in, so I'm stayin' for him til four." He scrutinized Chance's face. "You feel okay?"

"I'm fine," Chance dismissed, sitting down and forcing himself to take a bite of the peanut butter and jelly toast on the table.

Tucker stood behind him and kneaded his shoulders, which felt like heaven. "Don't spend all day with those fuckin' books," he said.

Before Chance could answer, Robert appeared in the kitchen. "Hey, I wanna get me some of that, McBride," he said. "Shanahan ain't the only one who's tense around here."

Tucker shrugged nonchalantly. "Don't come without a price, Diaz. Shanahan gives me sugar." And he bent down for a kiss, his tongue darting out to swipe at Chance's upper lip.

Robert pretended to gag.

"Whoa, hey, my eyes," Alex said from behind them. "Warn a guy, can'tcha."

Chance's relief on C shift showed up a blessed twenty minutes early and clapped him on the shoulder. "You're outta here, buddy," he said, and Chance was grateful.

Tucker walked him out to his car and watched as Chance slid behind the wheel. "You sure you're all right?" Tucker asked again.

"Headache," Chance admitted. "Need a nap." They'd been up twice during the night, once for a traffic accident on the freeway and once for a respiratory distress in the retirement community.

"Yeah, okay." He seemed doubtful, but didn't press it. Tucker leaned in for a hard kiss and a wink. "Be over later."

Chance drove home in a half-daze, and by the time he finally got there, his lack of appetite had turned into full-fledged queasiness.

Head pounding, he collapsed into bed and tried to remember what they ate at work last night. Oh, right – Double's crew had made a Thai chicken pasta that was better than anything Chance had eaten in a restaurant. He'd had two helpings.

Two too many, obviously, his stomach told him, and he wondered if the chicken had been bad. Steeling himself against the nausea, he turned over and tried to sleep.

***

Chance woke up abruptly three hours later and bolted for the bathroom.

Skidding to a stop in front of the toilet, he dropped to his knees and threw up the half piece of toast he'd eaten, as well as the little bit of water he'd drunk when he got home.

Panting, sweat breaking out on his forehead, he sat back on the floor and felt marginally better. Dinner from last night apparently wasn't agreeing with him. He looked up at the corner of the sink and reached up a hand to drag himself off the floor, swaying when he was finally standing.

His sheets were cool when he slid between them. It felt soothing to his head, which still ached fiercely, and he wished he had one of the bottles of water in his refrigerator. The kitchen was so far away, though.

Chance slept again.

He came wide-awake once more around two and made a second dash for the bathroom, this time barely making it before throwing up a little more water. Dry heaves followed after that, his whole body shuddering. Sinking back down to the floor, he reached up and managed to get down the bath towels hanging on the rack above his head. Chance folded them together for a pillow and stretched out on the bathroom floor, absorbing the feel of the cool tile beneath him.

The third time he woke up was to Tucker shaking him, a worried look on his face. "You're off?" Chance asked hoarsely, having no idea of the time.

"It's nearly five. How long you been lyin' here?"

"Dunno." He lifted his head and felt his stomach roll again. "You better move," he managed, before sitting up and pushing Tucker out of the way of the toilet.

He had nothing left to throw up, but his body unfortunately didn't know it. He dry-heaved a couple of times before bringing up yellow bile, wincing when it burned the back of his throat. He could feel Tucker's hand on his back, moving in slow circles, waiting 'til he was finished.

Dropping back down, he leaned his head against the wall and closed his eyes. "Thought it was from dinner last night," he said.

Tucker snorted. "Ain't from dinner. That flu's goin' around, remember? Think you can walk back to bed?"

Chance wanted to stay on the cool bathroom floor, but nodded. Using the wall to brace himself, he stood up on shaky legs. Tucker slid a strong arm around his waist and walked with him until he could sink onto the bed by himself, lying back with his legs still on the floor. "I feel like shit," he whispered to the ceiling.

"I know, baby," Tucker answered, pushing at his legs with an insistent hand until Chance groaned and swung them up on the bed. He closed his eyes and heard Tucker leave the room, then return.

"Here," he said, and Chance opened his eyes to see Tucker holding out a bottled water.

Chance grimaced. "Don't want it. Where were you at eleven when I was dying for water?"

Tucker grinned. "Was out protectin' lives and property, now wasn't I? You gotta drink some of this. If nothin' else, at least it'll give you somethin' to throw up."

"That's no incentive."

"Neither is bringin' you to the emergency room because you're dehydrated. Think of the embarrassment." Tucker sounded way too happy about that, and Chance opened one eye again to scowl at him.

"Gimme the fucking water." He took the bottle and drank two swallows, ignoring his stomach's protest but receiving a satisfied nod from Tucker.

"You take your temp today?"

"I don't think I even own a thermometer." Chance felt drowsy again and prayed the water would stay down long enough for him to sleep for a while.

"Christ. I'll try to steal one from work tomorrow." Chance felt a cool hand against his cheek. "You're pretty hot."

He turned into his pillow with a yawn. "Thanks. But I can't have sex with you right now, I'd probably puke on you."

Tucker snorted. "That would deserve a smack on the ass if you weren't sick. But you are, so I won't. You sleepin'?"

"Mmm," Chance mumbled in response, and then didn't hear anything for a long time.

***

Tucker woke him sometime after dark and insisted he drink more water, which promptly came back up with no warning. Tucker managed to dodge as Chance groped for the trashcan next to the bed.

"Sorry," Chance croaked, looking at the dark spot soaking into Tucker's long-sleeved t-shirt.

Tucker shrugged and pulled it over his head. "Jus' water."

Chance watched Tucker move to the dresser and hunt through Chance's shirts, and wished he could appreciate the sight of Tucker's bare back. His eyes traced the design of the tattoo on Tucker's right bicep, and he reminded himself to think about it again when he was better.

"You don't have to," he said softly, when Tucker returned from dumping out the trashcan. "I mean. Been sick by myself before, you know?"

Tucker looked at him. "Well, now you ain't by yourself."

"But why?" Chance insisted, not liking the vulnerability he knew he was showing.

"Why what?"

"Why are you …" he gestured vaguely at the bed, the trashcan.

Tucker huffed out an impatient breath. "Because I love you, you fuckin' idiot. God. Wouldya shut up and go to sleep?"

Chance did.

***

He slept through 'til morning, and when the alarm woke him up, his stomach had settled enough for him to think about going to work.

Chance changed his mind, however, when he ventured to the kitchen. Tucker glared at him and steered him right back to bed, threatening to call in sick for him "like your momma used to do when you were a kid" if Chance didn't do it himself.

He guessed his still-pounding head was enough reason to call in, anyway.

Tucker went off to work, muttering something about stupid surfers who didn't know when to stay in bed, and Chance slept most of the day. He tried a drink of Gatorade at noon and felt relieved when it stayed down. Chance guessed he probably still had a fever, judging from the glassiness of his eyes when he looked in the mirror and the chills that racked him every hour or so, but the nausea had receded. He figured he could handle everything else but the nausea.

Tucker had unearthed Chance's box of saltines from the cupboard and left them by the bed that morning. Chance gingerly ate a couple of them around dinnertime, ready to make his millionth dash to the bathroom, but they didn't make an appearance again.

He dropped back into bed at nine with some of his exam materials, but his head throbbed after only a few minutes, so he abandoned it in favor of sleep.

Chance didn't wake up 'til Tucker was crawling into bed with him the next morning.

The first thing he noticed was his stomach growling for food and his lack of headache. The second thing he noticed was the paleness of Tucker's face. "You all right?" he asked, voice scratchy from sleep.

Tucker gave a quick shake of his head. "Better get the trashcan."

***

It hit Tucker harder than it had Chance. He puked through the first thirty-six hours of it, sometimes so violently that his vomit was tinged with blood. Chance didn't start worrying until hour twenty-four, when neither of them had slept for more than a few minutes at a time.

"Goddamn," Chance said finally, easing Tucker back into bed after making their tenth trip to the bathroom in as many hours. "You want me to call one of the nurse educators for some Compazine?" The traveling nurses that taught the firefighter continuing education classes always had the anti-nausea meds at home.

"Couldn't keep it down," Tucker demurred.

"Oh, I don't know," Chance sighed. "They do make it in suppository form."

That earned Chance a weak middle finger. "The only thing I'm puttin' up my ass is you. Don' worry, baby, I ain't gonna die from a little pukin'. Done worse from booze." He managed a pale imitation of his usual grin, dimples barely making an appearance.

He kept it up for another twelve hours, throwing up any liquids Chance was able to coax down. By that time, Chance was worried enough to want to ignore Tucker's protests and throw him into the car, blankets and all, and drive his butt to the hospital for an intravenous line.

But as quickly as it had started, it stopped. Tucker drank nearly a full bottle of water around eight o' clock and kept it down before falling into an exhausted sleep. Chance breathed a sigh of relief and burrowed into the pillows next to him.

***

It had been three days since both of them had shaken off the last remains of the sudden flu and Tucker had yet to go home. Not that Chance cared – he found that he liked having Tucker there all the time. It was so easy to just reach out and touch him while they watched television or ate dinner. Having a warm, willing body in bed with him didn't hurt either, and Tucker was *always* willing.

So on the third straight day of having Tucker there, Chance said casually over breakfast, "You wanna move in?"

Tucker stopped chewing his cereal and looked up from where he'd been laughing at the comics in the newspaper. "Huh?"

"Do you want to move in," Chance repeated, enunciating sarcastically.

"I heard you."

"Well?" He shifted in his chair, already rethinking it.

"Why?"

"Because I love you, you fucking idiot," Chance said, repeating Tucker's exact words to him and already knowing it was true before he'd even spoken.

"Oh," Tucker said, and grinned hugely. "Yeah, I do."

Chapter Ten

December

The months wore on and winter finally arrived, bringing with it California's rainy season and putting Chance in a foul mood.

"Fucking rain," he said morosely, and returned to waxing his neglected surfboard.

Tucker watched him with a wry expression. "I think you got that seasonal affective disorder thing. You bitch and moan every time the sun ain't shinin'. Some day you oughta come back to Kentucky with me and see what real seasons are."

Chance's witty retort was to flip Tucker off.

The weather did afford him more time to study, however. Chance spent long hours at night with his test materials, cramming for the exam that was only six weeks away. He narrowly avoided having to spend the holidays with his mother and stepfather in Arizona by using the captain's test for an excuse.

"I'm sorry, Mom," he sighed into the phone one evening while Tucker was in the kitchen making tacos. "I really can't make it. I gotta study for this thing."

"Chancellor," his mother said in her haughtiest tone, "you did not come for Thanksgiving either. If I didn't know better, I would think you were avoiding spending time with your family."

He marveled at how she always knew. "That ain't it, Mom."

"Ain't?" she spat. "Since when do you use such hillbilly language?"

Chance winced. Seemed he'd been spending too much time with a certain hillbilly. "Sorry. There's a guy I, uh - " he paused there, knowing her reaction if he told the truth. "A guy I work with talks like that. Guess it's rubbing off." He ignored Tucker's derisive snort from the kitchen.

"Chancellor," she continued, "might it be too much to hope that you are not still ... fraternizing with men?"

"Yes, Mother," he ground out, "it would be too much to hope."

"Well. Perhaps if you moved to a less liberal area." She sounded as if she was sucking on lemons.

"Maybe if I register Republican," Chance said cheerfully. "Then the government could just beat the gay out of me."

"Chance, *really*," she said in a horrified tone. "It's only because I love you."

"How about Easter," he sighed finally, just wanting to get off the phone.

"We won't be here for Easter. Your brother has invited us to Colorado to spend the holiday with him and his girlfriend." She was switching from annoyed to hurt, going through the entire gamut of false emotion in hopes of eliciting some response.

"He invites you every year and you always make him come to you instead. How is Casey, anyway," he asked, trying to sound uninterested.

"He's been offered a partnership in the firm," she glowed. "He'll probably propose to Allison by Christmas."

Chance sighed inwardly. His brother was clearly going to be crowned "Best Child" at the next family get-together. He looked up as Tucker's head poked out of the kitchen.

"Chow," Tucker mouthed, thumbing over his shoulder, and Chance nodded.

"Mom, I hate to end this loving conversation we're having, but I'm eating dinner. Say hello to Frank for me, I'll call you in a few weeks." And he hung up on her.

"Wow," Tucker said when Chance entered the kitchen.

"You're telling me."

***

The rain continued, making things miserable for Chance at work as well.

"Fuck," he swore, stepping off the engine one day after a call and nearly slipping in the puddles of water all over the garage floor. His hair was drenched from the ride back, as his seat behind the engineer was completely exposed to the weather. And water had found its way under the collar of his jacket and had soaked the t-shirt under his gear. "I need a hot shower," he groused to no one in particular.

He received grunts of agreement from his crew and a smirk from Tucker. "You need more'n that," Tucker whispered on his way by, carrying his helmet in his hand. "A good blow'll cure what ails ya."

"Too bad I'm working, I can't go out and get one." Chance winked at him and watched Tucker's eyes get impossibly darker.

Tucker paused at the door to the greatroom and waited 'til the garage slowly emptied of wet, grumbling firemen. Putting his mouth close to Chance's ear, he whispered, "I've been so hard for you all fuckin' day. You think about teasin' me and your balls'll be blue for a goddamned month, Shanahan."

The fine hairs on Chance's arm rose at the whispered words in his ear. "Shower," he growled, pulling Tucker in for a kiss and using his other hand to grope Tucker's crotch. Yup – hard as steel beneath the yellow turnout pants, not unlike Chance's own cock.

The thing Chance loved best about their showers at work was the privacy. Each stall had its own floor to ceiling frosted glass door, impossible to tell who was showering behind each one. Their bathroom was big enough for each of the six showers to have significant room between them; voices did not often carry from stall to stall.

He reminded himself to write a letter someday to whoever saw fit to create their showers, but decided to leave out the part where it allowed his partner to suck his dick so beautifully with the relative security of not being discovered.

Tucker had snuck in about five minutes after Chance's water had started to warm him up, prick still hard. Chance could feel it now against the crack of his ass while Tucker slid two hands around his waist and down his hips, enfolding his cock with both hands and making Chance hiss against the steam and spray.

Tucker jacked him slowly from behind while Chance leaned his forehead against the tile and spread his legs and tried not to groan out loud. The other guys were calling to each other over the tops of their stalls, their voices loud and echoing in the bathroom, and Chance knew there were five more men waiting their turns for showers too. "Better hurry," Tucker whispered, and Chance could hear the grin in his voice. "Guys waitin'."

Embarrassingly enough, Chance didn't think it was going to be a problem. He was tingling already, his breath coming faster, and he began thrusting into Tucker's sure grip. But almost as soon as Tucker started, he stopped, and Chance whimpered out loud before he could catch himself.

And then Tucker was turning him, sliding down the front of Chance's body, and Chance slammed back against the wall as Tucker took his dick in his mouth in one smooth swallow. Chance gritted his teeth together and pressed the heels of his hands against his eyes, feeling his cock slide down the back of Tucker's throat.

"Oh God, oh God," he heard himself mutter when Tucker started doing things with his tongue that Chance had only seen in porn flicks.

Tucker pulled off his dick long enough to say, "You ain't gonna scream in here like you did last night, are ya?" and Chance almost came on the spot, remembering it.

He glared and pushed Tucker's head back where it was supposed to be, ignoring Tucker's barely suppressed chuckle. "Get busy, McBride."

Chance needn't have ordered it; Tucker began sucking him in earnest, flicking a talented tongue over the slit until Chance's knees were trembling and threatened not to hold him for much longer. He curled urgent fingers in Tucker's wet hair and sent him a silent signal, which Tucker picked up on immediately.

Tucker deep-throated Chance, pressing up on the underside of Chance's cock with his tongue, and then Chance was biting the inside of his cheek in an effort not to groan out loud as he came down Tucker's throat in heavy pulses.

Before Tucker could even get off his knees, Chance was sliding down the wall and fisting Tucker's prick, pulling him off fast and hard. Tucker didn't have much time to steady himself before he was biting at Chance's shoulder to muffle his whimpers, hands roaming over Chance's chest.

Tucker came with a soft cry that was lost among the other voices in the bathroom, his come falling hotly over Chance's hand and getting rinsed down the drain almost immediately.

Chance kissed him while Tucker was still coming down. "Could handle the rain if I got more of that," he mused, making Tucker laugh.

"Jus' have to ask, baby."

***

The weather cleared for a week and then started up again. Chance thought he might be getting used to being soaking wet for most of his twenty-four hour shift, but prayed for winter to be over anyway. Tucker just laughed at him and threatened again to take him to Kentucky to see what real winter was like.

It was drizzling, naturally, when the call came through about the small car fire on the busiest street in the neighborhood. Chance swore viciously as he stabbed the 'stop' button on the treadmill, and Tucker threw him a sympathetic look.

Rain started falling in earnest as they pulled up to the scene, blocking a lane of traffic. Ignoring the horns from other drivers, firefighters leaped off the engine and began dropping orange caution cones in front of and behind the rig.

Chance hesitated, knowing he should be with Alex, who was examining the flames coming from under the hood and trying to determine if they should use dry powder or foam. The rain was doing nothing to lessen the fire's intensity. Tucker had already jumped down and was talking to the frightened-looking elderly man who stood to one side, clutching his wife's elbow.

If only it wasn't so fucking wet and miserable.

That thought in mind, wondering if he could corner Tucker in the shower again after they got back, Chance stepped off the engine without looking into the street first.

Matt would tell him later that he hadn't actually stepped into oncoming traffic; he'd been behind the relative safety of the cones. But it didn't stop visibility from being poor, or the street from being slick, or the woman on her cell phone from being too distracted to notice that her lane was being cut off due to the large fire engine blocking it.

Chance stepped down with his left leg and before his right foot touched the ground, he was hit with something that had enough force to throw him back against the engine before sending him sprawling onto the wet pavement. He dimly registered screeching tires and the shouts of his crew, but they took a backseat to the pain blossoming in his leg. His upper thigh was one big mass of excruciating agony.

Before he could decide exactly what the hell had just happened to him, Chance figured he'd better get his ass out of the street. But attempting to push himself up on his elbows sent a fresh wave of torture through his leg and made things go dizzily gray. His head swam, and his stomach rolled over, and Chance was afraid he was going to be sick right there on the rain-covered road, so he lay back down and closed his eyes.

He wasn't sure if he'd blacked out or not, but nothing much had changed the next time he opened his eyes, except for the fact that Tucker was bending over his leg and Matt was prying open one of his eyelids and shining a penlight in it. Chance batted his hand away weakly.

"Hey!" Matt said, startled by Chance's movement. "Look who's with us. Stay awake for a little bit, all right?" His voice was perfectly calm and soothing, which Chance took to mean that something was seriously wrong. The calmer Matt was, usually the more dire the situation.

Tucker had jerked his head around to look at Chance, and Chance was startled by the whiteness of his face. Tucker's expression was nothing like Chance had ever seen: a combination of fear and horror.

"What's wrong," Chance asked, but it came out as only a hoarse whisper.

Tucker and Matt exchanged a look, and Tucker gave Chance a weak version of his usual grin. "Got yourself hit by a car, dumbass," Tucker told him. "Called for backup and a medic van. You hurt anywhere else?"

"Hit by a car," Chance repeated, trying to make the words sink in. Hit by a car? Huh. That was weird.

"Chancellor," Matt said firmly, "does your head hurt?"

"Yeah," he mumbled, realizing it. His head hurt like a bitch. "But my leg is killing me," he continued, raising his head from where it was pillowed on someone's turnout coat – probably Tucker's, since he seemed to have on just a t-shirt and suspenders – to look down at where the pain was centered.

"Chance, don't," Tucker said sharply, but the warning came too late.

White, glistening bone peeked at him through the ripped flesh in his leg. Chance stared at it impassively, feeling the pain and seeing the bone but not connecting the two events. *Compound fracture of the left femur*, his paramedic's mind thought, and then there was nothing.

Chapter Eleven

Ten days in the hospital passed in a haze of surgeries, doctors, and pain.

Tucker rarely left his bedside, calling in sick for three shifts. When Chance was conscious enough, he protested. "You should work," he said half-heartedly, but he didn't really want him to go.

"Shut up," Tucker said, and Chance didn't argue.

He'd had two surgeries on his leg, only one of which he remembered. The first one had been three hours after his arrival to the hospital, when he was still blessedly unconscious. The second had been four days later. He now had a steel rod with eight screws holding his fracture together. The doctor claimed he also had forty-eight stitches where the bone had pierced his skin and the surgery site was, but Chance had yet to see them as the wound was covered by a thick bandage.

Sleep and pain medication were his best friends.

His mother and stepfather visited, much to Chance's chagrin and Tucker's amusement. It was an uncomfortable two days. Tucker sat in the chair in the corner and smirked at Chance behind their backs, turning the full force of his dimples on Chance's mother whenever she looked directly at him. Which wasn't often.

She correctly deduced the nature of their relationship not ten minutes after arriving at the hospital and refused to speak to Tucker directly. Chance finally got annoyed at her obvious slights. "Mother," he said, "you can quit calling Tucker my 'friend', 'coworker', or 'acquaintance'. He's my partner, both at work and home, and if you can't even make the goddamned effort to be polite, then you can go back to Arizona and tell all your canasta-playing friends how rude I was."

He thought he heard Frank snort behind his newspaper, and Tucker threw him a wink from the door before stepping out into the hall, presumably to not laugh in front of Chance's speechless mother.

She found her tongue soon enough, unfortunately, and Chance braced himself for a good verbal lashing. But when she did open her mouth to speak, it was not what he expected at all.

"Your partner," she said quietly, and looked at the chair Tucker had vacated. "Does he – do you – are you both – " She stopped and examined the enormous diamond on her finger before looking up to meet Chance's eyes. "Do you have strong feelings for him?"

She wouldn't say the word 'love', it wasn't in her vocabulary. Chance nodded. "Yeah, Mom. I do. Sorry if it's not what you planned for me." And he was sorry, sorry for turning out to be everything she was against, but at thirty-six years old, he couldn't change it now. Didn't want to.

"Well," she said in a tone that brooked no nonsense, "then I expect both of you at Easter. Frank, let's go. Our flight out is in less than two hours."

Chance grinned at her as she leaned down to press a perfunctory kiss to his cheek. "See you in the spring."

***

Tucker took him home on a Tuesday night, settled him in bed, and made a general nuisance of himself by hovering until Chance barked at the man to back off. When Tucker looked at him, startled, Chance was instantly contrite.

"Sorry," he sighed, and lifted his arm in an invitation for Tucker to join him in bed.

Tucker gingerly lay down on Chance's right side, away from the bad leg, and snaked a careful arm over Chance's stomach. "Just wanna make sure you're okay," he said, and Chance heard the exhaustion in his voice. Apparently Chance wasn't the only one who hadn't slept well since the accident.

He turned his face into Tucker's hair and breathed deeply, reveling in the clean scent and so fucking glad he couldn't smell hospital antiseptic anymore. "M' better now," he murmured, and Tucker's arm tightened over his stomach.

***

Being bedridden was harder than it looked.

Tucker had to resort to bribery to keep him in bed. It usually entailed something of a sexual nature, not that Chance minded, but he itched to get up anyway, if only to walk into the living room. But Tucker held firm, reminding Chance of doctor's orders to put absolutely no weight on the leg for a week.

"That's what the crutches are for!" he protested, glaring when Tucker pushed him back into the pillows for the third time that day.

"The fuckin' crutches are for when you gotta take a piss. Christ, Chance, you're the worst goddamned patient on the planet." Tucker ran an impatient hand through his hair and shook his head.

Chance knew he wasn't making it easier on either of them, but he resented watching Tucker walk around the room on two good legs. The fact that they were having a run of nice weather didn't help either; Chance's mind kept turning to his abandoned surfboard in the garage.

To Chance's frustration, Tucker was smart enough not to go back to work until the doctor cleared Chance to hobble around on his crutches, keeping most of his weight off his leg. The first day Tucker returned to the station, Chance spent most of the morning limping from his patio to the living room and back again, just thankful for some sort of movement.

It exhausted him enough to sleep for three hours in the afternoon, and he woke up to the phone ringing shrilly. His caller I.D. showed it to be the station, so thinking it was Tucker, he answered accordingly. "Don't tell me you can't find anyone to blow you in the shower."

"I suppose I could," Matt drawled, "if it wouldn't get my ass fired."

Chance chuckled nervously. "Right. It was a joke. Hey, Matt."

"How's the leg?"

"Sucks. How's the shift?"

"The usual. Just thought I'd check on you, make sure you got your disability and workman's comp all taken care of."

Chance appreciated the gesture. Matt was only older than he was by ten years, but Chance liked the feeling of being looked out for. "Yeah, it's all fine. Tucker did most of it while I was in the hospital. He making trouble without me?"

Matt laughed. "Robert kept him busy all morning to distract him. Surprised he's not lurking over my shoulder right now, waiting to use the phone. You need anything?"

Two good legs, he almost said, then figured feeling sorry for himself was a waste of everyone's time. "Nah. Go save lives and property. I start physical therapy next week, so hopefully I'll be back before you've missed me."

It was wishful thinking, Chance knew, since the doctor had made noises about sixteen weeks being normal recovery time, but Matt played along. "Keep that attitude," he said gruffly. "And get your ass back to Eleven."

Tucker called that night around nine, sounding for all the world like he hadn't given Chance a second thought all day. "You okay?" he asked casually, but Chance wasn't fooled.

"No," he said, trying to sound as pitiful as possible. "My leg gave out while I was trying to cook dinner and I've been lying on the floor for two hours."

"What!" Tucker shouted into the phone. "Jesus fuckin' Christ, you shoulda called me as soon as you fell! Goddammit, I'm hangin' up and callin' Bonnie right now – " he stopped abruptly as soon as he heard Chance laughing.

"Easy," Chance said, still chuckling. "I'm messing with you. I'm sitting on the couch with Smokey."

"Ass," Tucker snapped, and hung up.

Chance waited until he had his laughter under control and called back, knowing Tucker was still in his probation year and would have to answer.

"Station Eleven," Tucker growled.

"You mad?"

Chance was greeted with silence.

"Aw, Tuck, c'mon. I was just playing." He felt slightly guilty now.

"You think leavin' you this morning was easy?" Tucker asked, sounding tired. "It wasn't. Been worryin' about you all day."

"I know," Chance admitted, and all of a sudden, he missed Tucker fiercely. "I'm sorry."

"You should be."

"Wish you were home," he said in the low voice that Chance knew made Tucker hard.

"Don't start," Tucker warned, his voice going husky. "Been runnin' calls all night. You make me start jerkin' off and sure as shit the alarm'll go."

"Maybe I'll jerk off instead."

Tucker groaned. "Man, I gotta go. This ain't gonna end well." And he hung up, leaving Chance harder than he'd been since the accident.

He was awakened in the morning by a warm hand and mouth on his cock, and Chance smiled sleepily. "Morning," he yawned, then arched his back as Tucker flicked a tongue over the head.

"Dreamed about you," Tucker said, sliding up Chance's body as carefully as he could, keeping one hand on Chance's dick.

"Yeah? Like what?" Chance murmured, curling his fingers into the bed sheets and thrusting into Tucker's hand.

"Like how I haven't felt you inside me for goin' on three weeks. Like how I had to jack off last night after just hearin' your voice. Like how suckin' and jerkin' is okay, but it can't compare to havin' you in me."

"Oh, God," Chance groaned, feeling his cock pulse at the words. "You know I would if I could."

"Been thinkin' 'bout that, too," Tucker continued, and now Chance could feel Tucker's erection pressing insistently against his thigh. "All you gotta do is lay on your right side."

Chance considered it, trying to use any brainpower that wasn't occupied with thoughts of his cock and how well it was being stroked. "I guess," he finally said, and Tucker's answering grin was satisfied.

He turned gingerly to his side, using two hands to draw up his injured leg and place it carefully on top of his good one. Tucker handed Chance the lube and a condom before turning around and fitting his back to Chance's chest, bringing Chance's cock in direct line with his ass.

They both moaned softly at the contact, and Chance couldn't help nudging into Tucker's crack, loving the friction and not realizing until now just how long it had been since they'd done this. Tucker pushed back impatiently, his left hand already pulling himself off. "God, yes," he was muttering. "Do it."

Chance slicked down the condom and lubed one finger, prepping Tucker but finding him more open than usual. "You been playing around without me?" Chance asked, putting in another finger.

Tucker glanced back over his shoulder, and Chance was amused to see a flush color his neck. "Been usin' a dildo sometimes," he admitted, and then he laughed when he felt Chance's cock throb against him. "Like the idea o' that? Gonna have to introduce you to the finer points of it," he teased, and Chance gave him a gentle bite on the shoulder. "Hold still, now. Lemme do the work."

"Hurry up," Chance demanded, and then couldn't help pushing forward despite the protest from his leg. He slid in like silk, easier than ever before, and he gasped against Tucker's skin. "So good," he ground out, and Tucker whimpered agreement, hand moving faster on his cock.

He held himself as still as he could. The warning twinges from his healing leg wouldn't let him thrust, despite his cock's insistence in that area. Tucker took care of it, however, easing back cautiously and then pulling forward, fucking himself on Chance's dick with agonizing slowness. Chance thought he might go out of his mind.

"Too long, " Tucker was murmuring, "oh my God, don't ever make me go that long again, I'll shrivel up." He clenched tight ass muscles around Chance's cock, and Chance sucked in a breath, willing it to go on forever.

Except his body was reminding him it'd been nearly three weeks, and who did he think he was kidding with trying to maintain some stamina? To his chagrin, Chance felt his balls draw up and knew he was going to shoot. "Damn," he whispered against Tucker's neck, his fingers clutching Tucker's thigh.

But he wasn't the only one. With a groan, Tucker's head fell back, and Chance felt his whole body tense. Thankful he wasn't going to embarrass himself alone, he squeezed his eyes shut and drove into Tucker deeply.

It happened about three seconds before Chance came. Tucker, forgetting everything else when he felt his climax, jerked back his elbow and connected solidly with the bandage on Chance's leg. Pain blossomed immediately, white-hot, blocking out anything else.

"Fuck!" Chance shouted, pulling out and throwing himself on his back, pressing his hands to his eyes. His head swam and he gritted his teeth, willing himself not to throw up.

Tucker, who had frozen the instant he'd hit Chance, was now on his knees next to him. "Oh, crap. Oh, fuck, I'm sorry," he babbled. "Christ, I'm an idiot. What the fuck was I thinkin', I'm sorry," he kept on. "You okay? Hey, say somethin', you want some ice? Oh, dammit all to hell, you're bleedin'."

Chance opened his eyes at that and glanced down. The pain was fading slightly but Tucker's words were true: there was a small crimson stain spreading across the wrapping on the inside of his leg. "Great," he said bitterly. "Wonder how many stitches you busted open."

"Let me check," Tucker said, already going to fetch the scissors and gauze they used when changing the bandage.

Chance lay with an arm thrown over his eyes and let Tucker clip away the dressing, wincing when he got close to the wound. "Fuck, be careful," he bit out, knowing he was acting like an asshole but in too much pain to care.

"It's okay," Tucker said after a minute. "None broke."

"Thank God for small mercies," Chance muttered, and made no move to help Tucker re-wrap his leg except for lifting it when necessary.

When Tucker was done, Chance kept his eyes closed and heard Tucker cleaning up the mess. It was silent for a while and he peeked out from under his arm to see Tucker standing by the bed, chewing on his lower lip. "You need anything?" Tucker asked cautiously.

Chance took a deep breath and let it out with a sigh. "To start this day over, apparently. Or pancakes, one of the two."

"Pancakes," Tucker nodded. "Got it."

Chapter Twelve

January

Physical therapy was slowly becoming the bane of Chance's existence.

"More weight on the leg!" his therapist Michelle would command, watching him limp as best he could up and down the stairs.

"Fuck you," was his usual retort, having learned early on that it took a lot more than profanity to offend her.

"Yeah, yeah. Don't think that cute fireman you live with would like that. *Put more weight on the leg!*"

Chance would grit his teeth and do as she asked and tried not to think about the cute fireman he lived with.

The frequency of their sexual activity had been steadily waning for the past month. Tucker had attempted fewer and fewer moves on him, and Chance had just let it go, more often than not his leg bothering him enough to override any desire he might feel. The temperature of their bedroom hovered just above frigid.

He thought sometimes, *if only.* If only therapy didn't tire him out so much. If only he had a little more energy. If only he could smooth out the crease that seemed to crop up more and more between Tucker's brows.

If only he hadn't been hit by a fucking car.

Bonnie picked him up from therapy on Thursday, although he hadn't been expecting her. "Tucker called me," she explained, opening the passenger door so he could struggle in. "Went to the store for stuff for dinner." Chance grunted at that, and Bonnie slanted him a sideways look. "You guys okay?"

"I guess," he shrugged, and turned up the radio.

Bonnie turned it back down. "What's 'I guess' mean?"

"It means yes, things are great. Okay?" He didn't like questions he had already asked himself and not found an answer for.

"Your attitude sort of sucks right now." She said it matter-of-factly. It pissed him off.

"Yeah, well, my life sort of sucks right now," he retorted, and turned the radio back up.

She didn't say anything else the rest of the way home, and when they pulled up in front of his condo, she didn't bother opening his door for him. "Out you go," she said cheerfully, and gave him her 'I'm annoyed at you' smile.

Chance glared back and shoved open his door, managing to get out and reach into the back seat for his crutches. "Thanks," he said shortly.

"Count your blessings, Chancellor," Bonnie said, just before he slammed the door.

The semi-argument made his bad mood worse. He limped into the house and lowered himself into a kitchen chair. Tucker walked in not long after, arms full of groceries. "How was therapy," he asked, yanking open the fridge and putting food away.

Chance reached out and snagged a beer from the open door before answering. "Inhumane. She made me go up the stairs four times."

"Good for her. Am I workin' for your next one?" He threw ingredients for spaghetti on the counter and nodded toward the shift calendar on the table.

Chance sighed and pulled it closer, not really caring who picked his useless ass up from the hospital. He couldn't fucking wait 'til he was cleared to drive. Idly he flicked through the calendar pages until he found January, and froze.

"Well?" Tucker asked, his back to Chance as he worked at the stove. When he got no answer, he turned around to look. "Hey. Do I work or not?"

Chance was staring at the date, circled in red pen. January twenty-fifth. His captain's exam. He'd forgotten, his regular life having been pre-empted by things such as learning how to get up and down the goddamned stairs.

In a fit of anger, Chance heaved the calendar across the kitchen and sent his beer bottle flying after it. The bottle crashed against the wall, and Chance saw Tucker duck reflexively as the glass shattered.

A stunned silence filled the room.

"The fuck was that?" Tucker finally said, eyeing the glass on the floor.

"The goddamned test was today," Chance said, feeling a muscle twitch in his jaw. "That fucking goddamned test that I studied my ass off for. And for what!" he finished with a shout. "For fucking what? So I could be idiotic enough to get myself mowed down by a goddamned car. Jesus Christ." He clenched and unclenched his fists on the table, wishing like hell he could get up and storm out, but his leg was too sore from therapy.

Tucker leaned against the counter and studied him. "You got next year," he offered quietly.

"Great," Chance laughed. "That's exactly what I want to hear. I can wait another damn year."

Tucker narrowed his eyes. "Quit yelpin' at me. I ain't the one who put you where you are."

"Oh, so it's my own fucking fault?" Chance asked, deliberately misunderstanding him, itching for a fight.

"Christ on the cross. I ain't gonna fight with you, Chance. All I wanna do is cook dinner and go to bed, all right?" Tucker sounded more weary than Chance had ever heard the man, but somehow he couldn't make himself stop.

"Oh, I'm sorry. Am I interrupting your comfortable life? Fucking sue me." He pushed back his chair and struggled to his feet, wincing when his leg protested fiercely.

Tucker slammed the wooden spoon he was holding into the pot of sauce, sending splashes of it onto the counter. "Jesus. I ain't gonna stay here and take this shit. Either you adjust your fuckin' attitude or I'm out." His eyes were dark and angry.

Chance opened his mouth to keep pushing, but as he did, a look at the furious expression on Tucker's face made all the fight go out of him. He heaved an enormous sigh and leaned one shoulder against the refrigerator. "Don't go," he mumbled, studying the floor.

Tucker didn't answer right away and Chance looked up, nibbling on the side of his thumbnail. "I get that you're pissed," Tucker finally said. "Shit. I'd be the same way, if it was me."

Chance bit back his response: *But it isn't you.*

"I get it," Tucker continued. "But goddamn, Chance. I ain't the enemy, you know?"

"I know." An apology hovered on the tip of his tongue, Tucker deserved to hear it, and yet Chance couldn't bring himself to say he was sorry. It seemed he couldn't bring himself to say a lot of shit these days.

Tucker either heard the unspoken apology or pretended he did. "Are you hungry?"

"Yeah."

"Then sit your sorry ass down and keep your mouth shut unless you're chewin'." He turned back to the spaghetti, and Chance did as he was told.

***

More than anything else, Chance mourned the beach.

He made Tucker carry his surfboard in from the garage, and he rested it on the coffee table, waxing and polishing it until it shone.

"That board's getting more action than me," Tucker commented one afternoon, watching Chance rub it down with a soft cloth.

"Hardly," Chance replied, ignoring the sexual reference. "Hasn't been in the water for over a month."

"Neither have you," Tucker pointed out. "Doctor said you could swim after four to six weeks. S'been almost seven."

"He meant the pool, not the ocean."

"What's the fuckin' difference?" Tucker picked up the remote to the TV and started flipping channels restlessly. Chance could tell he didn't really give a damn about what was on television.

"The difference is – " he stopped, not sure how to explain it to someone who didn't feel the same strong attachment to the water. Tucker looked over, obviously waiting for an answer. Chance sighed and scrubbed a hand over his face. "The difference is that I don't want to be in the ocean if I can't surf."

"So basically you're punishin' yourself."

Chance laughed without humor. "If you want to look at it that way." He turned back to his board and gave it one last swipe.

"What if I said I was goin' to the beach tomorrow, and I want you to go?" he said, with studied casualness.

"I'd laugh my ass off. It's the end of January, the water's freezing. And you've been to the beach exactly twice since we've been together." Not for lack of trying, though. Chance had tried to wheedle him into going during the summer, but Tucker hadn't shown interest.

"Don't wanna go in the water. Just wanna go hang out."

Chance threw him a suspicious look, but he was focused on the TV. "Fine. We'll go hang out."

Tucker got him up early the next morning, and they drove the four miles to the ocean, easily finding a close parking space due to the cold weather. Chance closed his eyes and took a deep breath of the tangy air, unwilling to admit to Tucker how much he'd missed it.

Tucker stayed close to him as they made their way down the small set of stairs to the sand, but Chance growled at him that he was fine. Tucker just shrugged and stuck close anyway. "You fall and break your fool neck and I'm the one who's gotta drag your ass back up the stairs."

They reached the sand, and Chance kicked off his flip-flops immediately, curling his toes into the cool grains. Tucker did the same, albeit more tentatively. Chance headed toward the water while Tucker hung back, wary. "Thought you said it was freezin'," Tucker said, eyeing the ocean.

The waves washed over his feet and Chance gritted his teeth. "Holy crap. It is." But it still felt fucking amazing.

Tucker ventured to where the sand turned damp, but no closer. "Just don't fall. If I have to get wet, I ain't gonna be so nice to you."

Chance laughed, real happiness spreading through him. He balanced on his good leg and used his other one to kick water at Tucker. "Baby."

Tucker shrugged but didn't budge. "Like I told you. You come back east with me for one winter, and we'll see who's callin' names then."

Chance shuddered when another low curl snuck up and covered his feet, licking at his calves. "Fuck, this is cold." But he didn't move, letting the tide cover his toes with wet sand when it snuck back out to sea.

He stood for at least ten minutes, watching the seagulls dart and dive over the ocean, missing the sea lions that sunned themselves on their rock during the summer. He dug his toes into the wet sand under his feet and breathed ocean air, letting it fill his lungs. He stood until his hair and sweatshirt were damp with spray and his teeth were chattering, and he still didn't want to leave.

Chance figured that since he couldn't feel his feet anymore, it was probably time to at least get out of the water and go sit on the sand for a while. Turning, looking behind him for Tucker, he meant to carefully extricate himself from where his feet were buried with sand. It was at that minute that a wave broke, not any higher than the rest, but still high enough to send him off balance.

Normally, he would have caught himself. All that had to happen was to get his leg under him for balance, but normally he didn't have a fucking steel rod implanted in it. Chance knew he was going to fall at least five seconds before it happened. "Shit," he got out, and then he was gasping as the freezing water soaked his shorts and shirt.

Almost before his brain could even register the shock, Tucker was hauling him to his feet and toward dry sand. "You okay?" he asked. "Damn, didn't think to bring a towel."

The water was chilling him, his clothes clinging and uncomfortable. His momentary joy was gone, replaced by the familiar bitter anger he'd felt for the past month. "Quit it," he snapped, yanking away from Tucker and scanning the sand for his flip-flops. "Not a fucking invalid."

"I know that." Tucker tried to keep the hurt out of his voice, which was worse than if he'd just let it through. He picked up Chance's shoes and handed them to him before stripping off his own dry sweatshirt and passing it over. "Put that on."

Chance didn't argue, peeling off his own wet one and slipping Tucker's on. It was warm and smelled of something vaguely spicy. He wanted to burrow into it, to just close his eyes and rub the worn fleece against his cheek and not be so helpless anymore. He cleared his throat and glanced down at his wet shorts, grimacing at the thought of driving back home. "Let's go," he said resignedly. "Don't know what in hell made me think this was a good idea."

Tucker's mouth tightened. "Right. Me either."

At home, he declined Tucker's offer of help and took a shower alone. He stayed in for nearly half an hour, not caring if he used all the hot water.

Chapter Thirteen

February

Things were inexplicably better for a couple of weeks. Chance made a concerted effort to be less of a dick, and Tucker picked up an overtime shift or two, resulting in him being out of the house for two or three days at a time.

They still weren't having sex.

Chance's sex drive had barely reared its head since the accident. He knew it was because of the overwhelming fatigue he felt most of the time, not to mention the constant pain in his leg. The pain itself was lessening, but by very slow degrees. Sex crossed his mind on occasion, but not often enough for him to want to do something about it.

He wondered if Tucker was doing something about it, though. There'd been plenty of days when Chance had seen Tucker's morning wood tenting the sheets before he'd rolled out of bed and hit the shower. Once or twice, Chance wanted to tell Tucker to just go out and get blown, but the thought of that made him sick to his stomach. If Tucker was getting anything on the side, Chance didn't want to know.

Chance figured Tucker pretty much deserved it anyway.

He thought he'd managed to successfully put it out of his mind – after all, he was a healthy male in his thirties, his sex drive had to make a reappearance sometime – until one night when he awoke from a sound sleep.

The digital clock told him it was just past midnight, and Chance had no idea why he was awake. Smokey lay sleeping peacefully at the foot of the bed, so it hadn't been a noise that startled him. Turning his head to see if Tucker was still asleep, he discovered only a vacant space. That was it, then – despite their strained relationship, Chance's subconscious still knew when Tucker was supposed to be there.

The light shining from under the bathroom door drew his attention, and he listened for a minute. No discernible sound came from there, however, and he wondered if Tucker was all right. He thought briefly of their bout with the stomach flu two months ago and made a face. "Tuck?" he called out, but his voice was husky with sleep and didn't carry far.

Sighing, Chance threw back the covers and got to his feet, ignoring his crutches in favor of hopping the short distance to the bathroom door. He knocked once before turning the knob, shouldering the door open. "Tucker?" he started, then trailed off.

Tucker stood at the sink, one hand braced on the countertop and the other around his cock. His dick glistened with lube and he had obviously been close to coming. Chance watched as a single, crystal drop of pre-come fell from the tip, leaving a long strand behind. "Um," Tucker said, clearing his throat.

"Yeah. Don't let me interrupt," Chance said, and slammed the door shut again.

He managed to get out to the living room and deposit himself on the couch, not knowing why he was suddenly angry. It wasn't like Tucker was looking for relief outside the relationship – not that Chance knew, anyway – and jerking off was certainly something both of them had done countless times, together and alone.

But Christ, he hated martyrs.

Chance didn't wait long.

Tucker appeared in the doorway after only a minute or two, an unsure expression on his face. "Yeah, so ..." he started, and then didn't know how to finish.

Chance just looked at him, wondering how, after six months of laughing and talking and fucking and loving, they were here at this point of not really knowing what to say to each other.

"Don't have to explain it," Chance shrugged finally. "Not like I was offended or anything."

"It's just – I was – I dunno. I woke up and was hard and ... yeah." Tucker sounded apologetic, which made Chance even madder.

"Yup. And Christ forbid you should ask for a helping hand," Chance replied, slowly figuring out the root of his anger.

"Aw, Chance, c'mon. Didn't mean nothin'. Didn't want to wake you up, and besides, it's been – " he stopped abruptly and Chance knew he wanted to say 'a long time.'

"Well. Remind me to get you a new crown of fucking thorns." And there he was again, provoking Tucker, stirring the pot and looking for an argument.

He got one.

"Look," Tucker said in a low, dangerous tone. "I told you already that I know things suck for you. You can't work, you can't drive, your leg hurts like a motherfuck."

"Don't forget the part where I don't want to have sex," he offered, making it worse on purpose. "Oh! And the part where the opportunity to advance my career was put on hold for a year."

A muscle jumped in Tucker's jaw, and Chance saw him clench and unclench a fist. "Yeah, I fuckin' know all that, Shanahan. And just like I told you before, I ain't the one that made all that shit happen. It's crappy, and I don't wish it for anyone, but you're makin' life hell for both of us."

"Oh, I'm sorry. Must be hell to be able to run on the beach. Must be hell to have to get in the car and drive somewhere. Obviously, I wasn't taking your feelings into consideration." The words bubbled up before he could check them, and he spat them out at his nearest target.

"How about the fact that you're just bein' a complete jackass?" Tucker finally shouted, and Chance had a flash of triumph from getting a rise out of him. "Fuck this shit. No fuckin' way I'm stayin' here to get crapped on every day."

"Fine," Chance replied bitterly. "Go spend the night at the station. Maybe you can finish jacking off there. Least you won't have the guilt of me lying in bed next to you while you do it. Actually," and here he paused, pretending to think about it, "maybe someone there'll be happy to finish it off for you. I think Brandon on A shift's been checking you out."

"Fuck you," Tucker said, his voice quiet. "Fuck you, Chance. I ain't spendin' the night at the goddamned firehouse. If I walk out, I'm goin' to a hotel, and then findin' a new place to live. Because you didn't fuckin' die, you just broke your goddamn leg, and almost two months of this is enough. I figured out when I was fourteen years old that I don't have to get shit on by people who claim to love me."

It was almost enough to make an apology come out, almost enough to make Chance bite back any remaining words and raise a hand to Tucker in supplication.

But his anger and hurt – however irrational – were still too close to the surface. "I don't need you," Chance bit out, and Tucker's expression closed.

"Right," he said, and turned back to the bedroom.

Chance watched a small spider crawl along the air conditioning vent and did not look toward the front door until after it had closed with a soft click.

Chapter Fourteen

April

"Good, Chancellor! Your best yet. One more set, and we'll quit for the day." Michelle gave him a proud smile that Chance was too exhausted to return.

His thighs ached from the squats he'd done for the past hour, not to mention the half-mile she'd made him do at a brisk walk on the treadmill. But the fatigue was good, even welcome. He'd worked harder at therapy over the past nine weeks than he'd worked at anything in his life.

It was the only time when he didn't think about Tucker.

His doctor was cautiously optimistic about his return to work sometime in May, and Chance intended to see it through. He'd never been so bored.

In some maudlin way, he liked to think about Tucker's and his day at the beach in January. He forced himself to go, though surfing was far from being on his list of approved activities. So he sat. He watched the other surfers in the water, lifting his hand in greeting sometimes, watching intently as the tide came and went and the waves made foamy blankets on the sand.

It was soothing, and brought him closer to the peace he was looking for.

The phone had turned into something hated. He shied away from it when it rang, more thankful than ever for the caller ID that let him avoid pretty much everyone. He only picked it up on the rare occasion that someone at work needed to talk to him, and oddly enough, he answered it for his mother, too.

He made his excuses about not coming to her for Easter, though, when she brought it up during her usual weekly call.

"It'd be hard on the leg, Mom," he lied, and it sounded lame even to his own ears.

She sighed. "Chancellor. You could at least give a believable excuse. I might even pretend to accept it."

His mother was anything but stupid, and he considered telling her about Tucker. But he held back at the last second, unwilling or unable to explain something that had spiraled out of his control so quickly. "Maybe Christmas, Mom," he mumbled.

"Call your brother," she said in answer. "He'd like to hear from you."

It was a li and Chance knew it, but he muttered an assent anyway and hung up.

He'd gotten used to the quiet of the house, and was even sleeping better at night, although five or six hours wasn't much of an improvement over three or four. But it was something.

On the nights when sleep was just impossible, Chance would prowl the rooms under the guise of exercising his leg, and think. It was only during the dark that he seemed to allow himself to do it; it was just too painful and real during the day.

He knew that Tucker leaving was completely, entirely his fault. He knew it the instant Tucker walked out the door, and he knew it with every day that went by that they didn't see or speak to each other. And now here they were, two months later.

Chance guessed he could find out things like where Tucker was living easily enough, but something whispered that he wasn't allowed to do that anymore. He'd been the one to drive Tucker away, it wasn't within his rights these days to know anything about him.

He was sort of holding out hope for when he returned to work. There was no way they'd be able to work together and not speak to each other, and then maybe Chance would find a way to say he was sorry. He had no illusions about the relationship part. They were finished, he'd done a fucking fantastic job of that, but Chance knew Tucker deserved an apology.

The fact that Chance was too much of a goddamned coward to pick up the phone and call the man really spoke volumes. Chance had had no idea he was that much of a chickenshit.

Chance kept in touch with Matt, who made the effort to call him once every couple of weeks and update him on firehouse gossip. When Chance was cleared to drive, they went for a beer once or twice, and it was nice to have someone to talk to.

Chance never said a word about Tucker, and Matt never asked.

So when Matt called one night toward the end of April, Chance was glad to hear from him. "Hey!" Chance said, putting his feet up on his patio railing.

"How you feeling?" Matt asked.

"Pretty good," Chance mused. "Today was a good day." And it had been, too. He'd sat on his surfboard in the water, paddling out and then lying flat on his stomach to ride back in. Just being in the ocean made things better. Sort of.

"Glad to hear it. Still planning on coming back in May?"

"Hell, yes. Don't replace me yet."

Matt chuckled. "No way, man. Be glad to have you." He cleared his throat and paused for a second. "You, uh. Talked to McBride?"

The way he said it so cautiously, Chance could tell he knew. Probably had known for a while. "Nope."

"It's over?"

"Yep. What did he tell you?" Although it was well within Tucker's rights to tell anyone who'd listen about what a piece of shit Chance had been, Chance sort of hoped he hadn't.

"That it was over." Matt didn't sound partial one way or the other.

"He say it was because of me?" Chance swallowed, realizing that talking about it to someone other than Bonnie was sort of painful. Bonnie just told him he was a complete asshole, not to mention an idiot, and Chance would agree and go back to watching TV.

"Nope. Said you guys weren't getting along, and he'd moved out. That true?"

"True enough," Chance said. "But it's cool as far as work goes. As soon as I get back, I'll put in for a transfer. There's a medic spot open at Station Nineteen, I think." It pained him to say, but he'd already promised this wouldn't be anyone else's issue but his.

"Not anymore," Matt sighed. "Been filled."

"Oh. Well, there's always C shift over at Station Six, I think they're looking for a guy." He supposed it didn't matter where he went, nothing would be like Eleven. Wouldn't make a difference anyway; Tucker wouldn't be there.

"Chance ... you don't have to transfer. Tucker took the spot at Nineteen." Matt sounded remorseful.

Oh. Well that took care of that, didn't it.

"Yeah?" Chance said, trying not to sound ... well, however he felt. He didn't know what that was, exactly. Upset? Disappointed? Pissed off? Betrayed? Damn, Tucker hadn't even bothered to call and tell him.

The absurdity of that thought hit him, and he wanted to laugh. Like he was entitled to know anything Tucker was doing.

"Couple of weeks ago," Matt was saying. "Had to get my approval for it, otherwise I wouldn't have known until he left. I asked him why, he told me about you guys, I signed his paperwork."

"Okay," Chance replied, still trying to formulate an appropriate response other than throwing something against the wall.

"But that's not the only reason I called," Matt continued. "Got a letter from downtown today."

Chance was only half-listening, still trying to wrap his mind around the fact that Tucker had managed to extricate himself completely from Chance's life. "'Bout what?"

"They're doing a second captain's test."

That got his attention. "No shit. Really?"

"Really. Apparently they only filled thirteen out of fifteen spots this time around. There were a lot of failed tests. They're offering it mid-July. Should I put your name in?"

Chance considered. It was three months away, he'd have ample time to prepare. And it would occupy his sleepless nights. What the hell, it wasn't like he had anything else going on. And if he failed? At least he'd know what the exam was like for next time. "Yeah, do it," he said. Why the fuck not.

"Good decision. It's what you need," Matt said, sounding happier than he'd been until now.

Not exactly, Chance thought, but made a noise of agreement anyway.

***

It was some sort of great cosmic joke that his sex drive returned with a vengeance. Chance hoped someone somewhere was laughing, because he sure as hell wasn't.

He woke up at three in the morning almost two months to the day after Tucker had walked out, sheets a sweaty mess, and his cock so hard it ached.

He couldn't be bothered with lube, it was too urgent. A lick to his palm, and he was bringing himself off, holding tight to the last vestiges of the dream that had managed to rouse him out of a sound sleep.

Tucker, mouth open and wet and hot on Chance's dick. Midnight-blue eyes glinting in the darkness. Flash of dimple. Sucking fast and hard, then slow and gentle, alternating until

*Chance wants to weep or beg or come or all three. And then he
doesn't have to do the first two because he's trembling and gasping
and pulsing in Tucker's mouth. Tucker swallows all of it and
Chance looks down to watch, meeting Tucker's eyes and getting a
wink in return.*

He came in about five seconds. It would have been
embarrassing if it didn't feel so fucking good. Chance let it wash
over him like water, his mind going blessedly blank at the point of
climax, just feeling and trembling until he lay spent.

The burn behind his eyes didn't register until after he'd stopped
shaking.

***

After a week and a half of jerking off pretty much every day,
Chance figured it was probably time to pay a visit to the Seagull. It
was only a measure of relief he was after, he told himself, it had
nothing to do with wanting the comfort of another warm body.
Might as well stop being a monk, and maybe it would make him
feel slightly more normal.

His leg was taking most of his weight now. It had been four
months, his doctor had proclaimed the break healed, and now all
that was left was strengthening the muscles that had torn. Therapy
was down from three times a week to just once, on Wednesdays.
He had felt a personal sense of triumph when his therapy was
reduced, and his mind automatically turned to Tucker, wanting to
tell the man, to share it.

It was time to start curbing those impulses.

So he found himself putting on a decent shirt and his most
comfortable jeans, but not bothering to shave his three-day-old
stubble. He hadn't been to the bar in nearly a year, but from what
he knew of the place, the patrons of the Seagull wouldn't give
much of a shit anyway.

Before he left, he considered calling Bonnie. She'd gone with
him a couple of times, pre-Tucker. They'd sit at a table together
and share a pitcher of beer and watch the asses of the guys playing
pool. Except he hadn't returned her calls over the past month, and
the last message she'd left on his machine told him in no uncertain
terms exactly which part of a horse's anatomy she thought he was
being. He figured Bonnie wasn't his best bet at the moment.

He sat in his car for a while in the parking lot, telling himself that yes, he really did want to do this, and no, he didn't really want to go back home and put porn in the DVD player instead. Even if he just found someone to talk to for a while, it would be okay.

The fact that he wasn't coping well with loneliness didn't escape his notice.

Cursing himself, he finally got out of the car and limped to the door, thankful that the doctor had, at last, given him the okay to ditch his crutches.

The place hadn't changed much. Small, understated room with music that was just loud enough to dance to, but not loud enough to make conversation impossible. Full bar that poured generous shots and made decent margaritas. Chairs, tables, barstools, the usual. Nothing much to differentiate it from straight bars except for the fact that its patrons were almost exclusively men. Nothing like the club scene in Los Angeles, either, thank God. Chance couldn't keep up with the frenetic pace there. He much preferred quiet places like this.

He made his way to the bar and leaned one hip on a barstool, taking weight off his bad leg and putting both elbows on the polished wood. "Jack and Coke," he answered, when the bartender pointed at him.

Chance nursed it for a while, not even looking up until he was halfway through his drink and the ice had started watering it down. Someone took a seat two stools away and he thought, *Here we go.*

Looking up, bracing himself to start the inane small talk that would hopefully lead to him not going home alone, he saw a fairly good-looking guy smiling at him. And it would have been okay, Chance thought, if only his gaze hadn't traveled past the guy to the people sitting at the small tables.

And if only he hadn't picked up on the low, smooth chuckle he knew so well; a laugh he knew would be accompanied by a flash of dimples under eyes that looked black but weren't.

If only.

If only you'd said you were sorry, you dumb fuck, then you wouldn't be here now, would you?

He sat frozen, only dimly aware when the man sitting near him shook his head and moved away. Chance couldn't tear his gaze away from Tucker, and in that moment, two things registered.

This first was that Tucker was drunk. Chance could see it in the glassiness of his eyes and the way he sprawled in his chair, limbs all loose and easy. The second thing was that Tucker was sitting with some kid who couldn't have been more than twenty-five, laughing and flirting and turning the full force of his smile on the smitten guy.

It frightened Chance a little bit, how much he wanted to put his hands around the other guy's neck and squeeze.

Get out, his inner voice warned, and Chance knew it was right. Better leave, just get out now, because any second, Tucker could turn just a fraction to his left and –

Damn it.

Tucker's eyes widened and everything stopped, or at least it seemed to. Chance couldn't hear music or other people, just his own blood thundering in his ears and his increased breathing.

Damn it all to fucking hell.

Chance knew he had to get out. Couldn't deal with this now, his heart was pounding too hard, and his breathing was coming fast and loud, felt like he was having a goddamned panic attack.

He meant to slide off the barstool carefully, but in his anxiety, Chance stepped down with his bad leg first. Pain shot up his thigh in a tight blaze, and his knee buckled, threatening to send him to the floor. At the last second he caught the edge of the bar with both hands. He managed to save himself from collapsing in a pathetic heap, but not before Tucker had seen his near miss.

Chance looked over to see Tucker half-out of his chair, the kid sitting with him forgotten. "No," Chance blurted out before he could stop himself, shaking his head abruptly at Tucker, his voice hoarse. If Tucker touched him, he wouldn't be able to handle it.

Tucker sank back down, but perched on the very edge of his seat, every muscle in his body tense. Chance let his eyes rest on Tucker's face for another five seconds before gathering his strength and moving toward the door.

At home, in the shower, he got shampoo in his eyes. It was a good excuse for the tears.

Chapter Fifteen

June

Summer, and Chance cautiously started finding his balance on his surfboard. It was like coming home, the first time he managed to take a small curl all the way into the shallows, and he hopped off his board with an enormously silly grin on his face. It had only taken six damn months.

Returning to work had been both easier and more difficult than he'd expected.

The first painful reminder was the fact that Chance came back almost a year to the day that Tucker McBride had first walked into Station Eleven. Twelve months made a hell of a difference, Chance had learned. The second jolt was that there was a new medic in Tucker's spot, but it was someone Chance had known for a while. His name was Jason Talbot, and he was a decent paramedic, so that part was okay.

Also okay was the warm welcome he received from the rest of his crew. They cooked him his favorite dinner his first shift back – medium-rare filet and red potatoes – and seemed genuinely glad to see him. None of them mentioned Tucker, with the exception of Robert, who cornered him after dinner and demanded to know what had happened.

"I was an ass," Chance said, hoping that would end it. No such luck.

"Of course you were," Robert said reasonably. "But why? And are you sure it's done?"

"Pretty sure," Chance sighed. "Haven't seen or talked to him since he left in February." His mind touched on their brief encounter at the Seagull, but Chance figured that didn't count for much.

"Why were you an ass?" Robert persisted.

It made him think. "Um. Because my leg hurt like a sonofabitch. And I couldn't do stuff I loved, like work or surf or - " he stopped there, not sure how Robert would take "or fuck my boyfriend."

"And McBride couldn't handle it?"

"No, he was good. He handled it really well for a while."
Chance felt the familiar guilt tighten his chest. "Then it turned sort
of bad after I started therapy, but he hung in there. And one night it
just … wasn't a good scene."

Robert studied him. "You give him any kind of apology?"

"No. I wanted to. But I didn't." He wouldn't make excuses for it
because there weren't any to make.

"He give you one?"

"Not really his fault for anything, is it?" Chance frowned, not
sure where this was going.

Robert shrugged. "What'd he do when you started pissing and
moaning?"

Chance thought. "He just let me do it."

"Seems to me like that was his fault right there. Why didn't he
beat the shit out of you?"

"What the hell was he supposed to do, Rob? I was sort of a
bastard."

"No argument here. But if'n you were living with me? I woulda
let you feel sorry for yourself for about a week. Then I woulda
gotten you drunk, gotten you laid, and told you to shut the fuck up.
And if *that* didn't work? I woulda kicked the living shit out of
you." He nodded with satisfaction.

"He sort of made an effort. Once." He hadn't thought about that
day at the beach for a while and was surprised to find that it still
stung.

"Once?" Robert said dryly.

Chance stared at him. For the first time in four months he
wondered if this could possibly be both of their faults. Not that
Tucker was to blame for Chance's completely dickish behavior…
but maybe the way Tucker had reacted to it was part of the
problem.

He thought back to that last difficult night, when he'd caught
Tucker in the bathroom, and the anger that had washed over him.
Why had he gotten so pissed off? He'd never dwelled on it before.

If he was honest with himself, really truthful, he knew the
answer. Tucker had – however unintentionally – enabled his
uselessness. And Chance had let him, had played along, and it had
been a self-fulfilling prophecy. Finding Tucker jerking off alone in
the bathroom instead of using what he had lying next to him – well.
It went back to the whole martyr complex thing.

But now who was the martyr, taking complete blame for their breakup?

He opened his mouth to ask Robert who the hell he thought he was, making Chance think this hard on his first shift back, but was interrupted by two soft dings of the alarm.

"Duty calls," Robert said cheerfully, and walked away whistling.

***

He picked up as many overtime shifts as he could when he wasn't studying for the upcoming exam. It occupied his time, kept his mind off the test, and gave him the opportunity to see what other crews at other stations were like. He would need the information if, by some chance, he passed his test. He'd be reassigned within the month, and Chance would want to know what kind of station he'd be coming into or what sort of guys he'd be working with.

So it happened that he found himself working overtime at Station Four with Tucker McBride.

They both arrived in the parking lot at the same time, ten minutes before their eight o'clock shift. Tucker saw him as soon as he opened his truck door and stood with one leg on the pavement and one still in the cab. "Hey," he said cautiously.

"Hey," Chance answered, and grabbed his gear out of the back of his car.

It had really never occurred to him that he might run into Tucker. Chance knew that the open spot that Tucker had filled at Nineteen was on B shift, so the days when Chance was at work, Tucker was, too. No real danger of their paths crossing.

Unless, of course, they both picked up some overtime at the same place. Damn.

They stood in the parking lot together, loaded down with helmets, boots, and turnouts, and just looked at each other. Chance finally broke the silence. "Seems like we could get through one shift without killing each other."

"Reckon," Tucker said slowly, watching another car pull into the lot. "Quiet station, anyway. Won't have to go out much."

Chance wanted to answer in an intelligent fashion, but all he could think about was the last time he'd seen Tucker. And from there, his mind went to the bad place of what had happened

Fireline

between Tucker and the other guy after Chance had made his not-so-graceful exit.

This was clearly not a good start to getting through a shift together.

"I'm going in," he said abruptly, and left Tucker standing by his truck.

Chance found the captain on duty drinking coffee in the kitchen. Station Four was small and fairly mellow, running just two or three calls a day. They used one engine, so the shift was comprised of only five guys. Not really conducive to ignoring somebody.

It was only twenty-four hours. He could do it.

"First one on the right," the captain said in response to Chance's question about which dorm he should use. "Or the one next to it, actually. Both empty today."

Great. That only meant that one was his and one was Tucker's.

He took the first room and dumped out his linens, busying himself with making the bed. A minute later he heard Tucker doing the same thing next door, and Chance wondered if Tucker still favored the blue sheets.

He was emptying some stuff into his locker when Tucker poked his head in. "The leg been okay?" Tucker asked.

"Hurts when the weather's cold," Chance said truthfully. "And sometimes I get muscle cramps in the middle of the night."

"Doc say that was normal?" He cocked his head.

"Yup. Gotta deal with it." It felt weird, having a regular, quiet conversation, but Chance figured they'd have to come to terms sometime. He guessed this was sometime.

Tucker nodded. "Okay. Good. Been wonderin'." And then he was gone, presumably off to see what was for breakfast.

***

The day passed slowly. Chance was careful to be in areas of the station where Tucker was not. He used the weight room and watched some television. The shift captain wanted ice cream after dinner, so they took the engine to the grocery store and wandered the aisles. Chance snorted at Tucker when he showed up in the checkout line with two pints of peanut butter cup.

"What," Tucker said defensively, clutching the cartons to his chest. "It's on sale."

"Better do some extra laps on the track," Chance said, his eyebrows raised. "I'm just saying."

Tucker scowled at him and went to put one pint back.

They got a call on the way back to the station. Tucker grouched that his ice cream was going to melt, but luckily they were cancelled by dispatch before they'd gotten halfway there. Chance hoped that if he passed his test, he wouldn't get placed at such a slow station. Guy could get lazy this way.

The rest of the evening was uneventful enough for Chance to be exhausted by ten. "Bed," he said to the others, who were laughing hysterically at Johnny Knoxville on TV.

"Night," one or two of them said, but Tucker just looked up at him with an unreadable expression.

His leg was giving him warning twinges that meant he wouldn't be able to actually sleep, so Chance read for a while until he heard Tucker moving around in the dorm next to him. Putting down his book and flipping the light off, he listened.

Even after four months, he could still see it as clearly as if he were in the same room. Tucker stripping his shirt off, muscles flexing in his back. The tattoo on his bicep that Chance had traced with both fingers and tongue. Smooth chest. Flat, tight stomach that ran down to his narrow hips. Chance closed his eyes and thought of the groove between Tucker's waist and thigh, the one that led straight to his groin and made Tucker laugh and twist away when Chance tried to suckle there. He wondered if Tucker had let anyone else discover that he was ticklish.

He knew Tucker wasn't sleeping naked, none of them did at work, but Chance pictured it anyway. Perfect, firm ass. Long cock that always seemed half-hard.

And speaking of hard. Fuck. Chance jerked his hand away from his own dick and flipped onto his stomach. Not gonna go there.

He didn't know he'd fallen asleep until he awakened with a soft yelp, the muscles in his leg twisting and knotting on themselves. The leg cramps he'd mentioned to Tucker were asserting themselves, but it was unusual because it had been such a low-activity day.

The best way to get rid of them, he'd found, was to walk. Chance got out of bed and stood gingerly on the leg, testing to make sure it wasn't going to spasm before padding quietly down the hall to the kitchen. Rooting through the freezer, he made himself an ice pack and bound it to his thigh with some of the ace bandages under the sink.

Chance made a lap or two around the kitchen and television room before noticing he wasn't alone anymore.

Tucker stood in the doorway to the hall, blinking sleepily. "You all right? Heard you get up."

Chance shrugged. "Cramp. No big deal." But his muscle chose that moment to remind him who was boss, and he winced involuntarily.

"You want me to … um. I could stretch it out for you?" Tucker sounded like he wanted to retract the offer as soon as he'd made it.

Chance opened his mouth to say no and found himself nodding instead. "That'd be good." He dropped onto the couch and eased his leg up, releasing the bandage and letting the ice pack fall to the floor.

Tucker sat down facing him, in line with Chance's thigh, and placed two hands just below his knee. Lifting gently, Tucker pulled Chance's leg toward the opposite end of the couch until Chance dropped his head back on the arm of the sofa and hissed in pain.

"Sorry," Tucker said instantly, lowering Chance's leg but not moving those hands.

"No, it's good. Do it once more." Chance gritted his teeth and closed his eyes, bracing himself. Tucker obeyed, pulling until Chance felt the knotted muscle suddenly loosen and relax. Breathing a sigh of relief, he opened his eyes and grinned. "Got it. Thanks."

Tucker smiled back. "You bet, baby."

The endearment, said without thinking but with a caress in his voice, hit Chance with a painful wrench. He lifted his gaze to meet Tucker's troubled expression. Tucker still had both hands on Chance's leg, and Chance realized wryly that he was hard again.

Tucker was, too, clearly indicated through his nylon gym shorts. "Tucker," Chance whispered in the stillness, "Tuck, I want … I can't …"

He wanted to finish, to find his way into the apology that had been too long in coming, but then Tucker was kissing him, stretching himself out over Chance, pressing their erections together, and Chance could only groan and kiss him back.

Chance wrapped one arm around Tucker's back and fisted the other hand in his hair, angling Tucker's head so Chance could invade his mouth with an eager tongue. He tasted so good, and the little whimpers he was making drove any rational thought out of Chance's mind.

He was just wondering how he could get them down the hall to his bed without breaking contact when Tucker suddenly shoved himself upward with both hands, scrambling off the couch. Chance blinked at Tucker, confused. "Hey," he protested.

Tucker licked his lips nervously and jammed a hand through his hair. "Can't," he whispered, pleading. "Can't do it again. I'm sorry, Chance, I thought for a minute about just gettin' off and not carin' about anythin' else, but it's you and that's different."

It stung that Tucker thought he'd just wanted to get off. "I didn't -" he started to say, but Tucker shook his head and held up a hand.

"It's different," Tucker said again, and the look on his face was miserable. "Been waitin' for you to say somethin' or call me or even leave me a fuckin' email or somethin'. But you let me walk out, just like I let you treat me like shit, and I ain't goin' back there now. It's been four months – *four fuckin' months, Chance!* – and I didn't hear a peep outta you."

Chance drew a shaky breath. Now was when he should say it, his conscience told him, when Tucker was standing there looking hurt and forlorn and pretty much breaking his heart. But even as he opened his mouth, Tucker was shaking his head again. "I don't wanna hear it now. Ain't worth much if I gotta force it, now is it?"

It was true, so Chance just looked at him. "You deserve better," was what finally came out of his mouth.

"Yeah," Tucker said sadly. "But so do you."

Chance watched him turn and disappear back down the hall. Sliding even further down on the couch, he contemplated the ceiling tiles until morning.

Fireline

Chapter Sixteen

July

Chance woke up at five-thirty on the morning of his exam and couldn't go back to sleep. Scenarios for the essays and options for the multiple-choice questions kept running through his head, things that might or might not be on the test. It was maddening, but he sure as hell was awake, so he got up and showered.

He wolfed down a bowl of cereal, and then regretted it when his nerves threatened to send it back up again. Smokey jumped on the counter and looked interested in the last remnants of milk, so Chance let him lick the bowl clean before leaving it in the sink and giving the cat a chuck under the chin. "Wish me luck," he said, and then snorted when Smokey lifted his leg to wash his crotch. "Thanks."

He dressed in his usual t-shirt and shorts and left the house with time to spare, arriving at battalion headquarters fifteen minutes before nine. Chance briefly considered opening up one of the study guides he'd thrown in the back seat, then figured it wasn't worth it. He either knew his shit or he didn't.

That thought in mind, he left the car and crossed the shady parking lot, already feeling the warmth of the day. Through the double doors, smiling at the woman who'd sat behind the front desk for more years than he'd been alive, and down the hall to Conference Room Twelve. Six guys were already there, looking either nervous or confident depending on how many times they'd done this, and Chance nodded at the ones he knew.

The room filled up with almost fifty other men before nine o'clock, and Chance knew he'd be fighting both their seniority and experience. A captain Chance knew from Station Two came in with the bundle of exams and grinned at all of them. "Quit looking like you're going before a firing squad, take a deep breath, and just write what you know. Bring me your booklet when you're done." He paused for a minute, then said, "The department wants you to pass. No one's here to purposely fail you, so keep that in mind. Ready?"

There were mumbled assents. Tests were distributed, pencils were tapped nervously against desks, and then the room fell silent.

Chance scrawled his name across the front, set his jaw, and opened his booklet.

His leg was protesting the inactivity by the time he was done. It took him an hour and a half to complete the entire thing, which was exactly half the allotted time. He wasn't the first to be finished, but there were still a fair number of guys left when he handed in his test and walked out into the sunshine.

He drove straight to the beach and surfed for the rest of the day.

***

Two and a half weeks later he received two identical letters, one at work and one at home.

Dear Chancellor,

Thank you for your interest in becoming a captain for the Oceanside Fire Authority.

We are pleased to inform you that your score on the captaincy exam was 192 out of a possible 200. This places you as the second-highest scoring test during the round. Should you wish to pursue this opportunity, your promotion will be effective on the fifteenth of August and you will be assigned to one of the two open captain positions in the department. Please inform us of your decision as soon as possible.

The badge-pinning ceremony will take place on August the fifteenth at five o'clock p.m.

He read it twice, his gaze lingering on his score, then a third time to make sure he hadn't misunderstood.

He'd passed?

He'd passed. And was going to be promoted.

Chance's thoughts turned instantly to Tucker, wanting to share his joy and relief, before he remembered. Funny how after this long Tucker was still the one he thought of first.

He called Bonnie instead before he did something stupid.

***

Chance hadn't worn his dress uniform in over a year, not since the funeral he'd attended for a firefighter who'd died off-duty in a skiing accident in the mountains.

He picked one of Smokey's hairs off the sleeve of the dark blue shirt and leaned in to study his reflection more carefully. He straightened his tie, wishing he'd thought to break in his new boots. He could already feel a blister forming on his heel, and he hadn't even left the house.

Bonnie came up behind him and turned him around so she could remove the badge that was pinned over his heart. "Don't need this," she smiled at him. "They'll give you a new one."

He took it from her and fingered the black elastic band that encircled it, a tribute to all firefighters who had lost their lives on September eleventh. "Thanks," he said simply. "You know. For volunteering to pin, and all."

She brushed his thanks away. "Like I'd let anyone else stand up there to pin your badge. I pinned you the first time, didn't I?"

Chance grinned at her. "Yeah, you did. Surprised I didn't pass out from blood loss."

She blushed. "I was nervous! I didn't mean to stab you with it."

"Just be careful tonight." He set his old badge down on his dresser and reached for his hat, holding it carefully by the brim while he used his sleeve to polish the silver Maltese cross on the front.

"You look good," Bonnie said softly. "Tucker would be -"

"Don't, Bon," Chance said, his tone sharp. "Not now."

She gave him an inscrutable look and nodded, brushing a speck of lint from his tie. "We better go."

They decided that Bonnie would drive her car so she could leave if the after-ceremony party went too long, so Chance slid into the passenger seat.

"Oh, you're fine," she snapped as they pulled up to the City Hall building, and Chance tried to check his uniform one more time in the visor mirror. "Pretty enough to eat."

They made their way through the center of the building, following the signs to an outdoor courtyard where rows of chairs were set up before a small stage and podium. The first two rows were marked with a small 'reserved' sign. Chance knew that this was to be the only badge ceremony for the year. The original had been postponed when the quota hadn't been filled, so the guys who had passed the previous test were also attending with their families.

He took a seat in the second reserved row so Bonnie could sit directly behind him.

It was still sort of not-real, and Chance shook his head. He felt Bonnie put a supporting hand on his arm and squeeze. He was glad to have her there, to at least have one person stand up for him. The other guys getting their badges had several family members in attendance, and Chance was grateful he wasn't alone.

"They're gonna do it in alphabetical order," he said over his shoulder to Bonnie. "But they have all the badge-pinners come up at once. So you might have to stand for a while until they get to S."

"I've done this before," she said, glancing around the courtyard. "Hey, isn't that your captain?"

Chance turned in surprise to see Matt coming up the aisle toward him, dressed in the same uniform as Chance and grinning broadly. "Hey!" Chance said, pleased. It was a B shift day, and Chance had had to take a vacation day to attend the ceremony. He hadn't expected to see anyone from work.

"Hey yourself," Matt said easily, dropping into the chair next to Bonnie. "You got a badge-pinner?"

"Yes," Bonnie said, eyeing Matt. "He does."

Matt grinned at her. "Just checking. Matthew Perkins, ma'am." Chance watched with amusement as Matt took off his hat and gave her a nod of acknowledgement.

Bonnie narrowed her eyes. "Bonnie White. And if you call me ma'am again, I'll hit you with my cane."

Matt laughed out loud and sat back in his chair. "Noted."

It started shortly after that. Three city councilmen gave boring speeches on how noble a job firefighting was, to which no one listened but everyone pretended. Then they went on to praise the fifteen candidates for the captains' positions, noting their excellent work in the department as well as their outstanding results on the two previous exams.

Finally, the candidates were asked to rise from their seats and the badge-pinners were invited to come forward and stand in a small group on the stage. Mothers, fathers, wives, sons, and friends were among them, pride shining in their eyes. Chance stood where he was and watched Bonnie lose herself in the group onstage while she waited for his name to be called.

He was tenth on the list, stepping onto the stage and shaking the hands of the city council members. The department chief handed him his badge and Chance moved over to the small crowd of people, waiting for Bonnie to make her way to the front so he could give it to her to pin.

Except when the crowd parted slightly, it wasn't for Bonnie.

Chance's throat went dry as Tucker stepped forward, holding his hand out for Chance's badge. Their eyes locked and Chance's arm came up of its own accord, placing his badge into Tucker's waiting fingers.

Tucker looked gorgeous, and Chance greedily drank in the sight of him. His dress uniform was just a shade lighter than his eyes, his boots polished 'til they shone. He'd had a haircut, Chance could see under his hat, and his cheeks were baby smooth from a fresh shave. When Tucker took the final step forward to put his badge in place, Chance could smell his cologne and shampoo.

He stood motionless while Tucker pinned him, hands fisted at his sides. "Why?" he murmured, low enough for Tucker's ears alone.

"Proud of you," Tucker answered, his voice husky and rich.

Tucker's hands lingered for a fraction of a second after he was finished – or Chance could have imagined it, he was too overwhelmed to know – before he stepped back, allowing the next person to come forward.

Numbly, Chance returned to his seat, refusing to let Tucker out of his sight. He craned his neck to watch him come off the side of the stage and stand near the door that led back inside. He was sort of aware of Bonnie sitting down behind him, a huge smile nearly splitting her face in two.

It ended ten minutes later, the rest of the candidates proudly displaying their new badges on their chests while they were all sworn in as captains. Chance barely heard the oath he was supposed to be taking and it was a struggle to keep his eyes forward, sure that the instant he took his gaze off Tucker, he would disappear.

It was finally over. Turning abruptly, Chance's heart stopped in his chest when he saw the empty space where Tucker had been standing.

But then it was all right, thank God, because Bonnie was nudging him and gesturing toward the back of the courtyard and Chance almost sobbed in relief. Tucker sat in the last chair in the last row, his hat on his lap and one arm flung casually over the back of his seat.

He stood up as Chance approached, fiddling with his hat brim. "Hey, Cap," he greeted.

Chance smiled slightly. "Sounds weird."

"Sounds good."

He nodded in agreement and couldn't think of anything else to say that didn't start with either "why" or "kiss me", so he stayed quiet.

"So I was thinkin'," Tucker started, and then stopped. "Shit. Don't know what I'm supposed to say."

"I'm sorry," Chance said suddenly, and then it was a rush of words that tumbled out before he even knew what was coming next. "Tuck, I was an asshole, and you didn't deserve any of it. I should have said sorry right from the beginning, but I was so wrapped up in my own stupid head, I couldn't see how bad I was hurting us by being such a dick. And then you were gone, and I didn't think you wanted anything to do with me so I didn't call, and it got harder and harder the longer it was, and then - "

"Whoa," Tucker finally interrupted, stepping in close and putting a finger over Chance's lips. Chance wanted to lick it. "Wasn't just you. I jus' let it all build up and then exploded, when I shoulda been talkin' to you all along and not lettin' you feel so damn sorry for yourself all the time. Wasn't much of a supportive partner, was I?"

Chance arched a brow. "You been talking to Robert?"

Tucker shrugged gracefully. "Maybe. When he found out I transferred, he dragged me out to have a drink and find out what happened. Nosy bastard."

Chance sighed and closed his eyes, leaning in just a fraction so their foreheads touched, not caring who was looking. "Come home with me," he whispered. "Been so long, Tuck, I need you." He swallowed and added one final word. "Please."

Tucker brought up a hand to rest at his waist. "Let's go."

***

Chance didn't remember the ride home in Tucker's truck, his hands and mind too full of lean, rangy fireman. Tucker had pushed him back against the wall as soon as they'd gotten through the door, mouths meeting with an urgency Chance hadn't felt for months.

"Missed you," Tucker was murmuring against his cheek while those fingers worked the buttons on Chance's uniform. "Missed you so fuckin' much, God, you don't know."

"I do know," Chance answered, fisting Tucker's shirt in one hand and dragging him down the short hallway to his bedroom. "Need you."

Tucker stopped him in the doorway again, struggling to get their clothes off, and Chance cursed all the buttons and zippers that were making things difficult. He finally managed to toe off his boots and shoved Tucker to the bed to do the same. When they were at last naked on top of the sheets together, Chance found himself suddenly shy and unable to meet Tucker's eyes.

"Hey," Tucker said, his tone sweet and questioning. "Backin' out on me?"

"No! God, no." He punctuated this with a kiss that left Tucker gasping against his mouth. "It's just been a long time. Didn't think we'd get here."

"Yeah," Tucker replied, his eyes growing impossibly darker. "Missed you, all the time. Wondered if I'd done the right thing, wanted to come back the next day." The words caught and he looked down, playing distractedly with the fine hairs on Chance's forearm.

Chance reached out a hand and curved it around Tucker's jaw, bringing his head back up and catching the wetness clinging to his lashes. "Love you," Chance breathed, kissing him, pushing him back into the pillows and stretching out on top. "Love you. So sorry," Chance whispered between gentle kisses, "so fucking sorry."

"Me, too," Tucker confessed, his voice breaking, though Chance could tell he was struggling to hold back his emotion. "Love you too."

There were no more words for a while after that, just the sound of their breathing growing harsher as they touched and savored and groped, hands moving with urgency. Chance gasped when Tucker rolled his hips upward, putting pressure where he needed it. It had been so long. "More," Chance managed, and Tucker complied, doing it again and again until Chance was afraid he'd come just from that.

Shaking his head, firmly telling himself that there'd been too many times Tucker had made him come just from a little grinding, Chance levered himself upward and pointed toward the nightstand. "Drawer," he ground out.

Tucker offered up dimples before reaching over his head to the drawer and extracting the lube. "No condoms in here," he said, craning his neck to see.

Chance took a deep breath. "It's okay."

Tucker's eyes widened. "Yeah?"

"Yeah. But …" Chance paused, mind going back to the night he'd seen Tucker in the Seagull, laughing and flirting with someone else. "Just need to know. You been safe?"

Tucker frowned. "That would imply I'd have been with someone other than you."

"Um. Yeah, but that night? When I saw you?" His cheeks grew hot. He hadn't considered the possibility that nothing had happened.

The corner of Tucker's mouth turned up. "Oh. That was just Chris. Rookie at Nineteen. Found out he liked guys, just took the kid out for a drink is all. Wasn't nothin'." His eyes glittered up at Chance. "Not my type. I kinda like 'em tall and bossy."

Chance couldn't not kiss Tucker then, biting at that soft upper lip and thrusting his tongue inside, sweeping and growling low in his throat until Tucker was laughing and kissing him back. "Want you," Chance said again, so softly he wasn't sure if Tucker heard.

"Then do it." Tucker pressed the lube into his hand and spread his legs a little, offering.

"Wait," Chance said, setting the lube aside and sliding down Tucker's body, licking at his cock when he passed, but not settling there. Tucker raised his head to see where Chance was.

"What're you – oh, *holy hell.*" He arched up off the bed when Chance tongued him. "Christ, Chance!"

Chance smiled to himself and did it again, tongue brushing over the sensitive hole before darting inside for a taste. "Oh, sorry," he murmured mischievously. "I'll stop."

"Don't you fuckin' *dare.*" The tone was strained and needy and Tucker was trembling with the effort to not buck up again.

Chance decided Tucker needed to lose a little bit of that tenuous control.

Getting down to business, he made his tongue into a point and shoved it as deep as he could, inhaling the sharp, unique scent that was Tucker. Twice more he did it until Tucker's restraint broke and he shoved himself upward to meet the small thrusts, one hand on Chance's head and the other on his own cock. "Oh God, oh God, oh

God," Tucker started chanting to himself. "Chance. More, God, gonna come in a second, hurry."

Chance looked up. "No," he said sharply, stilling the hard jerks Tucker was making on his dick. "Not before I'm in you."

Tucker inhaled and froze, eyes pleading. "Then do it. Can't wait, please."

Chance figured he better obey, considering he himself was leaking pre-come everywhere, and his hands were shaking. Quickly he slicked two fingers and then his cock, easing one finger at a time into Tucker until the other man was writhing beneath him. Drawing his hand out and pushing Tucker's knees back, Chance swallowed and positioned himself at Tucker's entrance.

Oh, Christ. Just touching Tucker like this, with no latex between them, threatened to kill Chance before he'd even started. Better do it all at once.

So he did, having coated himself with enough lubrication that he just slid in like butter, causing both of them to gasp at the same time.

"Did you think about this?" he asked, leaning down to pass his tongue over the corner of Tucker's mouth. "Did you want me like this?"

"Oh fuck yes," Tucker bit out. "Jus' about every damn time I jerked off. It was you, it was always you."

He tried not to move, to savor the feeling of being skin to skin, but it was damn near impossible when Tucker started to clench around him. "Don't," Chance whimpered, which of course encouraged Tucker to do it again, and then it was all hopeless. Chance managed four good thrusts before he felt the edges of his fingers start to tingle and his balls grow tight. "Now," he growled.

Tucker squeezed his eyes shut and cried out, coming without ever touching himself, painting Chance's abdomen with hot streaks.

Chance thrust in one more time, reveling in the feel of no barriers. With a wrench and a shudder, he let it go, coming harder than he ever had in his life.

They lay tangled up in sheets and each other for a long time afterward. Chance just didn't see the necessity in getting up when Tucker was kissing him, drawing patterns on Chance's arm, dimpling at him. "'Bout killed me," Tucker said lazily, his eyes dark. "Could feel you. It was amazing."

"You're amazing," Chance said truthfully, then blushed. Wasn't like him to make romantic declarations.

But Tucker just grinned and nuzzled his cheek.

"Want you back here," Chance said. "Ain't right without you."

"Better not let your momma hear you say 'ain't'," Tucker teased.

"I'm not kidding," Chance insisted. It was suddenly imperative Tucker believe him. "Want you with me, Tuck."

Tucker looked at him, indigo eyes glittering in the dark. "Wanna be with you."

"Say you'll do it," Chance pressed. "Say you'll move back." He took Tucker's hand in his, threading their fingers together and clenching tightly.

Tucker leaned up to offer a kiss, his lips barely brushing Chance's. "Yeah. I'll do it."

Chance let out a breath he hadn't known he was holding. "Tomorrow."

Tucker laughed, a sound Chance knew he'd never get tired of. "Okay, okay. Tomorrow." He paused, let a grin curve the corner of his mouth. "So fuckin' bossy."

End

Flashover

Tory Temple

Flashover: (noun) The point at which all combustible materials in a room ignite simultaneously.

Chapter One

"Hey," Tucker McBride said over the sound of the surf. "Hey! Look!"

Chancellor Shanahan watched as Tucker managed to scramble from a sitting position to get one knee underneath him on his new board. Still clutching the sides, he rode the small wave until it broke beneath him and sent him headfirst into the water. Chance grinned, inordinately proud. "Almost," he said, when Tucker's dark head surfaced.

"Almost?" Tucker sputtered, stretching out on the board and paddling back to where Chance sat astride his own surfboard, bobbing in the water. "Fuck 'almost'. I was awesome."

Chance laughed at his sulky look and reached out a hand to Tucker's wetsuit, catching the neoprene and drawing Tucker up next to him in the water. "You were awesome," Chance agreed, dropping a saltwater kiss on Tucker's mouth and running his fingers through Tucker's wet hair. "But you'd be more awesome if you let go of the board and actually stood up."

Tucker broke away and gave him a shove, sending them both into the ocean. Chance came up laughing, flinging an arm over his board and treading water. "Aw," he teased. "You gonna cry?"

Tucker tried not to smile, but the dimple in his cheek gave him away as usual. "All right, yeah. I got a ways to go. But I'm doin' good so far, huh?"

Chance ducked under his board and surfaced next to Tucker. "Yup," he murmured, just before darting out his tongue to swipe at Tucker's upper lip. "You're doing good."

Tucker grinned against his mouth and kissed him back, snaking a foot around Chance's calf and bringing their crotches into contact beneath the calm water. Chance could feel him already at full-mast beneath the rubbery foam of his wetsuit. "Don't guess fuckin' in the ocean is a good idea," Tucker said with a sigh,, still rubbing suggestively against him.

Fireline

Chance shuddered. "God, no. Salt and sand in places you don't want to think about."

"Then I wanna go home."

Chance laughed. "Insatiable."

"Yeah," Tucker agreed cheerfully, and began to paddle toward shore. "Gettin' cold anyhow. What's for dinner?"

Chance hesitated, hoping to catch one more swell to ride in, but the tide was going out and his sore leg was making itself known with warning twinges. It had been nearly a year since he'd broken it while on a call, but it still ached when he surfed too long or put too much pressure on it. He followed Tucker reluctantly. "Don't care. Got chicken at home, I think."

They reached the shallows and splashed their way onto the sand, shivering in the cool fall afternoon. Peeling off wetsuits, they rubbed down with towels and hefted their boards under their arms. "Gonna be too cold for the water soon," Tucker observed, but Chance shook his head.

"No way. Never too cold for that."

Laying their boards in the back of his truck, Tucker snorted. "How come you start shakin' if the temperature falls below seventy degrees, but you can surf in fifty-five degree water?"

Chance shrugged and hopped in the passenger seat. "Don't know," he said when Tucker slid behind the wheel. "Cause I'm not thinking about being cold when I'm out there, I guess. Turn up the damn heat."

"Bossy," Tucker muttered, using his favorite word to describe Chance, but obeying the command anyway.

They were home shortly, Chance's condo only a few blocks from the beach. Tucker was ready to head inside but Chance stopped him with "Boards," and Tucker heaved a sigh.

"Okay, okay. God forbid they should stay outside for a night."

Chance glared as he lifted them from the truck bed. "Respect your board, man. You think these things were cheap?"

Tucker took the surfboards from him, leading their way into the house. "I know. You done told me a hundred times."

Chance waited for him to store the boards in the front closet before catching Tucker's hand and tugging him down the hall to the bathroom. "If you take care of your stuff," he explained, stopping halfway there and pressing Tucker against the wall, "it makes me happy."

Tucker grinned. "Oh, I can take care of your stuff, all right." He kissed Chance, mouth still tasting of sand and sea.

Chance kissed him back, suddenly hungry for him, hips thrusting forward against Tucker's wet swimsuit. It was like this a lot of the time, he'd found, the two of them always wanting and horny. Not that Chance was complaining; he just sort of marveled at it every now and then. They'd been together nearly a year and a half – if you counted the five-month breakup in between – and Chance still couldn't get enough of Tucker.

Tucker was holding Chance's hips in place as they kissed, the vee of Tucker's crotch nestled snugly against Chance's thigh. He could feel Tucker's cock, full and solid in his wet bathing suit. "Shower," Chance murmured, but Tucker shook his head.

"No," he grinned, and pushed his cock up suggestively. "Here. Bet I can make you come in your shorts."

It was not a bet Chance wanted to take. Tucker had proved his skill many times, reducing Chance to nothing more than a trembling bundle of want, ruining lots of pairs of jeans. But protesting was futile – Tucker only saw that as a challenge – so Chance just set his jaw and snaked a hand down to cup one of Tucker's firm ass cheeks. "Fine," he dared. "You're on. But I bet you spill first."

Tucker wisely kept his mouth shut, but his eyes showed merriment. Chance ignored his gleeful expression and kissed him instead, grinding on Tucker in the slow way that Chance knew drove him crazy.

It worked, for a while. Tucker's head fell back and he gripped Chance's hips tightly, letting Chance suck up a mark on his salt-crusted skin. Chance kept pressure on Tucker's groin, letting his leg rest just so between Tucker's thighs and trying his damndest not to grind down himself.

The pulse in Tucker's neck increased under Chance's tongue, feeling like a small, fluttering bird, and Chance felt a flash of triumph. Not so impervious after all, it seemed, despite Tucker's best intentions to stay detached. Chance let his tongue trace the shell of Tucker's ear, ignoring the tiny grains of sand he could feel in his mouth, and then took a sharp nip.

Tucker inhaled and jerked involuntarily before shaking his head. "Oh, no you don't," he muttered, hauling Chance up against him and starting a seductive rhythm, moving his hips in a circle while keeping Chance flush against his cock.

Chance squeezed his eyes shut tight and cursed himself for making yet another bet he was going to lose. However, the feeling in his dick and Tucker grinding on him soon made him not care. He concentrated on Tucker's panting breaths and figured he wasn't going to go down alone. "Together," he managed to say, one arm tight around Tucker's back and the other hand tangled in his hair.

"No," Tucker ground out. "You. First."

Time to fight dirty. "Together," Chance whispered again, trying his best not to come when his wet bathing suit slid over his cock in just the right way, "because feeling you come is the hottest thing ever, the way you just let it go all over my hand and it's all warm and it smells like you and – "

Bingo.

Tucker whimpered and fisted the material of Chance's t-shirt tightly in one hand as he went completely still. Chance felt the faint pulsing beneath their swim trunks, and then the blood was rushing in his ears and he forgot about Tucker's orgasm because his own was crashing down.

"You cheated," Tucker complained later, under the warm spray of the shower. "You talked dirty. Your momma know you let filth like that come outta your mouth?"

"I did not," Chance protested. He turned Tucker around to drag the washcloth over his back, making Tucker arch and roll his shoulders. "And besides, I fucking have to cheat with you. You're too good at that. Make me all embarrassed and shit, like I'm some high-school kid who's got no stamina."

"So you admit you cheated. Man, Cap, and here I thought you were all honorable and stuff." Tucker shook his head and sighed dramatically.

"Oh, don't give me that 'honorable' crap. And don't call me Cap at home." It had been three months since Chance had been promoted to captain in the Oceanside Fire Authority, and Tucker only called him Cap when he wanted it to rankle.

"You working tomorrow?" Tucker asked, as they shut off the water and reached for towels.

It was hard keeping their respective schedules straight ever since Chance had switched to where the empty captain's spot was. It was a good arrangement, though, giving them some nights off together and some alone.

Just by pure luck, the A shift captain in Chance's own station had wanted to work closer to where he lived, so when a slot came up, he transferred, and Chance had been able to stay on at Station Eleven. It was a little weird being in a place of authority at the same station where he'd been a rookie almost ten years ago, but he was getting used to it. And since Tucker had kept his own spot at Station Nineteen, there was no danger of Chance being Tucker's boss. All the better for both of them.

"Yeah," Chance said, picking up Tucker's towel from where he'd left it in a damp heap on the floor. "Come by for dinner, if you want. My turn to cook."

"I get enough of your cookin' at home." But he softened the remark with a kiss, trailing his hand over Chance's bare ass as he wandered to the chair where he'd dropped his track pants that morning. Slipping them on, he turned back to Chance. "Wanna grill dinner?"

"We could," Chance said slowly. "Or." He crossed the room, reaching out for Tucker and wrapping both arms around his waist. "We could play."

"Play," Tucker said instantly, dragging Chance to the bed and pulling him down.

Chance snorted. "You're so easy."

"And you're so fuckin' bossy. Help me get my damn pants off." He kicked ineffectually at them.

"Who's bossy now?" But Chance yanked at Tucker's waistband, getting his pants at least to his knees.

Tucker shoved them all the way off and Chance could see he was hard already, cock standing out away from his belly. God, he was easy.

Chance loved it.

He slid down and wasted no time in taking Tucker deep, letting Tucker hit the back of his throat while Chance sucked as hard as he could. Tucker arched. "Christ," he hissed. "Wasn't ready."

"I know," Chance said on the upsweep, sucking relentlessly just at the head. "That was the idea."

Tucker mumbled something unintelligible that could have been "more" or "harder" or any one of the dozen words he usually gritted out during sex, but it didn't matter. Chance knew what he meant.

Chance took minutes to lick him with soft, wet strokes, coating him liberally with spit and Tucker's own pre-come, loving the taste and smell of him. He ignored his own erection as best he could, no easy feat since he was hard enough to hurt, but sometimes it was just for Tucker. Giving was as good as getting, especially when the recipient was as appreciative as Tucker always was.

And Tucker was appreciative now, slamming a hand down on the bed and arching his back, trying to get words out but only managing to groan instead. Chance thought he recognized his name, but everything else was unintelligible.

And when Tucker shuddered under his mouth and came without making a sound, it was what Chance wanted. He took it all down greedily, inhaling the sharp, intoxicating scent, feeling his own prick twitch without even being touched.

It was just an added bonus when Tucker roused himself enough to wrap his fist around Chance's cock and jerked him quickly, using the rough, tight strokes that Chance loved. Chance took a breath and came in a rush, spilling hotly over Tucker's hand and soaking the newly washed sheets.

"Damn, baby," Tucker mumbled a while later. "I gotta be ready 'fore you do stuff like that. Otherwise I come faster'n anything."

"Welcome to my world," Chance said wryly, blushing inwardly at all the times Tucker had gotten him off in sixty seconds or less.

"Can't help that, now can I?" Tucker asked, shaking his head. "You're just so needy. And easy. And bossy. And – " He let out a yelp and didn't finish his sentence when Chance leaned over and bit down on a flat nipple.

"You saying you don't like it?"

Tucker sobered instantly, reaching up a hand and brushing a thumb over Chance's cheek. "I love it."

"Yeah. Don't you forget it, McBride."

Chapter Two

The drive home from work that normally took sixteen minutes took him less than ten. Chance prayed he wouldn't get a speeding ticket, then glanced at what he had in the front seat next to him and decided a ticket would be worth it. Dropping one hand to his crotch, he tried to adjust his jeans so that his cock wasn't quite so uncomfortably tight.

Bursting through the front door, he started shouting for Tucker before he'd even dropped his gear bag. The house was still and silent and Chance remembered with a grimace that it was just after eight in the morning. On Tucker's day off. Which meant he was probably asleep, or had been until Chance started yelling.

Chance shouldered the bedroom door open, holding his prize behind his back. Tucker had the pillow over his head with both hands. "Shut up," he mumbled from beneath it.

Chance crawled onto the bed and pushed the pillow away. "Sorry," he said, punctuating it with a kiss. Mmm. His favorite thing: warm, sleepy fireman.

"You don't sound sorry," Tucker grumbled, rolling over and burying his face in his discarded pillow again.

"I'm not," Chance agreed easily. "And you won't be, either." He paused. Tucker didn't stir. "Tuck. Are you listening?"

"No. I'm sleepin'."

"Okay." Chance sighed, and brought out what he was holding from behind his back. He let the links clink together softly and waited.

Sure enough, Tucker looked over his shoulder. His hair was tousled with sleep and Chance wanted to pounce on him. "Whatcha got?"

He held them up and watched Tucker's eyes go wide. "These," he grinned.

Tucker turned all the way over and sat up. "Cuffs? You got handcuffs? Are they real?" He made a grab for them, but Chance held them out of his reach.

"Yeah, they're real. You know Sandy? That blonde cop? Works nights and stops by the station sometimes?"

Tucker nodded, but kept his eyes glued to the handcuffs. Oh, this was going to be easy. "Yeah," Tucker said, clearing his throat. "Sandy. The cop."

"She came by last night to use our head. Left her belt on the table while she peed and Dan thought he'd be funny and lift her cuffs. By the time I figured out he had them, she was gone. I had dispatch radio her, but she said she had another pair in her car and she'd come by and get 'em next week sometime. So ..." He grinned, dangling the cuffs in front of Tucker's glazed expression. "I brought them home. What do you think?"

Tucker's answer was to grab Chance's free hand and drag it down to his lap. He slept naked, so Chance found a handful of warm, silky, hard cock. "That's what I think," Tucker answered, and then groaned when Chance squeezed. "Who gets to wear 'em?"

"Well," Chance said, not sure how it would be received, "I was thinking you."

Tucker's expression grew wary, but Chance felt Tucker's cock twitch under his fingers. It made his own dick pulse in answer. He was ready to back down if Tucker didn't want this, because pressure in the bedroom was never good, but then Tucker licked his lips. "Okay," he agreed, and the dazed look was back in his eyes.

Chance jumped him then, pushing him back into the pillows and straddling him. They kissed deeply, tongues sweeping and driving, and Chance found himself grinding Tucker into the bed, his cock demanding attention. Hard and wanting, and Tucker tasted like morning, Chance's favorite flavor next to caramel fudge.

He was wondering if maybe they should just get off fast, something to dull the bright edges and then concentrate on the real stuff, when Tucker reached over and snagged the handcuffs. Dangling them in front of Chance, he cocked a brow and said, "Well?"

Chance sat up, still straddling Tucker's hips. He took the cuffs and fingered the cool metal, warming it under his palms. "We have to be careful," he said unnecessarily. He knew Tucker knew the dangers of real police cuffs. "Bondage cuffs would be safer."

"And yet," Tucker said, rolling his hips upward and making Chance gasp, "not as hot." He slowly lifted his wrists over his head and held them against one of the wooden slats in the headboard.

Chance swallowed hard and brought the handcuffs up, clicking one cuff around Tucker's left wrist before threading the other one through the gap in the wood. He clicked the other metal ring around Tucker's right wrist, and there he was. Cuffed.

Tucker glanced up and pulled slightly, testing the strength of the wood and metal. They both held fast, allowing little to no movement except for up and down. "All right?" Chance asked, hoping he wouldn't drool when he spoke.

Tucker grinned, both dimples flashing. "Don't have no choice. You got me."

"Yeah," Chance said. "Looks like I do." And Chance leaned down again, holding Tucker's head in place with both hands and practically swallowing him whole, licking and sucking at his mouth. Oh, God, this was hotter than he'd expected.

Chance backed off slightly, moving down toward Tucker's feet and shoving all the sheets and blankets out of the way. When there was nothing blocking his view, he just sat and stared.

It was a gorgeous sight: Tucker, naked and hard and wanting, pretty wrists bound to the headboard. Chance reached down to take his own cock in hand and realized he was still fully dressed. Shedding clothes fast enough to make Tucker laugh, Chance was soon blessedly naked and kneeling once again over Tucker's flat stomach, pressing a kiss to his navel and giving his cock a squeeze.

"Want you," Tucker whispered into the quiet of the bedroom, his eyes dark and glittering.

Chance nodded and met his gaze, at once understanding the trust passing between them. "Tell me if they start to hurt," he said, reaching up for the small bottle of lube in the nightstand.

"They're fine," Tucker said absently, arching his neck on the pillow as their cocks brushed. "Oh, *damn*, we shoulda done this a long time ago."

Chance murmured in agreement and poured a generous amount of lube into his palm, dropping the bottle and reaching down to coat Tucker in one stroke. He hadn't realized just how hard Tucker was until he touched the man.

Tucker was barely controlling his trembling, all muscles tensed. His cock was maybe harder than Chance had ever felt, steel beneath his touch, already leaking a small drop of pre-come when Chance brushed the head with his thumb. He glanced up to see Tucker's eyes closed, lashes making dark crescents on his cheeks, teeth creasing a dent in his bottom lip. "You okay?" Chance asked, ignoring the leap his own dick made.

Tucker's answer was a sharp, single nod, but as soon as Chance began to stroke him, he gasped out, "Fuck," and came in hot, sticky pulses over Chance's stomach.

Chance blinked in surprise, but let him ride it out, milking him until Tucker winced and shifted away, suddenly too sensitive to touch. Chance waited till he opened his eyes before cocking a brow and saying dryly, "I take it bondage is your thing?"

A blush spread its way upward, staining already flushed cheekbones. Tucker grinned bashfully. "Sorry. Was sorta intense." He started to reach for Chance before remembering, the cuffs biting into his wrists.

Chance watched as Tucker's cock, which hadn't completely softened, twitched and began to fill again once Tucker realized he was still bound. "Oh, yeah," Chance said softly. "Bondage is definitely your thing." With difficulty, he stopped himself from just throwing himself across Tucker and rubbing off right there on Tucker's hip. Better to do this right.

Using the spunk on his hand as more lube, Chance leaned forward and took both of their dicks together in a firm grip. He jacked them both slowly until Tucker was back at full staff and Chance was biting the inside of his cheek in an attempt to stave off orgasm, trying not to listen to the soft, crooning noises Tucker was making. The handcuff links were clinking together and Tucker was pulling against them desperately, unmindful of the raw spots they would probably leave on his wrists.

"Easy," Chance warned, but Tucker tossed his head on the pillow.

"Screw easy," Tucker moaned. "God. Do it, Chance, fuck me before I come all over you again. Hurry up."

Now, there was an offer not to be refused.

In one quick move, Chance pushed Tucker's legs back and sank in so deep he swore he was never getting out. Chance stayed absolutely still, and it occurred to him that he could feel Tucker's pulse from inside, the rhythm surprisingly steady. The whole sensation of it was powerful and Tucker had given that to him; had relinquished total and complete control and had put his trust in Chance.

It was beautiful and terrifying at the same time.

He started to move slowly, supporting himself on his arms and angling his thrusts in order to touch Tucker's prostate with each surge forward. Tucker had gone completely motionless, back arched and hips tilted, sweat breaking out on his brow and wrists straining at his bonds. Chance had to look away or risk shooting just from the sight of it. "Come on," he whispered to Tucker. "Let it go."

Tucker didn't move, didn't give any indication he'd even heard Chance speak, aside from a muscle twitching in his jaw. Chance grew slightly alarmed. "Tuck," he said, breaking stride despite his body's protests to just slam in until he came. "Hey. Look at me, would you?"

Tucker opened his eyes and Chance could see that his pupils were dilated enough to almost completely block out the indigo color. All that was left was a thin ring of midnight blue around the black. "Chance," he whispered, and then clenched his jaw, the muscles straining in his forearms.

His desperation was evident and Chance couldn't – wouldn't – deny him. Chance hadn't known when they started that Tucker would respond this way; they'd never played at restraining each other before. Seemed like maybe it should be something they did more often. "What do you want?" Chance murmured, his voice husky.

"Oh, God, just get me off, please, *please.*"

Tucker rarely begged.

Sinking back down into him, Chance let their torsos touch, trapping Tucker's prick between them. "Like this?" he asked, holding his breath, feeling Tucker twitch and clench around him. He rubbed against Tucker with more weight, feeling Tucker slippery and warm against his stomach, and took one, two, three more strokes before Tucker cried out something that could have been a prayer or a curse. Tucker came in huge, liquid pulses over both of them, trembling hard enough to shake the bed.

Chance held off long enough to watch Tucker while he came, to see his eyes roll back and his mouth open, and then let go himself. He bit back a groan and buried his face in the hollow of Tucker's shoulder. He tried not to let his weight sag, especially since in the back of his mind he knew that Tucker was still bound to the headboard, but in the end, his limbs gave way and he collapsed.

When he finally did manage to lift his head, he found Tucker staring at the ceiling, a blissful look on his face. "You all right?" Chance asked groggily.

Tucker grinned slowly, sleepily. "Mmm. I'm good. 'Cept my arms hurt."

"Damn!" Chance heaved himself off Tucker and reached for his pants, scrabbling in the front pocket for the key. "You should have poked me or something."

"With what? My dick?" He rattled the chain slightly, smiling.

"You've done it before." Chance inserted the key and the handcuffs clicked open.

Tucker dropped his arms with a wince, rubbing his wrists. "Man. Shoulders'll be sore tomorrow."

Chance captured one of his hands, turning it palm-up to examine Tucker's inner wrist. The tender skin was red and abraded and Chance could see one or two places where it was chafed enough that scabs were going to form.

"Ouch," he said softly. "We need to put something on this."

"Nah," Tucker shrugged, trying to wrest his arm away. "S'okay. Quit fussin'."

"Stay there," Chance commanded. He climbed off the bed and glared over his shoulder.

Tucker gave a long-suffering sigh, but stayed put, stretching his arms over his head and then out in front. Chance could almost see the word *bossy* forming in Tucker's brain. Tucker kept quiet, though, so Chance went to the bathroom and poked around in the medicine cabinet. Unearthing a tube of antibacterial ointment, he returned to the bed and held out a hand for Tucker's wrist.

Tucker snorted, but held out his arm anyway for Chance's ministrations. "It's not as bad as it looks. Ouch!"

Chance raised a brow at him, smoothing ointment over the raw spots. "You shouldn't have pulled so much. I knew we shouldn't have used real ones."

Tucker shrugged one shoulder. "It was hot." He pulled out of Chance's grip and laid back, holding the covers open for Chance to crawl in. "Wow," he said when Chance yawned widely enough for his jaw to crack. "S'only nine in the mornin', baby. You tired already?"

"Up three times last night," Chance mumbled, suddenly drowsy. It had been a rough night for his crew. They had had emergency calls at midnight, two, and four a.m. Chance hadn't bothered to go back to sleep after the last one, opting instead to use the station's weight room while it was empty.

"Aw," Tucker said sympathetically, and Chance felt a hand in his hair. "Sleep a while, yeah? Gotta gear up for round two."

"Your wrists couldn't handle any more today," he whispered, nearly asleep.

"No," Tucker said thoughtfully, "but yours could."

Chapter Three

Some shifts just weren't worth going in for.

Chance slammed his helmet back into his seat on the engine and threw his turnout jacket on top of it, not bothering to hang it up in his locker. Wouldn't fucking matter anyway; they'd just get another idiot call for another idiot reason that had nothing to do with any medical assistance.

The last two calls had reached new levels of ridiculousness. First there had been the family that had returned home from vacation at midnight, only to hear what they described as a strange hissing noise coming from their upstairs bathroom. Fearful that it was a gas leak, they dialed 911 and the operator had dispatched Chance's engine.

It took Chance's crew five minutes to determine that someone had left an electric toothbrush on in the bathroom, thereby explaining the "hissing" noise. They all rolled their eyes at each other while somehow managing to keep straight faces, although Chance noted that Jim had to turn his back when Chance presented the vibrating toothbrush to the chagrined owner.

He'd finally fallen asleep again when the alarm dinged around two in the morning, this time dispatching them to a small home in the nearby retirement community. An elderly woman had gotten a pacemaker installed a few days prior, and an insistent beeping had woken her up. Chance would never understand why the public's first instinct was to call for emergency assistance rather than a family member, but knew there was no sense in getting frustrated by it.

Unless, of course, it was two-fifteen in the fucking morning and the beeping noise turned out to be the woman's clock radio.

Even the woman herself refused to believe it until Chance held the offending radio up to her ear. It made it even harder to keep a straight face when Chance realized that Jim couldn't just turn his back but had had to actually leave the room when Chance raised his voice and said, "Ma'am, it's your radio!"

He slept restlessly for the remainder of the night, coming wide-awake the next time his pager beeped, although it was the other engine's turn to go out. Morning found him irritable and tired. All he wanted to do was crawl in bed and sleep, preferably with Tucker next to him.

He forgot until morning that he'd agreed to stay late for the captain on C shift. A nine-hour holdover kept Chance at work until five o'clock that evening. His relief finally showed up and clapped him on the back and thanked him for staying. The crew offered him dinner, but he declined in favor of getting home, since it was Tucker's turn to cook. Chance usually didn't pass up the opportunity to let Tucker put good southern chow on the table.

Thin winter darkness had set in by the time he got there, and he briefly wondered why the front light wasn't on. Neither was the foyer light, and the rest of the house was dark as well. Chance would have thought Tucker wasn't home, but his truck was parked out by the curb and his wallet and car keys were on the kitchen table.

"McBride," he called out on his way down the hall, "you better have a damn good reason why this house doesn't smell like dinner yet. Unless you want to go out, which is cool -"

"Turn the fuckin' light off," Tucker barked from the bed, interrupting Chance's sentence.

Startled, he flipped the light back off and stood in the doorway. "You okay?"

"No."

He made his way over in the near-darkness and hesitated at the side of the bed. "What's the matter?" He could just make out Tucker lying on his back with what looked like a towel filled with ice over his eyes.

"Migraine. Christ, don't make me talk." His voice was strained.

"Migraine. Really?" His own tiredness and slight headache vanished. Clearly they were nothing compared to what Tucker seemed to be feeling. Chance was surprised; he'd had no idea Tucker suffered from migraine headaches. At least, he hadn't had one in the past year and a half they'd been together.

Tucker didn't answer and Chance sat down gingerly on the edge of the bed. "You got meds for it?" he asked, not sure how Tucker wanted him to handle it.

"Expired. Too late to take 'em anyway, probably gonna start pukin' soon. God, *please* don't make me talk."

Chance winced in sympathy and reached over for the trashcan, wanting to do something to help, but not knowing what. He had an odd, unsettled feeling as he eyed Tucker and didn't know how to put a name to it, didn't like the fact that this was something he hadn't known about Tucker. "You want me to stay?"

"No."

"Okay." Chance got up and shoved his hands into his jeans pockets, hesitating, wanting to say something else but respecting Tucker's wishes not to make him talk. "Gonna go make dinner, if you need me."

Tucker didn't answer, so Chance left him alone in the dark bedroom and went to see what he could find to eat.

Searching through the fridge turned up enough ingredients for a decent chicken casserole, so he threw them together and stuck it in the oven to bake. He sorted through the mail, one ear tuned to the bedroom, and then wandered into the living room to turn on the television. He found a football game and muted the sound.

True to Tucker's word, within minutes Chance could hear him retching into the trashcan that had been placed near the bed. Chance went to the bedroom and sat down next to him, one hand rubbing soothing circles on Tucker's back until the tense muscles relaxed and Tucker dropped back down to the bed. "Okay?" Chance murmured.

Tucker nodded shakily. "Gonna get better now," he whispered. "It's always bad 'til I throw up."

The 'always' part was what was bothering him, like this was something he should have known, especially if it happened often enough for Tucker to be familiar with the pattern. Chance ran a hand through Tucker's sweat-damp hair and studied him. "You gonna sleep?"

"Maybe," Tucker mumbled, already halfway gone.

Chance stayed for a while longer, squeezing the muscles in Tucker's neck and using his thumb to press into the hollow at the base of Tucker's skull. Tucker heaved a huge breath and Chance felt the tension drain out of him slowly, until he was limp and pliant under Chance's hand and his breathing was even.

The beep of the oven timer drew his attention, so Chance left a drowsing Tucker to rest while he went to eat. His casserole wasn't bad, if he said so himself, and he downed two helpings in front of the TV.

Tucker produced himself an hour and a half later, weaving unsteadily in the doorway of the living room and blinking against the light. Chance leaned up to turn the table lamp off. "Better?" he asked, and Tucker nodded with relief.

"Yeah. Thanks." He made his way carefully to the couch and sat down, leaning his head against the back cushion and closing his eyes.

"You hungry?"

Tucker nodded. "Yep. Gimme a little while, though. My stomach says 'food', but my brain says 'no way'."

"Got it. Come here." Chance tugged at Tucker's shirt, urging him to lie down. He did so with a sigh, turning to his back and laying his head across Chance's lap. Chance played with the strands of Tucker's bangs, letting the silky hair slide through his fingers as he watched the end of the game on TV.

"Momma used to do that," Tucker murmured, almost asleep again. "Was 'bout the only thing that would make the headache go away. She'd play with my hair and put me to sleep."

"You had migraines when you were little?" Chance asked, his fingers stilling in Tucker's hair.

"Don't stop," Tucker said, shifting his head in Chance's lap to get his attention. "Yeah. Momma had 'em, too, the doc said it was genetic. I started gettin' 'em when I was about ten. Sucked."

"You never told me," Chance said, and hoped he didn't sound as whiny as it felt to say.

Tucker shrugged. "Haven't had one for a couple years. Since before you. Kinda weird, I dunno where this one came from. Used to happen when I was stressed."

"Stressed, huh? Everything okay?"

He yawned. "Guess so. Don't got nothin' to be stressed out about, really. Was just a random headache."

It was completely unnecessary for Chance to feel so unsettled by that information, but he didn't know how to stop dwelling on the fact that there was something about Tucker he hadn't known or been able to help with. It bothered him enough to remain silent for the rest of the night, though he kept his fingers tangled in Tucker's hair while they watched television.

Much later, after eating and showering, Tucker had clearly made a remarkable recovery. The erection Tucker was grinding into Chance's thigh was a good indication, and Chance paused from where he was sucking up a healthy-sized hickey into Tucker's

Fireline

neck. "Anything else you need to tell me about yourself?" he asked, not even knowing where it was coming from. "Criminal record or anything?"

Tucker stopped moving and looked down at him, confused. "Huh?"

Chance at once felt ashamed. It wasn't Tucker's fault. "Nothing," he muttered, and set back to work, one hand finding its way into the smooth space between Tucker's asscheeks.

He managed not to think about it the whole time he was receiving a very enthusiastic blow job, but when Tucker was sleeping soundly next to him, Chance wondered about it.

Chapter Four

He managed to push the remaining uneasiness away after a few days, when Tucker showed no further signs of having any other secrets Chance didn't know about.

"No," Chance mumbled in protest when the clock radio on Tucker's side of the bed went off at six-thirty. He curled into Tucker and tightened the arm he had over his waist. "Don't go. Call in."

Tucker chuckled and ran a hand down Chance's bare hip. "That don't sound like you, Captain Shanahan. What happened to 'get your ass outta bed, you gotta work'?"

"That was only when we were partners."

"You said it three days ago." Tucker's hand crept around to palm Chance's ass and pull him in closer.

"Did I? I forgot." He nudged his hips up, meeting Tucker's morning wood with his own stiff cock, and groaned appreciatively.

Tucker clucked his tongue and then suddenly there was empty space, cool air rushing over Chance as Tucker lifted the covers and got up. "Sorry, Cap. Told Dave I'd come in early for him. Save that for me, okay?" He winked and then disappeared into the bathroom and Chance was left with a good-sized erection and a slightly disgruntled feeling.

The sense of irritation stayed with him long after Tucker had left and Chance had finally dragged himself out of bed. A quick jerk in the shower hadn't helped any, and neither did the less-than-average waves he rode for an hour. He tried going for a run in hopes that the exercise would clear his head, but just ended up back in the shower with his hand around his cock for the second time that day.

Finally, sometime after it grew dark, he just gave in to the inevitable and got in the car. Fuck, Tucker had showed up countless times at Chance's station looking for a grope, it was only right Chance return the favor. He knew he was neatly side-stepping the fact that he'd told Tucker he wouldn't mess around at work since his promotion, but damn. Tucker didn't often leave in the morning without either of them getting off.

Fireline

The closer he got to Nineteen, the better he felt, and Chance caught himself whistling softly along with the radio by the time he pulled into the lot. He parked next to Tucker's truck and studied the outside of the station. Smaller than Station Eleven, it ran only one engine with a crew of five guys, but they were fairly busy. However, the rig was currently in the garage, so Chance knew they were there.

He adjusted himself inside his nylon track pants when he got out of the car, his cock somehow knowing that Tucker was in the immediate vicinity, and strolled through their garage. Chance knew they'd all still be hanging around after dinner, probably watching TV or doing dishes. There wouldn't be anyone near Tucker's bunk, he hoped. They could always come out to the parking lot as a last resort, too. It wasn't like the bed of Tucker's truck hadn't seen its share of screwing around.

He pulled open the door to the main room just off the garage and walked in, eyes searching immediately for Tucker. There were a couple of guys at the sink, cleaning up from dinner, and Tucker's captain, Rich, sat in one of the recliners near the TV. "Shanahan," he said with a lift of his chin. "S'going on?"

"Looking for McBride," Chance said, keeping his tone neutral, aware of the men in the room who didn't know he and Tucker were together. Rich knew, and although Chance had never asked him directly, Tucker had said he was fine with it.

"In the other room with the small TV," Rich answered. "Didn't want to watch in here. Chris must be in there too."

Chance paused. He knew who Chris was. The guy was nearing the end of his rookie year with the department, and was also the same one that Chance had seen out with Tucker when he and Tucker had been apart. The incident had been discussed, and Chance had taken Tucker at face value when he'd said nothing had happened, but Chance was still irrationally watchful where Chris was concerned.

He'd never tell Tucker that, of course, since that was the last thing Tucker needed to be gloating over.

Chance knew which room off the kitchen Rich was referring to; Tucker had dragged him in there more than once in hopes of getting a quick fondle: the only thing the room held was a television and sectional couch that went from wall to wall. The door was closed and he could hear the TV inside, so Chance knocked once and then opened the door.

The first thing he registered was that yes, Chris was definitely in there with Tucker. The second thing he registered was that they were sitting awfully close together. Slouched, really, and Chris had a leg thrown over Tucker's thigh as the two of them laughed at whatever was on TV and shared a bag of chips.

They both looked up when the door opened, Chris quickly disentangling himself from Tucker and pushing himself to a more upright position. Tucker blinked in surprise and rose from the couch. "Hey!" he said, sounding pleased. "Didn't know you were comin' down."

"Apparently not," Chance said calmly, and Chris had the grace to blush.

Tucker looked behind him at Chris and then back at Chance. "We were just watchin' the game," he said, studying Chance's face. "They wouldn't let us watch in the other room. Rich has to watch Jeopardy! every night."

"Mmhmm," Chance said, proud of himself for keeping the anger in check. For now. "Guess I should have called first." He turned to leave, but Tucker stopped him with a hand on his arm.

"Chance," he implored, "it ain't what you think."

"What do I think?" he asked, curious to see what Tucker would say.

Tucker's mouth thinned and he pushed Chance back through the doorway, leaving Chris on the couch and pulling the door halfway closed behind him. "I think *you* think I'm flirtin' around on you as soon as your back's turned."

He wasn't doing this here. Hell, he didn't want to do it, ever. Abruptly, he detached himself from Tucker's grip. "You have no fucking idea what I think," he bit out, and then he really did go, stomping back out through the kitchen and ignoring Rich's goodbye.

Chance had time to feel sorry for himself on the ten-minute ride home, starting with the revelation earlier in the week that there were apparently still some things he didn't know about Tucker, continuing onto this morning with Tucker leaving him alone and horny, and ending with the nice surprise he'd just found. By the time he got to his house, the 'feeling sorry for himself' part had turned into 'really pissed off' instead, and he went straight to the refrigerator.

He uncapped a beer and pointedly ignored the blinking light on the answering machine. The beer went down easily, and so did a second one, and by the time he was halfway through his third, Chance knew he wanted something stronger. He yanked open the cabinet over the sink and found Tucker's bottle of Jack Daniel's. Perfect.

He at least made himself get down a whiskey glass from the cupboard and splashed a small amount of soda in with the JD, gulping it back and relishing the burn. He finished it standing over the sink and then poured another, bringing it into the living room with him and flopping down in front of the television. Smokey jumped up next to him and sniffed carefully at his glass, recoiling when he smelled the strong liquor and giving Chance a disdainful look.

"Don't you fucking start," Chance muttered at the cat.

He started feeling the effects toward the end of the second healthy glass. The room tilted just a little when he got up to take a leak, and then suddenly he was restless and wanted to get out. Driving anywhere was out of the question, of course, and he was just wondering if he'd be arrested for being drunk in public if he decided to walk to the beach when the phone rang.

Sober, he would have let the machine get it. Halfway drunk, answering it sounded like a good idea, so he did. Not like Chance didn't know who it was; the number on the caller ID showed up as Oceanside Fire Authority.

"What," he snapped into the phone.

"Stormin' off and not lettin' me explain was a shitty thing to do," Tucker said immediately.

"That wasn't the place to discuss it," Chance said, and discovered the half-empty beer he'd left on the table. He downed it right then, not bothering to move the receiver away from his mouth.

"What're you drinkin?," Tucker asked, a note of suspicion creeping in.

"Beer. Bourbon. More beer."

"Great," he muttered. Chance didn't answer, so Tucker kept going. "We'll talk about it tomorrow."

"Maybe," Chance shrugged. "Should give you 'nough time to figure somethin' out." He could hear himself slurring and didn't care.

Tucker sighed heavily into the phone. "Jesus, Cap, it ain't like that." His pager started beeping then, and Chance could hear the faint ding of the alarm behind him. "Fuck," he spat. "Jus' be home in the morning, all right?"

"Maybe," he said again. "'Less there's waves."

Tucker hung up on him.

***

His head hurt when the alarm woke him at seven and he felt slightly nauseous, but he dragged himself out of bed anyway and winced at his reflection in the mirror. Bloodshot eyes and dark circles underneath did not a pretty picture make.

Normally he would have plopped himself right back into bed to nurse his hangover, but he made himself pull on swim trunks and get his board out of the front closet. There was a tiny second when he paused by the front door, wondering if maybe he should just forget his pride and be there when Tucker got home, but then he remembered the sick feeling he'd had when he'd seen Tucker and Chris cozied up together and abandoned that idea.

Chance let the ocean soothe him, in the way it always did. There wasn't anything to think about out there except the water and the security of knowing there was always another wave. He surfed for longer than his usual hour, well past the point when he would usually have gotten tired or cold and headed towards shore.

He was shaking and his fingers were numb by the time he finally gave it up and swam in, not bothering to strip off his wetsuit before strapping down his board to the surf rack on top of his car. He threw down a towel on the front seat and got in, scattering wet sand everywhere, but not caring about anything except getting warm.

He'd at least stopped shivering by the time he got home and he paused before getting out of the car. Tucker's truck was in its usual spot and Chance knew he must have been home for at least an hour, since it was after nine. He wondered how pissed off Tucker was at finding the house empty. Chance hoped the answer was 'a lot'.

He couldn't avoid it forever, despite wanting to, so he steeled himself and headed for the front door with his board tucked protectively under his arm. Shoving open the front door, he went straight to the closet and put his board away, listening to how quiet the place was and assuming Tucker was probably sulking in the bedroom.

Except when Chance turned around, Tucker was leaning against the doorway between the kitchen and the living room, arms crossed and an unreadable expression on his face. "I asked you to be home," he said to Chance quietly, and that was Chance's first clue that Tucker was beyond just pissed off. Tucker was never quiet about anything.

"Good surf," he replied, keeping his tone neutral.

Tucker narrowed his eyes and pushed off from the doorjamb. "I wanna know why you think I'd fuck around on you." Tone a little louder now, and Chance wondered if he was on his way to yelling.

Chance opened his mouth to answer and then closed it again when he realized he had nothing more to go on than the vague, unsettled feeling that had been with him all week. It didn't stop him from recalling how he'd felt when he saw someone else touching Tucker, however, and that just rekindled his anger from last night.

"Saw you both tangled up in each other. Didn't have to think anything, did I?"

The flash of guilt on Tucker's face said more than anything Chance's imagination could have come up with. Chance would have turned away at that point, his stomach hurting, but Tucker stepped forward and laid a hand on his arm. "Okay, yeah. I see how you coulda thought somethin' was goin' on. But I swear, Chance, I don't ever make moves on that guy; he's the one who's always touchin'."

"So you thought hanging out with him behind a closed door was still within our boundaries?" It struck him that he sounded ridiculous; they had no defined boundaries.

Tucker was obviously thinking the same thing, because his brows drew together. "What the hell are our boundaries?"

Another question he didn't know how to answer. Fuck, Chance hated nothing more than being caught unprepared. "I don't know," he snapped. "I guess I was insane to think we sort of had an unspoken agreement not to screw around."

"Fuck you," Tucker retorted immediately. "You can just fuck right off if you seriously think I was messin' around on you. Christ, Chancellor, ain't you gonna give me a little bit of credit?" He shook his head in disgust and folded his arms. "Jesus. So fuckin' sick of takin' blame all the damn time."

Well, now that was something Chance hadn't heard before. "The fuck does that mean?"

"It means you judge first and ask questions later. It means it might be nice if that trust that you're yellin' so hard about was extended to both of us. And maybe that 'unspoken' agreement should get spoken, don'tcha think?"

Chance was hit with two big realizations at once. The first was that Tucker was right; he deserved more credit than Chance was giving him. After all, Chance wasn't so stupid that he didn't know his suspicions had no basis in fact. He never said emotions were logical, after all. That was the main reason he didn't like them.

The second realization was that Tucker was trying to talk to him about exclusivity. Chance couldn't remember them ever discussing it before. Once Tucker had moved in permanently, Chance had just sort of assumed that they weren't fucking around on each other and that their relationship was long-term.

But he knew what people said about assumptions.

"So what's our agreement?" he said before he thought better of it. Statements like that only left him open to vulnerability.

Tucker glared. "Whaddya want it to be?"

Chance blew out an impatient breath. "Tucker. Do you want to play this game, or do you want to settle this?"

"Shoot, Cap, I ain't playin'. I'm sayin' I know what I want, but I ain't the only one who counts around here. Whyn't you tell me what you're thinkin' and we can go from there?" He shrugged and stuck his hands in his back pockets, and Chance was struck by how easy Tucker was making it sound.

He stared at Tucker for a few seconds. Tucker did nothing but arch a brow and stare right back, waiting. "I'm thinking," he started, and then stopped again, turning the words over in his head and wishing he was better at this.

His confusion must have been evident on his face because Tucker stepped forward and rested his hands on Chance's crossed arms. "It don't gotta be this hard, baby," he murmured, and the blue in his eyes reminded Chance of rain. "You just gotta say what you want."

"I want you," he said in a rush, afraid to say it, but more afraid of what would happen if he never did. "I don't want there to be anyone else. I don't want anyone touching you and I want anyone who tries to put their hands on you to know that you belong to me. That's what I want." Chance had to look away from Tucker's steady gaze and concentrated on the front of his t-shirt instead, worrying at the edge of his bottom lip with his teeth.

Tucker's eyes darkened and one dimple made a fleeting appearance. "There you go," he whispered, leaning in for a kiss. "Ain't so tough to say, is it?"

Fireline

He almost forgot what they were talking about in favor of wrapping tight arms around Tucker and kissing the man, but then Chance realized he'd been the only one to say anything. "Hey," he mused, pulling back. "What about you?"

Tucker grinned, slow and lazy. "You ain't figured that out by now?"

"I had to say it," Chance reminded him.

"Okay," Tucker said, and his look turned smoky. "I want you. I wanna come home to you and know you're waitin'. I don't want you to ever want anyone else but me. I wanna know I ain't ever gotta worry about where I lay my head or who I'm layin' next to, because I want it to be with you." He brought up a hand and curled it around Chance's neck, tugging Chance forward until their foreheads touched. "And I want somethin' that reminds me of that every day."

Chance blinked. "Like what?" God, he hoped Tucker didn't mean rings. They couldn't wear them at work anyway. Plus, just saying the word "ring" was hard enough, never mind actually wearing one.

Tucker caught the look Chance had made at his hand and rolled his eyes. "Please. Do I look like the jewelry-wearin' type to you?" He snorted in disgust and Chance laughed.

"Okay, yeah. But I know you're thinking something, you have that expression on your face that I don't usually like." Chance studied Tucker with a practiced eye.

"Lemme make a phone call," Tucker said suddenly, breaking away and heading toward the bedroom. "Stay here."

Chance obeyed, if only because he realized his hangover had disappeared and he was famished. "Can I make breakfast?"

"Whatever," Tucker's voice came floating down the hall. "I need five minutes."

An hour later saw them both showered, shaved, stomachs full, and in the front seat of Tucker's truck. "Now, will you tell me?" Chance asked, growing warier by the minute.

"You just hang on a bit and then you'll know." It was all Tucker would answer in response to Chance's questions.

Chance finally just shut up and stared out the window at the familiar streets they were navigating. At least it was somewhere in town; Tucker didn't seem to be headed toward the freeway. Chance watched as they passed restaurants and strip malls and finally pulled in to the small shopping center where he usually went to get

Smokey's cat food. "Here?" he asked doubtfully, his eyes passing over the pet store, the bookstore, the tattoo place, the pharmacy, the … oh, wait.

His gaze darted back to the tat shop and then to Tucker, who sat grinning at him and tapping the steering wheel. "Let's go."

"You want me to get ink?"

"I want us to get ink."

Chance frowned and looked at the shop again. Chance knew Tucker had a guy there who had shaded in the tattoo he'd gotten back in Kentucky. Chance had just never considered getting one of his own before. The idea actually didn't sound unappealing, though, especially if it was something symbolic that he and Tucker were sharing. "Okay," he said quietly, not missing the significance of the whole thing. "Let's get ink."

***

It hadn't hurt in the way he'd expected it to. There was a stinging burn while Tucker's guy – Diego, his name was – had outlined the Maltese cross in black ink on Chance's bicep, and then a sharper, longer sting when he'd shaded it in, but all in all it had been a tolerable sort of pain.

Tucker sat down next, laughing and joking with Diego, and Chance had watched while Diego had made one small adjustment to the tattoo Tucker already sported. The fireman's helmet in the middle of his cross now bore the initial "C" across the front, nearly identical to the "T" on the helmet of Chance's matching tattoo.

He looked at it again in the bathroom mirror, lifting up the edge of the plastic wrap that had been taped over it to see the detail of the design.

"Don't touch that."

Chance glanced up in the mirror to see Tucker leaning in the doorway of the bathroom, watching. "You took yours off already," he pointed out.

"Mine ain't got as much skin that needs to heal. You can take it off before bed." He came in and stood behind Chance, resting his chin on Chance's shoulder and meeting Chance's eyes in the reflection. "So whaddya think?"

"I think I like it," he said softly, leaning his head against Tucker's. "It's sort of … permanent." Except there was no 'sort of' about it, and that was the part he liked.

Fireline

Tucker nodded. "That was the idea."

They looked at each other for a long time in the mirror, Tucker's arms hooked around Chance's waist, until Chance turned his head to kiss him. "I know I was a dick," Chance murmured against Tucker's mouth, but Tucker shook his head and didn't let him say anything else.

They stood in the same position for long minutes until Chance felt Tucker grow hard against his ass. He shifted slightly in Tucker's embrace, meaning to turn and face him, but Tucker tightened his arms. "No," he whispered to Chance. "Stay this way. Watch in the mirror."

Chance felt his cheeks heat immediately. "Aw, come on."

"For me," Tucker said, and damn if he didn't know just what to say to make Chance obey his every wish.

It didn't take much more than unzipping two sets of shorts before Tucker was reaching over to the medicine cabinet for the lube and sliding wet fingers into Chance. Chance would have closed his eyes then to savor the feel, but Tucker squeezed one hand around his cock and said, "No, look. I want you to look."

So Chance looked, the last of the embarrassment fading away as he felt Tucker line himself up without ever breaking his gaze in the mirror. Their eyes stayed locked as Tucker eased in to the hilt, one hand on Chance's waist and the other making perfect strokes on his cock. "Us," Chance whispered, darting a fast glance down to the fresh ink on his arm and back up. "You and me. Just us."

"Just us," Tucker repeated, pulling out with a sigh and then gliding back in. "Just us, always. Promise."

"Promise."

Chance felt as if he was floating and grounded at the same time. Tucker's eyes in the mirror kept him rooted where he was, but the hand on his cock and the small brushes over his gland were sending him soaring. He would have likened it to finding the perfect wave, but there really was nothing else that compared to how he felt when he and Tucker were connecting on more than a physical level.

Tucker's teeth were against Chance's neck then, eyes still holding Chance's in the mirror as he sucked up a bite and brought dark blood to the surface of the thin skin. Chance knew Tucker was leaving another mark, not as permanent as the one on his arm, but a sign of possession nonetheless, and Chance felt the muscles in his thighs begin to tremble with the strain of holding off his orgasm. "Tucker," Chance said by way of warning, hands gripping the countertop, knowing if Tucker had a mind to do it, he could keep Chance on the edge for hours.

The hand on his cock sped up, teasing with nimble fingers at the head and tracing the heavy underside while Chance fought to keep his eyes from closing. "You're gonna look," Tucker murmured to him. "I wanna see you when you come."

Chance could only nod and suck his bottom lip into his mouth, biting down hard enough to bloody it and straining for the release that Tucker wouldn't let him have until Tucker was good and ready. Tucker's hand was tight around his cock and Chance jerked into his fist, feeling the push and pull behind him start to get a little shaky.

He wouldn't have thought that watching himself would be so hot, but now that Tucker had made him look, he couldn't tear his gaze away. Chance noted how their muscles flexed and stretched against each other and he started to see details of his own body that he normally never looked at. The way his tan contrasted with the skin below his bathing suit line. How he grew taut whenever Tucker's fingers tightened on him. It was an experience Chance hadn't had before, one he'd never considered as erotic, and he filed it away to remember for later.

It only took one more sweet tug on his dick and Chance was coming, hard and messy against the countertop, Tucker's name on his lips and a hot stare burning into him in their reflection. Chance ran a finger through his own come pooling on the sink and lifted it behind him, to Tucker's mouth.

The instant Tucker darted out a tongue to catch the taste, Chance felt him freeze and suck in a breath. "Oh, goddamn," he groaned, and then Tucker was trembling and gasping and coming hard enough to make him lean a hand over on the counter for support.

They traded kisses and touches and whispers while they cleaned up, and that night after dinner, Tucker took him back into the bathroom and carefully peeled off the bandage over his tattoo. Chance watched silently as Tucker used gentle fingers to put ointment on the ink, pressing a kiss to Chance's shoulder when he was finished.

"Just us, always," Tucker said again, repeating their words from earlier. "Promise."

"Promise," Chance whispered, watching him in the mirror. "Always."

Fireline

Chapter Five

Their daily routine was constant for a while. Chance had settled into it so well that he didn't realize how much he appreciated the monotony until something disrupted it. His first clue that their relatively calm life was about to change came one night while he was at work, about five seconds after Tucker showed up at Eleven looking for him.

He'd been studying the day's call printouts, getting them ready to be sent to headquarters, and he was about to check the computer to see if he'd been scheduled for any overtime for the month. Then Jim, the other paramedic, had paged him to the front.

Chance wandered out to the kitchen and raised his eyebrows at Jim in a question. Jim nodded toward the row of reclining chairs in front of the TV, and Chance smiled to himself when he saw the back of Tucker's dark head. "He all right?" Jim asked.

Chance's grin faded. "Why wouldn't he be?"

Jim shrugged. "Didn't say much when he came in. Asked for you and then sat his ass down."

Chance knew that his crew was aware of his relationship with Tucker. While he wouldn't call them gay-friendly – the fire department was kind of like the military in that regard – Chance would go so far as to say that most of them were tolerant. He could live with tolerant. Chance did his job, Tucker did the same, and they kept their private lives just that: private.

So he didn't feel weird when he motioned toward the door with his head, silently asking Jim for some privacy. Jim nodded once and left. Chance knew he'd keep the other guys out as long as he could.

He approached cautiously, crouching down in front of Tucker. Tucker sat forward in his chair, elbows on his knees, staring at the floor. "Hey," Chance said softly. "You paying a social call, or did you want another blow job in my bunk?"

It had been risky and stupid and so, so hot. They'd screwed around plenty at work before Chance had been promoted, but Chance had put a moratorium on it after he took the captain's position. It had been easy enough to stop since they were no longer at the same station, but once in a while Tucker appeared at Eleven during A shift to see if he could sweet talk Chance into anything. Last time, it had worked.

Tucker managed a faint smile and then it was gone, barely brushing his lips before vanishing. Chance grew slightly more alarmed, but he waited.

Tucker took a breath as if he was about to speak, then exhaled and shook his head. Mutely, he looked at Chance. The despair in his eyes was frightening, and Chance's unease grew to full-fledged fear. "Tucker," he said, placing a hand on Tucker's arm, "you gotta tell me. You're scaring the shit out of me."

Tucker swallowed and nodded. "Yeah, sorry. Still tryin' to wrap my mind around it. Um, Tim died."

Chance's brow furrowed. "Tim. Your uncle Tim?"

"Daddy's brother, yeah."

Chance thought for a minute. There was no love lost between Tucker and his uncle; Tim had made a few incestuous grabs at Tucker when he'd been a teenager, after his father died. He'd been the reason for Tucker leaving his family's farm at eighteen and then eventually getting out of Kentucky altogether. Tucker rarely spoke of him, or about his home in general. Chance had a feeling there was a lot more to it than what Tucker had chosen to tell him, but he'd never pushed, and Tucker had never 'fessed up.

"Okay," Chance said slowly, still unsure of why Tucker looked so bleak. "You get the call today?"

"Hour ago," Tucker confirmed. "Chance … it was some attorney. The farm belongs to me. It's always belonged to me, ever since Momma died. I never knew it. She told me she'd changed the will after Daddy died to make Tim the beneficiary, and I didn't give a shit because by then I hated that fuckin' farm. All I wanted was to get the fuck away from him. I guess she changed it back. She wouldn't have told me because she knew I'd have given her hell." He paused, twisted his fingers together. "I gotta go there."

"So Tim knew that the farm didn't belong to him this whole time? And he never tried to get in touch with you?" Chance suddenly had a thousand questions that Tucker probably wasn't ready to answer.

"Why would he? So I could come home and run him off? The lawyer said that he had my address and everything on file from Momma and he had no idea I didn't know about the farm. Tim told everyone that I'd taken off, which was true. And that I'd told him to handle everything, which wasn't true." He shook his head, pressed his lips together. "And now I gotta fuckin' go back there. Gotta take care of a mess of shit."

"I'm going with you," Chance said immediately.

Tucker smiled half-heartedly. "Y'can't. Probation, remember?"

Fuck. Tucker was right. There was a probationary period of one year for all newly appointed captains, and taking vacation time was definitely not a good idea. Chance cursed softly. "For how long?"

He shrugged. "Dunno. A month? Six weeks? Hafta figure out what the fuck to do with the goddamned place. Oh, Jesus, Chance, I don't wanna go back there, it took me for fuckin' ever just to get outta there and I can't – " He stopped short as Jim and Chance's engineer, Trey, came in, talking loudly. Jim threw Chance an apologetic look and Chance knew he'd tried to stay out as long as he could.

"Outside," he said to Tucker firmly, and tugged on his arm. Tucker rose obediently and stuck close as Chance led him out the door. Chance could practically feel him vibrating with anxiety.

They crossed the lot to Tucker's truck. He had backed into a parking space, so when Chance opened the driver's door, they were mostly hidden from view behind it. Tucker sat sideways behind the wheel; his feet on the running board, and Chance fit himself into the vee of Tucker's legs. Resting his forehead against Tucker's, Chance blessed the early fall darkness.

"It's all right," he murmured. "We'll work it out. Figure out what to do."

Tucker drew a shaky breath. "Don't think there's a 'we' this time, baby. I gotta go alone, gotta deal with it." He was twitching visibly, fingers drumming on his thighs.

Chance studied him for a moment. "Maybe not a 'we'," he said, "but there's still an 'us'. Don't forget that." He leaned in and kissed Tucker hard, not caring if they were at work. The only thing that mattered was calming him down enough so Tucker could drive home, and they'd work out the details in the morning.

But Chance hadn't expected Tucker to grip Chance's shirt in one hand and his belt in the other. Tucker hauled Chance up against him and started kissing Chance back desperately. He darted his tongue into Chance's mouth and then pulled away, breathing hard, fingers still fisted in Chance's department sweatshirt. "Don't wanna go," he whispered.

"I know," Chance answered, his chest feeling tight.

Tucker pulled him down again, kissing him with urgency. "Don't wanna go," he repeated, lips moving against Chance's. "Wanna stay here with you."

"Hey," Chance said, smoothing his hair off his forehead. "You have to calm down. I can't let you drive home like this."

"Worked up," Tucker said, and swallowed hard. "See?" He took Chance's hand and dragged it down to his crotch. Sure enough, he was stiff in his jeans.

Chance shook his head. "How do you do that?"

"It's a gift," Tucker answered, still breathing heavily.

Against his better judgment, Chance squeezed, making Tucker's head go back and eyes close. "This is the wrong place," Chance whispered.

"God, I know," Tucker groaned. "Come on, do it again. Please."

Chance darted a look toward the back door of the station and the row of kitchen windows that faced the parking lot. "You better keep an eye out," he muttered, and jerked open the button fly on Tucker's jeans.

Praying they wouldn't get a call, hoping against hope there were no fires, medical emergencies, or car accidents in the next two minutes, Chance reached in and drew out Tucker's cock. With a lick to his palm and the backs of his fingers brushing Tucker's stomach, Chance stroked him firmly.

Tucker leaned back on one hand and pushed his hips forward into Chance's grip, keeping his head turned toward the firehouse, although his eyes fluttered closed.

Chance swore under his breath and turned to watch the door, since Tucker obviously couldn't do it, and started pumping him with short, tight strokes.

Tucker put a hand on Chance's, gasping, and Chance felt his cock twitch and the resulting wet warmth. Tucker shuddered through it, gripping Chance's wrist while Chance milked him.

He lay back on the seat, dick softening against his abdomen, and reached over his head toward the glove box. Finding leftover napkins from the drive-through, Tucker sat back up and handed one to Chance.

Chance wiped the come from his hand, but when Tucker looked at him, he raised a finger to his mouth and licked. Tucker groaned. "You keep doin' that and I'll fuck you in the bed of this truck, Cap."

Fireline

Chance's cock leapt in his pants, but he gave it a firm mental 'no'. He let Tucker clean himself up a little before putting a finger under his chin and forcing him to meet his gaze. His eyes were still troubled, but clearer than they had been a few minutes ago.

"Better?" Chance asked, wishing they were at home.

Tucker took a deep breath and nodded. "Better. Thanks."

"Want to stay a while? There's peanut-butter-cup ice cream in the freezer."

"Nah, it's good. I'm good. Just … call me later, willya?" He sounded embarrassed to ask and Chance knew he didn't like the vulnerability. Neither of them was big on expressing emotion, which wasn't always to their advantage, or hadn't been during the course of their relationship.

But they were learning.

***

Chance found Tucker awake and staring at the ceiling the next morning. It was rare that he was up when Chance came in; he was a late sleeper on his days off. "Did you sleep?" Chance asked, shucking his clothes and crawling into bed.

"Yeah," Tucker said, but when Chance poked him in the ribs, he sighed. "No."

"Did you make arrangements?"

"Yeah. Put my days off work in the computer system, called the airlines. Flight out tomorrow. Cost a fuckin' fortune."

Chance's stomach dropped. "Tomorrow? Already?"

Tucker turned to his side and flung an arm and leg over Chance, burrowing his face into Chance's neck. "Sooner I go, sooner I can come back."

Chance closed his eyes. It was the 'coming back' part that was bothering him. "Tuck," he started, mentally kicking himself, "maybe you shouldn't."

"Shouldn't what? Go?" Tucker raised his head and looked at Chance.

Chance steeled himself. "No. I mean maybe you shouldn't rush back. Maybe you should stay for a while, see what you can do about getting the farm back together."

Tucker stared at him. "I'm not puttin' the goddamned farm back together. I'm sellin' the fuckin' thing and gettin' the hell out."

"You don't have to sell it. You lived there, you know what it takes to get it on its feet. Then you can find people to run it for you and come back here, yeah?" Chance hated saying it; hated to suggest anything that was going to keep Tucker from him longer than necessary, but he'd thought about it a lot during the night.

"You don't get it," Tucker said, his voice flinty. He sat up and flung the sheet aside, climbing out of bed. "I don't want anything to do with that fuckin' place, Chancellor." He jerked on a pair of sweatpants and t-shirt and grabbed his running shoes.

"Hey," Chance said, about to go after him, but Tucker turned around in the doorway and pointed a finger at Chance.

"Let it go," he bit out, and was gone.

***

Tucker stayed out all morning, and when he finally reappeared just after noon, Chance had paced a groove into the carpet.

He watched from the couch, nibbling on the side of his thumbnail as Smokey greeted Tucker at the door with a soft, purring meow. Tucker leaned down to chuck the cat under the chin before raising his eyes to Chance. Dropping his keys on the small table by the door, he approached the sofa and ran an impatient hand through his hair.

"I'm sorry – "

"I didn't mean – "

They stopped and grinned sheepishly at each other. Chance lifted his arm and Tucker dropped down next to him, curling into his side with a sigh. "Shouldn'ta taken off. Sorry."

"Shouldn't have pushed," Chance replied. "You'll figure out what to do."

Tucker didn't answer.

Chapter Six

The leaving part was more than Chance had bargained for.

He knew it would be hard to watch Tucker pack his suitcase. Knew it would be hard to see him take all his warmest shirts and sweaters out of his drawers and dig through the back of the closet for his old winter clothes. And Chance knew it would be really, really hard to watch him clear off the bathroom counter, putting his toothbrush and shaving kit in his backpack.

But when Tucker went to Chance's dresser and pulled out Chance's favorite, faded department sweatshirt, asking a silent question, Chance found himself dangerously close to losing it.

He nodded once, giving permission, but had to turn away when Tucker went to put it in the suitcase. Chance stretched out on his stomach on the bed, hugging a pillow to his chest and facing the headboard. He didn't say anything when Tucker crawled onto the bed and draped himself over Chance's back, burrowing into the hollow between Chance's neck and shoulder.

Chance turned in his embrace and enfolded him. He hooked an ankle over Tucker's calf and slid an arm beneath Tucker's shirt, spanning warm skin with his hand, letting Tucker work both arms under Chance's shoulders to gather him close. There were no words that Chance could find, so he didn't try, and the bedroom was quiet for a long time.

When they started moving together, it was unspoken and perfectly in sync. Their bodies lined up out of habit and want and it didn't matter which was which. The foot that Chance had hooked around Tucker's ankle kept him in place until Tucker squirmed and whispered, "Clothes. Can't get 'em off if you don't let me up."

Chance let him go only for the time it took to leave their shirts and sweats in a pile on the floor. He urged Tucker back on top, tangling a hand in that silky hair and angling Tucker's head so he could suck up a mark on Tucker's neck. He bit and nuzzled at the spot, knowing it would leave an angry-looking hickey for at least three days, but maybe that was his intent. To mark and claim and give Tucker something to look at in the mirror.

It was an unexpected turn-on, zinging right to his cock. They'd both been half-hard as they kissed, but now Chance felt himself swell to an almost painful erection, the need unfurling low in his belly. "Want you," he breathed against Tucker's neck, soothing the brand he'd made. "Always want you."

Tucker nodded, arms tightening around Chance, answering him. "How?"

"Ride me," Chance said, and then arched his neck when Tucker ground down on him. "Or you could just do that."

"Would rather feel you," Tucker whispered, already climbing over him to the nightstand drawer, searching for lube. He came back in a second, covering Chance again, sliding down, and all Chance could think when Tucker started stroking was "now" and "need" and "Tucker."

Tucker took his time with the lube, using too much and slicking it everywhere until Chance thought he'd go crazy with the firm stroking. "God, come on," he finally moaned, Tucker's answering grin his reward.

"Sometimes I want you to ask," Tucker said, rising to his knees and using still more lube to coat his own fingers.

Chance watched as Tucker reached behind and teased himself, widening his legs and inserting a finger with a soft "Yeah." Chance nearly stopped breathing when Tucker's eyes closed and he began fucking himself on his hand.

Chance almost didn't realize he'd been pulling on his cock until his balls tightened, giving him warning. Chance squeezed tightly at the base, one hand going out to grab Tucker's thigh and draw his attention. "You gonna finish on your fingers, or on me?"

Tucker's eyes flew open and Chance drew a breath at the glittering need in them. Kneeling over him, strong thighs around Chance's waist, Tucker lowered himself carefully onto Chance's straining dick until he was nearly sitting.

"Ah," they both exhaled together, and Tucker started to move. Up, down, and around, the same pattern over and over until Chance was tossing his head back and forth on the pillow, sweat beading on his forehead. Chance drew up his legs and planted his feet firmly on the mattress, angling his hips to drive upward, and Tucker hissed "Christ," between gritted teeth.

All the slick tightness around his cock made Chance whimper, despite pulling his lower lip into his mouth. It was an easy matter of reaching out to touch the tip of Tucker's prick, so hard it was nearly reaching his stomach, and then Tucker was coming, spunk falling in hot splashes over Chance's abdomen.

The convulsing warmth around his dick was enough to set Chance off. He thrust up once more and froze, a full-body shudder starting in his legs and moving upward, making him clench his fingers helplessly at Tucker's hips as they both trembled.

They were sweaty and sticky and tangled up and neither of them made any effort to move at all. Chance sort of hoped that if they stayed really still, tomorrow wouldn't come, and Tucker wouldn't have to go. Then he remembered that he was thirty-seven years old, not twelve, and gave up the childish wish.

"Gonna miss you," Tucker whispered some time later, after they'd disentangled just enough to lay side by side, arms still wrapped around each other.

Chance nodded, not able to meet his eyes. "Not forever. Just a month or so, yeah?"

"I hope. Yeah."

***

The airport didn't allow for emotional goodbyes, fortunately. Too many people, too much bustle. Security measures didn't even let Chance accompany Tucker to the gate, so they stood on the curb together and Tucker flung his backpack over his left shoulder.

"I'll call you as soon as I get in," Tucker said, studying his fingernails. "Should be about seven your time, I think."

"You renting a car?"

He shook his head. "Naw. That lawyer – Jackson or somethin' – s'gonna meet me. Farm should have a truck or two I can use while I'm there."

Chance nodded and swallowed, trying to find the willpower to just turn around and get in his car. He glanced up, ready to say goodbye, and then Tucker was dropping his backpack to the ground and wrapping an arm around Chance's neck.

Chance clutched Tucker back, squeezing his eyes shut and breathing in. They stood for a minute, oblivious to the people rushing past them, and Chance tried to memorize the feel of Tucker under his hands. It was difficult to come to terms with the fact that Chance had no idea when he'd be able to touch him again.

"God, I really don't wanna do this," Tucker mumbled into his neck.

"Listen," Chance said, holding Tucker's head in his hands and forcing their gazes to meet. "If you need me, you tell me. Fuck probation, fuck everything. If you need me, *you tell me.*"

Tucker opened his mouth to argue, but Chance gave a firm shake of the head, so he closed it again and simply nodded. "Got it."

Chance stepped back, shoving his hands in his pockets. "Safe trip, man."

Tucker gave Chance a halfhearted grin and picked up his bags. "Thanks, Cap."

***

The phone rang at five minutes past seven and Chance pounced on it, snatching the receiver from the cradle and startling Smokey out of a sound catnap. The caller ID identified it as Tucker's cell, but Chance would have known who it was anyway.

"Hey," he said, muting the TV.

"Hey," Tucker answered, and maybe it was the bad connection, but Chance thought he could hear defeat in that voice. "So I'm here."

"Flight was okay?"

"I guess."

He paused before asking, "What kind of shape is the place in?"

"Can't tell yet. Was dark. House looks all right, though. And there's a couple hands still here from when Daddy was alive, ones I used to trust. Talk to them in the morning." He yawned loud enough for it to carry through the phone.

"Go to bed," Chance ordered. "And call me at work tomorrow night."

"Bossy," Tucker said fondly, and it warmed Chance to hear the familiar joking tone.

"Just go," he replied, his voice gentle.

"Night," Tucker said, and then he was gone, and Chance was left with the dial tone loud in his ear.

It was only seven, too early for bed, and he'd already eaten dinner. He called Bonnie.

"Hey, Bon," he greeted her when she answered.

"Chancey," she said warmly. "What's up? Tucker working?"

He sighed. "Not really. Wanna come over?"

Her voice turned suspicious. "Are you fighting?"

Chance laughed. "No. If you come over, I'll tell you. I have ice cream."

"Oh, honey. Normally you know I wouldn't turn down ice cream, but Matt's taking me to dinner. Two-month anniversary." She sounded apologetic, but not about to break her date.

Chance had introduced Bonnie to Matt Perkins three months ago. Matt had been Chance's old captain at Station Eleven, someone Chance liked and respected, and the one who had encouraged Chance to take the captaincy exam. Matt and Bonnie had both attended Chance's badge-pinning ceremony, and two weeks later, Matt had asked Chance for her phone number. They'd been dating ever since, and from what Chance could tell, were getting along well. For the most part, Chance tried to stay out of it.

He grinned into the phone. "Oh, fine. Do your dating thing, or whatever you straight people do. Leave me alone to wallow."

"You don't impress me with dramatics, Chancellor," Bonnie said, and hung up on him.

The call improved his mood enough to turn on his stereo and drag his surfboard out of the front closet. Coating it with wax, he hummed along under his breath to the music during two rounds of polishing before realizing he'd been listening to Tucker's radio station. They'd had arguments about it before – Chance preferred alternative music or classic rock, while Tucker liked the twangier sound of southern rock. On the worst days, he'd listen to country music and laugh when Chance turned green.

"Takes me back to my roots," he'd say. "Didn't grow up listenin' to nothin' but Merle Haggard and Willie Nelson."

"So now's the time to improve your tastes," Chance would retort, but Tucker just grinned at him.

"Can take the boy outta the country, but can't take the country outta the boy. And I'd say I have damn good taste. You're here, ain'tcha?"

The discussions usually ended in simultaneous orgasms, so Chance was able to let it go. He smiled ruefully at himself now, not even having realized he knew the fucking words to the stupid songs. Tears and beers and broken hearts, whatever.

Chance finished waxing both his own board and Tucker's and was pondering doing the dishes in the sink before he realized he was putting off going to bed.

Not like he'd never slept alone. But for more than a year now, there had been Tucker, and tonight … well, tonight there wasn't.

The bed was emptier than he'd thought it would be.

Fireline

Chapter Seven

The first week found them talking to each other on the phone every day, sometimes more than once. Tucker usually called around eight p.m., California time, on Chance's days off. If he was working, Chance made sure he found a minute to call Tucker's cell to at least say good night.

Tucker sounded okay, as far as Chance could tell. It was difficult to get any information out of him. Tucker seemed determined to remain vague about what was happening on the farm despite Chance's pointed questioning.

"Jus' tryin' to get shit in order," he said on the fifth night he'd been gone.

Chance took a pull on his beer and propped his feet on the coffee table. "What kind of shit?" It was the same conversation they'd had for five nights.

"There's some legal issues."

That was new. "Yeah? Like what?"

"Like the fuckin' fact that Momma never legally put the farm in my name, even though she stated in her will that it should go to me." His voice was flat.

"So that means …?"

Tucker heaved an exasperated sigh, but Chance knew it wasn't directed at him. "It means it's gotta go through probate if I wanna sell it. And that could be, fuck. A long fuckin' time."

Chance sunk down and rested his head on the back of the sofa, staring at the ceiling. He traced the lip of his bottle with a finger. "Can you come home while all the legal shit's being sorted? And a realtor should be able to handle the sale. You don't have to be there."

"Depends how long probate is. If I can get everything straight around here, then yeah, I can come home. Jus' don't wanna get stuck flyin' back and forth, you know? Wanna make sure that when I come home to you, I'm stayin'." His tone was low and wistful and it went, unexpectedly, right to Chance's dick.

He shifted, trying to get more comfortable, plucking at the fleece of his sweats where it pulled over his crotch. "You in bed?" he asked, knowing it was nearly midnight there.

"Yup," Tucker confirmed. "Been sleepin' in one of the guest rooms. Didn't want to sleep in my old room. Too weird."

Chance reached over to the side table and clicked the light off, leaving the room in darkness except for the glow from the television. "What about the master bedroom? Gotta be bigger than the guest room."

Tucker was quiet for a minute. "Couldn't sleep in that bed," he finally said, and Chance felt a pang of guilt.

Chance was again struck by the fact that there was probably stuff he didn't know about what had happened while Tucker was growing up. He hadn't meant to bring up the past, however unintentionally. Tim had been the last one to sleep there and naturally Tucker wanted to avoid it. "Sorry," Chance said softly. "Forgot."

Tucker sighed. "It'd be okay if you were here. But I'm alone and it's weird. I just ain't used to sleepin' by myself if I ain't at work."

It was the same for Chance. If he wasn't working, Tucker should be sleeping next to him, easy as that. This separation thing was hard on both of them.

The fact that they were only at the beginning of it was making Chance's head hurt. He wasn't concerned for their relationship itself; after their breakup and then reconciliation earlier in the year, Chance knew they were pretty solid in that area. Matching tattoos had sealed that deal. It was just the unknown that was getting to him. He couldn't even picture the room in which Tucker was lying, since he'd never seen it, and Tucker had been so closemouthed about anything regarding the farm.

"So," Chance said slowly, cock still hard in his sweats, "you're in bed? Naked?"

He could practically hear Tucker's answering grin. "Too cold for that. This ain't California."

"What, there's no heat in that house?"

He laughed. "Oh, baby, no way. This farmhouse is near ninety years old; ain't no central heat or air or nothin'. Fireplaces keep the downstairs warm durin' the day, but at night you gotta use blankets."

Chance grimaced. "I'd hate it."

"Yeah, you would. You got that thin California blood."

He tried again. "What if I asked you nicely to get naked?"

The blankets rustled as Tucker shifted around. "Can't resist ya when you talk nice."

"There you go. Took you long enough."

"Dreamed of you last night," Tucker murmured.

Chance closed his eyes and flattened his palm against his dick through his sweats. A quick downward rub, coupled with the soft sigh Tucker made through the phone, sent him from three-quarters to full mast. "Tell me."

"Had a goddamn wet dream, if you can believe that." Tucker chuckled. "Guess you're never too old for that shit."

Chance groaned. For some reason, the visual sent a message straight to his sense-memory, and he was hit with the scent of Tucker's come. Spicy, warm, the barest hint of sweetness. "Tell me," he managed again. He pushed down the waistband of his pants and drew out his cock, heavy and hard in his own hand.

"I was suckin' you off," Tucker said, and he sounded distant as he remembered. "And I was just so horny, my God, all I wanted to do was just lay you down and rub off all over you."

Chance licked his palm and wrapped his fingers around his prick. He stroked slowly, wanting it to go on and on, listening to Tucker's soft words. "What did I do?"

"Oh, you were takin' it so nice," he answered, his breathing changing just the slightest bit. "Head back against the wall, mouth open, hands in my hair. So pretty." Chance heard him change the phone to the other ear and settle down into the bed.

"You jerking off?"

"In my dream, or now?" He was smiling, Chance could hear it.

"Now."

"What do you think?"

"I think yeah," Chance said, his hand speeding up the smallest bit, squeezing at the head and running a thumb through the moisture gathering there. "I think you're holding your balls in your left hand and stroking yourself with the other."

"Both right." A little more strained.

"And you want to come," he continued. "Like, you could come right now if I told you to, right?"

"Maybe."

"Don't."

He heard Tucker huff in frustration. "Bossy."

"Just listen, I'll make it worth it." Chance licked dry lips, hoping he could follow his own orders and not shoot everywhere. "Listening?"

"Yeah," Tucker panted, and Chance knew he was probably trembling with the effort.

"I'm gonna fuck you," he said, "and I'm gonna tell you about every single detail of it." His cock was *aching* now, so hard that Chance was afraid to keep stroking for fear that he wouldn't last. He held himself tightly instead, clamping down on the urge to just jack himself roughly until he spilled all over his hand. He tried to focus on what he was saying and not the deep breaths he could hear Tucker taking.

"God," Tucker groaned. "Can't do it, can't."

"Listen," Chance murmured to him gently. "You're stretched out on your stomach, right? And I've been rimming you. Your hole's all wet and open and slick with my spit. Sometimes a finger, sometimes my tongue, back and forth. Feel it?"

Tucker's muffled whimper was all the 'yes' he could manage.

"I want to get my dick in there so bad," Chance whispered. "And you're being all slutty and wanton, sticking your ass practically in my face." He took a risk and chanced a single stroke on his cock, gritting his teeth against the sudden, sharp pleasure.

"Chance," Tucker begged, "I gotta come, please. Please."

"Wait," Chance said sharply. "One more minute. Okay? Can you?"

"Tryin'."

"Okay. So I'm sliding over you, using your hair to pull your head back so I can suck a nice fat hickey into the skin on your neck." Chance gave up and started pulling his dick, clenching his ass on each tight upstroke. "And now I'm using too much lube so I can just slide in. You're so ready, Tuck, I don't even have to push; I can just slip right inside."

"Put your hand under me on the bed," Tucker groaned. "Jerk me off while you fuck me."

"What else," Chance answered, his voice thready.

"Do it slow. Like we can fuck all night, like we don't give a shit about anything. Slow, Chance, 'cause it's just us and no one else."

Damn. He hadn't taken into account how the raw need in Tucker's voice would affect him. Chance drew a shaky breath and knew that neither of them was in a position for this to continue. "You want to come?" he asked, knowing the answer.

Fireline

"The fuck do you think?"

"Tell me," he whispered, feeling his own orgasm build. The base of his spine was tingling and his toes were curling into the carpet.

"Let me come," Tucker nearly sobbed. "God. And you too, come with me so I ain't by myself."

It was a poignant request and touched something inside him, something he shoved away to examine later. "Go," he managed, giving himself permission at the same time. He managed two more strokes before it hit, leaving him a trembling mess with his come warm on his stomach.

Tucker was groaning on the other end, the relief evident. He fell silent after a minute, though Chance could hear him moving around, and Chance pictured him cleaning himself up.

He stripped off his sweats and used them to wipe up the mess on his stomach before getting off the couch and padding naked through the kitchen. Dropping his pants on the washing machine as he passed, he headed down the dark hall to the bedroom and crawled into bed. By the time he got there, Tucker's breathing had returned to normal. "Y'okay?" Chance asked.

"Better now," he answered with a yawn.

"Go to bed."

"Will. Hey," Tucker said suddenly. "Wait."

"Yeah?"

"I, um. Naw, nothin'." He sounded sheepish and bashful, two rare traits.

"You sure?" Chance didn't want to let him go; the loneliness was sure to be even more oppressive once Tucker hung up.

"I just. Love you, yeah? Night."

Chance smiled. They didn't say it that often. Neither of them was big on emotional displays. "Yeah. Same. Night."

Chapter Eight

The first time that more than a day passed where he didn't talk to Tucker, Chance didn't think much of it.

He had picked up an overtime spot and ended up working a seventy-two hour shift, which exhausted him. A small house fire, numerous car accidents, and a four-year-old girl sticking a fork in an outlet had kept them up nights. He had probably gotten a collective total of twelve hours of sleep for the entire three days.

It occurred to him as he sat at the breakfast table, waiting for his relief to show up, that he hadn't checked his voice mail. Chance pulled out his cell and looked at the display, only mildly curious when he realized there were no messages.

"The boy check in?" Jim asked from over his shoulder.

Chance shrugged and accepted the cup of fresh coffee Jim handed him. "Nah. He might have called the station, though, not my cell. We were too busy to answer the phone."

Jim yawned and nodded. "True enough."

It was true – they'd been crazy-busy for three straight days – but it niggled at him that he had no missed calls on his cell, nor any messages on the station's answering machine in his office.

Chance brushed it off as he drove home, his thoughts only on giving Smokey a scratch behind the ears and collapsing into bed. He'd call Tucker just as soon as he got some sleep.

***

He woke around one and lay there groggily for a while, feeling the cat against his back and hating the work shifts that knocked him out like this. It was a waste of a perfectly good day that he could have spent at the beach; the surf report last night had predicted three to four foot swells.

Chance was nearly asleep again when the phone startled him and he snatched it off the nightstand. "Hey," he greeted, sure it was Tucker without checking the caller ID.

"Dinner at my house Friday," Bonnie announced. "And hello. Are you finally home?"

Not Tucker. The disappointment was sharp. "Obviously I'm home. And what kind of dinner? You and me dinner or dinner where I have to wear nice clothes?"

"Dinner like with firefighter-type people. Matt says he has friends he wants me to meet. What's that about? I don't need to meet his friends." She sounded irritated and nervous at the same time.

Chance snorted. "You'll be fine. Do I have to come?"

"What the hell else are you going to do? Sit around and moon over your long-lost boyfriend?"

Point. "All right, whatever. Count me in."

"I already did. Seven, okay? And if they start talking about work, steer them to another topic. Preferably one where I can participate in the conversation."

He couldn't help but laugh. "It's all good, Bon. We can talk about shit other than work, you know."

"Chancey, just be there to back me up, all right? God. How did this get far enough along for me to be meeting his friends?" Bonnie sighed with exasperation and hung up.

He held the phone for a while, trying to will it to ring again of its own accord. Then he realized he was being idiotic, so he just punched in the familiar numbers and listened.

Straight to voicemail. Chance cleared his throat. "It's me. Sorry I didn't call, I worked a seventy-two and then crashed as soon as I got home. Call me tonight. Been thinking about you."

He hung up and went to go do laundry.

***

It was after ten when his phone finally rang.

Chance was in front of the television, as usual. The fact that he hadn't gone out since Tucker had left hadn't escaped his notice, but it was sort of hard to give a shit.

"Hiya," Tucker said, and it took Chance less than two seconds to discern he was drunk.

"Hi," he said carefully. "You been drinking?"

"Ayup," Tucker confirmed, popping the 'p'. "You?" He laughed at that, finding drunk humor in it.

"No," Chance said. "Work tomorrow."

"Whoops! I done forgot. Chancellor Shanahan's a captain now. You ain't never do nothin' wrong." His accent was thicker than Chance had ever heard it. He didn't know whether to attribute that to Tucker's intoxication or the fact that he'd been back in Kentucky for nearly two weeks.

"I wouldn't go that far," he replied. "Didn't I jack you off in the parking lot at work?"

"Riiiiight," Tucker drawled. "You're a reg'lar den of iniquity."

He ignored that. "So ... you been okay? Haven't talked to you."

"M'fuckin' great. And it's only been three days, baby. You missin' me?"

"What do you think? Smokey misses you, too. He sleeps curled up against your pillow."

"Aww. All we got here are the damn mangy barn cats. Fuck! No fuckin' cheese." He was rustling through something, probably the refrigerator.

"You're eating now? Isn't it, like, one in the morning?"

"So? Back off, I'm hungry. And I can't get decent Mexican food to save my goddamn life. Christ, I hate this fuckin' place."

Chance smiled to himself. Tucker had an affinity for authentic Mexican food, plentiful in southern California, but probably not so much in Kentucky. "I'll send you a pack of tortillas."

"Yeah, great. That'll make everything better," he slurred. "Jus' what I need. You're a hero."

He chose to ignore that, too, in the interest of the phone call hopefully ending on a good note. "Do you have snow?"

"Lil' bit. Too cold to stick and it don't snow much here anyhow. Oh, thank Christ, there's beer in here." The sound of a bottle being opened was audible through the phone.

"How the fuck can it be too cold to snow?" He'd never get people who lived in cold-weather climates.

"Maybe if you got your beach-boy ass out of the Golden State, you'd figure it out," Tucker said, after a swallow of beer.

Chance had had enough. "Fuck you, too," he snapped. "You're a shitty drunk." He slammed down the phone and unplugged it from the wall and before he went to bed he made sure his cell was off.

***

He forgot to plug the phone back in before he left for work in the morning, but he was still too pissed off to care.

Drinking was one thing. Chance was no teetotaler, he and Tucker had been drunk together plenty of times, and he'd even go so far as to say really, *really* smashed once or twice. It wasn't the alcohol that was bothering him.

They just didn't talk to each other like that.

It was an unspoken rule with them. If they were pissed at each other? Fine. Just don't say shit that couldn't be taken back. They'd had some fights in their time, had hurled insults and profanities at each other, and in the end it just resulted in bruised egos. They'd stopped fighting dirty when they'd gotten back together, and Chance felt they were better for it.

Apparently Tucker had forgotten.

Work kicked his ass, as usual, and Chance was glad. Kept him from dwelling on his anger. A car fire before dinner took longer to extinguish than normal and he hadn't realized he was barking orders at his crew until Jim ventured into his office after they got back to the station.

Chance was glaring at a newsletter from headquarters in the office he shared with the two other captains on B and C shifts when Jim knocked.

He glanced up and lifted an eyebrow. Jim was a good paramedic and a partner he could trust. "S'up?"

"You were kind of a dick on that last call." Jim wasn't one for mincing words, a quality Chance usually appreciated.

He blinked. "Yeah?"

"Yeah. Kind of a dick all day, really. You got something on your mind?"

"You ain't supposed to talk to your captain like that," he said, with an attempt at humor.

"You say 'ain't' a lot these days. And you might be my captain, but I still have to work with you. Missing the boy?" Jim leaned against the doorframe as if he had all the time in the world to discuss Chance's asshole behavior.

Chance sighed. He tried not to pick up Tucker's horrid grammar, but sometimes it slipped in under the radar. "No. I mean. Yeah, but. Things aren't so great right now."

"Cause he's gone, or what?"

"I guess. We got into it last night on the phone." He stopped there, unwilling to reveal the details.

Jim nodded slowly. "Yeah, I get it. Sorry, man." He pushed off from the doorjamb and ambled away, presumably to help the other engine's crew with dinner.

Chance watched him go. Jim's willingness to leave a man be was one of the things Chance liked best about him and made him so easy to work with. He briefly thought of Robert Diaz, a firefighter and friend on B shift. Robert was a good guy, but too nosy for his own good. He would have needled at Chance until he spilled the whole story, and then Chance would have been irritated at the intrusion.

Being alone until his mood improved was the better option for everyone.

***

He turned his phone on in the car on the way home. Chance had purposely left it off for his shift, and he was sort of afraid to check his messages for fear he wouldn't have any.

A shower cleared his head. He plugged the wall phone back in before sitting down with a bowl of cereal and checking his cell.

Two voicemails, both from Tucker. One last night and one this morning, just before he turned his phone back on. Good. Chance listened to them both twice and decided to go surfing.

The waves were average and the water was freezing. Even his full wetsuit couldn't block the November chill for longer than an hour, so he drove back home with the heat on high and his teeth chattering.

The answering machine was blinking. Chance listened.

"Um, hey. Checkin' to see if you're home yet. You're prolly at the beach -" Chance couldn't help smiling at that, Tucker did know his habits pretty well – "so just, y'know. Call me. If you want."

He called.

Tucker answered on the first ring, sounding hopeful. "Are y' mad?"

Chance sighed. "Would you be?"

"I'd be fuckin' furious." He laughed humorlessly. "M'sorry, man. Was drunk and stupid."

"Pretty much," Chance agreed, then let him off the hook. "Forget it. I have."

Tucker was quiet for a minute. Chance listened to him take a deep breath and suddenly missed him fiercely. "Okay," Tucker finally said. "We're square?"

"Square."

Chapter Nine

November wore on and, thankfully, Chance had a shift over Thanksgiving, which spared him from an extremely uncomfortable holiday at his mother's house. She was less than pleased when he called to let her know, and she demanded his presence for Christmas.

He brushed her off with a 'maybe' and didn't bother telling her that Tucker might not be back by Christmas. Not that that would be a deterrent at all. He knew she'd prefer it if he came by himself anyway. For Thanksgiving, she'd have to content herself with his younger brother Casey and his fiancée. Chance was pretty sure it wouldn't be a hardship for her and that he wouldn't be missed all that much.

Tucker being gone was getting old.

They were down to talking only two or three times a week. Tucker remained more close-mouthed than ever about the farm, and Chance finally just stopped asking questions he wasn't getting answers to. He couldn't stand the frustration and helplessness for much longer.

The fact that they'd had several more conversations while Tucker was drunk bothered Chance as well. Tucker hadn't been quite as loaded as that first time, but he'd usually had four or five beers by the time he'd finally get around to calling. Enough to slur his speech the tiniest bit, and enough to make Chance say something.

"You drink every night?" he asked, when it had taken six rings for Tucker to answer.

"Just about. Ain't just me, it's Ned and Coop, too. They make me. Peer pressure." He sounded as if he was trying to stifle a laugh and Chance could hear other laughter in the background.

He dropped it, because it only reminded him how powerless he was.

They managed decent phone sex every once in a while, but that too was getting old. It sure as fuck wasn't a substitute for the real thing. Chance wanted the connection, the physical presence, the touching. He wanted *Tucker*.

Chance's imagination and fantasies were more detailed than ever. Tucker on his knees, on his back, on his stomach. Lips, tongues, and hands all played a role in Chance's jerk-off daydreams, not to mention revisiting the time with the handcuffs and also the time he blew Tucker in the tillerman's seat of the new fire truck.

Not like he had a shortage of material. It was just the act itself that was getting lonely. A guy could only jack off so many times before he started wanting a little more, but it was so hard to stop himself when he woke up at six a.m. with raging morning wood.

Like now, for example. Chance glanced over at the clock, hoping it was at least seven and he'd managed to sleep a little later, but nope. Old Faithful had woken him up at his usual hour of six.

No sense putting off the inevitable. The lube hadn't strayed far from where he and Tucker usually kept it, under the pillow. Just to the nightstand, which was close enough. A palmful of it started him off and it only took a stroke or two to tell him that it wasn't going to take long.

Some mornings it did. Some mornings he could draw it out for fifteen minutes or more; stroking and fingering and playing with himself while he thought of blue eyes and flirty dimples. Long, slow pulls on his cock while he imagined being in Tucker's ass, strokes that would bring him to the edge and then he'd pull back and make it last longer. Letting it build and build until he thought he'd die if he stopped himself one more time. Until finally he couldn't take the torture, and then he would squeeze his eyes shut and come in great, shuddering jerks that left him trembling for long minutes afterward.

But this morning wasn't like that, he could tell already. He must have been dreaming before he woke up, because his cock was already hard enough to nearly stand up straight, even while he lay flat on his back. Chance took advantage of it.

He watched his own hand as he milked clear drops of pre-come from the slit, gathering them with his thumb and mixing with lube to slick himself up further. His eyes fought to close, but Chance resisted it, wanting instead to see himself shoot, to watch himself like Tucker sometimes did.

"Wanna watch you come," Tucker'd whisper. "Wanna see it." And it would usually just send Chance right over the edge he'd been teetering on.

His tongue snaked out to wet his bottom lip and he could feel his ass clenching with each hard tug on his prick, closer and closer and then closer still. One thought of Tucker's hot, pretty mouth on his cock and bam, there it was – a fast, fierce orgasm that left come spilling hotly over his fingers and landing warm on his stomach.

It was a testament to the state of things when a good wank left him lonely instead of satisfied.

***

It ended up being just a single phone call toward the beginning of December that set things in motion.

Chance had tried Tucker's phone twice during the week and had only gotten voicemail. He was sick of talking to an automated message. He'd hung up both times, knowing the missed call would show up on Tucker's phone, but he'd received no call in return.

Until this morning, when his own cell had started vibrating on the floor next to his bunk at work.

He came awake instantly, not even sure at first what had woken him up. He strained to hear the squawk box on the wall outside his dorm to see if his engine was being called before he realized that it hadn't been the alarm that startled him.

Groping around for his phone, he squinted at the time display on the front. Four-thirty. "Christ," he whispered. Then he looked again, unsure he'd seen the correct phone number on the caller ID. Nope, he'd been right the first time: Tucker's phone.

"Hey," he answered, keeping his voice low, aware of the men sleeping around him.

"This Shanahan?" an unfamiliar voice asked.

A faint sense of alarm pervaded his grogginess and he pushed up on an elbow. "Who the fuck's this?"

"Coop," came the answer, and Chance vaguely remembered Tucker mentioning the name. "M'thinkin' there's some shit you oughta know." His accent was pure drawl.

"Where's Tucker?" he demanded, getting out of bed and heading down the hall to the kitchen, where he could speak more loudly.

"That there's the shit you oughta know about. Seein' as how you're his roommate and all." There was a slight emphasis on 'roommate' and Chance was aware that this guy knew some or all aspects of their relationship.

"Where is he?" Chance asked again, standing in the dark kitchen and looking out the window towards their small basketball court. "He okay?"

"He will be," Coop said, and Chance could practically hear the other man's eyes rolling. "Jus' needs to be cleaned up a little. Gonna have a hell of a shiner, though." He sounded as if he was turning slightly away from the phone, perhaps to look at the subject of the conversation.

Chance cleared his throat and spoke very softly. "If you do not tell me in the next three seconds what happened to Tucker, I will hang up and have the police dispatched to wherever the fuck you are. *Where is Tucker?*"

"Now, now. Calm down, son. McBride's right here, passed out cold in his own bed. Stumbled in about fi'teen minutes ago, holdin' his ribs and had blood all over his shirt." Coop paused and chuckled, although Chance couldn't see any humor here at all. "Was spittin' mad an' drunker'n I ever seen him."

"Okay," Chance said slowly. "And?"

"And so I mopped the dang blood off his face – was thinkin' at first that he broke his nose 'cuz of all the blood, but it doesn't look like it – and stripped his shirt. Was gonna try to get his useless ass in the shower, but he fell into bed afore I could do much more 'cept get his boots off." Coop cleared his throat and spat, at least doing Chance the courtesy of turning the phone away from his mouth.

"Fighting," Chance said, sinking into a chair. A feeling of dread was creeping into his stomach, making him nauseous. "Damn it."

"Ayup," Coop confirmed. "Prolly at that faggot – I mean, uh. That there queer bar he goes to."

It was telling that Tucker was in a place where "queer" was considered more PC than "faggot". Chance was beginning to see a clearer picture now of what Tucker had had to go back to. "Yeah. He goes there a lot?"

"Nah," came the answer. "S'been a couple times. Mostly he just stays home and drinks with the hands. I done tole him not to go up there last night. The townies've been staking it out jus' to make trouble." Coop paused and Chance could hear a door closing, as if he'd left the room where Tucker was sleeping.

Chance took a deep breath and let it out slowly. "I appreciate the call. You do know he'd be pissed if he knew, right?"

Coop laughed, a hoarse sound that told of years of cigarette smoking. "Shit, son, course I know. But I'll tell ya one thing. The way he talks about you? Makes it sound like you're the second comin' of Christ. Figured if'n I called you, you'd figure out a way to straighten the sonofabitch out."

Chance closed his eyes and leaned forward until his forehead rested on the back of the chair he was straddling. "Don't know what the fuck to do," he confessed. "He doesn't tell me anything these days." It occurred to him that he was talking to a complete stranger, but at least he'd learned more about Tucker in the last five minutes than he had in the past three weeks.

"Seems to me the boy ain't gotta tell you nothin' for you to still know he's in trouble."

It was true.

***

Matt drove him and Bonnie tagged along in the back seat.

"You'll feed Smokey?" he asked, feeling guilty about leaving the cat home alone for over a week.

"Yes, yes," Bonnie brushed him off impatiently. "And water your plants and get your mail. You asked me three times already."

"Okay, but sometimes he loses his catnip mouse under the couch, so can you check if you don't see it?"

"Chancey, God! I can handle it and Smokey can, too. He'll be fine."

Matt snorted and Chance glared at him. "Maybe you should do it instead of her."

"Allergic to cats," Matt grinned. "You get your shifts taken care of?"

"Yeah. Took two days off, which gives me just over a week out there. Don't want to take another day, but if I have to, I have to." It hadn't been a smart thing to do, taking two shifts off during his probation year, but what choice did he have? It was for Tucker.

"You shouldn't get any flack for it," Matt said. "But I'll cover you if you do."

Chance nodded and turned back to the window. Bonnie sat forward in her seat and rested her chin on his shoulder. "You'll call us and let us know? How Tucker is, I mean."

He didn't turn from the window, but he could feel both of them eyeing him. "Soon as I figure out what the fuck is going on."

Matt pulled smoothly up to Chance's terminal and wormed his way into a spot near the curb. Putting the car in park, he studied the steering wheel for a minute. "McBride's no idiot, Chance. Just needs to get his head straight."

Chance looked at both of them, throat tight. "Yeah. Appreciate you guys."

Bonnie kissed his cheek and Matt clapped a hand on his shoulder. "Stay in touch."

Chapter Ten

The frigid air was a shock as soon as he let the automatic doors of Louisville International close behind him. Somehow Chance hadn't believed the internet when it had told him the average December temperature in Kentucky was thirty degrees.

He sure as hell believed it now, as he waited under the car rental sign for the shuttle that would take him to the lot. Burrowing deeper into his old, brown leather jacket, he was grateful for both the extra t-shirt and the sweatshirt he had on. He'd better get his ass to the store for some real winter clothes instead of the faux California-winter stuff he had in his suitcase.

It had been a simple matter of taking the address Coop had given him and finding directions from the airport. The town Tucker had grown up in, Brandenburg, was only fifty miles away. Chance snagged himself a small, clean pickup truck at the rental place and threw his bag in the bed, rooting around in it for his CDs before hopping behind the wheel and flipping the heat on.

The drive was easy. Chance had glimpses of the Ohio River from time to time and couldn't help making comparisons to his ocean. The river seemed flat and gray, the small whitecaps reminding him of spit on a sidewalk. There was no power in it like the ocean, no color, no visible movement. He stopped looking at it after a while and used the time to think instead.

Except thinking wasn't really to his advantage, Chance discovered. All it did was bring up the shit he hadn't thought through. Coming here without telling Tucker had the potential to go very badly, especially if Tucker was drinking as much as he suspected. Not to mention the fighting … It just didn't sound good, any of it, and Chance was apprehensive about what he'd find when he finally got to the farm.

The rural roads were winding and small, but the directions he had were fairly accurate and he found himself turning down a little dirt road sooner than he'd expected. He passed several fields with the stubby remains of tobacco plants and recalled Tucker telling him that the plants were cut in late summer, stripped in the fall, and brought to auction in December. Chance was just wondering if there was something else that could be grown in between tobacco seasons when he came over a small rise and stopped the truck short.

A gorgeous, three-story farmhouse sprawled out in front of him, its wrap-around porch the first thing to catch his attention. Chance whistled softly between his teeth as his gaze traveled upward. White paint with green shutters and a green front door, wooden slats, shake-shingle roof. The firefighter in him shuddered at all the wood, but the aesthetic part of him appreciated the near century-old beauty of the structure. It didn't look in too bad shape, either. Someone had obviously been caring for it.

He let his foot off the brake and coasted down the driveway, coming to a stop behind a truck that couldn't have seen a highway in a good thirty years. He hoped this wasn't the one Tucker had been driving. A quick scan of the area through the windshield gave the impression the place was deserted, though the fat Australian Shepherd sleeping on the porch was obviously getting fed by somebody.

The dog lifted its head when it heard the truck door slam and sleepily watched Chance cross the yard. It lost interest and laid its head back down when Chance climbed the wooden steps. "Aren't you cold?" Chance asked it, but the dog just closed its eyes in response. "Good answer," he muttered. "Sleep the cold away."

No doorbell, but a big brass knocker instead. He banged it hard against the door and waited, a mix of emotions making him slightly ill. Anticipation, nerves, and uneasiness all combined to make a knot in his stomach. Seemed he spent a lot of time with a stomach ache these days. Chance totally had no problem with blaming Tucker for that.

He'd really had no idea who was going to answer his knock, but when the door finally opened, Chance was still surprised to see a stranger. Baggy jeans, plaid shirt with a thermal underneath, well-worn work boots. He spoke around the toothpick in his mouth. "What?"

Chance blinked at him, unprepared for someone other than Tucker. "Uh. Hi. I'm Chance Shanahan." He hoped the name would be enough to spark recognition in whoever this was, because he sure as hell didn't feel like explaining how he'd come to be standing here.

Luckily enough, the man squinted his eyes and nodded. "You're the roommate."

Chance shoved his slowly numbing fingers into his jacket pockets. "That what he calls me?"

The man shifted his toothpick from one side to the other. "That's what I call you."

Ah. So that's how it was around here. Chance hunched his shoulders and thought that if he didn't get warm in the next ten seconds, his balls would never recover from the shock. "Can I come in? I need to see Tucker."

"Reckon," the man said calmly, and stood back. "Name's Coop." He put out a hand for Chance to shake. "Whoo doggies. Your fingers are frozen, son."

Chance kicked the door shut behind him and jammed his hands back in his pockets, relishing the warmth he could feel emanating from the fireplace to his left. "Yeah. Tucker was right, this sure as hell isn't California. Need to get myself some gloves."

Coop snorted in response and motioned toward the fireplace room. "G'wan in there by the fire, son. Got a pot of coffee on. How ya take it?"

He almost said "nonfat milk with two Equals" before remembering where he was. "Milk and sugar," he tried, and received a barely concealed eye roll. Chance guessed "black" would have been a more acceptable response.

The dog had shuffled in behind him, so Chance followed it to the warmth of the fireplace. The dog lay down on the hearth with a sigh and Chance sat himself on the well-worn sofa. Coop appeared momentarily and Chance gratefully wrapped his fingers around the steaming cup he was handed.

They sized each other up for a minute before Coop finally spoke. "McBride's pro'lly out in the barn with the horses."

"You have horses?" Chance felt more like a fish out of water every minute he was here. "Like, for riding?"

Coop blinked. "Mostly for fertilizer. McBride takes Blue out for a ride every day, though. Surprised he was up so early this mornin', after ..." He trailed off and feigned great interest in his coffee cup.

"After?" Chance prodded, getting frustrated with having to drag information out of everyone.

"After tyin' another one on," Coop finished with a shrug. "Boy's been drunk and ornery at least four nights a week since he's been here. Always up and out the next day, though, hangover or not. He drink that much out there with you?"

Chance shook his head. "No. Sometimes, maybe, if it's a night when we don't have to work the next day. But he's too conscious of his job to do it all the time. And he doesn't have a reason to, I guess."

Coop nodded. "His granddaddy was chief for Louisville Fire. He tell you that?"

"No. He never mentioned it." Chance had the feeling that this man knew a hell of a lot more than he did about Tucker.

"Walter was always bringin' Tucker toy fire engines and shit when he'd visit. Tucker thought he was the greatest thing ever made, and then he died in a barn fire when Tucker was only five. Hank – Tucker's daddy – always swore he'd never let his boy have anything to do with the fire service. Guess it's good he dropped dead before he saw his kid right there in the thick of things."

Chance set his cup on the scratched coffee table. "He's a good fireman. He loves it."

"Never said he didn't, son. Jus' lettin' you know how things were around here." Coop said it calmly, but Chance could hear the underlying message. Chance was the stranger here, and until he proved himself one way or another, he'd stay the outsider.

It didn't matter. The only thing that mattered to Chance was seeing Tucker and finding out exactly what the fuck was going on around here, and the sooner the better.

"So ... the barn's nearby?" Chance didn't want their reunion to be under Coop's watchful eye, mostly because he had no idea how it was going to go. A feeling in his gut told him to be wary.

"Back of the house. Y'all can go through the kitchen." He thumbed over his shoulder. "Cotton here can show you."

The dog lifted his head at the sound of his name and slowly got to his feet, tongue lolling out. He cocked an ear at Chance.

Chance nodded his thanks to the man and made his way through the farmhouse, boards creaking under his feet and the dog's nails making soft clicking noises as he walked ahead. Out the back door – god*damn* it was still fucking cold – and down the steps, and then Chance could see it was a simple matter of crossing the large backyard to the white and blue barn.

The dog led the way, looking back every now and then to see if Chance was following, and when he reached the open barn doors he wasted no time in trotting through.

Chance stopped at the doors and listened. Somebody was obviously inside, since they were whistling something tuneless while they worked, and Chance could hear the soft clinking of what he assumed were bridles. Or whatthefuckever went on a horse.

He might have waited forever outside the doors like a damn coward if he hadn't heard Tucker's voice. "Hey, Cotton," Tucker said to the dog. "Whatcha doin' away from the fire? Lazyass." Tucker's voice had a hint of affection and Chance heard the dog's collar jingle as Tucker probably gave his neck a scratch.

Chance mentally cursed himself for being so chickenshit and stepped through the doors. "He was showing me where you were."

Tucker's head whipped around so fast it would have been comical if not for the look of utter disbelief on his face. "You're fuckin' kiddin' me."

Chance wanted to leap on him and wrestle him to the ground, ensuring Tucker would never be out of touching distance again. He settled for putting his hands in his jacket pockets until he was more sure of his welcome. "Hey."

Tucker dropped the brush he'd been using on the horse and advanced a step or two, putting him within pouncing length. Chance clenched his hands into fists in his pockets and waited.

The silence stretched on long enough to be uncomfortable. Chance was aware of Cotton lying down with a sigh and the horse – presumably Blue – snorting softly and stamping an impatient foot. "You gonna say anything?" Chance finally asked.

"No," Tucker said, and reached for him.

Their mouths met with urgency and Chance clutched at him, relishing the feel of Tucker, warm and solid. Tucker's hair was longer and Chance could wrap it around his fingers, the silky curls sliding under his palm. Their tongues met and fought and soothed, teeth nipped and lips tasted, and Chance couldn't get enough of him after nearly three weeks of going without.

They were both hard beneath their jeans, rubbing up on each other, hands grabbing at each other's waists. Tucker's head fell back as Chance nuzzled his ear. "Missed you," Tucker murmured into the stillness of the barn. "Missed you, missed you, missed you."

"Missed you back," Chance whispered, and then they were kissing again.

He was just wondering frantically if there was an abandoned stall or something he could drag Tucker into when Tucker broke the embrace and pushed away. Chance reached for him instinctively, already bereft with the loss, but Tucker shook his head sharply and stepped back. "No. Wait."

Chance looked at Tucker in incredulity, chest heaving. He was about four seconds away from creaming into his jeans and his brain was sort of occupied with that thought. "The fuck?"

Tucker made a futile adjustment in his own jeans and winced when his hand came in contact with his erection. His nostrils flared and Chance could see his color was high; sure signs he was aroused. Not like the bulge at his crotch could be mistaken. But when he finally spoke, his tone was low and hard and put Chance on the alert immediately. "What in hell are you doin' here?"

All the rehearsed responses sounded idiotic, so he told the truth. "Heard you needed help."

Tucker's eyes narrowed. "Don't remember sayin' that."

"Didn't hear it from you. Which sort of pisses me off, by the way, since you said you'd call if you needed me."

"Who the fuck says I needed you? M'doin' fine." He crossed his arms defensively.

"Not what I heard. Heard you were drinking and fighting."

"Fuckin' Coop," he muttered, and dug the heel of his boot into the dirt floor. "Was one fight, which I won. Got jumped, what the fuck was I supposed to do?"

Chance took a tentative step forward. "Tuck, come on. I shouldn't have let you come out here by yourself to begin with. And don't fucking tell me you're happy here, because I know different, and goddamn, I just missed you, all right?" He ran a frustrated hand through his hair and didn't know what else to say.

Tucker's expression softened, but his posture remained rigid. "I get that you want to help, Chance. And I missed you so fuckin' much, 'specially at night."

It hit Chance then that being alone was probably the main reason Tucker had started drinking so excessively. It was too painful to examine further, so he shoved it away and let Tucker finish.

"But this ain't the place for you," he said, and the heaviness in his voice was unlike anything Chance had heard from him before. "I gotta be here by myself and deal with it alone, and you gotta go back home."

"No." He wasn't going anywhere.

Tucker blinked. "The fuck, no? There ain't nothin' for you to do here. It ain't your business."

"Oh, fuck you!" Chance's anger snuck up on him quickly, sending heat into his cheeks. "What the shit do you think I came here for? *You're* my goddamn business, you asshole, and don't think for one goddamn minute I'm turning myself around and trotting back home because you ordered it!" He ended in a near shout, loud enough to cause the dog to lift his head and stare.

Tucker moved close enough so that Chance could see his ridiculously long eyelashes and had to resist the urge to lick him. "Look," Tucker said, and Chance could hear the barely controlled fury, "you don't know shit about this place. Go the fuck home and go back to your beach and your cat and your happy life, all right? Leave well enough alone."

"Don't you fucking talk to me like I'm an idiot. That's your life, too, and you know it. Now you either get on the goddamned plane with me, or I'm staying. I'll sleep with the fucking horses if I have to." God, he'd freeze his balls off, but he wasn't going home.

Tucker shook his head. "Do whatever the fuck you want, California boy," he sneered, and turned to walk away.

It happened fast enough that Chance couldn't piece it together later. He went for Tucker's arm, intending to grab him, but Tucker wheeled around and tried to jerk away. His elbow came up and caught Chance squarely in the nose. Before the blood could even start to flow, Chance reacted. He drew back and let fly a right hook that caught Tucker on the jaw and sent him reeling into the side of the barn.

Tucker swore at him and pushed off the wall instantly, throwing a punch that grazed Chance's cheek. Chance reached out to get him in a headlock, but only succeeded in holding him for a second before Tucker slipped out of Chance's grasp and tried to hit him again. Chance was ready for it, though, and ducked just in time, coming back up to send one more punch that knocked Tucker into the door of a stall.

Tucker shook his head, dazed, and slid carefully down the wall to sit in the dirt. Chance was kneeling next to Tucker in an instant, ignoring his own blood that he could feel warm on his mouth and chin. "I'm sorry," Chance babbled, putting a careful hand on Tucker's jaw and turning his head to examine his pupils. "Christ, Tucker, I didn't mean it, I'm sorry." His knuckles burned slightly and Chance wanted to hit something else, preferably the wall.

Tucker brought up a hand to gingerly touch the spot on his jaw where Chance's fist had connected. "Damn." He leaned over and spat on the ground, his saliva tinged with red. Looking up again, he noticed Chance's face. "Oh, *damn*," he said again, and used his thumb to wipe some of the blood from Chance's upper lip. "What the fuck are we doin'?"

Chance closed his eyes and shook his head. "I have no idea."

Tucker got carefully to his feet, holding a hand out. Chance grasped it and stood. "Come on," Tucker said with a sigh. "Let's go mop you up."

Chapter Eleven

Coop was refreshing his coffee when they both came in, trailed by Cotton. He glanced up and raised his eyebrows at the blood covering Chance's face, but merely brought his cup to his lips and remained silent.

Tucker went to the freezer and pulled out an ice tray, dumping several cubes into a plastic bag and holding it against his jaw while he shoved some paper towels at Chance. Chance wet them at the sink and tried to clean himself up, but found it difficult to see what he was doing without a mirror. Tucker watched him for a minute before sighing and shoving him into a chair. Tucker tilted Chance's head back and used the wet towels to scrub at his face. "Didn't break it," he said, examining the bridge of Chance's nose with gentle fingers.

"Ouch," Chance said, and swatted at him. "Hope you don't manhandle patients that way."

Tucker looked down at him, the faintest trace of a smile tugging at his lips. "Don't manhandle anyone but you, baby."

The sight of his dimples and straight, white teeth was like an aphrodisiac to Chance. It was sort of embarrassing, really, how fast Tucker could make him hard. Especially considering they'd just been punching each other.

Their gazes were hot on each other as words trailed away, each of them trying to communicate silently. Only the clearing of someone's throat made them look up.

"Supper's at six," Coop said as he strolled out of the kitchen. "Don't be late or you don't get none."

"Six," Tucker whispered, leaning his forehead against Chance's. "That gives us – " he paused and checked the clock on the wall – "an hour and ten minutes." Tucker reached down and cupped Chance's cock through his pants. "I only need about three."

Chance reached up and yanked Tucker down into the chair, straddling his lap. He kissed Tucker fiercely, hips surging upward as Tucker ground down and whimpered into his mouth. "Need you," Chance said between kisses, hands clutching at Tucker's waist. "Need you right now, Tuck, please."

"Upstairs," Tucker panted, "come on." But he didn't move, he just started up a rhythm of sliding back and forth over Chance's dick, and Chance cursed all the clothing. And yet, he couldn't stop either, because it had been nearly a month and God, it just felt too good.

It built and built until Chance could only lower his head and try not to cry out while Tucker ground down on him. He gripped Tucker's ass with both hands and pulled Tucker in tightly, cussing at the denim that separated them. His cock was more than happy about the private lap dance he was getting, however, and Chance knew he was done for.

"Gonna shoot," he gasped, as Tucker bit down on the soft spot under his jaw.

Tucker's breathing changed and he wrapped one arm tightly around Chance's shoulders. The other hand gripped the back of the chair and he put his mouth on Chance's ear. "Don't scream," he murmured, and just like that, Chance felt him come.

Tucker jerked up hard against him and went still, riding out the faint pulses that Chance sensed more than felt, and then Chance was clamping his lips together and bucking up into his own climax.

Chance came down slowly, his trembling subsiding a little as Tucker buried his face in the side of Chance's neck. "*Now* we're goin' upstairs," Tucker mumbled with a downward nudge.

He felt his cock stir. "Show me."

Tucker clambered off him without a word and tugged at his hand, so Chance followed through the hallway and past the room with the fireplace. Up the stairs to their left, and Chance had time to glimpse another whitewashed staircase to the third floor before Tucker was yanking him down the corridor into the last room on the right.

It was large enough to hold a queen-sized bed and not much else. A five-drawer dresser and a nightstand in the corner took up the rest of the space. Chance could see why Tucker preferred to stay in this small guest bedroom instead of the master. There was nothing personal about it, nothing to remind him that he was staying in the house he'd grown up in, and clearly that was his preference.

Chance fell onto the bed and dragged Tucker down with him. The initial urgency had calmed a little, but Chance still had a frantic desire to touch bare skin. They'd left their jackets downstairs, so Chance just had to tug at Tucker's flannel to pull it from his waistband. Once it was free of the jeans, Chance let his hands roam underneath, touching and soothing whatever skin he could reach.

Tucker was trying to do the same, but with less success since they were tangled up in each other. Chance sat up briefly and pulled his sweatshirt and t-shirt off together, grimacing at the bloodstains that now decorated the front. Jeans, boots, and tennis shoes soon followed, and when they were naked together, they couldn't stop touching.

"Didja think about me?" Tucker whispered, lips closing over one of Chance's nipples.

He sucked in a breath and nodded, arching up to try and brush his cock against Tucker's hip. "Every damn night. Don't you ever fucking go off and leave me again."

Tucker murmured something Chance couldn't hear before sliding down Chance's body, leaving a trail of moist, open-mouthed kisses as he went. Chance felt himself melting, leaving himself open to Tucker's ministrations. He nearly came off the bed, however, when Tucker's mouth sank down wetly over his cock and gave one long, hard suck at the head.

"Missed this," Tucker paused to say, dimples flashing up at him. "Missed the way you taste, the way you smell, the way you feel under my hands."

"What else," Chance murmured, throwing an arm over his eyes and letting himself be lulled by Tucker's voice and the soft, gliding tongue on his cock.

"Now, if I talk, I can't get to work, can I?" Tucker pointed out, and proceeded to suck him slowly.

"Oh, God," Chance breathed, all his nerves bunched and wound. Tucker was fucking fantastic at giving head. "Yeah. Not fast, all right?"

"All's you gotta do is lie there. Quit bein' bossy and just enjoy it."

Chance complied. His fingers dug into the comforter when Tucker licked his balls and then squeezed gently, keeping a hand on them while Tucker got back to work on Chance's prick.

He couldn't help thrusting up the littlest bit into Tucker's mouth, trying not to go too deep, but unable to keep still when that talented tongue was doing things to his slit. "Harder," he begged, "suck me harder."

Tucker paused to lick Chance's balls again and then his own fingers. At the same time as returning to Chance's cock, Tucker worked the tip of a finger into his hole, Chance moaned even louder. God, he really hoped Coop had left the house, or dinner was going to be one hell of an uncomfortable meal.

Tucker slid one finger all the way in and crooked it slightly, brushing Chance's gland and making both of them groan. The vibrations around his dick made Chance shudder hard enough for Tucker to do it again, humming low in his throat and not stopping until Chance cried out. "Oh, shit," he managed, and then he was coming hard enough to see white streaks behind his eyes.

He hadn't finished shuddering before he was flipped to his stomach and Tucker had his face buried in Chance's ass. Chance groaned when he felt a warm tongue on his hole and slid both hands under the pillow, hugging it to his chest and arching his back.

Tucker rimmed him 'til Chance was nearly hard again. He was sort of surprising himself with his record recovery time between orgasms, but then again, it was Tucker. Not so unusual, especially when the man was doing things with his mouth that were turning Chance inside out, working his tongue into a point and licking Chance everywhere.

Tucker urged him to his knees with a whispered, "Up, baby. Need to fuck you, to feel you. Dreamed about it, jerked off to it, wanted it all the time."

Chance swallowed tightly and nodded, bracing on his hands and knees. "Same. Couldn't sleep, most nights."

There was no lube, but Tucker had gotten him wet enough that it wasn't needed. Chance relished the slight burn anyway; it made this more real, more solid. Too many nights he'd woken up with the last remnants of a dream teasing him, telling him Tucker was warm and sleepy next to him in bed.

Chance had reached out too many times to empty space.

"Oh, yes," Tucker murmured as he pushed in, hands flexing at Chance's waist. "Yes. Perfect."

Chance dropped his head and thrust back just the littlest bit, enough to make Tucker brush his prostate on each down stroke. He hissed when Tucker found the right rhythm and ground down, each thrust deeper than the last, pushing Chance forward with each pounding stroke.

"Tight," Tucker was gritting out. "Always so tight. God, you feel so good, Chance, I ain't gonna make this last."

Chance didn't think he'd be able to come a third time, so it didn't matter to him how long it lasted because all he cared about was feeling Tucker in him, around him. But Tucker wrapped a hand around his cock anyway and leaned over his back.

"You're comin' with me," Tucker whispered, and Chance shook his head.

"No," he whimpered, thrusting into Tucker's grip regardless. "Can't."

"Yes," Tucker said firmly, and hit Chance's gland at the same time he squeezed the head of Chance's dick. "Again. Right now."

And apparently Tucker was right, because Chance came for the third time in an hour, so hard that his vision blurred a little at the edges and his muscles trembled. Over his shoulder he could hear Tucker groaning "Oh, fuck, fuck, fuck ..." and then Tucker was coming, too, pulsing hotly into Chance and holding on tightly enough to leave red marks.

Shaky muscles gave out and they collapsed together. Tucker didn't move and Chance didn't want him to; wanted to feel him strong and solid on top. Tucker was running a hand lazily up and down Chance's arm and Chance let himself be lulled by it, tempted to give in to the sleepiness that was threatening him.

Chance thought they'd both fallen asleep when loud voices and boots on the hardwood below startled them.

"Dang," Tucker groaned. "Dinner."

"Can we skip it?" Chance wasn't up to meeting anyone, and besides, staying naked in bed with Tucker was much more appealing. Chance wiggled slightly underneath Tucker, making him sigh with regret.

"Prolly shouldn't. Coop more'n likely told 'em you were here, they'll be waitin' for us at the table." He didn't sound thrilled about the prospect, either.

"So ... is this gonna be weird? Should I be ready?" Chance really wasn't in the mood to deal with a bunch of homophobes, but for Tucker, he would.

Tucker shook his head as they cleaned up and dressed. "Nah, they're all right. S'probably just Ned and Johnny anyhow. The others got wives and families and don't stay for dinner most nights."

They trooped downstairs together and Tucker led the way into the dining room. Three men sat around the huge, oak table that could have easily held ten people. Coop didn't bother looking up as they came in, but the other two gave Chance a slow once-over.

Both of them were near Coop's age, Chance guessed. Grizzled and lined, they all looked older than they probably were, but Chance wasn't fooled for a second. Their eyes were sharp and their bodies lean and they could most likely hold their own in any kind of fight. He held their gazes steadily and made sure not to look away.

"Johnny and Ned Whitmore," Tucker said, sitting himself down and taking a heaping scoop of mashed potatoes. "Brothers."

Chance reached across the table and gave each of them a firm handshake, noting the rough, work-worn skin and realizing that Tucker's hands were starting to feel the same way. "Chancellor Shanahan."

"No cracks about the name," Tucker said sharply, and they both looked mildly disappointed.

They gave Chance a slight nod and a "How do," and that was the extent of the conversation between them.

He sat in the chair next to Tucker and followed his lead, helping himself to mashed potatoes, fresh green beans, and a large slice of ham. Talking was at a minimum for most of the meal, except for Tucker asking questions about how the tobacco stripping went that day and how soon they could be ready for auction.

It was all foreign to him, the whole concept of farming and the way of life in general. He ate silently while he listened to Tucker ask pointed questions about grading and baling, things that Chance had no familiarity with at all.

"Fish out of water" was becoming more and more accurate.

Apple pie that sure as hell didn't come from a store topped off the meal, and Chance wondered if he'd be able to go for a run tomorrow. He was betting there was no gym available and if meals were going to continue in this vein, he'd better keep up with his workouts. He was planning on staying as long as it took to figure out what was going on with Tucker.

Ned was saying something about hiring migrant workers as they brought their dishes to the kitchen and Chance was startled by Tucker's firm, "No fuckin' way."

"Now you listen here, pup," Coop spoke up, and Chance had to hide his grin. Pup? He'd remember that one for later. "Strippin's already gone on too long," Coop continued, and Chance recognized Tucker's stubborn set jaw. Coop didn't know what he was in for.

But then again … maybe it was Tucker who didn't know what he was in for. Coop kept talking, and something in his voice brooked no argument. "I been strippin' tobacco for your fam'ly since a'fore you was born. Strippin' shoulda been finished two weeks ago and our bales packed up and headed to auction by now."

Johnny added his two cents. "Man's right, Tucker. Ain't our fault the local boys what used to help all got themselves thrown in jail or addicted to crank or can't be assed to show up for two days in a row. We gotta have help if you want any fuckin' profit off this year's crop."

"Profit that's gonna get eaten up by migrant workers chargin' too fuckin' much for a day's labor!" Tucker complained, dropping his dishes in the sink with a clatter.

"You look here," Coop said, slamming his hand down on the countertop. "I don't give two shits if you do own this fuckin' farm now. You can't come back here after more'n ten years and tell me what's the what about this place. I dealt with your goddamned uncle runnin' this farm into the ground, knowin' your daddy was prolly spinnin' in his grave. Well, now Tim's dead and I plan on doin' right by your daddy."

They faced off in the large kitchen, the three men against Tucker. Chance stood to the side, silent, absorbing both the discussion and the tension in the room. It was only his intimate knowledge of Tucker that let Chance see how close the man was to the fine line between control and explosion.

Tucker chose control. Flinging the dishtowel he was holding onto the floor, he stalked by Chance and out the back door.

Fireline

Chapter Twelve

Three heads turned in Chance's direction. He really had no idea what they expected him to say, or if he was supposed to go chasing after Tucker. Tucker was the last person on earth who made dramatic exits expecting to be chased.

"S'pretty much the norm around here," Coop finally said, turning back to the sink and letting the water run. Ned and Johnny flanked him and started a neat assembly line of dishwashing.

"Where'd he take off to?" Chance asked, approaching the sink and leaning over to pick up the forgotten dishtowel.

Coop motioned with his chin toward the window, where Chance could see a light shining from the barn. "He went out the back, which means he went to the barn. He'll spend an hour or so with the horses and a six-pack, then he'll come back in and finish up with the Jim Beam."

"That's his usual thing? Takes off to the barn?"

"Varies. If he goes out the front, means he's crossin' the river and goin' on up to that bar he likes in Indiana." Coop cleared his throat and Chance caught the look they all surreptitiously gave each other.

"A gay bar," he clarified, and there was a lot of shuffling around, but no talking. Chance rolled his eyes. "Christ. No fucking wonder he drinks almost every night, if no one can stomach the thought that he likes dick."

"Kentucky ain't like California," Coop reminded him. "'Specially not Brandenburg. This here's a small town, Mister Shanahan, and everyone knows everyone else's fuckin' business. We ain't as progressive as you folks out on the west coast."

It was a reminder that Chance took a lot for granted and helped to calm his temper. "So does anyone go after him, or does he stew by himself?"

Ned laughed. "He don't want anyone goin' after him. Might have to share his beer."

Chance shook his head and resisted another eye roll. "I don't want any of his fucking booze," he said, and grabbed his jacket from the coat hook near the back door. He opened the door and shuddered when the chill December air hit his face. It had to have dropped fifteen degrees since the sun went down, and he made another mental note to get himself a real jacket and gloves.

Braving the cold, he followed the warm, yellow light to the barn and wandered in. The horses – three of them, he counted – turned their large heads in their stalls and whickered softly in greeting. Chance put a hand on the nearest one's velvety nose and glanced in, but only horse and straw occupied the enclosure.

He moved to the next one and did the same thing, but was met again with no success. It was only when he reached the third stall that he found what he was looking for.

Tucker raised a beer in greeting. "Didn't think it'd take you this long."

Chance unhooked the stall door and glanced warily at the horse that was sharing Tucker's space. "They said you wouldn't want company. Then I said screw what you wanted, I was coming after you."

"Just push Blue on the rump, he'll move over for you. And they were right, usually I don't want company."

Chance sat down next to him in the straw and leaned back against the wall. The stall was warmer than the rest of the barn, probably because of the heat from the horse. "And this time?"

"This time you're here."

Chance leaned over to kiss him then. The tip of Tucker's nose was cold, but his lips were warm, as was the tongue that poked out to swipe at Chance's mouth. He tasted of cheap beer and Chance pulled back to look at the can in Tucker's hand. "Tell me that's not Coors in the yellow can."

Tucker looked at it and shrugged before downing the rest of the beer and crumpling the can. "Sorry. Ain't got your Heinekens at the ready." He tossed the can in the corner where Chance noticed two others already waited.

"That your third already?" He reached for one, more to keep Tucker from drinking it than from any desire for the disgusting pisswater. Chance popped the top and took a swig, grimacing at the taste.

"Gotta keep warm somehow," he said. "Of course, now that you're here, I could think of better ways." He raised his brows and grinned.

Chance's cock stirred, as usual, but he ignored it for the moment. "Oh, we'll keep warm," he said, "but I wanna talk first."

Tucker rested his beer in the straw and rose to his knees. Before Chance could stop it, Tucker had managed to push him to his back and was straddling him. "No. First we screw around, then maybe we'll talk." He lowered his head and took Chance's mouth in a punishing kiss, one that Chance couldn't help responding to.

He threaded his fingers through Tucker's hair and held fast, slanting his head so their mouths could align. Tucker moaned into the kiss and started grinding against him. "Want you," Tucker muttered against Chance's neck.

Chance gave in to the inevitable and hooked an ankle over Tucker's calf. "Same," he murmured back, "but I'm not getting naked in a goddamned freezing cold barn."

Tucker grinned down and shook his head. "Don't gotta." He slid down enough to undo Chance's fly and then his own, drawing their cocks out and holding them together.

Chance closed his eyes and thrust forward, his hands settling lightly on Tucker's thighs. He let his whole body go loose and pliant and made Tucker do the work, jacking them both until they were panting, their breath mingling as puffs of smoke in the cold air.

Tucker's teeth nipped at his neck, his jaw, his ear, and Tucker's hand never stopped moving. Pre-come leaked from both of them, coating and sliding and warming their dicks as he stroked, and Chance was twisting and straining beneath him. "Gonna come like this," Chance warned, his voice tight.

"Tha's the idea, baby," Tucker answered.

Chance's balls drew up at the low, growly tone and he felt a tingle begin at the base of his spine. Slamming a hand down on top of Tucker's, Chance helped him speed up until they were both grinding desperately into Tucker's closed fist. "Now, *now*," Chance hissed, but Tucker was coming before he was.

"Oh, goddamn," Tucker groaned, jerking helplessly, and then Chance arched his neck and shot all over their joined hands.

Chance had forgotten they weren't alone until the horse snorted and turned its head to gaze at them soulfully.

Tucker glanced up and started laughing. "Don' give me that look, Blue. I done watched you fuck them fillies plenty a' times."

Chance eased to a sitting position and followed Tucker's lead in using the clean straw to wipe his hands. He tucked his prick back into his jeans and watched Tucker pop another beer open. "Now are we talking?"

"You can talk. I'm drinkin'." He proved his point by downing half the can.

"That's what I want to talk about. The fuck's with all the booze, man?" Chance leaned back against the wall and tried to ignore the cold air.

"Oh, don't give me that hypocritical shit," Tucker dismissed. "I seen you drunk more times'n I can count."

"Tuck, come on. You know it's not the same." He huffed out a frustrated breath and banged the back of his head against the stall wall. "Christ, Tucker, it's me. What the fuck are you afraid of? You know you can talk to me."

The fourth beer can crash-landed with the others and Tucker didn't reach for a fifth. He sat cross-legged next to Chance and stared at the straw floor. "Ain't afraid of nothin'."

Chance inched closer and slid a comforting hand onto Tucker's thigh. The misery was radiating off Tucker in waves, so much so that Chance could practically touch it. It gave Chance a tightness in his chest that he didn't know how to put a name to. The fact that there was something he couldn't make better for Tucker was frustrating and frightening at the same time. "Then … what?"

A myriad of things crossed Tucker's face in the span of a few seconds, and for a minute Chance thought Tucker was going to actually going to tell him what he wanted to know. Then Tucker's expression shuttered closed and he rose to his feet. Staring down at Chance, his jaw hard, he said quietly, "You shouldn't have come, Shanahan. You don't belong here."

He left Chance sitting alone on the floor of the stall.

***

Someone had left the light on over the stove, although the rest of the house was dark. Chance knew it wasn't that late, but he figured 'early to bed, early to rise' was probably the way of things around here. He didn't even know if Coop slept in the house or if he had another bed to go to.

Cotton snuffled at him from his bed in the corner of the kitchen and Chance stopped to give him a scratch. The dog sighed gratefully and thumped his tail. "Least someone's happy to see me," Chance whispered, and then rolled his eyes at himself. He'd been down the self-pity road before, when he'd broken his leg, and it hadn't done anyone any favors.

The important thing wasn't him, in any case. It was Tucker.

He made his way through the kitchen and passed the dining room on his right. To his left, before the stairs, was another short hallway. Although the stove light didn't carry into it, Chance turned that way. It ended at a small room and Chance felt along the wall for a switch. He found the light and clicked it on, blinking against the glare.

It was a small, wood-paneled office that had to have belonged to Tucker's father. Framed pictures lined one wall and Chance grinned at a nine-year-old Tucker holding up a small fish he had obviously just caught. Tucker's favorite fire department cap sat on the desk, telling Chance he'd taken over the space since he'd arrived. There were scattered papers and files everywhere and Chance didn't pretend to understand any of them, since they mostly seemed to be concerning this year's crop and auction prices for tobacco.

Another look around the office didn't turn up much and he was reluctant to go poking through stuff that was none of his business. He wasn't going to find answers here. Chance didn't think he was going to find answers anywhere unless Tucker gave them to him.

He climbed the stairs and was wondering if he should check out one of the other bedrooms to sleep in when he noticed the light. Tucker's door stood open, so Chance took it as a welcome and approached cautiously. He poked his head around the doorframe and waited.

Tucker lay on his back, arms folded behind his head. He glanced at Chance and then back at the ceiling. "Hi."

"Hi."

"You can come in," he offered, sliding over on the bed to make room, so Chance crawled onto the bed. Tucker turned to the side to face him. "Sorry. Seems all I do is 'pologize these days."

Chance brought up a hand and brushed the back of his knuckles against Tucker's cheek. "I'm not the enemy, Tuck."

Tucker looked at him, his eyes dark and serious. "Not intentionally."

Chance didn't think deciphering his meaning or arguing the point would do either of them any good right this minute, so he settled for kissing Tucker softly and pressing their foreheads together. "Maybe we should sleep on it."

"Considerin' you're gettin' your ass up at the crack of dawn with me to help strip, then, yeah. We better sleep." He gave a wan grin.

Chance eyed him. "What do I have to do?"

"Show you tomorrow," he yawned. "You gonna sleep with all those clothes on?"

"You said there's no central heat." But he kicked off his tennis shoes anyway and started undoing his jeans.

"Naw. But there's two of us. We'll make our own." Tucker started shedding clothes, too.

They crawled naked and shivering between cold sheets. Tucker turned over and Chance hauled him up tight against his chest, wriggling around until Tucker's ass fit snugly against Chance's cock. His dick twitched slightly, but he discarded the idea when Tucker yawned again and relaxed against him. Chance wasn't sure he'd be able to perform, anyway. His prick had seen more action today than it had in a month.

Chance was exhausted both mentally and physically, but he was still on west coast time and his mind refused to let him rest. Too much to consider. Too much to worry over. Too much to be unsure of. He cursed internally about it all, because he didn't live his life this way. His whole life was about control. It was one of the main reasons he'd decided to become a captain for the department; it was another place in his life he could be in charge, in command. In control.

Long after Tucker had fallen asleep, warm and heavy against Chance's chest, Chance lay awake and thought.

Chapter Thirteen

Chance figured he must have fallen asleep sometime, because otherwise he couldn't have been awakened so well by the hot, eager mouth on his cock.

"Still dark," he muttered, his brain fuzzy.

"Six a.m.," came the answer in between licks.

"Jesus. That's …" Chance tried to compute the time difference, but between the blow job and his exhaustion, his neurons weren't firing. "Really fucking early."

He received no answer, but only because Tucker's mouth was otherwise occupied. Chance gave up trying to think. He began moving with Tucker, arching his back and thrusting up gently, still half-asleep and losing himself in the hazy pleasure.

It was only another minute or so before his thought processes registered his impending orgasm. Planting his feet firmly, Chance reached down and tangled his fingers in Tucker's hair. "Right there," he managed, and then he was coming in slow, steady pulses that left him a little shaky.

Tucker licked him clean and then knelt over Chance, tugging at his own cock until Chance heard him groan quietly and felt Tucker's spunk land warm on his stomach. He collapsed next to Chance and leaned up to kiss him. "G'mornin'."

"Morning. Gonna sleep some more, okay?"

Tucker snorted and sat up. "No you ain't, baby. You're here, which means you're helpin'. Need every pair of hands we can get if we want to get that fuckin' tobacco to auction."

***

By the third day, Chance thought his arms might drop off his body.

Tucker had taught him how to strip the speared tobacco plants and separate them into different grades. Chance stopped pretending he could tell the difference and just threw the leaves into whatever pile Tucker told him to.

He'd gotten a few sidelong glances from the other men on the first day while Tucker was instructing him on what to do, but Chance just shut his mouth and did what he was told. He worked hard enough over the course of three days to make them nod approvingly at him when they all walked out of the tobacco barn and up to the house.

They threw together sandwiches and Chance wolfed down two of them. He downed a bottle of water and started in on the potato chips when Tucker gave him a nudge. "Go easy on chow. We got 'nother four hours and you don't want your belly crampin' up from the nicotine and cold air."

Chance reluctantly shoved the chips away from him. "This what you've been doing every day?" The answer should have been obvious; it was all he'd done since he'd gotten there.

Mack – one of the younger, quieter hands Chance had met the first day – answered that. "Only been strippin' for a week. Had to stack the plants and let 'em sweat for a few days after they were cut."

Yet more language that Chance didn't understand. It was becoming painfully obvious that he didn't know shit-all about farming. Now, firefighting? That was different. He sort of wished there was a burning building or something nearby. Then maybe he wouldn't feel like such an ignorant dumbass.

But Tucker gave him a wink and flashed his dimples when they headed back to the stripping room. "Doin' fine, Cap. Keep up the good work and I'll give ya a rubdown later."

It was a good incentive.

***

They stopped at four on the dot. The men threw down their gloves and grunted goodbyes at Tucker. Coop went with them, mumbling something about bowling night. Chance had no idea how they could lift their arms to heft a bowling ball. He didn't think he'd even be able to jerk off right now.

Not that he'd have to, judging by the way Tucker was leering at him.

"Big ol' house all to ourselves," he said casually, as Chance dragged himself up the stairs. "Whatever shall we do?"

"Shower," Chance said firmly. "I'm freezing my ass off. And I stink like those plants."

Fireline

"Then let's get wet." Tucker hustled him into the bathroom next to their bedroom – funny how it was suddenly *their* bedroom after only seventy-two hours – and Chance sat down on the closed toilet seat. He held out a foot to Tucker and made pleading eyes.

"Help," he said.

Tucker chuckled and yanked Chance's tennis shoe off, peeling his sock and wrapping a warm hand around his chilled toes. "Gotta get you a good pair of boots," he said, doing the same to the other foot. "And warmer socks. I mean, for as long as you're here."

Chance ignored the veiled reference to him leaving. He was supposed to be back at work five days from now, but he was no closer to getting Tucker back home with him than he was when he got here. Chance had no idea what he was going to do on Friday when he was supposed to leave.

Steam began to fill the small bathroom and the warmth slowly penetrated his frozen fingers. Chance got enough feeling back in his hands to lift his shirt over his head, and when he got it off, he noticed Tucker had left the room.

He appeared again as Chance was about to step into the shower, holding something behind his back. Chance paused, one foot in, and raised a brow.

Tucker grinned at him and Chance could see a flush covering his bare chest, and one glance south proved Tucker had something on his mind. "Just get in," Tucker motioned with one hand. "Be right there."

Chance narrowed his eyes, but the warm water was too hard to resist, so he ducked under the spray. Tucker followed Chance after a minute and Chance moved aside to let him in the water, running a hand down his chest while Tucker wet his hair.

Chance pulled back to just admire him as Tucker let the water sluice down. He'd always taken care of his body; they both had to because of work. But all the manual labor Tucker had done over the past month had changed it slightly. Leaner, tighter, the muscles harder and more defined. Chance glanced approvingly at the six-pack he sported, each ridge standing out. He reached out a finger to trace his favorite spot on Tucker: the groove between abdomen and hip that led diagonally to Tucker's groin.

Tucker twisted away with a chuckle and grabbed his wrist; it was a ticklish place. "Don't. Got other things you can touch."

"But I like that spot," Chance said, yanking his arm out of Tucker's grasp. He pressed it with his thumb and delighted in

Tucker's laughter, realizing he hadn't heard it in much too long. Chance kept it up for a while, wriggling his fingers in the narrow groove while Tucker laughed and tried to dodge him.

Tucker finally managed to make Chance stop by pushing him against the tile and kissing him, pressing his hard-on into Chance's hip and pinning his arms over his head. "Quit it, you big fuckin' bully," Tucker said with a smile.

"Me! Who's the one that worked my fingers to the bone for three days? You're a damn slave driver." Chance opened his mouth for Tucker's tongue and felt his cock rise to the occasion, pushing insistently at the soft skin of Tucker's inner thigh.

They were breathing hard when Tucker finally broke away and gave Chance a long look. "Want you to fuck me."

"Yes." Like he needed any coaxing. He turned Tucker to the wall and drew his tongue over Tucker's shoulder blade, tasting water and the fresh skin beneath. Tucker rolled his shoulders and shuddered, spreading his legs. Chance positioned his cock to rub in the crack of Tucker's ass, grabbing the bar of soap to help him slide more easily. He made no move to push inside yet, wanting to draw it out.

Tucker let Chance do it, bracing his hands on the tile and dropping his head. Chance reached around to hold Tucker's cock in his hand, jacking Tucker slowly while Chance rubbed off on him, loving the feel of being so secluded in the small shower. Shower sex was always his favorite, maybe because of the water and the slickness and the small, tight space. Chance readily admitted to having a water kink.

He felt along Tucker's crack until his finger touched Tucker's entrance. Tucker bucked back onto his finger, making both of them gasp, and Chance leaned over his shoulder. "You grab the lube?"

Tucker straightened up and made a move to reach outside the shower. "Yeah. And, uh. Got somethin' else, too." He handed Chance the nearly empty tube of lubricant and brought something else in with him.

Chance looked at what he had in his hand and raised both eyebrows. "Dildo?"

Tucker shrugged and Chance could swear there was an honest-to-Christ blush staining his cheeks. "Yeah. Use it on me?"

"Oh, *hell,* yes." He grabbed the smooth dildo out of Tucker's hand and attacked Tucker's mouth, hard and needy and eager.

Tucker's breathing was ragged and desperate as their tongues fought and hands slid over silky, wet skin. "God, need it so bad, need you," he muttered, fingers dancing over Chance's cock.

Chance took a deep breath to steady himself and tried to find a bit of distance. "Easy," Chance whispered, calming Tucker by pushing his wet hair back from his face. He followed his hand with sliding kisses over Tucker's cheeks and forehead. Tucker closed his eyes and leaned into it, his lashes making points on his cheeks, the steam and heat and arousal staining his skin pink.

Chance turned Tucker slowly to face the wall, raining open-mouthed kisses over his shoulders and spine. "Hot," he murmured against Tucker's skin. "You are so hot when you're like this."

"Like what?" His head fell back and he spread his legs, leaning against Chance's chest.

"Needy. Horny. Wanting."

"Only for you," he groaned.

Chance reached for the soap dish where he'd stuck the lube and managed to coat his fingers and the dildo at the same time. Dropping the tube, he circled a finger around Tucker's hole and slid the tip inside, feeling Tucker clench around him before relaxing. "More?" he asked, not being able to help sliding his cock against Tucker's hip.

"More. A lot more. Please." His voice was thready and Chance could see his fingers flexing on the tile, searching for purchase.

Chance took the dildo and touched it to the back of Tucker's neck. "Feel that?"

Tucker shuddered and moaned. "Yeah."

He drew it down further, following the bumps and ridges of Tucker's spine, until it rested in the hollow just above his ass. "And that?"

"Yes. Yes, come on, my God." He was whimpering and thrusting forward into thin air, his cock so hard it nearly stood parallel to his body.

Chance positioned the rubber head at Tucker's entrance and brought his mouth to Tucker's ear. "Gonna make you come apart," he whispered, and Tucker could only groan in response.

Slowly, carefully, he inched the dildo in, paying careful attention to Tucker's body language. It was tricky when Chance couldn't experience it himself, but he could feel Tucker under his hands and that would have to suffice. "Okay?" he asked.

"There," Tucker begged, "right there, go deeper with it."

He obeyed, pushing it in nearly to the hilt and tilting a bit to reach Tucker's prostate. Chance imagined he could feel it brush the gland and Tucker cried out, bucking backward and then thrusting forward. He did it again, and then again, until he was fucking himself on it and all Chance had to do was hold it still for him.

Tucker was gorgeous and Chance fed greedily on him, feeling sort of like a voyeur while Tucker worked himself, but Chance didn't care. He was beautiful. Chance could see the muscles bunch and cord in his back and realized Tucker was straining, reaching, concentrating so hard that he was shaking. "Chance," he pleaded, and that was all he had to say.

Chance slid a hand over his hip and wrapped fingers around Tucker's cock. "Go, baby," he coaxed, borrowing Tucker's favorite endearment.

"Fuck," Tucker got out, and then he was shuddering and trembling and coming hard enough to make Chance have to pin his upper body against the tile so he wouldn't fall.

When he was finished, Chance eased the dildo out and dropped it to the shower floor. He turned Tucker to face him and started to slide against the solidness of Tucker's thigh, the sound of Tucker's moans still in his ears.

Tucker splayed a hand over his ass, holding Chance close, and when Chance finally came it was with a groan that felt torn out of his chest.

They let the shower soothe them for a while before reaching for soap and washcloths. Gently, with slow, easy touches, they washed sore muscles and then each other's hair until Chance felt like Jell-O. He wanted dinner, bed, and Tucker, in that order.

If the purple smudges under his eyes were any indication, Tucker was equally worn out. They moved quickly to the bedroom to dress, shivering. Tucker sat down heavily on the bed and leaned against Chance's shoulder, smiling up at him. "Was good," he said, his tone light despite his exhaustion.

Chance kissed him and nuzzled his cheek. "Shoulda told me about it before. I'll add it to your list."

"List of what?" He heaved himself off the bed and held out a hand.

Chance let Tucker pull him up. "List of kinks. It's getting longer."

Tucker grinned and swatted his ass on their way downstairs. "You're at the top of it."

Fireline

Chapter Fourteen

Chance discovered the next night that alcohol wasn't the only thing in which Tucker had been indulging.

The house was empty again. It had been empty for three out of the four nights Chance had been in Kentucky, and neither he nor Tucker thought it was coincidence. Clearly, their relationship was uncomfortable for Coop and the others. Chance had been careful to keep a respectable distance from Tucker while they were in the presence of the men and although Tucker had grinned and winked wickedly at him behind their backs, he, too, had kept his hands to himself.

Not that Chance didn't appreciate the alone time. It had allowed for some very creative, not to mention high volume, sex. He blushed, thinking about how loud Tucker had made him shout this morning.

He glanced up to see Tucker watching him from behind his father's desk. "Somethin' on your mind?" he teased.

Chance blushed harder and shook his head, slouching lower in the easy chair. "You got much longer? I can go up and call Bonnie."

Tucker sighed and sat back in his own chair. He had his fire department cap on backwards and it made him look like a teenager, although with hot, four-day stubble on his cheeks and chin, Chance was hard-pressed to think of him as young.

Tucker glanced down at the scattering of papers on the desk and grimaced. "Have to call Jackson."

"What's he say about how probate's coming?"

"Two more months at best, six at worst. Then I gotta get busy on sellin' this place, which could be another four or five months. Dependin' on who's buyin'." The defeat in his voice was becoming a regular thing, and Chance hated it.

"Still think you can come home. No reason for you to be here when there's people that can do it for you. Can't you put Coop in charge of the crop, at least?"

Tucker looked torn. "Maybe. Dunno. I just feel like … damn, Chance, Momma left it to me, you know? And even if I sell, I feel like I gotta be here while it happens. And I can't just let Daddy's crop go to shit, even though it's so small. Tim didn't give a fuck about this place and I ain't gonna be like him." He propped his chin in his hand and scowled down at the paperwork.

It was difficult for Chance to understand, since for years he'd felt no real loyalty toward his own family. He supposed he loved them in a vague way, and he did make the effort to call his mother and get monthly progress reports on his younger brother. His father had taken off when he was three, so there was no regret or love lost there, either.

But clearly it was important to Tucker.

Tucker sighed in disgust and pushed back from the desk. "Screw this for tonight. I'll call him tomorrow and have him come out for a meetin'." He paused and looked at Chance thoughtfully. "Know what I need. You feel like relaxin' with me?"

Chance lifted his eyebrows and grinned. He knew what Tucker's preferred method of relaxing was. It usually involved some form of getting off. "Sure."

Tucker laughed. "Not what you're thinkin'. But yeah, that too, later." He stood up and Chance followed him to the kitchen, where Tucker dug around in the drawer by the stove.

When he pulled out a small plastic bag of what looked to be an herb commonly used in cooking, Chance knew exactly what it was. "Weed?"

"Weed." More digging in the drawer revealed a book of papers and a lighter, both of which Tucker deposited on the counter. "You in?"

Chance thought about it. He'd been high plenty of times in college – you couldn't go to school up in northern California without getting stoned on the good shit that came down from San Francisco or Humboldt county, but since he'd gotten hired for Oceanside he hadn't touched the stuff. It just didn't hold the same appeal anymore now that he wasn't twenty years old.

But Tucker was looking at him so hopefully that Chance couldn't turn him down. "Yeah, all right," he shrugged. "Roll it."

Tucker grinned. "Good boy."

Chance watched him quickly and expertly roll a fat joint, licking the paper to seal it. "New at this?" Chance asked with a hint of sarcasm.

Tucker shrugged. "Not much else to fuckin' do out here, if you ain't noticed by now. C'mon, let's go sit by the fire."

Cotton trailed them as they went into the family room and grabbed some cushions from the couch. Dropping to the floor, Tucker lit the joint and took a long hit before passing it to Chance and then lying back.

Chance inhaled the sweet smoke, feeling it press on his lungs and likening it to being caught in a fire. Even through his breathing apparatus, there was always the faint pressure of the smoke behind his mask. He finally exhaled with a rush of light-headedness and was proud of himself for not coughing. He guessed he'd inhaled enough smoke over the years to get used to it.

They passed the joint back and forth until Chance felt the buzz steal over him, which didn't take long. "Good stuff," he commented, and his words felt sticky in his mouth.

"Ayup," Tucker agreed, eyes fixed on the ceiling. "Mack brings it. Got me high my first night back, bless his ever-lovin' heart."

Chance thought maybe that was sort of significant, like he didn't think Tucker should be smoking pot or drinking or fighting or any of the shit he'd been doing since he'd been here, but his brain had slowed down to a crawl and he couldn't find the point. "God bless Mack," he said, and burst into giggles.

"Oh, don' make me start," Tucker warned, and then dissolved into laughter as well.

They rolled around on the floor, laughing 'til tears streamed from their eyes and just when Chance thought it was over, he caught sight of Cotton watching them very seriously from the couch. That brought on a fresh round of giggles that lasted until Tucker swatted him with a pillow. "Shut up. Stop laughin'."

"Okay," Chance said seriously, and did. It occurred to him that he was hungry. "Want food. Order me a pizza."

Tucker stared at him like he'd lost his mind. "Pizza? Ain't no pizza delivery service out here, man."

"Oh, right," Chance said miserably. "Still want food."

"For chrissakes," Tucker muttered, and got up. Chance watched him weave unsteadily to the kitchen and then return with a bag of bread and jar of peanut butter. "San'wich. Here." He dropped the food next to Chance, who tore into the bread and didn't bother with the peanut butter.

Tucker crawled over to Chance and lay down with his head on Chance's stomach. Chance tangled a hand in Tucker's hair while he ate the best piece of white bread that God ever made, then started on another. What had been wrong with pot, again? Besides the illegality factor, he couldn't think of anything.

He didn't know he was hard until Tucker's hand reached out to close around his cock. Chance arched at the brush of fingers on the material of his nylon track pants. Tucker slid the palm of his hand slow and easy over Chance's erection, rubbing and flattening and pushing. "So horny," Tucker whispered above the crackling and popping of the fire. "You feel it?"

Oh, God, did he feel it. Chance wanted to melt into the ground and let Tucker just get him off with a few quick rubs over his pants. He nodded and sighed and tried to do exactly that, but Tucker gave a low chuckle and slid on top of him. "You're participatin'."

He was too stoned to do anything but nod. Chance's limbs felt like honey, all warm and easy and loose, but when Tucker gave a slow, deliberate grind, cock to cock under the layers of clothing, Chance managed to bring up one arm to encircle his waist and hold him close. "Tuck," he murmured, not sure what he was going to say.

"Shh," came the answer against his lips, just a small brush of air before Tucker plunged his tongue inside.

Chance held onto Tucker's head with two hands, fingers curling into Tucker's scalp, and fucked Tucker's mouth with his tongue while his hips thrust forward to find pressure.

They were moaning in unison, but it sounded very faraway to Chance's ears, everything was muffled and filled with quiet. Sensation was the only thing that mattered. And Jesus Christ, he was more stoned than he'd ever been in his life.

Tucker slid down and took Chance's pants with him. Good thing they were track pants, so all he had to do was lift his hips, otherwise Chance wasn't sure he'd have been able to get them off at all. All his functioning muscle groups seemed to have taken a vacation. And no underwear in the way, thank God.

Chance felt himself kissed everywhere, slow brushes of tongue and lips, Tucker's mouth sucking at spots hard enough to bruise. He thought hazily that maybe he should be reciprocating, but couldn't make himself do more than keep a hand caught in Tucker's hair.

Tucker's knuckles grazed Chance's cock and then were replaced by his mouth, sucking and tasting the head and gathering up all the fluid Chance was leaking. It was so good and hazy; Chance felt distanced from it while at the same time had never felt more alive in his skin. He was suddenly aware of the heat from the fire and the sweat beading on his brow.

Tucker was working him so slowly Chance wanted to die. One lick up with the flat side of that tongue, then whole mouth on the down stroke, opened wide enough for Chance to feel the head of his cock hit the back of Tucker's throat. Quick, steady sucks at the tip, tongue pushed into the slit and then gone again, until Chance was moaning and twisting on the carpet.

He felt strong hands on either side of his waist, holding him still. "Don't thrash, baby," Tucker murmured. "Rug burn."

"Can't help it," Chance replied, and wasn't embarrassed at all about the whimper in his voice. "Want more."

"Ask and ye shall receive," Tucker whispered, and took hold of the base of Chance's dick in strong fingers. He lowered his head again, bobbing up and down while jacking Chance at the same time, and Chance wanted to know how Tucker could be so stoned and still doing that.

And then it didn't matter, nothing mattered except his cock being hard enough to hurt and the fingers Tucker was slowly inserting in his ass, using only spit for lube. There was one brushing his prostate, not pressing or stroking, just brushing it maddeningly and Chance started twisting his hips in an effort to make Tucker do it again.

He didn't know what to concentrate harder on, the fingers in his ass or the mouth on his dick or the hand on his balls, and he let out a frustrated groan. All of his skin was on fire, aching with whatever magic Tucker was weaving and whatever the *hell* had been in that weed to make him feel like this. A thumb pushed gently against his perineum and Chance knew that was it, game over, and waited for his orgasm.

Except Tucker was too good at this to let him come so easily.

He took his thumb away just when Chance would have needed two more seconds of the pressure and Chance cried out in protest. "Hey!"

"Shh, baby," Tucker murmured against his skin, the words low and soothing. "Gonna give it to you, promise. Trust me." Tucker stroked a hand down Chance's hip, calming him, before going back to the maddening game of suck, lick, pull back.

Chance wasn't sure he could take much more of it, his skin was crawling and goose bumps were rising despite the heat from the fire. His senses were alternating between alert and dull, the pleasure part of his brain trying to fight off the drug to experience everything.

There were light, tickling strokes on his balls, and somewhere either his mind or his dick decided it had had enough. Chance slammed both hands down onto the carpet and bucked up hard into Tucker's mouth, the fire at the base of his spine sending out shocks that reached all the way to his fingers and toes. He came hard enough to make the room tilt at the corners and everything at the edges of his vision went blurry and gray.

He was still shuddering with small aftershocks when he felt his legs pushed back. A warm hand swept through the come on his stomach and coated his entrance with it, one finger brushing inside. And then Tucker was pushing into him, pure heat and so, so hard, and Chance marveled at how the hell he'd lasted this long with a hard-on like that.

There was a slow pull out that made Chance gasp and Tucker threw his head back and muttered soft profanities. "So tight," he hissed through clenched teeth. "Fuck. Thought I could go longer, but – " He cut himself off when he pushed back inside, head down now and eyes squeezed closed. Tucker came without another word, fingers biting roughly into Chance's thighs and rocking fast and hard against him.

When Tucker finally pulled out, he reached for his t-shirt to clean both of them up. Chance was still too heavy-limbed to help Tucker, so he stared at the ceiling while Tucker took care of it.

Tucker dropped back down next to him and threw an arm over Chance's chest, studying him carefully. "You're pretty," Tucker said seriously.

Chance turned his head to look at him, startled. Tucker didn't like that word and rarely used it. He thought back to the first time he'd ever called Tucker pretty and gotten his head bitten off. "What? Shut up."

"You are." He reached out a light finger and traced the bridge of Chance's nose, then ran the pad of his thumb over Chance's cheek. "You got a pretty face. Ain't no one told you that before?"

"Besides my mom? And 'pretty' wouldn't be a word she'd use, anyway." He could feel his high receding slightly, the world righting itself at the corners again.

"You got green eyes," Tucker said absently, his thumb still stroking the arch of Chance's cheek.

"Hazel."

"They change. They're hazel when you're in a bad mood. They're green when you're tired. Or horny." He grinned. "Or stoned, like now. Bright green."

"You don't know what you're talking about." Chance looked back at the ceiling, embarrassed. He never thought much about his own looks and it was disconcerting to have Tucker studying him so closely.

"Sure I do. Got eyes, don't I? Look at you every damn day and say to myself, "How the fuck'd that boy get so pretty?" And you're always tan, even in the winter. Your skin's always got that tone to it."

Chance rolled over and shoved a hand against Tucker's mouth. "Shut up. You're the pretty one with your goddamned dimples and those fucking dark blue eyes. Could charm anyone in existence with that southern drawl."

Tucker darted a tongue out to lick Chance's palm. "Don't wanna charm anyone in existence. Just wanna charm you."

"You did." He yawned widely and pillowed his head on his arms. "M'tired. How come you're not tired?"

Tucker glanced at him and snorted. "M'thinkin' it's been too long since you had yourself a good smoke."

"And I'm thinking you've been doing this too much if you're not as high as I am."

Tucker shrugged, unconcerned. "Like I said. What the fuck else is there to do out here?"

Chance watched him in the dying light of the fire and didn't say anything.

***

It took him two days to recover.

Chance felt gritty-eyed and vaguely ill for almost forty-eight hours, and the nicotine in his system from the tobacco plants didn't help matters. By Thursday afternoon, feeling slightly better, he called Matt.

"Not coming home tomorrow," he said quietly, and shut the door to the bedroom. His voice probably wouldn't carry through the house to where Tucker was meeting with Jackson in the office, but he wasn't taking chances.

"That bad, huh?" Matt asked, concern lacing his tone.

"Well … not on the surface," Chance sighed. "If you didn't know the guy? You wouldn't think anything's wrong. But it's all the shit he isn't saying, plus all the bad habits he's picked up. It just weirds me out."

"So how long?"

Chance glanced at the business card-sized shift calendar he kept in his wallet. "Clear me through mid-January. That gives me a month."

"You might get written up," Matt warned. "But I'll see what I can tell headquarters. Family emergency or some shit."

"Thanks, man. Appreciate it."

Chapter Fifteen

Tucker didn't put up the expected fight when Chance told him he wasn't going home, which actually bothered Chance more than if he'd argued.

He shrugged and looked out the window of the front door, watching the lawyer drive away. "You can stay as long as you want, man. Ain't my hide that's gonna be tanned when you get back to work."

It was an abrupt change of heart from his earlier "I don't want you here" speeches. Chance eyed him. "You don't mind?"

Tucker turned from the door and then leaned back against it, crossing one booted foot over the other and looking for all the world like a southern redneck. "What's to mind?" he asked, accent thicker than ever. "Gettin' my dick sucked firs' thing in the mornin'? Wakin' up to your ass pressed against my cock? Shoot, baby, ain't nothin' to mind about you stayin'." He grinned.

Chance raised his eyebrows in surprise. "Yeah? Thought you'd be more wound up about it."

Tucker's grin faded and he leveled Chance with a stare. "You don't make any more fuckin' noise about me leavin' and there ain't nothin' to get wound up about."

Chance stared right back. "This isn't where you belong."

"You're wrong."

***

Tobacco stripping went on for another week and nothing changed. They went to town one day, to get Chance some decent winter clothes, and it didn't snow, but it was still in the thirties every day. Chance thought he'd never be warm again. The only time he wasn't freezing his balls off was when he and Tucker were in bed and there was another body he could curl up against.

He grew to hate the tobacco plants.

They finally finished stripping nine days before Christmas and got all the tobacco bales stored in neat piles. The big, dry bushels covered one wall of the barn. To Chance, it looked like a hell of a lot, but the men all grumbled about the smallness of the crop.

Tucker just stood back silently and looked at the bales and gave no clue as to what he might be thinking.

They all stood around and slapped their gloves against their jeans until Coop finally cleared his throat. "Well, since we ain't gettin' this shit to auction afore Christmas, I'll see y'all in January."

Chance looked up, surprised. "January?"

Tucker finally spoke. "Auction stops a week before Christmas. They start up again after the first of the year."

Chance furrowed his brow. "So what do we do now?"

A slow grin spread over Tucker's face. "Now we celebrate."

***

They ate dinner in town at the small diner before heading out on the interstate. Chance slouched in the passenger seat and watched the river as they drove: a big, black, silent ribbon beside them. "It's not like the ocean at all," he said softly.

Tucker glanced out the window at it. "Nope."

He missed the beach more than he thought possible. A year ago, when he'd broken his leg and had been forbidden to surf for several months, it had been bad. But it wasn't like this. Then, he could at least get in his car and go to the ocean. He had sat on the sand and watched the waves and felt a certain peace from it, although he had still yearned to be in the water. But now … now, Chance could sense how far they actually were from his beloved Pacific and it left a strange void in him.

"Lots of jet skiers in the summer," Tucker commented, reading his mind. "But I guess it ain't the same as surfin'."

"Nothing's the same as surfing," Chance replied.

They drove in companionable silence for a while, Tucker humming along with the radio now and then. Chance caught himself murmuring some of the words, too, and Tucker laughed at him. "You gone country, Cap?"

"God. Let's hope not."

It was only another ten minutes or so before they crossed the Indiana border. Chance didn't think the landscape changed much, though it was hard to tell in the dark. Flat fields, rolling highway, and always the endless Ohio River beside them. Monotonous. But he supposed it was just a matter of opinion, since he was used to a different type of geography.

They could see the bar coming long before they pulled up, since the lights shining from the windows were the only ones for miles. The music pulsing through the walls was barely audible except for the low, thumping beat and Chance sat up straighter. Maybe this was what they needed. Just a night together with no distractions. And if it happened to be at the only gay bar in three counties, all the better.

They crunched through the gravel to the door and Tucker hooked an arm around Chance's neck. "Need me a beer, the dance floor, and you."

Chance grinned and planted a kiss on him. "Same. Maybe two beers, though."

The music assaulted them as soon as they walked in. Tucker headed straight for the bar and Chance followed him, shouldering through the crowd and trying to take in the feel of the place.

Gay bars, in his experience, could have very different atmospheres. His preferred bar at home, The Seagull, was quiet and unassuming. It didn't have live music, just a muted jukebox in the corner that had been there for years, and wasn't much of a pickup place unless you were really looking. Then there were the clubs in Los Angeles that were all about who could be seen with whom and who had a shinier shirt on and how many times you could visit the back room in an hour. Chance hated them.

This bar seemed to be in between and pleasant enough. Guys were sitting at tables or on barstools and the dance floor was full but not packed. A DJ was up on the small stage in the corner, nodding his head in time to the music he was playing. Chance noted that Heineken was among the display bottles on the shelf behind the bar. Things were looking good.

They looked even better when Tucker handed a cool, green bottle over his shoulder. "Drink up, baby. Know you've been missin' em."

"You have no idea," Chance said, taking a long swig of his favorite beer. It tasted like heaven after the swill he'd been drinking here.

"Usual for you?" Chance heard the bartender ask, and looked over to see Tucker grin.

"Do me right, Scotty," Tucker dimpled, and accepted what looked like a stiff Jack Daniel's and Coke. The bartender smiled at Tucker and leaned his elbows on the bar.

"There you go. Heavy on the Jack, light on the Coke."

"That's my boy," Tucker winked, and Chance rolled his eyes.

Scotty leaned over even further. "Got an early shift tonight," he said conspiratorially. "Save a drink for me?"

Chance would have been happy to lurk behind Tucker and listen to the show, but Tucker reached around and yanked him forward. "Ask him," Tucker said to Scotty, tilting his head toward Chance.

'Crestfallen' didn't begin to describe the look on the bartender's face. "Aw, shoot, McBride," he said, straightening up and glancing at Chance. "You're a fuckin' tease."

Tucker made a pouty face and turned to Chance. "You hear that? Scotty says I'm a tease." He stuck out his lower lip and batted his eyelashes.

Chance slid a hand around his neck and pulled Tucker in for a kiss, plunging his tongue deep and running his fingers up to cup the back of Tucker's head. Chance held Tucker in place while he kissed him hard, and when he pulled back, he ended it with a lick to the corner of Tucker's mouth. Chance turned to the bartender and shrugged. "He doesn't kiss like he's teasing."

"Oh, fuck me," the bartender breathed, watching them both. "I'd let you both tease me any day. Or night. All night." He wet his lips and looked at Tucker. "What do you say? You guys play?"

Tucker met Chance's eyes. "Do we?"

Chance looked directly at Scotty, but spoke to Tucker. "No," he said firmly. "We don't."

Tucker didn't bother answering Scotty himself. He grabbed Chance by the front of his shirt and dragged him to the dance floor, wrapping the hand that wasn't holding a drink around Chance's waist. He hauled himself up snugly against Chance's crotch and started a slow, grinding rhythm in time to the music. "So," he said, mouth close to Chance's ear, "we don't play well with others, huh?"

Chance felt goose bumps go up his scalp at the breath in his ear. "Nope. I never did, in school. Teachers were always telling my mom I didn't listen well or take directions, either."

Tucker chuckled. "The not takin' directions part I believe. So damn bossy."

Chance meant to say something else, but all that came out was a moan when Tucker's hand crept down to his ass and squeezed. His cock pushed insistently against the rough denim of his jeans and he'd forgotten until now that he wasn't wearing underwear.

And he was so fucking glad he hadn't when Tucker's fingers popped the top two buttons of his fly and crept beneath the waistband. Chance dropped his mouth to Tucker's neck when he felt a sure brush of a hand against the head of his cock. He darted his tongue out to touch the silky skin below Tucker's ear, smiling when he felt the tiny hairs stand up.

His cock throbbed almost in time with the music and he pushed forward eagerly, frustrated when he realized Tucker couldn't get his hand in much farther. Tucker's own cock was a hard ridge against Chance's hip as they moved together, each seeking more friction and pressure.

Tucker took a gulp of his drink and kissed Chance again, his tongue cool from the ice and tasting of sharp bourbon. He began to pant, his one free hand pulling out of Chance's jeans and roaming over the bare skin under Chance's shirt. "God, could come right here," Tucker muttered, pressing himself as tight as he could against Chance's thigh.

Chance darted a look around. "Fuck, where's the bathroom?" he hissed, not sure he could even detach himself long enough to find it.

"Why – oh," Tucker breathed. "Yeah. Bathroom. Back a'the house." He curled his fingers into Chance's waistband and yanked him off the dance floor, heading toward the back. They dropped their drinks on an empty table and Chance noticed that Tucker was getting appreciative glances as they moved through the crowd. Yeah, let them look – he was the one who was going to have Tucker's dick in his hand in about five seconds.

There were two small restrooms in the dark hallway. Tucker glanced up at the one with the figure of a woman on it and pushed inside. "Don't guess we'll be bothered in here," Tucker mused, and then Chance found himself pressed with his back to the wall.

"Gimme," Tucker muttered, scrabbling at Chance's fly, tongue darting out to moisten his lips. "Damn. Fuckin' buttons won't undo."

He jerked roughly at Chance's jeans until Chance chuckled and pushed him away.

"Quit it. Let me." He managed to get his fly open enough for Tucker to draw his cock out and Chance sighed with relief.

Tucker tried to keep a hand on Chance's prick while getting his own jeans open and only succeeded in frustrating both of them. "Dammit. Dammit!"

"Here," Chance whispered, steadying him. He flicked open Tucker's fly and his cock nearly leapt into his hand, hard and leaking. "Damn. You been packing this all night?"

Tucker made a sound between a laugh and a groan. "Pretty much. Oh God, do that again."

Chance nuzzled into his neck and stroked him again, harder. He closed his eyes when Tucker reciprocated, cock leaping at the thought of Tucker hard as steel all night. "Fast," Chance demanded, hips thrusting forward into the tunnel of Tucker's hand. "Do it fast, come on. Wanna spill all over you."

"Keep talkin'. Don't get enough dirty talk outta you," he said, pulling at Chance's dick while jerking forward into Chance's hand.

"Want you to make me come," Chance whispered, "and then we're going back out to that dance floor to give them all a show. Gonna grind so hard on you out there, we'll make them all cream in their jeans. Okay?"

Tucker was panting now, one hand rucking up Chance's shirt to play over his nipples while the other continued to pump him. "Christ, yes. Yesyesyesyes."

"And then," Chance continued, sucking in a breath when he felt his balls draw up, "then we're going home and I'm gonna fuck you into the mattress, gonna pound you till you're walking funny and –"

"Gonna come … *now*," Tucker managed, and then shuddered within the circle of Chance's arms. Chance felt the hot spunk spill over his hand and didn't need any more coaxing. He bit back a groan and shot everywhere, his come falling on Tucker's cock and the front of his jeans and then spattering on the floor.

They took deep breaths in unison, trying to come down, and then Tucker reached over to the paper towel dispenser. He shoved two paper towels at Chance and then turned to the sink to clean up.

They grinned at each other in the mirror, color high in both of their faces. "Need me a drink," Tucker said.

Chance made a noise of agreement as he pulled the bathroom door open. "M'thinking I need more than one. Have to make up for all the pisswater beer you made me drink."

Fireline

Two hours later, Chance was happy, horny, and well on his way to drunk.

They'd been dancing all night, sometimes with other guys, but mostly together, making out on the dance floor like teenagers. Chance had had at least three beers and two good-sized shots of tequila, poured generously by Scotty.

"If'n I get you plowed, maybe y'all will reconsider playin'," he grinned, but Chance could tell he didn't really mean it.

Tucker showed up to haul him back to the floor. Chance barely had time to clunk his shot glass back on the bar and give Scotty a wink before Tucker was pressed up against him, cock thick and heavy in his pants. Chance's own cock twitched. "Thinkin' it's about time we hit it," Tucker said, his hand combing through the sweat-slicked hair at Chance's nape.

Chance nudged up close to Tucker, sliding his hand down to cup Tucker's bulge. "M'thinking I agree. How much you had to drink? 'Cause I sure as hell can't drive."

"Just two, baby. You think I'd endanger your precious ass?" Tucker dangled the keys at Chance and shook his head. "Dang, Cap. You sure don't think much of my moral standards."

They were laughing as they stumbled through the front door – well, Chance amended, Tucker didn't really seem to be the one who was stumbling – and stopped halfway across the parking lot to kiss and grope each other.

"Think I might puke," came a disgusted voice that rang clear across the lot.

They jerked apart and Chance looked around for the source. He was aware of Tucker standing warily next to him, hands loose at his sides. "Caffrey," Tucker said calmly, and something in his tone put Chance on the alert.

"Don't even say my name, you disgusting queer," he sneered, pushing off from where he and three other guys had been leaning on Tucker's truck. "Faggots like you don't get to say my name."

Chance felt his sobriety come crashing back, the happy buzz of earlier draining away like rain in the gutter. He stayed close to Tucker and eyed the four men approaching them.

"Looks like McBride's found hisself another cocksucker," one of the others spoke up. "And dang if he ain't just as pretty as you, McBride."

Tucker tensed and Chance put a hand on his arm. "Wait," he warned Tucker in a low voice. "Wait and see."

"Don't you fuckin' touch each other where I can see it," the one Tucker had called Caffrey said. "Not unless you're askin' for a fist in the mouth."

"Seems like you're gonna give it to us anyway," Tucker shrugged. "So I might as well go first." And before any of them could move, Tucker hauled off and punched him.

Caffrey's head snapped back and Chance caught a glimpse of bright red blood before everything else exploded. *Goddammit, Tucker,* he had time to think, and ducked a fist aimed at his nose. Another one from the left caught him on the cheek and Chance swore when he felt his skin split open. The guy must have been wearing a ring.

It had been a damn long time since he'd been in a fistfight, the scuffle he and Tucker had had not included. Chance surprised himself by letting his rage take over, something he was usually very careful to control. But he had gone from minding his own business to being called a cocksucker in a matter of seconds, and he really didn't think he should be responsible for his own actions at the moment.

At least, that's what he told himself as he dragged one of the assholes off of Tucker and gave the man a good blow to the gut, feeling a strong sense of satisfaction when the guy crumbled to the ground.

Things were okay for a while, even though the four-to-two odds were definitely not in their favor. Chance delivered a kick to the ribs to ensure the one on the ground stayed there, just as Caffrey wrapped an arm around his neck and began to choke him.

"You're a worthless piece of shit," Caffrey grunted in his ear. "Cocksuckers like you don't deserve to live. You're goin' straight to hell, you disgusting freak, and I'm just doin' God's work if'n I'm the one to send you."

Chance would have rolled his eyes at the religious hypocrisy, but his vision was getting a little blurry from lack of oxygen. He tried to look around to see how Tucker was faring, but when Caffrey squeezed harder, Chance felt himself sink to his knees.

Even then, he probably would have been able to bring an elbow around to get Caffrey in the stomach, but one of the other men took the opportunity to kick Chance hard in the groin.

Fireline

Pain that had no equivalent blossomed in his crotch and spread outward, making his head reel and his stomach clench. He would have keeled over on the gravel if Caffrey's arm wasn't still around his neck. As it was, Chance knew he was going to throw up and he scrabbled desperately at Caffrey's wrist, trying to make him let go in time.

It didn't work, but through the hazy agony, Chance felt a small measure of satisfaction when he puked all over the guy's arm. At least it made him let go.

But the satisfaction was short-lived when Caffrey hissed, "You stupid fuck," and delivered a sharp kick to his ribs. Chance dropped to all fours and willed himself not to hurl again, even though his balls were still aching enough to make him nauseous. Out of the corner of his eye, he could see a booted foot draw back for another kick, but it never came.

He sank into a sitting position and spit on the ground, trying to rid himself of the foul taste in his mouth and shifting uncomfortably at the pain in his crotch. No fucking way was he using his equipment for a while. Chance realized it had gone quiet and glanced up to see where everybody was.

Tucker's arms were pinned behind him by one of the bartenders who had come out to see what the commotion was. Blood dribbled from the corner of his mouth and he had a darkening bruise on his left cheek, but otherwise looked okay. The other four men were being held by various people who had all been inside the bar and all of them looked a sight worse than Tucker. Chance had a moment of gratification when he noted Caffrey's slowly blackening eye.

He met Tucker's gaze when they heard the sirens in the distance.

Chapter Sixteen

It didn't matter who had called the cops; the only thing that mattered was that Tucker had thrown the first punch, and that now they were handcuffed and sitting in the back of a car. Chance's throat was tight and his mind was racing.

They were actually being goddamned arrested. Jesus fucking Christ, was there nothing better for the police to do on a Thursday night in Indiana? Chance's jaw clenched so hard it ached. If the stupid fuckers who'd cornered them decided to press felony charges ... well, he and Tucker were screwed. They could both lose their paramedic licenses and Chance was in serious danger of being demoted.

And all because Tucker had swung first. *Shit.*

He stared out the window as they drove, completely ignoring Tucker sitting beside him. Chance could not remember another time in their year and a half together when he'd been so furious. And Chance could tell Tucker knew it, too, since he hadn't opened his mouth for the past ten minutes. Good. Let him sit there and bleed.

They were both bleeding, actually, since Chance could feel the slow trickle down his cheek from where the skin had separated. Fantastic. That should give him a nice, respectable scar. "Fuck," he cursed under his breath, unable to keep silent any longer.

Tucker heard him. "You gonna stay pissed?" he whispered, unwilling to draw the attention of the two officers in front.

Chance turned his head and cocked a brow at Tucker before looking out the window again.

"Yup," Tucker muttered. "Y'are."

***

The jail was small, with only five holding cells and a drunk tank. The officers had the foresight to put Caffrey and the others in the cell furthest from Tucker and Chance, although there were only about fifty feet between them anyway and they had to endure catcalls and name-calling through the bars. The big-bellied sheriff finally yelled at them to shut their yaps.

Rubbing the red places on his wrists, Chance stalked to the bench along the wall and plunked himself down on it. He used the back of his hand to scrub at his cheek, wiping the dried blood on his jeans and cursing inwardly at the vomit on his ruined shirt.

Tucker approached cautiously. "You okay?"

Chance looked up at him with disbelief. "Am I okay? Let's see. I went from being happily buzzed and thinking I was going to get laid to getting my cheek busted open and my balls kicked in. I puked my guts out all over the parking lot and then got arrested by the Indiana State Police for defending myself, and all because you hit first. Now I'm sitting in a fucking jail cell in goddamned Indiana, wondering if I'll have a job when I get back home, and I have to take a piss. No, McBride, *I am not okay!*"

He ended on a shout that he hadn't even known was building. Tucker's eyes widened and Chance had time to see him chew uncertainly on his lower lip before turning away and going back to the front of the cell. He put his arms through the bars and rested his elbows on the crossbar and Chance saw him lean his head on the metal gate.

Damn it.

He sat for a full minute, telling himself not to get up, but his gaze kept straying back to Tucker's slumped shoulders. Finally, Chance pushed himself off the wooden bench and approached Tucker. He leaned a shoulder against the bars and tilted his head, trying to see Tucker's expression. "Hey. Didn't mean to yell."

Tucker shook his head, staring at the cement floor. "Yeah, you did."

"Yeah, I did, okay. Shouldn't have, though. Least not here."

Tucker turned toward Chance, but kept his eyes on his shirt. "Was my fault," he said heavily. "I know. You should be furious."

"I am."

Tucker nodded and swallowed tightly. He glanced up for a brief second and met Chance's eyes before darting his gaze back to the floor. "Look, I just ..." he stopped and studied his fingernails, a furrow between his brows. Chance waited. "I don't like you seein' me like this," he finally said. "You shouldn't be here." He gestured at the tiny cell, but Chance knew he meant more than just the jail.

"Neither should you," Chance said softly, but Tucker shook his head.

"Naw, you don't get it, man. This is me, this is what I'm about. This is what I grew up with and what I'm always gonna be. Trouble. And comin' back here just cements it, you know?" He looked exhausted and beaten, both physically and mentally.

Just like that, Chance's anger dissipated. He was pretty sure it would surface again when they were home and warm and clean and had some privacy to yell at each other, but for now, all he wanted was to wrap Tucker in an embrace and whisper words of comfort.

He settled for nudging Tucker's booted foot with his own. "Hey," he said in a low voice, and waited till Tucker was looking at him. "You may be trouble, but you're my trouble. Got it?"

Tucker's eyes were dark and miserable, but he nodded.

***

They ended up being held till morning. Neither of them slept, they just sat together on the narrow bench, shoulder to shoulder, and endured it.

Coop showed up at eight with Jackson, the lawyer who'd dealt with the estate, even though he'd said during their one phone call that it was outside his area and he would have to send someone else.

"Got good news for you," he said as they walked out into the sharp winter sunshine. "Y'all aren't bein' charged with a felony. Gonna be class A misdemeanor battery, and even that's only because that guy Caffrey was whinin' about a broken nose."

Not a felony, thank God. It would go on his record and Chance knew for sure that he was going to get written up and reprimanded, but neither he nor Tucker would lose their paramedic licenses.

Coop shot Chance a look as they piled into Jackson's sleek black sedan. "You was supposed to keep him outta this kind of trouble," he accused. "Not help him do it."

Chance leveled Coop with a stare. "I'm his partner," he said evenly, before they both got into the car. "Not his mother."

But he still felt guilty.

***

He let Tucker take a shower alone when they got back. Chance thought about going in with him after a few minutes, but he was so

Fireline

grateful to be lying on a soft bed instead of sitting on a hard bench that he couldn't move.

Chance was almost asleep when he heard the water shut off and then Tucker moving around the bedroom. "Feel better?" he asked, without opening his eyes.

"Thousand percent better," Tucker answered, and Chance felt the bed dip as he sat down. "Go, baby. Get clean."

He sat up with a wince and tried to carefully peel off his jeans without any further damage to his balls. Tucker bit his lip, but stayed quiet while helping him, sliding his jeans down and using an easy touch to examine Chance's groin. Chance stared at the ceiling. "I don't want to look."

"S'not so bad," he mused. "Little bit of bruisin'. Bet it hurts like a bitch, though."

Surprisingly, the ache was receding. Not so surprisingly, it was being replaced with arousal, since Tucker was touching him so gently. "It's getting better."

"So I see," Tucker grinned, as Chance's cock filled. "But you get nothin' till you're clean. Go."

He went.

If there could be religious experiences in showering, Chance thought he might be having one. He could practically feel the dirt and grime sluicing off him as he used the hottest water possible. The cramped jail had left a sticky, uncomfortable feeling on his skin and he scrubbed down three times with the fragrant bar of soap before he really felt like he'd washed the stink off himself. The shampoo stung his eyes, but he didn't care; it was a reminder that he was finally getting clean.

He stepped out of the shower and grimaced at the pile of disgusting clothes he'd left on the floor. Chance didn't even want to touch them long enough to throw them in the hamper, so he left them where they were and figured he could get them later.

Right now, there was a bed to fall into and a warm body to curl around.

Tucker had drawn the curtains over the small window so the room was dim. Chance could make out his form under the blankets, curled in on himself, his back to the door. Chance dropped his towel on the dresser and crawled in next to Tucker, fitting his chest to Tucker's back and snaking an arm over Tucker's waist.

There was silence for long minutes, though neither of them was sleeping. Chance could feel Tucker breathing steadily and concentrated on the rise and fall of his chest, the simple normality of it. He splayed his hand out as wide as he could, feeling the taut muscles of Tucker's stomach, his pinky finger going into the narrow dent of Tucker's navel.

He had just dropped his lips to Tucker's shoulder when Tucker spoke in a near-whisper. "Chance."

"Mm?"

"I'm sorry."

Chance took a deep breath and closed his eyes. He let it out slowly, mouth still against Tucker's shoulder. "Yeah. I know."

"No," Tucker said, and his voice was raw. "No, you don't know." He turned in Chance's embrace and hid his face in the hollow of Chance's throat. Chance could hear him swallow twice in an effort to speak. "I never wanted this," he finally whispered. "Didn't want to come here, didn't want you to follow me, didn't want you to see who I really was, and what I came from."

Chance tightened his hold on Tucker and shook his head. "I keep telling you. You're not like this place. You don't belong here any more than I do."

He took a shaky breath. "Don't matter. I'm just sorry, man. So fuckin' sorry." He ended on a choked whisper and Chance could feel him shaking.

"Don't, Tuck," Chance said, his heart aching. "C'mon, shh." He couldn't do more than hold Tucker tightly, knowing he was crying and not able to do anything to make it better.

Tucker clung to him for a long time, tears dampening Chance's neck and the pillow beneath them. He didn't make a sound, except for the occasional gulp of air as he tried to compose himself, but the tears continued to fall relentlessly.

Chance murmured incoherent words into Tucker's hair as he cried. He didn't know what he was saying and it didn't matter, Tucker probably wasn't listening to him, anyway. The only thing that mattered was offering comfort.

The kisses Chance was pressing on Tucker's forehead and cheeks landed on his mouth when Tucker looked up with wet eyes. Chance kissed him gently, softly, treating him as if he was fragile when he knew Tucker was anything but. Chance darted out a tongue to catch the salt hovering on Tucker's lashes, following it with sliding kisses over his eyes and then to the corners of his lips.

Tucker breathed out slowly, remaining completely still except for the tightening of his fingers on Chance's waist. Chance tangled his fingers in damp hair and angled Tucker's head up for another kiss, tasting and touching with his tongue. There was too much to say with mere words, so Chance tried telling Tucker with his hands and mouth instead, soothing and calming both of them.

There was anger and fear under Tucker's surface, Chance could taste it. It was raw and needy and exposed. Chance tried to take it away; didn't like the tight, hoarse feeling below their kisses, so his mouth grew more desperate and opened even wider for Tucker's tongue. Tucker looked up at him and those eyes were dark, the pupils dilated enough to leave only a thin ring of blue around the black.

He felt the desire build in spite of himself, in spite of the fact that maybe this wasn't the time. But Tucker was rocking gently against him as they kissed, cock stiffening on Chance's hip, and Chance was helpless against the need as his own erection grew.

"Need you," Tucker said against his mouth, the words nearly inaudible. "Need you, please."

"How?" Chance asked, pushing back, cock sliding along the vee of Tucker's crotch.

"Don't care," he murmured, head going back as he ground down harder. "Just need you in me."

Chance detached himself long enough to reach for the lube. Tucker turned to his stomach and clutched a pillow to his chest, spreading his legs and presenting a perfect ass. Chance ran an appreciative hand over it, letting his fingers linger in the crack and running his thumb down to sweep over Tucker's hole.

And then Chance's fingers were inside, coating Tucker liberally while listening to the soft sounds he was making as he rubbed against the bed. Chance yanked his fingers out and replaced them with the head of his cock, nudging gently at the opening until Tucker groaned and thrust backward with one sudden movement.

Chance found himself buried balls deep, his arms trembling with the effort to hold himself up, while Tucker moaned beneath him. "Move," Tucker managed, trying to thrust backwards.

It was slow and languid for a while, Chance moving with ease and caution mixed together, trying to draw out the gratification. Tucker thrust against the bed and Chance watched his fingers flex and tighten on the pillow he held, trying to determine from the whiteness of his knuckles how close he was to coming.

It turned out that he didn't really have to guess. Leaning forward to pass his tongue along Tucker's shoulder blade made him press up on Tucker's prostate, sending a shudder through both of them. Tucker let out a soft cry and wriggled backwards, trying to get Chance to repeat the action.

Every wriggle of Tucker's ass brought Chance a little closer to release, so he braced one hand on the bed and worked the other one beneath Tucker's stomach to his swollen cock. He only had time to wrap his fingers around it before Tucker was coming with a jerk and a shudder, pressing his forehead into the pillow and gasping.

The convulsions pushed Chance into climax almost immediately and he came with Tucker's name on his lips.

The bed was soft and the blankets warm, creating a cocoon for them as they curled into each other. Their hands met and Chance brought their entwined fingers to his mouth, kissing Tucker's knuckles. "Better?" he asked, his eyes growing heavy.

Tucker yawned widely enough to make his eyes water. "Dunno. Too tired to tell. But I think so."

Chance snuggled into him. "Get back to me later."

They slept tangled up in each other, and when they woke up for dinner, Chance knew he'd dreamed. He couldn't remember what.

Chapter Seventeen

The December days passed and Christmas arrived, bringing with it the first snow that Chance had seen since he'd been there.

He stood in the kitchen on Christmas morning and looked out the back window, watching fat flakes land on the roof of the barn and longing for his beach and his ocean. Tucker came up behind Chance and rested his chin on Chance's shoulder. "It's pretty," Chance said absently.

"Pretty to look at," Tucker agreed. "But that's about it."

"And cold."

He chuckled. "And cold. Told ya I'd get you out here to show you what real winter was like."

Chance kissed Tucker's temple. "I knew you had an ulterior motive in coming back here."

"Gotta go out to the barn in a bit to make sure the bales aren't dryin' out. Or freezin'." He stared glumly at the falling snow.

"Never ends, huh?"

"Nope. S'why I always thought farmin' wasn't for me – no downtime. Too hard of a life."

Chance studied him. "And now? You think different?"

"I think I ain't got no choice." He shook his head as if to clear it. "Got somethin' for ya," Tucker said, straightening up. "Go start a fire and I'll be right there."

Damn. He had barely remembered it was Christmas, much less had time to get Tucker a present. "I don't have anything for – " he started, but Tucker waved him away.

"Don't matter, baby. I got you, that's all the present I need." He left him with a kiss, so Chance wandered into the other room to start a fire.

Cotton had just sunk down next to him with a sigh when Tucker reappeared, holding something behind his back. He plopped down onto the carpet next to Chance and handed him a package hastily wrapped in newspaper comic pages. "Sorry 'bout the wrappin' paper."

Chance grinned at him. "It's perfect." He tore into it eagerly, forgetting his usual dislike for organized holidays and feeling absurdly pleased that Tucker had gotten him a gift. He left the paper in a ball on the floor and lifted up a navy blue sweatshirt.

It was similar to his own fire department sweatshirts, but on the back, instead of having "Oceanside Fire" written below the Maltese Cross, the bright yellow letters read "Louisville Fire Authority".

"Hey," Chance said softly. "That's cool." It was traditional for fire departments across the country to trade shirts when visiting another station. Chance himself had department t-shirts from several different states, including Hawaii, and his favorite one was from a friend of his who had moved to Australia.

"Check the front," Tucker told him, tugging it out of his hand and turning it around. "See?"

Chance grinned hugely. "Chance" had been embroidered on the left breast in yellow thread that matched the back. "You sew that on yourself?" he teased, running a finger over the obvious machine embroidery.

"Yep," Tucker nodded. "Slaved over a hot sewin' machine for hours."

"Well. It was worth it." He pulled off his flannel shirt and put the new sweatshirt on, liking the way the fleece on the inside felt against his bare skin.

"Yeah? You like it?" Tucker looked hopeful and young.

"Love it." Chance wrapped fingers in Tucker's shirt and brought him closer, kissing him soundly.

He could feel Tucker smiling against his mouth. "There was somethin' else in there for ya."

Chance looked at the crumpled paper on the ground. "Really? I didn't see anything." He grabbed the paper and started pawing through it.

Tucker leaned back on his hands and crossed his legs at the ankles, waiting. "It's small."

He was right, it was small enough that Chance almost didn't see it drop out of the newspaper onto the carpet. He caught it out of the corner of his eye and picked up a small leather band with three metal snaps.

It didn't register immediately. Chance examined it, noting how supple the leather was and thinking for a second that it was some sort of bracelet. Then he realized, no, too small to fit around his wrist ... oh. Goddamn.

Chance looked up to find Tucker watching him, a dimple peeking out from one cheek. "Know what it is?"

His prick twitched in his sweats. "It's a cock ring."

"Uh huh." Tucker didn't say anything else, but his dimple deepened.

Chance studied it more closely. The snaps were undetectable on the inside, leaving just a smooth, leather band. It was cool and light in his hand, and all of a sudden Chance couldn't wait to get it on.

He unsnapped it and held it out, letting it dangle from his fingers. "Put it on me."

Tucker sat up and snatched it out of his hand. "Took you long enough to ask."

They shimmied out of their clothes while trying to kiss and touch at the same time. Chance's cock throbbed again and he gave Tucker a warning. "Better get that on before I'm fully hard."

"That's why it's adjustable," Tucker laughed, but pushed Chance back, anyway, and straddled him. With gentle fingers, he lifted Chance's quickly hardening dick and brought the leather strap down around the base. Fastening it on the second snap, he tugged a little bit to test it. "How's it feel?"

Chance lifted his head and looked, watching as his cock began to stand up and away from his body. It was pretty fucking hot, looking at the black stripe that was quickly tightening just above his balls. "Feels ... amazing," he murmured, laying his head back down and gesturing for Tucker to stretch out on top of him.

Tucker complied, muscles stretching and lengthening as he covered Chance's mouth with his own. Their tongues met in a familiar dance and Chance wanted to crawl inside him, wanted to get underneath Tucker's skin and turn him inside out. "Gonna make it good," Tucker whispered, tongue tracing the shell of Chance's ear. "You ain't gonna know what hit ya."

Chance groaned and rocked up against him, cock fully erect. The ring prevented any blood from leaving his dick, so he felt fuller and more swollen than ever before. Every small touch against him sent shocks to his nerve endings and he wasn't sure how long this was going to last.

Tucker moved down his body with agonizing slowness, stopping every few inches to lick or suckle at any skin that caught his interest. To Chance's frustration, this meant every area except his prick, which was practically pulsing with every beat of his heart. The leather binding around the base only emphasized the throbbing. "C'mon," he groaned. "Don't do this to me. It's Christmas."

Tucker chuckled against his belly. "Patience." Tucker slid a little lower, mouth finally in the right area, and Chance sighed in relief when he felt a warm tongue on his cock.

Tucker's tongue moved down to his balls, passing over the cock ring and then back up, lips pressing lightly on the head. Chance's hips came off the ground when he felt Tucker's tongue dart into his slit and then away, and he tried thrusting up again.

He tossed his head in frustration when strong hands came down on his hips, holding him still. "Not yet," Tucker said. "Go easy. Let me."

Chance let out a shaky breath and tried to relax. He let himself go limp, hands to his sides and legs falling slightly open.

"There you go," Tucker murmured approvingly. "Good boy." He lowered his head again and Chance saw him dart two fingers into his mouth, wetting them. Chance closed his eyes and waited to feel Tucker probing at his hole, but when he didn't feel anything, he cracked open an eye.

Chance was in time to see Tucker reach around and push both fingers into his own ass, neck arching beautifully as he rode his fingers for a minute. Chance held his breath while he watched, fingers curling into the carpet and his cock standing nearly perpendicular from his body.

He wanted to come so badly that he nearly wept when Tucker lifted himself up and in one smooth motion impaled himself on Chance's dick. They both gasped in unison and Chance's eyes rolled back in his head. Everything got hard and hot and tight all at once; he'd never been able to feel Tucker so intimately before. The leather ring enhanced every ripple of muscle, every clenching stroke Tucker made, until Chance thought he had to either come or die trying.

Tucker rocked up and down on Chance for the longest time, eyes closed in concentration, and Chance tried to watch his face for a distraction. He needed something, anything to take his mind off the torturous pleasure that both enticed and mocked him. Everything was on edge and tingling. And yet, his climax still eluded him.

When Tucker took his own cock in his hand and started stroking off over Chance, Chance heard himself make a strangled sound. "Can't come," he whimpered, hands beating at Tucker's thighs, fingernails digging in. "Want to so bad, please." He thought he might even feel tears burning at the backs of his eyes, but by this point he couldn't have cared less.

Tucker put a strong hand on his chest. "Hang on," he instructed, and reached his other hand down. With a practiced flick of his wrist, he snapped open the cock ring and pulled it off.

Chance's orgasm exploded out of him with enough force to rock them both. He was helpless against it, not able to do anything but ride it out and clutch at Tucker's thighs with shaking fingers. Tucker had been right; Chance didn't know what hit him. He could hear Tucker making soft, low noises in his chest as he pulled at his own cock and then there was warm spunk on Tucker's stomach and Chance was still shuddering.

The crackling of the fire was the only noise in the room for a long time after that, except for Cotton's soft snores. "That dog can sleep through anything," Tucker mused after a while, and they both laughed.

"Yeah. Smokey never sticks around, you know?"

Tucker nodded. "I know. You make too much noise for his poor, sensitive kitty ears."

"Me? What the fuck about you? You're the one who always has to talk during sex." Chance poked Tucker in the ribs and Tucker grabbed his hand, chuckling.

They rolled around and mock-wrestled for a while before settling into each other's arms again, letting the fire warm them. "Merry Christmas," Chance whispered, as Tucker drowsed with his head on Chance's chest.

"Mer' Christmas, baby."

***

The week between Christmas and New Year's was the most relaxing one yet. There was nothing to do about the tobacco, so Chance and Tucker spent most of their time either in bed or out with the horses. Chance made the mistake of telling Tucker he thought he might be getting used to the cold.

"Really," Tucker said, with an interested expression. "So you wouldn't mind bein' out in it for a while?"

"Depends," Chance said suspiciously. "What do I have to do?"

"Haven't been out on Blue for a couple of days," Tucker mused. "Wanna go for a ride?"

"On a horse?"

Tucker snorted. "Blue's my horse, yes."

Chance was doubtful. "Dunno. How do I stop?"

"Don't gotta worry about that. We'll double up on Blue, I'll do all the work." Tucker looked cheerful and Chance couldn't deny him.

"Okay," Chance said slowly, and Tucker let out a whoop and grabbed his Stetson from the hat rack by the door.

Tucker took off for the barn and Chance followed a few steps behind, not sure how or why he'd agreed to getting up on an animal that could potentially kill him.

Tucker was saddling Blue when Chance walked into the barn. "You can just swing up behind me," he said, pulling the cinch tight.

"I don't know," Chance said, eyeing Blue warily.

Tucker turned and leveled him with a stare. "Did I or did I not get my ass into the Pacific Ocean because you wanted me to?"

"You did," Chance admitted.

"And did I or did I not let you tell me how fuckin' easy surfin' is when you know goddamn well it ain't easy at all?"

He shuffled his feet, embarrassed. "Okay, okay. I get it."

Tucker reached out with a hand and yanked him closer, dropping a hard kiss on his mouth before swinging up onto the horse's back. "Get up on this fuckin' horse."

Chance knew enough to at least mount from the left side, so he put a booted foot on the block and swung up behind Tucker. Blue shifted underneath them, but stayed relatively still long enough for Chance to settle himself behind Tucker. It brought him right up close to Tucker's ass, his crotch nestled firmly against him. Maybe this wasn't so bad.

He nudged forward with his hips and could see Tucker grin at him over his shoulder. "Thought you might like that. Ready?"

"Ready," Chance nodded, his hands loose at Tucker's waist, and Tucker tapped Blue gently with his heels.

They took a slow, easy pace out of the barn and around to the front of the house, Blue's breath making puffs in the frigid air. Tucker kept the reins casually in one hand, the other resting easily on his thigh or pointing out landmarks to Chance as they walked. Chance could feel the horse underneath him, powerful and sure, and understood a little bit more about why Tucker loved to ride. Being out in the fresh air was different than sitting in a car, watching scenery flash by too quickly to appreciate. The scent of winter was crisp and fresh, another thing he would have missed if they were driving instead of riding.

They skirted the first tobacco field and then took a straight path through the second, Blue stepping carefully along the very narrow trail, even though there was nothing left in the field for the horse to hurt if he veered off the path. Tucker patted him approvingly. Then they were through the field and over the rise, moving down the hill toward the creek and then across it to the old riverbed.

They dismounted there and Tucker tied Blue, letting him search fruitlessly for any remaining weeds or grass. Chance sank to the ground with a wince. "Ouch. I'm not made for riding, I don't think."

Tucker tossed a handful of pebbles into the bed. "Just hafta get used to it. I miss ridin' a lot."

Chance was quiet, watching him pick little stones from the ground and throw them at the dead trees across the bed. The statement was so typical of Tucker these days. He proclaimed to hate Kentucky, but he missed riding. He hadn't wanted to come back here, yet refused to leave out of some sense of familial loyalty. Chance had spent nearly a month trying to figure it out and found himself no closer to answers than before.

"I miss the ocean," Chance finally said.

Tucker pushed his heels into the ground and propped his elbows on his knees. "You're gonna go back," he said in a low voice.

Chance had made no bones about that fact. "Well, yeah. I don't live here."

"I mean soon. You're not stayin' much longer, huh?" He stared at the ground.

"Tuck, I can't. I'm already risking things at work by being gone so long. And with what happened with the fight and all, well. You know I have to go back." Chance hated saying it, wanted to tell Tucker that no, he didn't have to go anywhere and he'd stay as long as Tucker needed him, but it wouldn't be true.

"I know." He looked over at Chance and a shaft of late-afternoon winter light glanced over his eyes, catching the indigo and showing the true color of his irises. "You want me to come back with you."

That had been the original intent. "Yeah."

"I got auction in a few days." But the excuse sounded weak to both of them. Chance knew Coop and the others were more than qualified to bring the tobacco to auction themselves.

"After," Chance said, holding his gaze. "Come home after." He swallowed and added another word, one he didn't often say. "Please."

It was quiet for a moment, the silence broken only by the jangling of Blue's harness.

"Maybe," Tucker said, looking back down. "Maybe after. I'll think about it."

Chance knew that was no kind of answer.

Chapter Eighteen

The new year came in with no marked difference from the old, except Chance had a lighter feeling that he attributed to the auction being almost here and gone. He knew the auction process would take two days, and as soon as it was done, he was planning on doing whatever he had to do to get Tucker on a plane back to California.

Chance just wasn't sure what that was, exactly.

At the moment, he thought his best bet was something along the lines of their current position. They were on the couch together yet again, Chance's favorite place these days because of the heat from the fire, both of them in t-shirts and sweats. They were making out lazily, cocks hard beneath their clothes but neither of them urgent or demanding. Side by side, tongues exploring and hips pushing gently, and Tucker was making soft, purring noises as they kissed.

"We just gonna do this all day, or get to the good stuff?" Tucker finally murmured, throwing a leg over Chance and fitting against his thigh.

"Oh, I don't know," Chance sighed, arching his neck when Tucker nuzzled into it. "This is good for me."

Tucker pulled back in surprise. "Really?"

He pushed his luck a little. "Sure, why not?" Chance shrugged. "I like making out. Reminds me of high school."

Tucker had the most adorably confused look on his face. "You just wanna kiss. You don't wanna … you know?" He waved his hand in the direction of their cocks.

"Maybe later," he said casually, tugging Tucker down again.

Tucker put his hands on Chance's chest and sat up. "Well, you got me all riled up now. If you ain't gonna take care of it, then I'll do it myself." He sat back against the arm of the sofa and pushed his waistband down enough to draw out his cock, thumb brushing over the head.

Chance swallowed. "Sure, whatever. If you have to, you have to." He put his hands behind his head and forced himself into a casual pose.

Tucker narrowed his gaze and Chance could tell he was trying to judge if Chance was serious or not. Then the corner of his mouth turned up and his eyes twinkled. "Sit there and watch, I don't care," he shrugged, and reached beneath him for the lube they usually hid under the cushion.

Oh, God. Maybe this was more than he bargained for. His eyes followed Tucker's fingers as he coated himself well, thumb again passing over the head and gathering up the moisture that had beaded there. Chance lifted his gaze to Tucker's face in time to see him sink even, white teeth into his lower lip.

"Sure you don't wanna?" Tucker whispered over the crackling of the fire.

Chance had to bite down on the soft skin of his inner cheek to keep from screaming out, "Yes, yes, Jesus Christ I want to." He shook his head once and hoped he looked calm. A glance downward, however, revealed his own dick tenting his sweats. Not much chance of hiding that.

Tucker gave him that wicked half-smile again and closed his eyes, fisting his cock. The soft, slippery noises his hand made against his skin carried easily over the fire, making Chance flare his nostrils and try to adjust himself without rubbing his palm over his own prick.

This was probably a form of torture in some countries. Chance cursed himself for it; he knew better by now than to entice Tucker into any sort of sexual contest. Not that he'd been enticing him, exactly, but Tucker could make anything into a challenge. Chance figured he was just going to have to sit back and watch for as long as he could.

Except just sitting back and watching sounded easier in his head. It would have been a lot easier, in fact, if Tucker didn't insist on furrowing his brow in concentration as he stroked. Chance licked his lips and wondered if he could get in a quick rub over his sweats, just to relieve a tiny bit of pressure.

He tried it at exactly the wrong time. Just as his palm flattened over his aching cock, Tucker opened those eyes and caught him. He arched a brow at Chance and a dimple flashed. "No, you don't wanna do this at all," he mocked softly, hand still sliding up and down his shaft.

Chance slammed both hands down on the couch, determined not to touch again. For at least a minute, anyway.

Tucker rolled his eyes and lowered his head, his breathing coming faster and his strokes getting harder and quicker. When Tucker started up the usual monologue, Chance thought he might come without ever touching himself. "Yes," Chance could hear him whispering, "good. So good, right there, gonna shoot everywhere."

He might have been able to stand it if his eyes hadn't narrowed in on the head of Tucker's prick appearing and disappearing through his closed fist. Chance's cock pulsed almost painfully as he watched it, mesmerized by the sight and sound. But even that might have been okay, if Tucker hadn't said, "Look," and swept two fingers over the pre-come on the head.

Chance followed his fingers as Tucker brought them up to his mouth, and when his tongue darted out to catch the taste of himself on his own hand, Chance gave up.

"Goddamn," he moaned, scrabbling at his waistband and yanking his prick out of his pants. He sat up and pushed Tucker's hand out of the way, sweeping up and down Tucker's dick just once to gather some of the lube that glistened there, and then lay back and lowered his fist to himself.

It took no more than three strokes before he was shuddering and groaning and coming, his spunk falling in hot splashes on his chest. Tucker knelt up and stroked off over him while Chance came, his own come soon mixing with Chance's and both of them crying out.

Tucker lifted his t-shirt over his head and managed to swipe up most of the mess with it before falling back down across Chance, kissing him and grinning against his mouth. "You should know better," he murmured drowsily.

"Yeah," Chance sighed, nuzzling into him. "I should."

***

Auction was three days away and things were busy.

Chance helped Tucker and the men stack the eighty-pound bales to ready them for transport. Each bale box had to be checked for moisture. The lower the moisture content, the better it would sell. Tucker tried explaining a bunch of other stuff, too, but stopped with a chuckle when Chance felt his eyes glaze over. He just let Tucker tell him what to lift and where to stack.

The night before auction, Chance helped Tucker curry Blue in the barn. He was unsure about the process of the next two days. "So … we can't load the trucks tonight?"

"Nope," Tucker said, his arm sweeping in long strokes over Blue's back and side. "Too cold. Bales'll dry out and freeze if we put 'em outside. They need the shelter of the barn for as long as possible."

"What time are we getting up?" he asked suspiciously, cupping Blue's velvety nose. This didn't sound good.

Tucker threw him an apologetic look. "Um. 'Bout five. Gotta get loaded up and on the road by six-thirty to get to Maysville on time."

Chance grimaced. "You know I expect some phenomenal head for this."

He laughed and threw Blue's brush in Chance's direction. "You don't gotta go to auction for that, baby. Here, brush Blue a bit, wouldya?"

Chance caught the brush and started on Blue's neck, ignoring the long-suffering look the horse gave him. "Five a.m.," he muttered. "Christ."

Coop, Johnny, Ned, and Mack all stayed for dinner. Tucker threw sheets and blankets at them around nine and told them to go make up their own beds because he sure as hell wasn't doing it, and they all trooped upstairs, grumbling. Coop chose to stay downstairs on the couch instead of sharing one of the rooms with two twin beds. Cotton gazed sadly at him when he settled himself on the sofa.

"Get your mangy butt up here," Chance heard Coop growl to the dog as he and Tucker made their way up to their room.

They showered together quickly, hands roaming and teasing but too aware of the men in the other bedrooms to get anything out of it. Hair still wet, they dropped into bed and Chance snuggled into Tucker's chest. "Too tired for it now," he mumbled, "but you owe me some sex."

He heard the answering rumble of laughter in Tucker's chest. "Noted."

***

He thought at first he was dreaming it.

The smell was so familiar, yet so foreign to his surroundings that it had to be a dream. There was no reason for him to be smelling smoke here in Kentucky; it was something he usually only experienced while on the job at home. The scent and sound was ingrained in him because of work.

So it had to be a dream, because if he was at work, Tucker wouldn't be warm against his back. If he was in his bunk at the station, two soft dings of the alarm would be sounding, telling them which engine needed to go into service, and the voices of his crew would be muted in the hallway as they made their sleepy way to the garage.

The terrified whinny of a horse finally brought Chance fully awake.

He blinked into the dark, disoriented, and then he heard it again. A frightened screaming that sounded eerily like a woman, making him sit straight up in the darkness and poke at Tucker. "Hey," he said urgently. "Tuck. Listen."

Tucker rolled over and squinted up at him. "Wassamatter?"

Chance was about to answer, but his attention was caught by a flickering at the window. Climbing out of bed, he crossed the tiny room in two strides and flung the curtain aside, revealing what looked at first glance to be the entire backyard in flames. A closer look showed that it was not, in fact, the whole backyard, but the tobacco barn.

Fire was also licking at the base of the horse barn, smoke pouring thick and gray into the night air. The smell of burning tobacco was unsettling the horses and as Chance stared in disbelief, one of them screamed again. It jolted him into action and he whirled around, searching for his clothes.

Tucker was doing the same thing, having seen the burning buildings over Chance's shoulder, and he jerked open the door to their room. "Fire!" he shouted down the hall, pounding on the walls. "Get the fuck up!" He whirled around and pointed at Chance. "Use the landline to call 911," he ordered, and then disappeared down the stairs.

"Wait for me," Chance barked after him, and cursed. He knew Tucker was headed out to the back and wasn't waiting for anything. Finally managing to shove his tennis shoes on, he raced down the stairs after Tucker and grabbed the phone from the wall in the kitchen. Speaking slowly and clearly, Chance gave the dispatcher the address and felt a strange sense of weirdness at being on the other end of the call.

The rest of the men tumbled down the stairs, pulling on jackets and grabbing gloves from their pockets. Chance followed them down the back steps and they all headed toward the blazing tobacco barn at a run, skidding to a stop just outside the doors. "No," Chance yelled, when Coop made a move to slide them open. "Don't touch it!"

Coop jerked his hand back and looked helplessly at Chance, his face panicked. "Where's McBride?" he shouted over the noise.

Christ. Chance darted a look around the yard, searching for Tucker and feeling his heart begin to pound when he couldn't be found. The heat was starting to penetrate Chance's thin flannel shirt and he longed for his heavy turnout coat and pants. It might be hotter than a bitch inside them, but at least he was well-protected.

"There," Ned yelled, and they all turned to see Tucker leading a horse out of the second barn.

Chance strode to his side, fury simmering. "Are you insane?" he asked. "The fuck did you go in there alone for?"

"Here," Tucker said shortly, and handed Chance the horse's lead line. He turned to go back to the barn but Chance caught his arm.

"You don't go in there by yourself," he barked, grip tightening.

"You ain't at work, Cap," Tucker snapped. "Let go." He yanked his arm away. "Gotta get the other two horses."

"Then we'll both go." Chance whistled at the men who stood in a huddle, watching the blaze eat up the tobacco barn. Coop trotted over and Chance handed off the line, then ran after Tucker.

He followed Tucker into the barn. The heavy smoke assaulted him immediately and he pulled his shirt up to cover his nose, searching through the dimness for Tucker. Flames had covered the back wall and were starting to lick up the roof and he darted a nervous glance at the dry bales of straw that were stacked three high.

Blue pranced alone in the last stall, eyes rolling at the fire that crept closer and closer. He danced away when Tucker tried to reach for his mane. "Goddammit, you big stupid animal," Chance could hear him mutter.

Chance slid in when Blue wasn't looking at him and went around to the horse's backside. "Move," he ordered the horse, and gave it a slap on the rump. Blue tossed his head and gave a half-hearted kick that Chance managed to dodge, but moved out of the stall into the openness of the barn. Once there, he scented the fresh air through the open barn doors and bolted for freedom. Chance hoped one of the guys outside would catch him.

Tucker turned back for the last horse, a small, sweet filly named Sabrina. She was snorting fearfully and her coat was damp with sweat when Tucker approached, Chance close on his heels. "Pretty girl," Tucker crooned to her, reaching out a hand. "Don't be scared, pretty."

Chance ducked under Tucker's arm and made a move to get behind her as he'd done to Blue, but Sabrina startled at his sudden movement. Wheeling around in the small space, she knocked him into the wall and came dangerously close to tramping on his foot. He hissed in pain as his ribs caught the edge of the stall door and Tucker's head turned sharply. "You okay?" he shouted over the crackling of flames, and Chance nodded and waved him away.

"Sabrina, *go*," Chance finally shouted, and smacked her on the flank. She whinnied in response and moved halfway out of the stall, reluctant to go further because of the heat and sparks beginning to shower down from the ceiling.

One of the bales of hay caught the sparks and began to burn, crackling ominously. Sabrina shied away from it, bumping into the side of the stall, and Tucker swore. "Fuck this shit," he spat, and grabbed Sabrina's mane. Using a bale of hay to boost him, he swung up on her back and kicked her hard with his heels.

Startled, she reared up on her hind legs and took two steps backwards, and for a moment Chance was terrified that she would succeed in throwing Tucker off. Chance flattened himself against the wall in an effort to stay out of the way, but at the very last second, one of Sabrina's hooves caught the side of his head on her way back down.

Things started to spin and Chance felt the wall tilt away from him. He put out a hand to break his fall and somehow managed to make it to the ground with no further injury. Squinting up through the rapidly thickening smoke, he saw Sabrina finally bolt from her stall and make it out the front door of the barn, Tucker still astride her.

Heat to his left made him turn his head and look. The blaze from the hay had started smoldering his shirt, and he thought hazily that maybe he should roll away from it before it blistered his skin.

The last thing he heard before the blackness was the distant sirens.

Chapter Nineteen

He woke up in the back of an ambulance. Chance thought at first they were headed to the hospital, then realized the back doors were open and they weren't moving. He blinked at the roof of the vehicle and lifted his head.

"Stay put, baby," he heard Tucker murmur, and Chance carefully turned his head to look.

Tucker sat next to Chance, dirt and soot smudging his face. His elbows rested on his knees and his hands were clasped so tightly that his knuckles were white. "The barn?" Chance managed, and winced at the pounding in his head.

Tucker stared at the floor and gave a half-hearted shrug. He motioned with his head toward the open door, so Chance lifted himself on his elbows and looked.

Only the skeleton of the tobacco barn remained.

The yard was crawling with firefighters and ordinarily Chance might have liked the opportunity to watch how another department operated, but his head hurt like a motherfucker and his arm was throbbing, too. He eased himself back down and held up his arm to eye level, noting the gauze that was loosely wrapped around it. "Burned?" he asked, his voice raspy from smoke.

"Not bad," Tucker said, voice still bleak and flat. "First degree, tiny bit of blisterin'. Should heal up good."

Chance closed his eyes and was quiet for a while, listening to the squawk of radios outside and the firemen calling to each other. The whinny and snort of the horses mingled with their voices and Chance was grateful they'd gotten out. "Anyone get hurt?" he thought to ask.

"You mean besides you?"

He opened his eyes and managed a weak grin. "I ain't hurt."

"You're sayin' 'ain't'. Your head's all loopy." Tucker said it fondly, but the worry was still there, along with something else Chance couldn't pinpoint.

"Surprised you didn't make them take me in," he said, although he had no idea how close or far the nearest hospital was.

"You were breathin'," Tucker answered with a chuckle. "Checked your pupils, gave you the rundown. Told 'em I'd sit with you for a bit. And I knew you'd be way more pissed if you woke up in the ER."

"I would've been."

"Yeah. Got yourself a concussion, prolly. Hafta wake your ass up all night long."

"Blame Sabrina, not me."

Tucker nodded and swallowed hard, his gaze straying to the scene outside. "The whole fuckin' barn," he said quietly. "Lost it all. The whole goddamned crop."

Fuck. The tobacco. Chance felt his stomach knot in sympathy. He put out a hand and rested it on Tucker's knee. "I'm sorry," he said, frustrated at the insignificance of the statement. He *was* sorry, sorry for all the work and sweat and blood that had burned up in a matter of minutes, and sorry that Tucker had to be the one to deal with this. Chance knew he hadn't asked for any of it.

"Not as sorry as I am."

***

It was nearly two hours later that the captain on duty pronounced the building free of hot spots. They'd managed to douse the flames on the horse barn before too much damage had been inflicted, and it looked like it could be rebuilt within a matter of days. In the meantime, they'd have to bring the horses to the farm's closest neighbor, an older man and his wife who'd long given up the tobacco trade and were now farming organic vegetables.

Chance's headache had receded enough for him to sit up and he sat now at the edge of the ambulance with his feet resting on the back bumper. A medic had been by a couple of times to check his vision and take his pulse, but Chance had spouted his own vitals at the guy and they'd left him alone after that. A slight concussion wasn't going to kill him.

He watched Tucker talk to the captain, nodding his head slowly and biting at the side of his thumbnail, recognizing the gesture as one Tucker made when he was tired or stressed out. Chance guessed both. They disappeared around to the back of the still-smoking barn and Chance turned his attention to the crew that was preparing to leave. Hose re-rolled, ladders lowered, helmets left carelessly on the ground or the step-side of the engine as they called good-naturedly to each other.

It was an odd feeling, watching it unfold so familiarly, but being a victim rather than a hero. Chance didn't know how to reconcile it with himself and maybe it was just his headache, but the confusion was warring within him. He was not supposed to be here, watching this from the outside, missing it and longing to be the one explaining to some poor soul exactly what they did to douse the flames. He knew the captain wasn't telling Tucker how the fire had started – that's what the fire investigator was for – but he and Tucker were probably back there checking for signs of arson anyway.

And then suddenly, sharply, Chance knew he was going home.

It was time. He'd been here nearly a month and he missed his condo and his job and Bonnie. He missed his cat and his favorite beer and wearing shorts in January and most of all, Chance missed his ocean. He missed the feel of his board, sleek and cool under his fingers. Missed the good swell that came in off Mexico's coast and catching a good set just before the tide went out. Missed the tang of the sea and the grainy texture of the sand and goddammit all to hell, he didn't want to miss it anymore.

He realized he couldn't make Tucker go. He'd tried his fucking best to convince Tucker, and talk to him and persuade him, but his stubborn streak was a mile wide and Chance was tired of fighting. He was just tired of everything.

Chance watched Tucker reappear from behind what was left of the building and shake the captain's hand. They said something to each other that Chance couldn't make out and then the captain heaved himself up into his seat opposite the engineer. The diesel engine started up and with a release of the emergency brake, they rolled slowly out of the yard and around to the front of the house.

Tucker hadn't moved from his spot. He looked at the remains of the barn one last time before turning to where Chance still sat in the back of the ambulance, and when their eyes met, Chance saw that Tucker knew.

He watched as Tucker approached and stood in front of him, arms crossed and eyes on the ground. "You're goin'," Tucker said at last, and it wasn't a question.

"Yes."

"I can't."

He wanted to say a hundred things right then. Chance wanted to beg him to come home, to forget about the damn farm and let the lawyers handle it, and to plead with Tucker not to resign himself to the kind of life he thought he deserved.

But none of it came out.

"I'll leave the light on for you," was all Chance finally said.

***

Matt picked him up, didn't ask any questions, and deposited him at his front door.

"Thanks," Chance said, wondering if there should be more to it.

Matt nodded and tapped his fingers on the steering wheel. "He'll come home, Shanahan."

Chance started to say something, then realized he didn't know what to say. Was he supposed to agree? Or confirm? He couldn't do it. He looked at Matt, who was calmly watching Chance war with himself. "We'll see," was all Chance could say.

He dropped his duffel just inside the door and said Smokey's name, anxious to see the cat. He got no response to his call, so he went on a search of each dark room, noting as he looked that his plants were still alive and there was no dust on his furniture. Leave it to Bonnie to clean up for him.

He poked his head in the bedroom and was met with the sight of his cat sitting regally in the middle of the bed, paws neatly placed in front of him and a haughty look on his face. "Aw," Chance grinned, sitting down on the edge of the bed, "don't do this to me, man. Sort of need the love right now." He put out a hand in supplication, inviting Smokey to sniff his fingers.

After what looked like a complicated decision process, the cat got up and padded over to Chance, rubbing the side of his face along Chance's hand. "There you go," Chance murmured to him, using his other hand to stroke the silky head. "Missed you too."

He lay back on the bed with his legs still hanging off the side and closed his eyes. The familiar feel of his own mattress beneath his back was comforting. He'd just lie here for a minute, he was so tired from traveling and the events of the last few days that someone could hardly begrudge him a few minutes of rest.

He fell asleep fully clothed, tennis shoes still on.

***

In the morning, the first thing he noticed was that he was hot.

Chance opened one eye and found himself buried beneath the covers, a habit he'd picked up in Kentucky to keep his nose from freezing. Usually he'd wake up in the pre-dawn light with his face tucked into Tucker's chest and the blankets over his head. Matter of survival, he'd told Tucker. No way was he gonna go out by freezing to death. Tucker would chuckle and kiss him and they would flex long, lean muscles against each other and find ways to get even warmer.

He closed his eyes again briefly, not expecting the sting. Throwing off the comforter, he let the cool air wash over him and wondered when he'd woken up long enough to take off his jeans and shoes. His bedroom was flooding with light now, making sleep impossible, so Chance heaved a sigh and sat up. Might as well get up and start pretending things were normal.

He didn't see the picture until he got out of the shower and walked back into the bedroom, running a comb through his wet hair and insanely grateful that he could wear only a towel without his teeth chattering and his balls wanting to crawl up inside his body. Chance thought he might have gone for a few days without noticing the change if he hadn't happened to look up at the picture that had hung over his bed for nearly eight years.

It had been an academy graduation present from Bonnie. The picture was of a firefighter's gear, including turnouts, helmets, and a toolbox with bootblack and a brush. Bonnie had had the original artist personalize it for Chance, with his last name printed across the bottom of the turnout coat and his station number written on the helmet. And then again, after he'd gone through paramedic school and gotten his medic license, she'd sent it back to the artist to have a caduceus painted on the wood beam where the coat hung.

Apparently she'd sent it back to the artist again. The difference was the toolbox. Chance had seen this same picture hanging in the homes of other firefighters, personalized with their own names and stations, and usually the toolbox had a small heart drawn on it with the names of their wives and kids. Chance never thought much about the fact that his toolbox would probably stay empty. He knew that kids weren't in his future, and as for getting legally married, well. That really wasn't in the cards either.

But the side of the toolbox wasn't blank anymore.

He walked to the side of his bed and leaned over to look at it, a finger coming up to touch the cool glass and the small print that spelled out "Tucker" in block letters. Chance touched it for a long time, rubbing it gently with his thumb and tracing the heart with a fingernail.

***

It was January and the water temperature was nothing close to what he would call warm, but that's what his full wetsuit was for.

Chance paddled out about halfway and then straddled his board, bobbing gently in the water and absorbing the reality of his ocean. The water was freezing and it was low tide, both of which he'd known before he started, and both of which would normally have stopped him from coming out, but this time he didn't care. He had missed it too much to give a damn about whether or not there were waves.

A small set surprised him and he rode it for a while, letting the sharp taste of the water sink into his tongue and skin and heal a little part of his psyche. He ducked under a wave and got salt in his eyes. It burned and itched and Chance savored it, brushing at his eyes with the back of his hand, but not really trying to make it go away, letting the sand cling to his lashes, liking the gritty feel.

An hour and a half in the freezing water finally did him in. He admitted defeat when he couldn't feel his toes and his fingernail beds had turned a nice purplish-blue color. The sky looked to promise rain, so he splashed onto the sand and peeled off his wetsuit. He shivered out of habit, but the cold here was different. California cold wasn't so knife-like, so piercing, as it had been in Kentucky.

Back home and another shower helped to warm his core temperature. There wasn't much in his fridge or cupboards to cook for dinner, so he settled for a tuna fish sandwich and some chips. He ate at the table, Smokey sitting on the opposite chair, watching him with interest.

A sole Heineken in the refrigerator was the best thing he could ask for for dessert and he savored it as he wandered into the living room to turn on the television. It was only when he put his feet up on the coffee table that he noticed the holiday card in a green envelope, addressed to him in Bonnie's feminine hand. He tore it open and used the envelope for a coaster as he read.

Chancey,

I miss you a lot this Christmas. I hope Tucker appreciates having you there for the holidays. You might have noticed your picture by now, I had the guy add Tucker's name because I figured it was time and I knew you'd never do it yourself. It was sort of a present for Tucker too, in a way.

I hope you both get what you need while you're there. And I really hope you can bring him back, since I know it's what you want. Merry Christmas, Chancellor.

Much love,

Bonnie

He read it twice and then folded it in half, running his finger along the crease. He'd call her tomorrow.

The phone didn't ring that night, but he didn't expect it to.

Chapter Twenty

Returning to work was a welcome distraction. Chance's first scheduled shift was three days after he got home and his crew greeted him with genuine smiles and slaps on the back.

"Finally, we'll get decent chow," Trey grumbled.

Chance chuckled. "What, the overtime captains didn't treat you right?"

Trey made a face and Jim nodded in agreement. "Had a lot of spaghetti."

"Then I guess we'd best get our asses to the store," Chance mused, "because I feel like some pesto pasta with goat cheese and sundried tomatoes for dinner."

Twelve firemen had never looked happier.

They shopped and answered three calls and Chance worked out with weights after dinner, purposely not recalling details of the first time Tucker had ever made a move on him right here in the station's small gym. A hard run on the treadmill helped with the not-recalling, and he was panting and sweating by the time he finally turned off the lights and went to shower.

He was poring over the day's call sheets in his office when Jim rapped on the doorframe. "Hey," he said. "Randy's trying to make cookies from scratch in there. Would you tell him he can't use baking powder as a substitute for baking soda? He doesn't believe me."

Chance smiled distractedly and nodded, eyes still on the computer printouts. "Be in there in a minute." When he could still feel Jim's gaze on him, he looked up. "What? Just don't let him ruin the dough, I'll be right there."

"McBride come back with you?"

He thought about lying and saying yes, but everyone would find out soon enough anyway. All they had to do was look at Tucker's schedule on the computer to see his spot at Station Nineteen was still open. "Nope."

"Stubborn sonofabitch, ain't he?" Jim was studying him, but not in an uncomfortable way.

Chance dropped his papers and steepled his fingers together, resting his chin on the tips. "'Stubborn' doesn't begin to describe it."

The corner of Jim's mouth curved. "Yeah. Had me a girlfriend like that once. Whoo-ee, she ran me ragged."

Chance laughed without humor. "Sounds about right. Although I suppose he'd say the same about me."

Jim nodded. "You give him some time, Shanahan. He'll come home."

Chance wondered why he couldn't be as sure as everyone else was.

***

Accepting a dinner invitation a few nights later with Bonnie and Matt was preferable to yet another overtime shift or lonely night at home, so Chance went. Besides, it was a restaurant he liked.

His stuffed sea bass was good and the drinks were strong. Conversation was easy between the three of them and, not for the first time, Chance realized how he appreciated being with people who just accepted him for who he was. To them, he wasn't a captain, he wasn't a son that didn't measure up, he wasn't gay, he just … was. And they had probably been the only two people in his life who'd made him feel like that. Until Tucker.

He sat back in his chair after dinner and watched the ocean just beyond the glass of the window. In the dark, the individual waves were hard to see, but the ocean itself was a constantly moving entity.

Chance broke his gaze from the sea in time to watch Matt take the last forkful of Bonnie's crab fettuccine. "She never lets me do that," Chance remarked, feeling mellow.

"She lets me do lots of things I'm sure you're not allowed to do," Matt said with an uncharacteristic leer, and Bonnie elbowed him in the side.

"Matthew! Jesus."

"We had sex twice," Chance offered, trying vainly to compete.

Matt snorted and drained his wineglass. "In high school. Like you knew what you were doing."

Chance took the good-natured teasing from both of them for another half hour, all the way through the raspberry cheesecake and the cappuccinos, until he finally put up both hands in supplication.

Fireline

"Okay, okay," he said to Bonnie with a sigh. "I get it. I was a less than acceptable substitute for whatever was missing in your life until this guy came along."

Matt looked pleased, but Bonnie was horrified. "Oh, Chancey, we didn't mean that! You weren't a substitute for anything; you're my best friend, and you know I love you, it's –" The rest of her response was cut off by Matt planting a fast kiss.

"He's shitting with you, Bon," Matt said gently.

She looked at him suspiciously and Chance shrugged. "Are you?" she asked.

"Possibly."

She threw a napkin across the table at him and grabbed her purse. "I'll be in the car," she informed Matt, and flounced away.

"Women," Matt muttered, in an age-old complaint.

"See why I prefer guys?" Chance shrugged. .

"Starting to see it, yes," Matt replied.

Chance turned his gaze back toward the window. "She likes you," he said absently, imagining he could see the tide.

Matt cleared his throat. "I like her."

Chance looked at him again. "It's a good thing. The two of you. There isn't anyone else I know that could handle her."

Matt let out a bark of laughter. "Most of the time, I can't. But thanks, Chance."

He grinned.

They dropped him off in front of his dark condo and Chance remembered for the first time all night that there wouldn't be anyone to greet him. It was an improvement; usually he was reminded of the emptiness of his place at least once an hour. Dinner and stiff drinks had apparently been good for him.

Maybe too good, since he found himself weaving slightly as he fitted his key in the lock. He was a little drunk. No work tomorrow, thank God.

He almost killed himself tripping over the bag by the front door. He let fly a stream of profanity and got mad at himself for not putting his gear bag away that morning, then remembered he was on a four-day break and had come home yesterday, not today. And he'd put his bag on top of the washing machine to do laundry.

"Language, Cap," a low, smooth voice scolded, and at once all of Chance's senses were on alert.

He wanted to say Tucker's name, to make the voice he heard turn into something solid and real that he could touch, but he was terrified that it was his own tipsiness playing a cruel joke. If he said Tucker's name and nobody responded, if he turned his head to look into the living room and there was no one sitting on the couch flashing dimples at him, Chance thought he might lose yet another part of himself that couldn't be returned.

He looked anyway.

Tucker slouched on the sofa, long legs splayed out in front of him. Smokey lay curled into his side. Tucker tilted his head at Chance and offered up a grin. "Hey."

"Hey," Chance returned dumbly, and moved to stand in front of him. "You're home."

"Looks that way."

"When?"

He checked his wrist for the watch Chance had given him on his birthday. "Hour ago."

"You didn't call me."

"You didn't call me when you decided to bring your ass east, either."

Damn. He was right.

Chance would have stood there longer, trying to figure out if Tucker was really sitting in front of him or if he'd had too much to drink, but Tucker interrupted his convoluted train of thought again. "So ... I don't get a better "Welcome home, Tuck," than that? Damn, Cap. Lost your touch."

And then, just like that, Chance was on him, pushing his shoulders down into the cushion while straddling Tucker's lap and trying to swallow his tongue. He was vaguely aware of making soft, needy sounds that he hadn't even known were buried inside until they came out, and Tucker had both hands tangled in Chance's hair to hold him in place.

Chance ground down hard, his cock driving all rational thought away. *Tucker,* was all his brain could manage to whisper. *Tucker's home.* He fastened his mouth to Tucker's neck and felt Tucker's head fall back against the couch as he suckled a mark into the skin and rolled his hips harder and harder.

"Chance," Tucker murmured into the dimness of the living room. "Hold on, baby. Move over for a second and I can ..." he trailed off as he tried to work his hand in between them to get at the button on Chance's jeans, but Chance knocked his hand away.

"Don't," Chance gasped, thrusting again. "Just let me."

"God," Tucker groaned, and then Chance was coming, Tucker's hands hard on his ass, pulling and pushing their crotches together as he shuddered.

A few deep breaths later, he lifted his head from the hollow of Tucker's neck and shoulder. "Welcome home, Tuck," he grinned.

"That's more like it. Now, you gonna take me into the bedroom to do this the right way?"

Chance glanced down, realizing both that he'd soaked his good jeans and that Tucker was still painfully hard. "Get up," he demanded, climbing off and yanking at Tucker's hand. "Get the fuck up and into that bedroom. Right now." He was still trembling, but his dick was already hardening again. "And if you call me bossy, I won't fuck you."

One wicked dimple peeked at him. "Well, now. Who said you were bossy?"

"Bedroom, McBride."

They barely made it through the doorway before tearing at each other's clothes, Chance still shaking with the need to touch him and ensure he was really here. Chance thought he might have popped a button or two off Tucker's shirt, but when he was rewarded with an expanse of rich, smooth skin, nothing else came close to mattering.

"Better tell me now if you don't want it rough," Chance warned, licking his fingers and teasing at Tucker's hole. "Because I don't think I'm really in a gentle kind of mood."

Tucker's answer was to reach up and pull Chance down for a kiss, his mouth saying wordlessly exactly what Chance wanted to hear.

He left Tucker only to reach for the lube, and when he slid back down Tucker was turning to his stomach. Chance stopped him. "No. Face me. Need to see you."

Tucker looked up at him and Chance thought he could easily fall forever this way, looking into eyes that appeared black, but weren't. "This way," Tucker nodded, agreeing softly.

Chance slicked them both and pushed in without asking permission, but the gasp it wrung from Tucker was consent enough. Chance watched as Tucker's eyes got impossibly darker and then rolled back when Chance angled up to reach his prostate. "Tuck," Chance murmured reverently, using one hand to push Tucker's leg back and the other to sweep his hair from his forehead.

"Hard. And fast. Don't mess around, Chancellor, you got me wound too tight," Tucker said, his voice strained.

Chance almost came a second time just from the words alone. Tucker usually kept up a steady monologue during sex, but most of the time it was simple muttering to himself rather than actual conversation. On the rare occasion when he directed his words right to Chance, it made Chance's brain melt. He was already having a hard enough time holding it together just from the sheer joy of having Tucker home. "Don't talk," he ground out.

Amusement warred with desire in Tucker's eyes. "Really?" he murmured seductively, arching his hips up to meet Chance's downward thrust. "So you don't want me to tell you how much I fuckin' love this? That the first night you left, I jacked off twice thinkin' about your cock?" He clenched tight muscles and threw back his head, gasping. "That I dreamed about lickin' your – "

Chance slammed his mouth down on Tucker's in a desperate attempt to shut him up, but the damage had already been done. His brain, overwhelmed with images from Tucker's words, sent a message straight to his dick and he felt his balls draw up. "Goddammit to hell," he managed, and then stiffened. Chance held himself perfectly still when he felt his cock throb, and everything he'd felt during the past month came pouring out with his orgasm.

The love and fear and anxiety was dangerously close to the surface when he came, trembling and shuddering, as Tucker wrapped strong arms around him and murmured into his ear. Chance felt it right down to the tips of his fingers and couldn't stop shaking from the force. He hung his head and sucked in a deep breath, jerking helplessly as the blood roared in his ears. Aftershocks came fast and hard on top of each other, so he rode those out, too, savoring all of it. It was only the nudge of Tucker's hips against him that reminded Chance he'd neglected his partner.

He held himself up with one hand and wrapped the other one around Tucker's prick, so hard and swollen by now that it was nearly weeping drops of pre-come. Tucker's eyes fluttered closed and his tongue came out to moisten his bottom lip as his hands fell away, letting Chance work him. "Yes," he breathed, a small wrinkle forming between his brows as he concentrated.

"Beautiful," Chance whispered to him, jerking him with tight, rapid pulls, just the way Tucker liked it. "You're so gorgeous when you're getting off. Show me you like it." Chance lowered himself to an elbow and pressed himself full-length against Tucker while he stroked, his body adding weight to his grip.

Tucker struggled not to cry out, but gave up the fight at the last minute. With a low groan, he arched up into Chance's hand and began to shudder. Chance could feel the pulsing in the silky skin seconds before he felt the slippery warmth under his fingers and he made sure to draw it out, to give what he could and to let Tucker savor it.

For a long while afterward, they lay and touched each other with hands that wouldn't stop trembling. Chance found himself repeating the same thing in a whisper: "You're home."

Tucker nodded each time, shaking fingers coming up to trace a line along Chance's cheekbone, his jaw, the soft skin just behind his ear. "Yeah. I'm home."

"For good," Chance insisted, nuzzling into his hair, breathing the fresh, clean scent.

"Yeah. For good."

Chapter Twenty One

Chance was so glad to have Tucker home that he was able to ignore the questions that were niggling at him. He was dying to find out what the fire investigator had discovered, as well as what had finally happened to get Tucker out of Kentucky. But the joy and relief of actually having Tucker back in his bed gave him the patience to wait. For a while, anyway.

He basked in the glow of having Tucker home for three days before testing the waters.

"So," he said casually, the night before Tucker was slated to return to work, "what did the investigator's report say?"

Tucker yawned and stretched and arched off the bed like a cat. He wore the sated and sleepy look that meant he'd just gotten blown, which was in fact what had actually happened. "Dunno. Lots of stuff. You know what they look like."

"Yeah, and? What kind of stuff?"

Tucker's eyes darkened slightly. "The usual. Point of origin, patterns and factors."

Chance rolled over and sat up. "Tucker. You know what I'm asking you. What was the cause?"

He huffed an impatient breath and got off the bed, yanking on sweats. "It was fuckin' arson, Chance. You know that as well as I do. How the fuck else would the goddamn barn start to burn in the middle of winter?"

"Who?"

"Who do you think?" Tucker's voice had an edge to it that Chance hadn't heard since he'd been home. "Little weasel Will Caffrey and his cronies."

Chance remembered the look of pure disgust that had been on the man's face when they'd been confronted in the parking lot of the bar, and didn't doubt Tucker was right. "They know that for sure?"

"Nope. Still 'checkin' into it'," he snorted. "You know how that goes. Everyone in that fuckin' town's got their hands in everyone else's back pocket."

Chance knew he shouldn't push, but damn it all, he was getting a little tired of not having his questions answered. "So … you're just letting it go? You know you have to make noise to get heard. I can call out there for you, see if I can throw my weight around with their department – "

"No," Tucker said, cutting him off.

"Why not? It won't hurt anything – "

"I said no!" he shouted, startling Chance. "Christ, Shanahan, let it go! Nobody's gonna give a shit about a tobacco farm that was on its way out five years ago! Tobacco farmers are a dyin' breed and that ain't even countin' the gay ones, you know?" He shook his head in disgust and looked suddenly exhausted. "I just ain't gonna fight that fight no more. Don't know where the fuck I even stand, where I'm supposed to be."

Chance bit his lip and wanted to go to him, but he could tell by Tucker's rigid posture that his touch wouldn't be welcomed. "A crime was still committed," he offered lamely. "I mean, they have to take legal action."

Tucker rolled his eyes. "It's all so fuckin' simple for you, Chance. You ain't never dealt with the shit I grew up with and I know that ain't your fault, but Jesus. Try to figure out that life ain't all been surfboards and palm trees for me, yeah?"

"I know it hasn't," he replied, and heard the anger creeping into his tone. His patience with the whole issue was apparently reaching its limit. "I'm trying to help you."

"Don't."

"Why the fuck not?" Chance said, his voice rising. "Isn't that what partners are supposed to do?" He really had no idea how they'd gone from sucking each other off to yelling at each other in a matter of minutes, but here they were, and he'd be damned if he wasn't going to get it all out now.

Tucker ignored that in favor of stalking across the bedroom to snatch his car keys from the dresser. He shoved his feet into tennis shoes without tying the laces and went to the door, turning at the last minute. "I know you want to help," he said in a low voice. "'Cause it's what you do, I get that. It's your fuckin' job to help people and give orders and make things right. But I don't need you to help me. I just need you to let me help myself."

The house was still and silent after he left.

Chance lay awake long past midnight and thought. When he heard Tucker come home and get sheets out of the linen closet, Chance let him sleep on the couch.

***

He didn't wake up until after eight the next morning and knew instinctively that the house was empty.

Tucker had gone off to work and left the rumpled sheets and blankets on the couch. Smokey lay in the middle of them, blinking sleepily at Chance when he wandered into the living room. Chance sat down next to him with a sigh, stroking the silky fur between his ears and inhaling Tucker's familiar scent. "Did you keep him company last night, Smoke?" he murmured. The cat glanced up at him and twitched an ear. "Well, at least one of us had a warm body to curl up with."

He did a lot of nothing around the house for an hour or so. It was only putting off the inevitable, and eventually he took his shower and got in the car. A short drive got him where he needed to be, so Chance parked and studied the outside of Station Nineteen. The engine was in the bay, meaning the crew was definitely there. Might as well do this thing.

He walked straight through the garage into the side door that let him into their kitchen. The captain on duty looked up from the table where he was reading the newspaper. "Shanahan," he greeted. "How's things?"

"Greg," Chance answered. "McBride here?"

He thumbed over his shoulder toward the back of the small station. "Been in his dorm all morning. Came in in a foul mood."

Chance nodded his thanks and headed that way. He turned the corner and stopped in the short hallway that held five rooms, listening to make sure no one else was hiding out in their bunk like Tucker was. Hearing only silence, he moved to the third doorway on the right and poked his head in.

Tucker lay on his bed, half-heartedly leafing through a firefighters' union journal. He looked up and met Chance's eyes. Raising a brow in question, he dropped the magazine to the floor and folded his arms.

Chance moved inside and pulled up the trunk at the foot of Tucker's bed. Sitting down, he rested his elbows on his knees and studied the carpet. "Hey."

"Hey."

No sense pussyfooting around it. "I'm sorry," he said simply, remembering a time when the words would have stuck in his throat and their communication would have started its usual breakdown. "You were right. I was treating you like a patient. I just want to make it better."

Tucker made a sound that could have been half laugh, half frustrated sigh and turned to his side. He propped his head up with a hand and studied Chance. "It ain't that I don't appreciate what you been tryin' to do."

"I don't know what I've been trying to do. Make you happier, I guess." Chance scrubbed a hand over his face. He knew they were getting better at working things out in their relationship, but that didn't mean it still wasn't damn hard. Or that Chance didn't have a bad habit of just wanting to close up shop and call it a day before they even got started with the "I'm sorrys".

"Me bein' unhappy ain't got nothin' to do with you, baby. You're jus' about the only thing that don't make me miserable or pissed off these days. S'why I came home, you know?" Tucker's words didn't hold the edge of anger anymore, which was a relief. Chance hated that most of all.

"I get what you're saying. At least, I'm trying to get it. But, Tuck, you have to talk to me about some stuff. You can't just appear back home after I spent a goddamn month in Kentucky trying to get you here and you refused to go. You see where I'm having a problem?" He braced himself, waiting for either stony silence or a minor explosion.

He got neither. "I know," Tucker said quietly, and Chance looked up in surprise.

"Yeah?"

"Yeah." He put out a hand and played with a frayed hole in the knee of Chance's oldest, most comfortable jeans. "You're off tomorrow?"

"Yep. Till Friday."

"We'll talk tomorrow."

Chance nodded and felt the tension lift, even if just a little. He looked up to find Tucker studying him. "What?"

Tucker grinned and reached out to grab Chance's shirt, pulling him down until Chance had to brace both hands on the edge of the bed to avoid falling off the trunk where he was sitting. "You're gettin' better at this apologizin' shit, Cap."

"Don't call me Cap."

Tucker just chuckled and kissed him, tongue darting out to swipe at Chance's upper lip.

It was only the sound of the alarm that broke them apart. Tucker swore under his breath and heaved himself off his bunk, trailing a hand through Chance's hair on his way by. "Wanna ride along?"

"Hell, no. It's my day off."

"Fine," Tucker sulked. "Go home. I'll see you in the morning."

***

He came home on time, just after eight in the morning. Chance was leaning against the counter with a bowl of cereal when Tucker walked in and Chance studied his face. "Did you sleep?" Chance asked, knowing it would make a difference.

"All night," Tucker nodded. "Had a call after dinner around nine, then nothin' else."

"Did you eat this morning?"

The corner of his mouth curved. "Yes, Momma. I slept, I ate, I even brushed my own teeth."

Chance looked down, chagrined. "Sorry."

Tucker walked over, took the bowl of cereal from his hand, and fitted himself into the vee of Chance's legs. "No fixin'," he reminded, before placing a soft, open-mouthed kiss on Chance's top lip.

"No fixing."

They kissed for a while, hands tangling and tongues searching, and Chance liked it. It had no urgency or demand to it, neither of them were hard or expecting more than the simplicity of lips and tongue. Nice. Maybe they should do it more often.

They ended by pressing their foreheads together. Tucker was close enough that Chance could feel the blink of his lashes. "So … I'm guessin' we're goin' somewhere to talk?" Tucker said.

"Beach."

"Shoulda known."

***

For as much as Tucker pretended not to care, Chance knew Tucker liked the ocean. What the hell was there not to like, anyway? It smelled good, it sounded like thunder, and you could play in it. And despite the constant motion and shifting tides, Chance found it soothing. It helped him think, in any case.

They sat far up on the sand, away from the frigid winter water. The sky threatened rain, but it was probably still a couple of hours away, so they were all right. Chance dug his toes into the cold sand and played with the fringes on the edge of the blanket. Next to him, Tucker uncapped a bottle of water and lay back, staring at the houses on the cliff just above them.

The only sound for a long time was the cry of one sad seagull.

"It ain't all that dramatic," Tucker finally said. "Dunno why I didn't just tell you before."

"Maybe that's what we're gonna figure out," Chance shrugged, looking back over a shoulder at him.

He wasn't looking at Chance, his eyes still on the houses. Chance knew which one in particular had caught his attention. The white one, the one with the entire back window as large as two rooms, that looked out over the ocean. From ground to roof the glass stretched, allowing the owners an amazing view of the water. Tucker always looked at that one.

"So we lost the crop." His voice was low, barely discernible over the sound of the surf. "Fifteen thousand dollars, probably."

Chance nodded; he knew. He lay back on the blanket next to Tucker and folded his hands on his stomach, listening.

"And then you left. And I sorta went on a bender when you were gone." He paused there and Chance looked over and met his gaze.

"Bad?"

"Bad." He didn't need to say more; Chance could figure it out. "Talked myself into all kinds of ridiculous shit, like how you'd run off 'cause you couldn't handle the whole scene and I should just quit the fuckin' department and stay in Kentucky and run the goddamned farm into the ground like Tim did. Shit like that." Chance opened his mouth, but Tucker held up a hand. "Now, don't go gettin' all uptight like you do. I know that crap ain't true. Knew it every morning when I had a hangover that wanted to kill me. Was only at night when I was too drunk to fuckin' stand up that I got all maudlin."

There was a lot Chance could say, but Tucker didn't need to hear any of it. So he held his tongue and waited.

"I got pissed at you," Tucker continued, his voice dropping even lower. "I got pissed for all kinds of reasons that had nothin' to do with you. I was mad at you for comin', and then leavin' me just when I needed you not to."

Something inside Chance tightened and he felt guilt wash over him, but Tucker reached out a hand and rested it on Chance's own. "I know you're lyin' there all guilty and shit. Quit it. You gotta know by now this ain't about you, baby. It's me."

He knew, but it still twisted his heart.

"So then," Tucker continued, and something in his tone made Chance raise his eyes to Tucker's face. "I went back to Indiana. Got completely blitzed just sittin' at the bar, didn't have any fuckin' idea how I was gettin' home since I sure as shit couldn't drive, and then along comes this rodeo cowboy. All tall and dark-haired and white teeth."

Chance could feel his gorge rise along with the fury and had to make a concerted effort to tamp them both back down. "Whatever you're gonna say, you better say fast," he gritted out.

Tucker smiled softly at him. "Didn't do nothin'. You don't need to piss in a circle around me."

He relaxed a little, but not much. "Just tell me. And try to leave out the part where some guy takes advantage of your drunk ass."

Dimples flashed, quick as the tide, then gone again. "He tried. And I was so sloppy drunk I could barely stand, plus bein' all mad at you for leavin', that I prolly woulda gone. But you know who stood up for me? Scotty."

"That bartender?"

"That's the one. Stopped the guy in his tracks, hauled me off to the back office, and let me pass out on the floor 'til morning. Left my keys and a note on the desk."

"Note?"

"'Get your fuckin' ass back to the surfer'," he said with a chuckle. "But I didn't need him to tell me. I jus' knew. Had to get the hell out, 'cause damn, Chance, nothin' ain't right without you."

Chance turned to his side and reached out an arm. Tucker slid closer into Chance's embrace and tucked his head under Chance's chin, fingers coming up to play with a loose thread in Chance's sweater. "So what's the rest?" Chance finally asked him, when Tucker didn't seem inclined to say any more.

Tucker took a deep breath and let it out slowly, head still tucked down. "Coop sat me down. Wants to take care of the farm. Wants to buy it, actually, and convert all the tobacco fields to vegetables. Ain't nothin' to be gained from tobacco farmin' no more anyway."

"That's … a good thing, isn't it? So why not just let him buy it?" It sounded good in theory, but Chance had a feeling there was more.

"He can't afford the whole thing. And I can't afford to sell at a price he can manage. So, he asked if … if he could buy half. And we'd be part owners together."

"So, he'd run it?" Chance was starting to see why Tucker was so torn.

"Yeah. He'd run it and consult with me if he had to and I'd have to go back once or twice a year. Maybe less, dependin' on whether or not they could just fax shit to me that needed to be signed." He was talking into the front of Chance's sweater, his words muffled.

"You want to tell me why this is so hard to figure out?" He thought he knew, but unless Tucker could give voice to it, it didn't matter what Chance knew at all.

Another deep breath. Then, "It means I gotta hold on to somethin' I spent near twenty years tryin' to get rid of. It means I'm tied to that farm for good and I gotta go back there at least once a year. Don't know, Chance. Just don't know if I got it in me."

It was another reminder that there were things in Tucker's past that he wasn't sharing. He might never share them; Chance knew that now. It couldn't be coerced out of him, not until he was ready, if ever. But it was Tucker's story to tell.

Chance held him close and let Tucker just lie there and breathe, knowing there was nothing he could say that Tucker hadn't been thinking for the past several days. It wasn't the time for fixing, Tucker had told him. What was he supposed to do? Oh, right. Be there to help Tucker fix it. Okay. "When do you need to decide?"

"Couple weeks, I guess. Coop said just to call him when I was ready. Don't know if I'm ever gon' be ready."

"I'd go with you," Chance said softly. "You don't have to go back by yourself. Once a year, shit, those vacation days are easy."

"I know you would," he murmured. "Ain't worried 'bout that."

It was the unspoken worries that bothered Chance, the ones Tucker either wouldn't or couldn't give an explanation for. "You think on it," was all Chance finally said.

Chapter Twenty Two

It took Tucker five days to figure things out, and during that time Chance forced himself not to say a word about it. It wasn't easy, but he tried.

They worked and had dinner and kissed and jogged on the beach and had sex and did all the normal things they'd always done and Chance wasn't sure if it was real or just a cover. He went with it, though, his heart lightening when Tucker would flash him a smile or his eyes would twinkle. There wasn't much to fake there.

On the fifth day, Tucker came to him while Chance was examining a new scratch in his surfboard. "Hey," Tucker said, and something in his voice made Chance look up immediately, board forgotten.

"Yeah?"

"Called Coop. It's done." The look on his face was caught between apprehension and relief and Chance had no fucking idea what it meant.

"Okay," he said hesitantly, standing up to face Tucker.

Tucker twisted his fingers together and a furrow appeared between his brows. "Still don't know if it was the right thing. Don't guess I'll ever know, huh? Just gotta deal with it."

Chance took a deep breath and tried to keep his patience, when what he really wanted to do was either shake Tucker until he clarified himself, or yell at him. Neither one was really a viable option, so he said calmly, "Tucker. Did you tell him yes or no?"

Tucker blinked, then grinned sheepishly. "Oh! Sorry. I told him … I told him yeah. I'd do it." He swallowed hard and searched Chance's face, waiting for a reaction.

It was Chance's turn to blink. He hadn't quite thought Tucker would go through with it, and now Chance wasn't sure what kind of reaction Tucker was expecting. "Oh, hey," he said. "Congratulations. I think. You okay?"

Tucker appeared to think that over, nibbling on the side of his thumbnail. "Don't know yet. Gotta see how it plays out, I guess. But Coop says he don't need me there for a while and he can sort out the paperwork and fax me the shit." Tucker glanced up at Chance, eyes twinkling. "So, yeah. I think I'm okay." He stepped closer and nuzzled at Chance's neck, hands coming up to slide around Chance's waist.

Chance snorted, but moved into his embrace, already responding to Tucker's nearness. "Yeah, feels like you're okay to me." Chance reached down and traced Tucker's cock lightly through his jeans, watching as his eyes fluttered closed, hiding the indigo at which Chance never failed to marvel.

There was a jolt right down his spine and into his cock and both of them wordlessly sank to the floor. Impatient fingers pulled at fabric and zippers until there were no more clothes in the way, no physical or emotional barriers between them, and Chance rolled them both to get Tucker straddled on top. "I'm proud of you," he said. "It was the right thing."

Tucker flushed pink, shrugging one shoulder even as he managed to grind their erections together. "Don't know 'bout that. Just gotta see."

Chance dug urgent fingers into Tucker's thighs. He wanted to do this right, possibly with more finesse than he was exhibiting, but the sweet weight on top of him wiped out all concentration and made him just rock upwards again and again until Tucker gave a half-laugh, half-groan.

"Ain't nothin' wrong with grinding," he grinned down at Chance, "but I was kinda hopin' to get fucked into the floor or somethin' along those lines."

Chance growled and flipped them fast enough to make Tucker's head hit the carpet with a soft thud. He leaned down quickly and put a fast, hard bite to Tucker's jaw, knowing it would show later and feeling his cock grow even stiffer at the thought. Tucker arched his neck and hissed in a breath and Chance thought to himself that no one should be that beautiful.

Chance took Tucker's cock in hand and started to jack him in the way he knew would get the fastest results. Good, firm strokes, watching as Tucker's eyes closed and his brows drew together in concentration, tongue coming out to rest on his bottom lip. Sure enough, Tucker's hand came down over Chance's and he shook his head. "Don't."

"Why not?" Chance murmured, not stopping.

"Because – oh, Jesus, that's good – because I'm three seconds away from shootin' all over you and I'd rather do it when you're in me." His nostrils flared and he thrust into Chance's hand, despite his pleas to stop.

Chance leaned down again and put his mouth near Tucker's ear. "But if you come before I'm in you," he purred low and soft, "then I can use it for lube."

And there it was: an indrawn breath and a muscle jumping in Tucker's jaw right before Chance felt his dick throb and the resulting slippery warmth spilling over Chance's fingers.

He let Tucker ride it out for a second, but then couldn't wait anymore. Chance palmed the slickness and coated himself with it, bowing his head as he moved over Tucker and pushed at one of his knees. Up and over and Chance took another kiss, wanting and loving the familiar taste. A sweep of his tongue over Tucker's mouth and Chance slid inside Tucker with no resistance at all.

Their eyes stayed locked through the first smooth thrusts. Tucker's gaze burned into him and Chance thought he could look at those eyes forever, watching the dark of those pupils edging out the midnight color. He put down a hand to find Tucker's cock still half-hard between them and wrapped his fingers around it, tugging Tucker back to fullness easily. "Again?" Chance whispered to him, and Tucker closed his eyes and nodded.

"Think so."

"I know so." It made Tucker shudder against him as soon as Chance said it, and Chance had to bite down hard on his tongue and mentally recall all the gauges on the engine's instrument panel in order not to come.

He made the mistake of looking down at Tucker's mouth, red and swollen and wet, and reached out a thumb to skim over that soft lower lip. Tucker opened for him and sucked Chance's thumb in, swirling a tongue over the pad and using teeth to bite down, and then the slick-slide of their bodies became desperate pushing and reaching until Chance had to bite back a whimper.

Tucker's cock rocked hard against his stomach and everything turned into just pressure and warmth and skin and Tucker and it was perfect. Chance's skin was suddenly electric, feeling little shocks run right up his balls and into every nerve ending he had, and Tucker's scent was everywhere when Chance finally broke, spilling into Tucker and coming hard enough to make himself dizzy.

Chance was aware, barely, of Tucker groaning under him and following him for the second time, and he made a mental note to ask later just how the hell Tucker was able to do that so fast. Chance was too wrung out right now to do anything but try not to fall on Tucker as he let his weight down.

Tucker coaxed him close with kisses to his shoulder and murmured soft words and Chance let himself be lulled by the sense of peace that stole over him. There was nowhere else either of them had to be and nowhere else Chance could imagine himself at that minute.

Turning just slightly, he nuzzled into Tucker's hair and whispered his name. Just his name, that was all, and received a sleepy wink and dimple in return.

It was enough.

***

"Now!" Chance shouted, paddling as hard as he could and watching Tucker do the same next to him in the water. "Ready?" he asked over the sound of the surf, and Tucker nodded with determination.

The swell crested just behind him and he could feel the wave, could sense when it was the right time to go from lying prone on his board to gathering himself into a crouch. He had spent months trying to teach it to Tucker, but it wasn't really something that could be learned. It had to be innate, you had to recognize the pull of the water and your body had to respond to it, and Chance couldn't remember a time when he hadn't known what it was.

He went from his knees to his feet and glanced to his left, watching with pride as Tucker copied him out of sheer force of will. Shaky, but managing to balance with one foot forward and one foot back, Tucker kept his center of gravity low and focused on the midpoint of his board like Chance had shown him hundreds of times.

It wasn't a long ride. Both of them angled left to run parallel to the beach, and just as Chance thought they might be able to take it all the way in, he saw Tucker's foot shift enough to send him off-balance. Sure enough, it sent Tucker's board nose down and he couldn't recover in time before taking a dive into the water.

Chance looked behind him just long enough to ensure Tucker surfaced, then rode a few more feet before jumping off himself and catching his board before it could skim past. The wave crashed just after that and then the ocean was calm enough for him to climb back up and straddle the board, sitting in the water as he waited for Tucker to catch up.

Tucker swam up to him, grin splitting his face and pleased as anything. "Well?" he asked, slicking his hair back from his face and looking expectant.

Chance shrugged, trying not to smile. "It was all right."

The grin faded. "'All right'?" he repeated. "You gotta be kiddin' me."

Chance sighed. "You fell," he pointed out, wondering how long he could keep it up.

"But ... I stood up!" Tucker spluttered, waving his arm for emphasis. "I did everything you told me to! And I didn't fall right away, I rode for a little bit, and ..." He trailed off and narrowed his eyes. "Are you just givin' me a hard time?"

Chance winked in answer and Tucker launched himself at him, pushing Chance off his board and shoving him down under the water. "Asshole," Tucker said gleefully when he surfaced, and Chance laughed and kissed him.

The tangy, salty scent of ocean was all around them and the strong California sun beat down on their heads as they wrestled in the water. And when Tucker nuzzled into the side of Chance's neck and murmured soft and sweet against his skin, Chance knew what it meant to have something that he never wanted to be without again.

End

Printed in the United States
75396LV00003B/63

9 781933 389998